Mountain of Peril

Faith in the Parks, Book 1

J. Carol Nemeth

Copyright 2018

Written by: J. Carol Nemeth

Published by: Forget Me Not Romances, a division of Winged Publications

Cover Design: Cynthia Hickey

ISBN-13: 978-1-0879-5264-2

Dedication

I would like to dedicate this book to the memory of my father, the Rev. James W. Pruitt and to my mother, Mary Sue Amick Pruitt. My parents instilled in my siblings and me the love of camping and the outdoors at an early age. I still remember our first camping trip in an old canvas army tent that closed by tying long strings at the door, and it had no floor. We slept on old army cots. I must have been three or four years old. We soon graduated to one with a floor and a zippered door where creepy crawlies were encouraged to stay out. My parents introduced us to the national parks and monuments as well as state parks, and we traveled from the mountains to the coast as often as we could. We climbed lighthouses, descended into caves, swam in the ocean, visited presidents (homes). We saw where man took flight. They took us places. I want to once again thank them for spreading our wings and giving us the love of travel. Thanks Mama and Daddy!

.

Acknowledgments

I owe my gratitude to Police Officer Ben Anderson for his information concerning police arrest procedure and to US Park Ranger Jamie Sanders of the Great Smoky Mountains National Park for answering my questions concerning Park Police procedures when dealing with poachers.

Thank you to Judy Blaha, R.N and Carol Cool, L.P.N at our local VA for answering my medical questions.

Chapter One

With a whistle on his lips, Jake Stuart rounded the corner of the ranger station. He pulled his keys from his pants pocket, prepared to flip the Closed sign by the door to Open as he did every morning. As he approached the front stoop, he froze. The whistle hung in his throat. He jerked back, a gasp slipping out. The decapitated head of a black bear perched on the floor of the porch stoop, a pair of severed paws positioned on either side of the head. Blood seeped from beneath the black fur of the head and ran across the cement stoop dripping into the grass. Jake tasted bile as his gut knotted. He clenched his fists and shook his head. Who would do such an awful thing? And why? The glazed eyes of the bear were haunting. This bear had died needlessly.

Avoiding the horrible mess, Jake stepped onto the stoop from the side and unlocked the station office. Grabbing the phone, he called his supervisor, Cal Bishop. He'd come out and assist in the processing of the crime scene. Because that's exactly what it was. He pulled his digital camera from the desk drawer. Photo-documenting the evidence was an important part of any investigation. After searching carefully, no vehicle tire tracks or footprints could be found. Too much grass and gravel and not enough dirt to hold a print.

By the time Cal arrived, the spring morning had warmed considerably and flies had found the bear head.

"Now that's not a pretty sight to greet you in the morning." Cal climbed out of his National Park SUV. "We're getting more and more reports of poaching lately, and out of season too. They took the carcass and left the head. Pretty disgusting."

"Yeah, well, this is different." Jake squatted down, pulled out his pocketknife and probed the fur for possible gunshot wounds. "This is more than just poaching. Someone's left us a strong message." But for what? A warning, maybe? Or a threat?

~

"What'd she say, Burt?" The elderly man turned to his companion where they sat on a bench in front of the old service station.

"I dunno, George. Can't understand her." Burt cupped his ear with his hand and leaned forward. "What'd ya say, young woman?"

Molly Walker stepped closer and raised her voice. "Sir, I asked for directions to Deep Creek Ranger Station." This was the first business she'd found open on this road and somehow she thought she'd gotten turned around. The two elderly gentlemen sitting on the bench in front of the station were why she'd stopped, but she wasn't getting very far with them.

"Sounds like gibberish to me, George. Can't make out a word." He turned his head toward the screen door beside him. "Hey, Bertha!" he called, hand cupped around his mouth like a megaphone. "Come out here a minute, would ya!"

Molly sighed as a large lady in a bright print blouse, orange-red curly hair and large dangly earrings propped open the screen door. "What ya bellowin' about, Burt? Oh, hello there," she added with a congenial smile upon spotting Molly.

"This here young woman wants something, and I can't understand her." Burt and George both shook their heads.

The woman rolled her eyes, "What can I do for ya, sweetie? You need help with the gas pump? It's not one of those newfangled ones, but it works. Some of the young folks can't figure it out."

Molly smiled wide. "No, thanks. I just need directions out to Deep Creek Ranger Station. I seem to have gotten turned around somehow."

"Oh, sure. Take this road into town then turn right at the courthouse. It's the big building with the gold dome." A touch of pride edged her words. She gave Molly detailed directions all the way to Deep Creek.

"Thanks! You've been a big help." Molly waved at Burt and George. "Thanks, fellows!"

"Who's Hank Bellows, Bertha?" George raised his bushy eyebrows.

"Never mind, George." Bertha huffed as the screen door banged shut behind her.

Molly followed Bertha's directions, liking the laid-back quaintness of the little town. It had that certain "Mayberry" feel to it. She half expected an old black and white to cruise past with Andy or Barney at the wheel. Turning right at the courthouse, she spotted two more elderly men sitting on a park bench, a checkerboard between them. Remembering Burt and George, she grinned. Laid back, indeed!

Small storefronts, a hardware store and an old drugstore lined the street. Taking another right at the old train depot, Molly left the town behind, passing small mountain homes along the green hillsides, a country store and the occasional mobile home. The North Carolina Smoky Mountains rose up from the valley she drove through, their smoky blue color beautiful against the brilliant blue sky. Spring had arrived in the Smokies, and the vibrant pink and white Laurel bushes were in full bloom. Redbuds and dogwoods peeked between the new green leaves sprouting on the poplar, maple and oak trees.

Molly spotted the sign for Deep Creek Campground and a surge of exhilaration knotted her stomach. She'd waited a long time for this. It was her first position with the National Park Service, and she was certain great-grandpa Murphy would've been pleased. Having trained for this very day, she was ready to begin her new career. Gratitude for how circumstances had worked out swelled in her heart. *Thank you, Lord.*

Turning right, she crossed a bridge that spanned a swiftly flowing creek then entered a large clearing in the woods. A small brown building sat near the center with a sign beside it that read Office. The early afternoon breeze stirred an American flag at the top of a flagpole.

Molly parked across from the office and exited her SUV, stretching stiff muscles and glancing around the quiet clearing. Strolling over to the little office, she opened the squeaky screen door, hoping Cal Bishop was in. As head ranger over the campground and this part of the park district, he was meeting her here to explain her duties.

The small front office was split by a wooden counter along the front, a desk holding a base station radio and a file cabinet positioned behind it. Mountain scenes and maps graced the walls while a tattered and torn backpack hung by the front door. An old coffee pot and tin can, both punctured and bent, hung from the backpack. Beneath, a sign read, Campers: Please Store Food Properly. A partition to the left of the counter indicated more office space.

A young auburn-haired man dressed in a National Park Service uniform leaned on the counter, grinning as Molly glanced around. His hair was short and freckles spattered across his nose. His name badge read "Craig Wilson."

"Can I help you?" A bright smile crossed his lips.

"I hope so." Molly returned his smile. "I'm looking for Cal Bishop. Is he in?"

"No, he's out in the campground somewhere. I can call him if you'd like."

"I'd appreciate that. My name's Molly Walker. I believe he's expecting me."

"Molly Walker!" He extended his hand to Molly. "You bet he is. He'll be glad to know you're here. I'm Craig Wilson. It's nice to meet you."

"I'm happy to meet you, Craig." Molly shook his outstretched hand.

"Hang on a minute. I'll call Cal." Craig reached for the base radio microphone on the desk, depressed the button and called out some numbers followed by Cal's name. "Guess who's here? Yeah, she made it. Come back?"

A deep male voice responded he was on his way.

"He'll be here shortly. I just made some coffee a little while ago. Would you like a cup?"

"I'd love some." Molly glanced around the office. The coffee maker sat on a small table near the desk. "May I help myself?"

"Sure. May as well. You'll be working here so make yourself at home."

"Thanks." Molly chuckled, filling an insulated cup. "Where are you from, Craig?"

"Montana."

"Wow! You're a long way from home. Been in the park service long?"

"This is my first season." He perched on the barstool behind the counter. "You're coming in a little late, I suppose."

Molly settled onto the rolling chair at the desk, sipping the hot brew. "I understand I'm replacing someone that didn't work out."

"Yeah, that was Howard, Cal's assistant ranger for the past two seasons. He took seriously ill. Don't know the whole story, but I don't think he's returning to the park service. Early retirement, I think." He shrugged his shoulders.

"So what do you do?"

"I'm a summer seasonal park aide. I'm still in college and working my way through, but I'll graduate next spring. The experience here will be good."

The screen door opened and a man of stocky build strolled in. He wore the gray shirt and dark green pants of the National Park Service uniform, and when he removed a dark green NPS ball cap and sunglasses, Molly noticed his sandy colored crew cut and bright blue eyes surrounded by laugh lines. Determining he was in his mid-forties, she stood as he approached with outstretched hand.

"I'm Cal Bishop," his voice deep and gravely. "Welcome to Deep Creek, Miss Walker."

"Please, call me Molly."

"Certainly, but you have to call me Cal. We don't stand on formalities around here. Come on back and have a seat. I have some things to go over with you." He led Molly behind the partition where another desk and file cabinet made up Cal's office. Through an open door to the left, Molly spotted what passed for a bathroom. It would be a tight fit, but certainly better than nothing.

"Did you have a good trip?" Cal motioned her to sit in a chair beside the desk while he took the rolling chair behind it. "Where'd you drive from?"

"From Charlottesville, Virginia. Except for a couple really bad storms that kept me alert, it was uneventful."

"They're predicting storms this evening. We need it. It's been a dry spring so far." As he chatted he drew a file folder from the desk drawer, removing several pages. "Here's a list of required uniform items and you'll get a uniform allowance, so that'll help you out."

He removed a small plastic bag stapled to the list then handed the list to her. "You can order by mail or online, but it takes a week or so to get your items. However, if you don't mind taking a drive, there's a store in Maryville, Tennessee that carries the NPS uniform shirts, pants and leather belt. You can also pick up the ball cap."

Cal pointed to his on the side of the desk.

Molly glanced at it. "What about the "Smoky-Bear" hat?"

He tapped the list in her hand. "It has to be ordered. Pick up some good hiking boots too. You'll need 'em."

Dumping the contents of the little plastic bag onto the desk, he picked up a little brass bar. "I took the liberty of ordering your name tag so you'd have it when you arrived." He handed her the name tag and a metal, shield-shaped badge. "This gives you your authority."

"When do I start?" Eagerness threatened to overwhelm Molly. Had he noticed her wiping her palms on her pant legs? It was hard to tone down her beaming smile.

Cal glanced at his wristwatch, a broad grin on his lips. Yeah, he'd noticed. "If you want to drive over to Maryville for your uniforms, go today. Then you can start in the morning. On your way, if you don't mind, you can deliver something to the remote Twentymile Ranger Station for me. I have some paperwork for Ranger Jake Stuart."

"I don't mind. Is it on the way?"

"Yep. You drive right past it to get to Maryville. Before you go, I'll take you up to the duplex where you'll lodge temporarily until you find a place." Grabbing a notepad, Cal drew a rudimentary map and handed it to Molly along with a manila envelope. "Here are directions to Maryville with Twentymile marked on it. This is the packet for Jake." Unlocking a drawer in his desk, he opened it and pulled out a Glock 19 9mm and a brown leather holster.

"This is your sidearm." He peered closely at Molly. "From your weapon scores, I see you know how to handle one of these."

"I didn't do too badly." Pleasure warmed Molly at his compliment. "Besides, my father made sure my brothers and I knew how to protect ourselves."

Cal nodded and handed her another form. "That's what I like to hear. Sign on the dotted line. This says you were issued the weapon. Just make sure the serial number matches the paper before you sign."

Comparing the numbers, Molly signed the form and returned it to Cal.

"Follow me and I'll show you to your quarters." Clapping his cap on his head, he led the way out the door.

~

After Molly and Cal dropped off her suitcases, bags and boxes at the little duplex up the hill from the office, Molly grabbed lunch at the drugstore in town then headed west toward Twentymile Ranger Station. The drive was pleasant with the road winding just past the edge of a huge lake and around hairpin curves. According to Cal's map, the lake was Fontana Lake. The scenery was gorgeous. Molly's family had visited the Great Smoky Mountains in her childhood, and she'd always loved the gentle yet mysterious smoky-blue mountains. Not nearly as tall as the Rockies or some of the other western mountain ranges, the Smokies had a quiet, peaceful beauty all their own.

Molly spotted a sign for Fontana Dam and another for Fontana Village. Having read up on the area before coming, she knew the dam, one of many in the area, was built by the Tennessee Valley Authority during WWII. The village was a summer resort with a lodge, swimming pools and hiking. It was located south of Fontana Lake, while the boundary to Great Smoky Mountains National Park lay along the northern shore.

With no time to explore the area today, Molly vowed to return on a day off to investigate further. Passing the entrance to the village, she descended a winding, wooded mountain road to the bottom where a bridge crossed a wide river. To her right, the sheer wall of Fontana Dam rose far above. A power generating station sat to one side. On the left of the bridge, the river flowed into another lake. Here in the valley below the dam, the road wound along the lake's edge on the left while on the right the wooded foot of the mountains rose up into the park.

Turning into a gravel driveway by a sign for Twentymile Ranger Station, she parked in the small lot in front of the building. Climbing out, she stretched, listening to the peace and quiet that enveloped her. A creek flowing merrily alongside the station, a gentle breeze rustling the trees and birds singing were the only sounds. Bright sunshine belied any sign of a predicted storm.

Molly stepped onto the small front porch and found a large wooden clock face with movable hands indicating the ranger would return in an hour. She glanced at her wristwatch. She couldn't wait that long. Not with an hour drive to Maryville.

Exploring the grounds, she hoped to find Jake Stuart. A long, dark green garage stood fifty feet behind the station. A light green NPS Jeep was parked in front beside a blue Ford Ranger. The gravel and dirt driveway wound past the station, the garage and on up the hill. It curved past a little brown shanty before disappearing around the bend.

Well, now what should she do? A faint sound came from up the hill. Was that a metallic ringing noise? Following it, she stopped at the little shanty only to find it locked. Twenty-five feet further an iron gate blocked the road that meandered into the woods. Ducking beneath the gate, Molly followed the road toward the sound of a faint voice, an occasional metallic ring and a horse nickering. Ahead she spotted a barn surrounded by corrals.

Shoving open one of the barn doors, she glanced around for the owner of the voice. Two horses and a mule stood in their stalls, softly nickering at her appearance. As they stirred, motes of dust danced in the sunbeams that slipped through the cracks above the rafters. The scent of hay and horses filled her nose.

"Hello?" she called in a soft voice. Frightening the horses would be a bad idea. "Anyone here?"

Molly approached one of the horses and stroked its head, crooning softly to it. "Easy, fellow. Where's the ranger, huh?"

The voice spoke again, louder this time. The owner switched back and forth between talking and humming in a deep baritone. Striding to the double doors leading to a corral, Molly found a man working beside a horse. Bent from the waist, he held the horse's back hoof between his knees, a hoof pick in his hand. With his back to her, he hadn't heard her approach. The horse noticed her and nickered, shifting his weight.

"Whoa, Billy!" A deep voice soothed. "Stand still, boy. We'll be done shortly."

"Excuse me," Molly said quietly. "Sorry to interrupt your work, but I'm looking for Jake Stuart."

Glancing over his shoulder in surprise, the man accidently allowed the weight of the horse's leg to slip from his grasp. Suddenly off balance, he fell forward, landing on his shoulder and knees.

"Oh, no!" Molly gasped, covering her mouth with her hands. "I'm so sorry. I didn't mean to startle you."

Picking himself up, he dusted off his pants and grinned. Molly wasn't sure if the red in his cheeks was from embarrassment or from leaning over too long. She had a pretty good idea which it was. Her hands still covering her mouth, she tried not to laugh, but found one working its way out.

~

Jake Stuart noted the woman was trying unsuccessfully not to laugh at him. "You know, seeing as how we've never met, I don't think it's very polite to laugh at me." His voice and face were stern, but his dark sapphire eyes shone with laughter. "Especially since *you're* the one who startled *me*."

"I truly am sorry, but if I'd shouted, would I have startled you any less?" The pretty woman chuckled again.

He shook his head. "I suppose you have a point. Did you say you're looking for Jake Stuart?"

"Yes, I am."

He surveyed her thoroughly, taking in the long brown braid hanging carelessly over her shoulder. The soft curve of her cheeks, and the dark chocolate eyes. Her lips were a delicate shade of pink, slightly compressed at the moment and compressing more and more as he observed her appearance. She wore a pair of blue jeans and a white button-down shirt with flowers embroidered on the collar.

"Do you know where he is or don't you?"

Uh-oh. A frown was forming between her delicate eyebrows.

Jake couldn't take his eyes from her. She blushed, and the pink color delighted him. Was that a Virginian accent he detected? Whatever it was, it sounded great coming from her.

"What do you need him for?"

Eyes narrowing, she lifted her chin defiantly. "That's none of your concern. I have something for him, and I need to give it directly to him."

He crossed his arms over his chest. "Well now, he never mentioned expecting you. I'm sure if he knew you were coming, he would've made sure he was here to meet you."

Boy, this was fun. He checked his grin as she crossed her arms as well and tilted her chin upward.

"Be that as it may, I'm still looking for him."

~

Molly jumped as the walkie-talkie propped on a nearby stump crackled to life. After the usual call numbers, a deep voice said, "Come in, Jake, this is Cal."

Whoever this man was, he glanced at the walkie-talkie then back at her. Was the call for *him*? "Come in, Jake. This is Cal. Do you read me?"

Molly watched with dismay as the man hesitated momentarily before reaching for the instrument and pressing the button, responding. "Cal, this is Jake. What's up?"

"Just wanted to let you know that Molly Walker will be by sometime this afternoon to drop off those papers you wanted. She's the new ranger over here. Should be getting there soon, I expect. Was going to call sooner, but got caught up in a situation here."

Jake's gaze flicked back to hers. "Thanks Cal but she beat you to it. She's already here." He shrugged, never removing his eyes from her face.

"Roger that, Jake. Talk with you later. Cal out."

"Jake out."

Molly spun on her heels and headed back through the barn. Glancing over her shoulder, she saw Jake yank off the leather apron covering his uniform and nametag. He tossed it on the stump, slipped the walkie-talkie into its belt holster, and hurried after her.

"Hey, wait up," he called.

She sped toward the station, wanting to put some distance between them.

Jake caught up with her just before the gate. Catching hold of her arm, he gently tugged her around. "You're quick, you know that?"

Molly turned her best blank expression on him and pulled her arm away. "Thanks."

"Look, I'm sorry. I shouldn't have led you on like that, but I guess I was little sore at being caught off guard and having fallen flat on my face. I think they call it male ego or something like that. Anyway, I know you didn't surprise me on purpose." One side of his mouth lifted in a crooked grin as his eyebrows rose. "Am I forgiven?"

Molly grinned at the "male ego" comment and knew she couldn't stay mad. She'd have to work with him some time or other. Best to get things squared and make life a little easier. Besides, she *had* laughed at him. She held out her hand. "You're forgiven, if you'll forgive me for laughing at you."

His large calloused hand engulfed hers then released it. "Done. Now let's start over. Hi, I'm Jake Stuart."

"Molly Walker. I have an envelope for you in my car. The one Cal referred to when he gave you away."

As Jake strode on long legs back toward the station, Molly tried to keep up.

He shortened his stride. To match hers? "Right. Needless to say, I wasn't expecting you. I knew someone was replacing Howard, but I didn't know who. It's been awhile since I've been over to Deep Creek." As they stopped by her car, Molly retrieved the envelope.

"When did you get to town?"

"Today. I checked in with Cal, dropped my things at my temporary quarters then headed here. He suggested purchasing my uniforms in Maryville so that's where I'm heading. He asked me to drop this off to save him a trip."

"You're heading to Maryville, huh?" Jake's eyes gleamed with interest. "Could I impose on you to pick up something for me?"

"Sure. What do you need?" Another errand for another ranger? Was she going to be a ranger or a courier?

Jake pulled out his wallet and handed her a few bills then removed a notepad from his shirt pocket. "I'll jot down what I need." As he wrote, Molly took the opportunity to observe him unnoticed. His thick black hair was cut short and neat. A very handsome man in spite of the faint scar marring the right side of his chin. When she'd first seen him at the barn she'd noticed his broad shoulders and his dark sapphire eyes beneath black brows.

She suddenly realized those same eyes were gazing at her now.

Uh oh. She'd been caught staring. Looking down at the paper he was holding out, she willed herself not to blush.

"R…right," she stammered. "I'll pick these up for you and drop them off on my way past. Will you be here?"

Jake's smile was bright against his tanned face. "I'll be here. When you live in the backcountry, there aren't too many places to go. If I'm not here at the station, I'll be up at the barn. I still have two more horses to shoe."

As Molly drove away, she was still embarrassed that she'd stared, much less been caught at it. What had come over her? Staring at a man wasn't her style. She shook her head and concentrated on the winding road.

Chapter Two

Jake watched Molly drive away then walked to the edge of the creek. With unseeing eyes he watched the water rush out to the lake beyond the main road. Suddenly feeling like he'd been hit upside the head, he scrubbed his hand down his face. Molly's presence in the barn doorway had been an unexpected and very pleasant surprise. Once in junior high when he wasn't expecting it, a kid had punched him in the gut, leaving him stunned and breathless. That same sort of feeling washed over him now, although he hadn't suffered a physical blow. Shaking his head, he strode back toward the barn. This was ridiculous! Maybe he'd bumped his head when he'd fallen and hadn't realized till now. No way. There wasn't anything to bump his head on and he sure hadn't hit the ground that hard.

Molly Walker. She certainly was a sight for sore eyes. *I've been in the woods too long. Maybe I need to go into town soon and get away from the peace and quiet.* He chuckled as he donned his leather apron again. Turning, he looked at the barn door half expecting to see Molly still standing there. Billy Boy, who had wandered across the corral, turned and whinnied at him.

"You're absolutely right, Billy Boy, I'm losing it." He led the horse back to where his farrier tool kit sat and retrieved the hoof pick. Positioning the horse's back hoof between his knees, he added, "She is beautiful, though, isn't she!"

Billy Boy bobbed his large head in agreement.

~

Tossing several packages into the back of her car, Molly left

Maryville and headed back to Twentymile. She was happy to have found what she needed but her travels were catching up with her. She just wanted to return to Deep Creek, throw some sheets on the bed and fall in. Unfortunately, it wouldn't be that quick. As she maneuvered the winding roads, she tuned the radio to some lively music, attempting to stay alert. There were more hairpin curves between Maryville and Twentymile than she'd ever seen. Every time she rounded a hairpin curve she expected to see her brake lights coming around the curve behind her.

When she pulled into Twentymile, she glanced at her watch. Almost six o'clock. She hoped she wouldn't catch Jake in the middle of supper. The front of the building was closed up and dark so she drove around to the back where light shown from the windows. This must be the living quarters. Climbing out of the car, she knocked on the back door. She'd only knocked once when Jake immediately yanked it open. But then he was expecting her.

"It's just me." She held out the plastic bag with his purchases.

"Come on in." Stepping back to let her in, he accepted the bag. She stepped just inside the door. It opened directly into a small country kitchen. Through an archway to the left a small living room was arranged with comfort in mind. Her nose honed in on a wonderful aroma, making her stomach growl.

"Here's your change. They had everything on your list and in the right sizes." She held out her hand.

"Thanks for picking them up for me." Jake held out his hand. As she placed the change in his open palm, her fingers brushed his. She dropped her gaze as her cheeks warmed. Could he tell? She busied herself with returning her wallet to her purse, trying to hide what surely were pink cheeks.

"You know, I just finished cooking supper and was going to sit down to eat. Would you join me? I don't claim to be the best cook in the world, but it's not bad."

Molly lifted her gaze and smiled. "It smells wonderful, and I'm sure it tastes just as good, but I really do need to get back to Deep Creek. I've had a couple very long days, and I still know absolutely nothing about where I'm staying. I dropped everything in the middle of the living room and left. I still have quite a drive ahead of me too."

"A raincheck, perhaps?" Jake grinned hopefully.

"Sure," Molly agreed. "I don't see why not." She turned to go.

"Goodbye, Molly Walker. It was a pleasure meeting you. I'll see you soon." Something in Jake's tone made that sound like a promise.

~

As Molly drove into Deep Creek, the predicted storm was threatening to erupt. Rain had begun and the sky was lit by lightning as thunder rumbled in the distance. Stopping in town, she picked up a takeout meal. When she arrived at her new home, Molly dropped down wearily at the kitchen table and ate part of it. After unpacking her new uniforms, she ironed and hung them, ready for work in the morning. Then she quickly made the bed and prepared to fall in.

Sliding between the cool sheets, her weary muscles relaxed. *Thank you, Lord, for keeping me safe. I've traveled a lot of miles today, but You were right there with me. Thank you for this job. As tired as I am, I'm excited about tomorrow.* She fell asleep to the sounds of the storm brewing outside.

~

When the alarm rang the next morning, it took Molly a minute to remember where she was. Her uniform hanging on the closet door brought it all back. Unfortunately she had no coffee, but after a hot shower, she was awake. Donning her uniform, she gazed at her reflection in the bathroom mirror as she pinned on her name tag and badge. Wow! This was really happening. She was a National Park Service Ranger. Something she'd wanted for a long time.

Too tired the night before to shop for something for breakfast, she finished the rest of her takeout. Buying groceries would be her priority after work. She braided her hair, slipped on her cap, grabbed her keys and locked the door behind her. As she strolled down the hill to the ranger station, she glanced around. The storm had left the air cool and crisp. What a gorgeous morning, proclaimed the cheerful bird's song. The sky was bright, even though the mountain tops were shrouded in clouds. Peace filled Molly's heart as she sent up a simple *Thank you, Lord!*

~

As Molly arrived at the station, Cal pulled into the parking lot.

"Morning, Molly," he greeted in his deep voice, an oversized travel mug in his hand. He gestured to her uniform. "How'd your trip go? I see you made it to Maryville."

"Morning, Cal. I had no trouble finding Twentymile or the store in Maryville. You give great directions."

"Good. How's Jake? Haven't seen him in a few weeks. One or the other of us is usually back and forth, but we've both been extra busy lately."

"Oh, he's fine," Molly evaded. Hopefully yesterday's silly incident would soon be forgotten and it would go no further than she and Jake. "We didn't talk long."

"He's a good man and a good ranger." As they entered the station, Cal drained his travel mug then set it on the counter. "Do you know how to use that coffee maker?" He nodded toward the one on the desk.

"Sure. Want me to make a pot?"

"If you don't mind. I'm a big coffee drinker and my cup is empty."

Molly chuckled and carried the carafe into the tiny bathroom, filling it with water. "No problem. I didn't have coffee at the duplex this morning, so I could use a cup myself."

"When Craig gets here, I'll show you around, and we'll go over your duties. There are more seasonals besides Craig. Kate Fleming comes in at noon and Joe Hernandez is on break. He'll be in tomorrow when Craig's on break. You don't have to worry about the schedule, I take care of that. A copy is posted on the bulletin board so you'll always know who's working." He pointed at the cork board on the wall beside his desk.

After switching on the coffee maker, Molly grabbed several dirty mugs and spoons and returned to the bathroom to wash them. "What will my schedule be?"

"Straight days for a few weeks till you're familiar with things. Then you'll pull some evenings too. The next few days you'll stick with me. I'm heading to Headquarters in Gatlinburg on Friday, and I want you to tag along. I'll introduce you to some of the staff that you're likely to deal with most."

"We went through Gatlinburg once when I was growing up. Is it still a tourist trap?"

"Oh, yeah, but we won't be going into town. HQ is on the edge of the park. Sugarlands Visitor Center is there. It's always busy."

Cal refilled his mug with fresh coffee and downed a swig.

The front door opened and Craig sauntered in. "Mornin'," he said in a cheery tone. "Great! Fresh coffee."

"And it's good too," Cal said. "Not like that sludge you make. Molly, I think one of your duties will be to make coffee in the mornings. This is good."

"Okay, it only takes a minute, but maybe I can have some help with the cup washing?" Molly laughed and aimed a pointed look at both men.

Cal chuckled, his voice gruff. "You're going to fit in pretty well, Molly. Craig, I think that's a polite but direct way of saying she isn't going to clean up after us."

"I think you're right." A mischievous smile spread over Craig's face. "We'll get Kate to do it."

Cal raised a brow and chuckled again. "Knowing her, that won't fly."

"Kate sounds like my kind of person," Molly grinned.

"Yeah, you'll like her," Cal said.

"What's not to like?" Craig released a heavy sigh.

"Our Craig is smitten, but Kate doesn't know it." Cal sipped his coffee. "She treats everyone the same."

Molly patted Craig's arm in sympathy. "Hang in there, Craig. Perhaps one day she'll realize you care."

"Come on, Molly." Cal topped off his mug and replaced the lid. "We have places to go and lots of things to see. Take it easy, Craig. Don't let the campers give you a hard time. Call if you need us."

~

Campers were stirring throughout the campground, slowly bringing it to life. Some headed out for day trips to explore the mountains and tourist locations while others lingered around their campsites relaxing. Cal and Molly rode through, stopping occasionally to visit with folks along the way. Some had specific questions while others just wanted to shoot the breeze.

Cal parked the SUV beside the horse barn where the ranger horses were stabled. "The four horses in the front paddock are for ranger use and the two in the rear paddock are for maintenance use."

"I assume the ranger horses are for hiking trail and backcountry patrol?" Molly exited the vehicle. "What do the maintenance crews use horses for?"

"They take them up to maintain the backcountry campsites. We have a lot of backpackers come through, some on the Appalachian Trail that crosses through the middle of the park, some just camping for a few days. Unfortunately, use causes erosion of sites, so we have to limit the number of people using them at a time. They apply for a permit to stay at each site. The maintenance crew maintains those sites just like they do the sites here in the campground."

A chorus of nickers rose from the horses as Cal and Molly approached the paddock gate.

"I'll go over the permit process later," Cal continued. "There's one thing about horse patrol. A lot of our backpacking campers don't think we really patrol the woods, but we do. Heavily. Either on horseback or on foot."

After introducing Molly to the horses, Cal showed her the tack room and the food supply. "The seasonals feed the horses and you'll check to make sure the feed and hay don't run out. We get our supplies from Smokemont, the North Carolina park HQ near Cherokee. When orders come down from Gatlinburg, they go through Smokemont. We'll stop on the way to Gatlinburg Friday and I'll show you around. Do you ride?" He nodded toward the horses.

"It's been awhile, but I used to ride a lot."

"Good. You'll be riding backcountry patrol as well as hiking foot patrol. These are well-trained horses, but occasionally they get mischievous." Cal patted the neck of the nearest horse before heading back to the SUV. Molly followed him. "Next I'll show you the trailheads then we'll drive the 'Road to Nowhere'."

Molly cast him a puzzled expression.

"Don't worry. You'll see." He grinned.

Cal drove Molly up the gated road further into the park, showing her several trailheads and the paths to the waterfalls. Mountain laurel and redbud bloomed along the roadbed while the morning sun shone bright beams down through the treetops, leaving patches of golden sunlight dappling the dirt road.

Molly loved hiking and vowed to check out the trails and waterfalls the first chance she got.

Leaving the campground they wound through the valley, over low hills, past houses and barns scattered across peaceful countryside. After several miles they re-entered the park.

"This is the North Shore Road or better known as the 'Road to Nowhere," Cal said. "Fontana Lake is a manmade reservoir and when they constructed it, the plan was to build a road along the north edge of the lake, ending at Fontana Dam which was built in the 1940's. But due to lack of funding and some broken promises by the government, the road was never finished."

Cal cautiously maneuvered a series of hairpin curves. "It would've been about thirty-five miles long but only six miles were finished with a 1,200 foot tunnel at the end. The road stops on the far end of the tunnel. A lot of the locals felt betrayed, with good reason. They were promised access to family cemeteries that are now within park boundaries, but because the road was never finished, their only means to get to them is by horse, boat or hiking for miles."

The road wound through the mountains, the lake below making an occasional appearance through the trees. Cal pulled to a stop by another gate blocking the road.

"Where's the tunnel?" Molly asked curiously.

"Around that bend." Cal pointed beyond the gate. "Come on, we'll hike to the entrance."

Hiking along the paved road, they arrived at the entrance of a large two-lane tunnel, pitch black inside except for a small light at the other end. Molly could just make out the opening at the far end of the tunnel.

"Wow. To get this far and then quit. What a waste."

"Yeah. For years there've been rumors that occult groups meet out here in the tunnel and do whatever occult groups do, but we've never found any evidence. Urban legend, most likely. Occasionally we'll find the remains of a campfire. Probably nothing more than illegal camping or poachers."

"Looks like someone's been here recently. Take a look at that." Molly pointed to a black pile of something several feet inside the tunnel at the edge of the darkness.

Approaching cautiously Cal tugged a small flashlight from his leather utility belt.

"That's not good." With a heavy sigh, he lit up the object. The bright beam illuminated a pile of black fur. Returning to the edge of the tunnel, he picked up a long stick lying beside the pavement. When he flipped the fur over, it was obvious it had recently been skinned from an animal.

"Bear. Poachers have been here."

Sadness filled Molly at her first encounter with poaching evidence. "That's terrible."

"It's one of the biggest problems we have in the park. So much land and not enough rangers, and the poachers know it." Tugging his cell phone from his pocket, he snapped a few pictures of the furry remains. "I'll have to write up a report on this. Reports are something you'll need to get used to doing. We write 'em up for everything." After a fruitless search for more evidence, Cal returned to the SUV, brought back a large garbage bag and bagged the skin for disposal.

On the return trip to Deep Creek, Cal explained more about Molly's duties and the happenings around the park and the campground.

Molly had noticed Cal's wedding ring the day before. "Do you and your family live in the park?"

He nodded. "We live in quarters up past where you're staying. Pam and I have three kids: two boys and a girl. I'll introduce you to Pam. She keeps busy with the house and kids most of the time."

"I look forward to meeting her. Maybe I'll run up one evening if you don't mind."

"Not at all, if she doesn't come down to see you first."

Chapter Three

Molly had been home less than ten minutes when a knock sounded at the door. In the middle of changing out of her uniform, she quickly donned jeans and a T-shirt and hurried to answer it.

A tall woman with short blond hair had her hand raised to knock again as Molly opened the door.

"Hi, there. You must be Molly Walker. I'm Pam Bishop, Cal's wife. Just wanted to welcome you to the neighborhood, such as it is." Pam offered a cheerful laugh.

Molly opened the screen door. "It's nice to meet you, Pam. Come on in."

"Thanks." Pam entered the small living room, taking a seat on the couch. Molly caught her glance at the pile of suitcases and boxes. "You're already working and you haven't even had a chance to unpack. Cal doesn't think about those things. He's been super busy lately, and he's just so happy to have you here to share the workload."

"It's okay." Molly chuckled. "I know he's anxious for me to learn the ropes around here. Besides, these are temporary quarters. I'll be searching for a place on my days off."

Pam glanced around the plain room. "It's a shame they can't decorate these a little more attractively, but because they're temporary quarters, the seasonals tack things on the walls and don't always take care of things. The park would rather spend their budget elsewhere, so they remain a bit…rustic."

Molly's gaze circled the room. "It'll do for now. Do you know of any apartments nearby?"

"Not right off, but we get the newspaper. I'll check it for possibilities."

"That'd be great. Can I get you something to drink? I haven't had a chance to grocery shop, but during my lunchtime, I ran to the general store down the road and grabbed a few things. I have diet drinks, water and coffee."

"I'll have a diet."

In the tiny kitchenette at the end of the room, Molly pulled two sodas from the little fridge and grabbed two glasses. "Here you go."

"Thanks. I hope you don't mind me dropping in like this. I know how it is to move someplace new and no one care one way or the other. Cal and I make it a goal not to let that happen with the staff here. We've had our share of moving since he joined the park service, and he's a military vet as well."

"I don't mind at all." Molly took the armchair beside the couch. "It's nice to have someone stop by and say hello. Cal mentioned you have kids."

"Yep. Scott's eleven, Kelly's eight and Brian's five. We've been here for four years, so it's all that Kelly and Brian can remember."

They chatted for a while then Pam set her glass on the coffee table and stood. "I've really enjoyed this, Molly, but I better run. I still have to prepare supper. Cal's probably home by now and starving. Maybe if I wait long enough, he'll have it ready when I get home, huh?" She snickered. "Not a chance."

~

Over the next week, Molly familiarized herself with the routine at Deep Creek. She met and worked with Kate Fleming and Joe Hernandez, the other two seasonals. She hit it off with Kate, a petite young woman with long auburn hair always arranged in a ponytail. Her sunny disposition was a draw to everyone around her. Joe, a young Latin-American from New Mexico, was quieter than Craig and Kate, but very friendly and helpful.

The maintenance crew consisted of Bill Hopper, a fiftyish man, who had served with the park for nearly thirty years. He was born and raised in the Smoky Mountains. Molly soon discovered most NPS maintenance personnel were local folk. The other crewman,

Frank Raven, was a thirty-something Cherokee Indian who lived on the Qualla Boundary bordering the park. It didn't take long for Molly to notice the two were laid-back, never in a hurry and their motto was "we'll get to it when we have a chance." Or at least that's what Bill said. Frank rarely spoke. She concluded they'd most likely missed a lot of chances.

One morning as Molly and Joe Hernandez manned the ranger station, a man burst through the office door.

"I can't believe it!" He yelled, shaking his head in disbelief. "I just can't believe it."

Stepping to the counter, Molly asked, "Is there a problem, sir?"

"A problem?" he bellowed. "You bet there is. A bear ransacked our campsite last night. He destroyed our cooler, tore up all our food packages and ate our food. It's a mess! Now, you tell me, Missy, have we got a problem?"

Glancing at Joe, she saw him roll his eyes. Missy? Really? "Sir, when you checked in, weren't you informed of the possibility of bears roaming the campground and the absolute necessity of storing food properly?"

"I don't need someone in a uniform telling me how to camp. I've been camping for fifteen years. We've never, I repeat, *never* been attacked by bears before. You tell me why that is."

"Well, sir," Molly used her most authoritative voice, "I'd venture to say you've been fortunate before now. If you've camped in any national park where bears live then you've been informed of the dangers. This park is just one of many where bears are a problem. For many years the park service has advised campers to store their food supplies properly. Unfortunately, not everyone listens and they find themselves victims. Bears tend to follow the path of least resistance, and if food is left available, they'll take it."

The man sputtered angrily. "How dare you blame me for this! If you people would keep your bears in the woods where they belong then this wouldn't happen!"

Joe spoke up. "Sir, I checked you in yesterday and gave you the warning about proper food storage. You signed your registration card acknowledging you understood the warning. I'm sorry, but this is your own fault."

"Why you…!" sputtered the irate man. Molly watched his face turn a mottled shade of red. Was he going to pop a gasket?

Stabbing a finger in Joe's face, he demanded, "I want to see your superior! Now!"

"*I'm* his superior." Molly planted her hands on her hips. "Let's head to your campsite and check it out then we'll take it from there." Grabbing her cap, a walkie-talkie and her ticket book, she motioned the man out the door. "Which site are you in?"

"D-15!" he yelled over his shoulder as he stalked up the road.

Molly drove the park pickup slowly to the campsite, arriving before the man did. Surveying the damage, she thought he deserved what he'd gotten. A large cooler was knocked over on the ground, puncture holes in the lid and sides. The ripped open remains of food packages were scattered across the ground. A cardboard box was shredded, the remains of non-perishable food containers trailing from it.

"See?" The infuriating man huffed to a stop beside her. "Look what he did to our campsite!"

Molly's perusal took in the pop-up camper apparently unscathed. "Sir, the fact remains you stored your food outside in an unapproved manner, evidence that you failed to follow park regulations. I'd consider you fortunate he didn't do more damage. When bears find food so easily, they sometimes search further, going through campers and vehicles looking for more. You or someone in your party could've been seriously injured. I'm going to issue you a citation for this. We have regulations for a reason."

"A citation? You mean a ticket?" He exploded "Well…I won't accept it!"

Reaching to the side of her utility belt, Molly removed her walkie-talkie from its holster. Without another word to the man, she stepped a few feet away and called Cal.

"Go ahead, Molly." Cal responded.

"Cal, I have a situation in the campground. Are you available?"

"Just stopped at the office. Be right there."

"Thanks. I'm at D-15."

True to his word, Cal arrived in less than three minutes. Parking behind Molly's pickup, he climbed out. He scanned the campsite, clearly understanding what had happened. He nodded to the man then turned to Molly.

"What's up?"

While waiting for Cal to arrive, Molly began filling out the citation. She handed it to Cal without a word. He glanced at it then turned to the camper.

"Sir, did you refuse this citation?"

"I certainly did." He nodded, belligerence marring his face.

"Well, sir, either you take responsibility for what happened here and take the citation, pay the fine and move on, or I'll have to arrest you. It's that simple."

"Arrest me? You would arrest me over this?" Incredulity and perhaps a touch of fear pushed out the anger. He waved a hand toward the mess. "Why don't you give the bear the citation?"

Cal released his handcuffs from his belt, holding them in his hand. "I've given you the choice. Either you comply or I'll arrest you. It doesn't take a genius to see that your neglect caused this situation. Your driver's license, please."

Molly expected the man would again refuse, but instead he extracted his wallet and removed his license, handing it over. Cal filled in the necessary information, ripped out the citation and gave it and the license to the man. Reluctantly, he accepted them. "Sir, directions for paying your fine are on the back. As you can see, we have a copy that we keep on record. If you don't pay it, you'll be hearing from us." Cal handed the ticket book to Molly. "Come on, Molly, let's go."

Back at the station, she turned to Cal. "Thanks for your help."

He tossed her a wink. "Don't worry. It'll get easier, but then that kind is never easy. If I were a betting man I'd say he'll be checked out of here first thing in the morning." He turned to Joe sitting behind the counter. "Hey, Joe, How long are the folks at D-15 supposed to stay?"

Joe thumbed through the rack on the wall beside the counter with all the campsite numbers. Beside each number was a card with the camper's information. He found D-15. "They're paid up till Sunday. Tomorrow's Friday. Think they'll give up two days?"

Cal nodded. "In a heartbeat."

~

The next morning as Molly patrolled the campground, she wasn't surprised to find D-15 empty. Picking up the radio mic, she called the station. "Hey, Joe, did D-15 check out yet?"

After a pause, Joe responded. "Nope. Their card's still here."

"From the looks of things, I'd say they're gone, but leave the card till this afternoon, just in case. If things get busy and we need the site, go ahead, but hold out as long as you can. After all, they did pay for it. Over."

"Roger that. Over."

She drove up to the barn to spend a few minutes with the horses and to check the feed supply. Parking her truck, she grabbed a plastic bag, climbed out and approached the horses as they were eating their oats. "Hi, fellows," Molly crooned in soothing tones. Having made friends with them over the last few days, they nickered as she approached. When she pulled carrots from the bag, the horses abandoned their feed and trotted over.

"Uh huh. I've got you figured out. You just love me for my carrots. I'm on to you fellows." Opening the corral gate, she stepped inside, latching it behind her. The horses crowded around as she stroked their velvety muzzles and scratched their foreheads. Feeding each of them several pieces of carrot, she laughed. "Boy, I haven't had this much attention in a long time."

"Well, you can't blame them, you know," a voice spoke from behind her. "Who wouldn't give attention to a pretty lady."

Startled, Molly whirled to find Jake Stuart, forearms folded on the corral fence, a grin on his face. She turned back to the horses as her cheeks warmed.

"What are you doing here?" she asked as casually as she could. What was he doing here? She fed the horses the remaining carrots, stalling till her cheeks cooled. Then turning, she approached the fence. She attempted to ignore the increased rhythm of her heartbeat as her eyes met his. How ridiculous. She'd only met him once.

"I'm headed to HQ in Gatlinburg. Cal mentioned he was going tomorrow. Thought I might save him a trip."

"He's over on Noland Creek right now. There was a report of gunshots out there this morning."

"Poachers?" he asked, all traces of humor gone.

"He thought it was likely. I haven't heard from him since he left an hour ago."

A pensive expression crossed Jake's handsome face. "Maybe I'll ride over and see what's happening, if anything. Been to Noland Creek yet?"

Molly shook her head. "Not yet. Cal pointed out the entrance to the road when he showed me the 'Road to Nowhere'."

"Want to ride out with me? We can drop your truck at the station and tell Joe where we're heading." He hesitated. "Or did you have specific plans for today?"

"Not really. Just exploring the area."

"Well, come explore with me, my lady." He swept a grand bow and grinned.

~

Driving down the North Shore Road in Jake's Jeep was different than driving it in the SUV. Molly ignored the fact that the driver might have something to do with the difference.

"How long have you been at Twentymile?"

"This is my first year. I worked two years at Smokemont and one at Cades Cove. I also worked at the Grand Canyon for a year."

"Why didn't you stay at the Grand Canyon? I'd think that would be a sought after assignment."

"Oh it is, for most rangers, but I like the mountains better. The Smokies in particular hold a mystical appeal, like they've held secrets and tales for centuries just waiting for folks to discover. They have…personality." He paused, glancing at Molly. "Sounds silly, huh?"

Molly shook her head. "Not at all. That's how I see them." She turned her gaze out the window. "I remember visiting sometimes in my childhood and youth and thinking how many stories these mountains would tell if only they could speak. You have no idea how excited I was when I was hired on."

"Because of the mysteries these mountains hold?" Jake lifted a skeptical eyebrow.

"Well, they've always held a fascination for me and their beauty is… well…spectacular. But I have an even greater connection to them."

"What kind of connection?"

"My great-grandfather Cameron Murphy was the park ranger stationed at Deep Creek CCC camp back before the park was dedicated. He attended the dedication by Franklin D. Roosevelt long before it became a park campground. And Deep Creek is where he met my great-grandmother Jillian Spencer. She was a reporter with the *Asheville Citizen* and covered the story of the dedication." Molly flashed Jake a grin. "From what I understand she was quite a go-getter in her day."

"A woman reporter in 1940? I'd say so." Jake turned an appreciative gaze on her. "That's pretty amazing. So your great-grandfather was the first ranger at Deep Creek?"

"Yep." Pride filled Molly's voice. "That's why I wanted to work there."

"That's a very interesting connection you have. I guess not too many people can say that."

Jake turned the Jeep onto a dirt road that meandered down and into the forest. He parked at an iron gate beside Cal's NPS SUV. Climbing out, they stood listening, but the only sounds were the birds singing, the rustle of the breeze in the treetops and the distant sound of rushing water tripping over rocks in Noland Creek.

"Come on, let's find Cal." Jake motioned toward a path and led the way. It was fairly clear but wasn't one that visitors used often. Originally it had been an early roadbed used back before the park was established.

About ten minutes down the trail, an old wooden house that hadn't seen paint in nearly a century stood near the creek

"You can still find structures that belonged to the original landowners that sold out to the park." Jake seemed to know a great deal about the area. "Most were torn down or fell down, but some still remain."

"Why do they leave them standing?"

"Mostly the maintenance crews use them, but occasionally the rangers do, particularly for stakeouts. So, they're kept up for safety reasons but nothing is wasted on appearance."

"Where do you think Cal is?" Molly peered around the wooded area.

"Right here." Cal's voice preceded him as he approached from the side of the house. They turned as he strode toward them.

"Hey, Cal," Jake said. "Haven't seen you in a while, but I didn't think I'd have to take to the woods to find you."

"I know," Cal chuckled. "You just can't keep me out of these woods. What are you doing here?"

"I'm on my way to HQ and thought I'd see if you need anything delivered or brought back."

Removing his cap, Cal wiped his forehead with a handkerchief. "Well, I was planning to go tomorrow, but if you're going today,

I'll send what I have with you. Was going to take Molly to show her around and introduce her to some folks she'll have contact with. Why don't you take her today and show her around?"

Jake looked at Molly. "Ok with you?"

Molly would've felt more at ease going with Cal, but she didn't seem to have a choice. "Sure. If Cal's positive he doesn't need me at the campground today." She half hoped he did then wondered at her uneasiness. Jake had never done anything to make her uneasy, except to cast those dark sapphire eyes in her direction. Was that it? How silly. He couldn't help being the owner of such amazing eyes.

"Naw, the kids can handle it. And I'm done here so I'm heading back to the station."

"I guess I'm with you." Molly turned to Jake.

"Great!" A grin tilted his lips then faded. "By the way, Molly said gunshots were reported out here this morning. Find anything?"

"No but my source is pretty reliable," Cal chuckled.

"Oh, yeah? Who's that?" Jake asked as they returned to the vehicles.

"My wife," Cal responded.

"Pam?" Molly's voice rose in surprise. "Why was she out here?"

"She walks out here sometimes in the early morning. Sometimes she goes up Deep Creek, sometimes other places. She heard shots fired from the direction of the park this morning but never saw anything."

"If it was poachers, maybe they didn't get what they were after," Jake said. "She didn't see any vehicles or anything?"

"Nope. Nothing."

"Well, the shots support the evidence that's been building the last couple of months. What are your plans?" Jake opened the passenger door of his park Jeep for Molly.

Cal thought for a minute. "You and Molly head on to HQ. This afternoon when you get back I might have an answer for you. But I need to do some thinking."

Chapter Four

Does this happen often?" Molly buckled her seatbelt as Jake turned the Jeep onto the paved road.

"Too often," Jake's face was grim. "Unfortunately, there aren't enough personnel to patrol. So a lot of illegal hunting takes place in the park, and they usually get away with it."

"So why hunt in the park? There are State game lands all around it."

"You have to go back to the park's history to understand why. Great Smoky Mountains National Park wasn't made up of land grants from the government like most parks. The land belonged to people since the first families settled here. Several logging companies owned land here as well, but they were destroying rather than managing it."

Jake shifted gears as he took a sharp curve. "Anyway, the government bought out those families and the companies. They were paid and relocated outside park boundaries. Even though this all took place in the 1930's, some folks don't forget. Many felt the government robbed them, and a handful of their children and grandchildren still feel the land is theirs. Most just want to feed their families, but some have never forgiven the government. You almost can't blame them. Almost."

"So they don't appreciate that the park service is preserving the land as well as their heritage? If it had been left to the lumber mills, there wouldn't be much left by now."

"True, but instead of teaching their kids that, some just pass on their grievances." Jake paused then added, "But understand, it's not everyone who was bought out. Most accepted the park and have benefitted from it. The tourist trade through all four seasons boosts the local economy."

"What do they poach?"

"Bear and deer, both native to the Smoky Mountains, and the wild boar which isn't native, although they live within the park boundaries.

Molly focused on the scenery outside the Jeep window and grew quiet. Jake glanced at her but remained silent. She seemed lost in her own thoughts.

After several miles of silence, Jake broke into her thoughts. "This is the Qualla Boundary Cherokee Indian Reservation, another tourist attraction."

Molly spotted several Cherokee Indians dressed in brightly colored feathers and headdresses in front of a few shops lining the main road through Cherokee. A variety of signs and billboards for restaurants and shops alike beckoned visitors to come in and spend their money. The Oconoluftee River ran through the middle of town, paralleling the road. Leaving the reservation and its commercialized atmosphere behind, they re-entered the park. The road wound through wide open grasslands. Trilliums, pink lady slippers, and little brown jugs as well as other wildflowers bloomed in profusion.

Jake pulled the Jeep to the edge of the road and suggested Molly roll her window down. He then pointed to the edge of the meadow where two large animals grazed.

"Are those elk?" she whispered as she followed his suggestion.

At his nod, she sat silently watching in amazement as a huge bull elk soon walked out of the trees and joined the two grazing females. He strutted around a bit then reared his head and the forlorn bugle of the elk pervaded the quiet of the meadow.

Molly's delight at the spectacle filled Jake with a pleasure that left him breathless. *What in the world is that about? So she was beautiful and adorable and….Ok, enough of that.*

Jake started the Jeep and pulled back onto the road then pointed out an old pioneer farmstead that had stood for over a century and a half. Just past it was a large stone and wood building with a parking lot in front.

"That's the Oconoluftee Visitor Center. The farmstead is what the typical Southern Appalachian pioneer farm was like way back when. It's a live history working farm. Park personnel dress in period costume and give demonstrations of the lifestyle of the times. When you get a chance you should check it out. It's pretty interesting."

"I'll do that. What's in the visitor's center?"

"More information on the park, the farmstead and the Smokies in general."

The road paralleled the creek for several miles as it climbed slowly upward. The sun shone through the trees, dappling the road and the creek bed with bright spots of sunlight.

"It's so beautiful and peaceful through here." Contentment filled Molly's voice as she extended her arm out the window letting the wind lift and flutter it.

"Yeah, it's a nice drive, unless you're in a hurry to get to HQ and you get behind a slow moving park visitor. Then it's best to just sit back and enjoy the view. There aren't too many passing spots on this road. When we get up near the summit, tell me what you think it looks like. That is if you can see it." He chuckled.

"What do you mean?"

"It could be perfectly clear down here but up in the higher elevations it can be very foggy. It's not unusual to run into dense fog up there. Hence…."

"I know." Molly laughed. "Hence the name Smokies."

"You got it." He laughed along with her.

~

After a while Molly noticed a change in the terrain as they climbed higher and higher. Instead of the hardwood trees in the lower elevations, evergreens became predominant. Fortunately the gorgeous scenery wasn't marred by fog, and the mountain tops could be seen for miles.

"Canada!" Molly snapped her fingers suddenly. "It reminds me of Canada."

"That's right. Up here the climate is quite different. Pretty awesome, huh?"

"It certainly is."

At the summit, Jake pulled into a parking lot and turned off the engine. He pointed back at a road they'd just passed. "That's the Clingmans Dome Road. Eight and half miles up there's a large observation deck that rises above the treetops. It's a steep climb on a paved path from the parking lot, but the view is worth it. The road's closed in winter because it gets treacherous." He indicated the parking area where they sat. "This is Newfound Gap. An amazing view, huh? This is where FDR dedicated the park in 1940. Bet your great-grandpa enjoyed the view during the dedication."

"I don't know." Molly shook her head doubtfully. "I have a feeling he had his eyes on my great-grandmother."

"Well, if she was as pretty as her great-granddaughter…." Jake's words trailed off.

Molly's cheeks grew warm. She chose to ignore the compliment and drank in the scenery instead. "No wonder they picked this spot for the dedication. I could just sit a while and enjoy this view."

Jake chuckled softly as he cranked the Jeep. Yep. He'd noticed her evasion of his words. They'd warmed her heart as well as her cheeks, but it was best not to encourage him. She was here to get her career started. Great-grandpa Murphy would've wanted her to keep her eye on the ball, wouldn't he?

As they descended the curvy road through the mountains, Molly tried to glimpse below where the edge of the road fell away.

"Quite a drop," Jake laughed. "Don't worry. We don't lose *too* many rangers or visitors that way."

Eventually the road joined another creek in the lower elevation, winding along the banks until they reached the Sugarland Visitors Center. Jake drove around behind and parked in front of the large stone and wood headquarters building.

Once inside, Molly realized most personnel wore the NPS uniform while some dressed in civilian clothes. Jake led her through several offices, introducing her to people. After attempting a mental note of names, Molly finally gave up. There were just too many.

They descended to the basement of the building. In the back corner, Jake opened a door, allowing her to enter first.

"Hi, Paul." Jake tossed a wave to a young man behind a counter. A shock of dirty-blond hair spilled over his forehead and black-framed glasses encircled his bright blue eyes. A cordless microphone headset was attached over his head. On the desk in front of him sat an elaborate communications system. He jumped up when Jake called his name and held out his hand.

"Jake, my man, how's it going? What are you doing in this neck of the woods? Aren't you a little far from home?" A wide grin split Paul's face.

Jake grasped the outstretched hand, shaking it vigorously. "Yeah, well, you know how it goes. I have to come out of the woods sometime. If nothing else, just to see people."

Paul cast appreciative eyes in Molly's direction. "I know you didn't find her in the woods." He waggled his eyebrows.

Molly laughed softly as her cheeks flamed.

"Not exactly. This is Molly Walker, the new ranger at Deep Creek. She just started this week. Molly, this is Paul O'Brian, one of the park dispatchers. When you call HQ by radio, this is one of the folks you'll be communicating with."

"It's nice to meet you, Paul." Molly shook his outstretched hand.

"The pleasure's all mine." Paul waggled his eyebrows again. "You can call me anytime."

"Do his eyebrows always do that?" Molly asked in mock concern. "A nervous twitch, maybe?"

With a bark of laughter, Jake shook his head. "Pay him no mind. He sits in the basement corner and has very little human contact. So when he does, he can't control himself. He's harmless, really."

"I'll keep that in mind." Molly chuckled.

Paul's frown failed to disguise his twinkling eyes. "Well, that's definitely the pot calling the kettle black. Look who doesn't come out of the woods much. Ha! He prefers his horses to humans, you know."

"Well, I came out just so I could see you," Jake grinned.

"Sure you did." Paul's nod was skeptical. "Nobody comes just to see me. What are you doing here, anyway?"

"I have an appointment with Tom. I brought some reports that Cal and I have written up. Poaching in our area is on the increase. We've got to get a handle on it and put a stop to it."

"I wish you luck." Paul crossed his fingers. "That's a never-ending battle. We have the same problem on this side of the mountain, but I don't need to tell you that."

"Yeah. Well," Jake held up the manila folder, "we need to get over to Tom's office. It was great seeing you, Paul. If you're ever on my side of the mountain, drop in for a visit."

"Hey, you know it, man," Paul replied agreeably. Turning back to Molly, he held out his hand. She reached to shake it, but he drew it to his lips. "And, Molly my dear, I hope you'll come back to see me. My heart won't beat again until you do." His words dripped syrupy sweet.

Molly pulled her hand pointedly from his grasp and affected the same drippy tone. "Oh, I'm sure I'll be back. But you'll have to get help for that heart problem. I don't think I'm the answer." She winked and turned to leave.

Stunned, Paul stared momentarily then grinned at Jake. "Hey, I like her, Jake. She's alright."

"Yeah, well, she's on to you, Paul. She's got you figured out already. See you around."

And with that, they left. Just before the door closed, Molly turned and gave a quick saucy wave.

"He's something else," she stated as they returned to the main floor.

"He's a good guy," replied Jake. "He's just crazy, that's all."

~

Molly wasn't prepared for the man sitting behind the superintendent's desk. When Tom Cramer's secretary showed her and Jake into his office, Molly was expecting a large and possibly tough man. After all he was in charge of the whole park, right? He had to be tough. Perhaps he was, but he certainly wasn't big. A good half foot shorter than Jake's six-foot height, he had a wiry build. His thick mustache was gray as was his hair, or what remained of it. Wire framed glasses sat low on his thin, straight nose. As they entered the room, he stood and came around his desk.

"Jake! It's good to see you." He shook Jake's hand warmly then turned to Molly. "And who might this be?"

"This is Molly Walker, Sir. Deep Creek's newest ranger. Molly, this is Tom Cramer, Superintendent."

"It's a pleasure to meet you, Molly." He shook Molly's hand. "Cal mentioned you were coming. How do you like working at Deep Creek?"

"It's a pleasure to meet you, too, Sir." Molly smiled. He might be slightly built but he had a heck of a handshake. "I like it very much. The other rangers and aides have been a big help while I'm learning the ropes. I enjoy working with them."

"I'm glad to hear that. But please, call me Tom. Everyone does." He indicated the sable-colored leather chairs placed in front of his desk. "Please, have a seat. You too, Jake. No need to stand around when we can sit."

After they were seated, he continued. "Jake, what brings you here? Besides to show our new ranger around. Anything interesting happening at Twentymile?"

Jake nodded grimly. "Unfortunately. There's new evidence that the poachers have been busy." He handed the manila envelope across the desk to Tom. "Here are the reports that Cal and I have written up for you. One in particular is disturbing. A little present left on the station porch at Twentymile about two weeks ago. Cal's working on a game plan and said he'd call you in a day or so to talk it over with you."

"I hate to hear that. They hunt all winter and then just when you think things slow down, they don't." Tom shook his head sadly. "Things are just as bad in the summer. Worse really, because we have the summer visitors who are put more and more in danger and don't even know it."

"I'm sure you've already thought of hiring more personnel and getting them into the woods," said Jake.

"Yes, I have, but the Department of the Interior isn't allowing a big enough increase for hiring. They just don't have it. Still, we may be able to work something out." He picked up the manila folder. "I'll add your reports to what I've gathered from other rangers and consider the big picture. Tell Cal I'll wait to hear from him. Perhaps if we all put our heads together, we'll come up with something."

"Right, Tom. It was good seeing you."

"You too, Jake. Molly." He turned to her as he stood behind his desk, "I'm very glad to meet you. I don't get down to the south districts as much as I'd like, so stop in and say hello when you're up this way. I like to keep in touch with my rangers."

~

As Molly and Jake exited the building, a feminine voice called Jake's name. Glancing back, Molly spotted a tall blond in a cream-colored blouse, tight brown skirt, and black high heels following them out the door. The woman caught up with them and threw her arms around Jake's neck, giving him a tight hug.

"Jake, darling, it's so good to see you." She smiled devotedly into his astonished face. "Why haven't you come out of those silly ol' woods sooner? I've missed you!"

"Celeste!" Jake exclaimed.

Molly noticed the heightened color in his face as he reached back and grasped the woman's hands, pulling them down from his neck. "Celeste! How are you? It's been a while." His expression changed from astonishment, to uneasiness to irritation, all in about two seconds.

"You're telling me," she pouted. "I never see you anymore."

"Yeah, well, I stay pretty busy."

He looked extremely uncomfortable to Molly.

"Celeste, this is Molly Walker. Molly, Celeste Payne, one of the secretaries here at HQ."

Molly extended a hand toward the tall blond. "It's nice to meet you, Celeste."

Celeste barely gave Molly a second glance and completely ignored her outstretched hand. "Likewise, I'm sure," she murmured, turning back to Jake. "Come on, Jake. When are you going to call me? I've been waiting, you know."

Shunned, Molly dropped her hand. "I'll wait in the Jeep. Take your time, Jake." She hurried away, eager to escape the scene playing out on the porch.

~

Jake scowled with distaste. "That was pretty rude, Celeste. Molly's new to the park. You could've at least welcomed her properly."

"Oh, Jake." A pout tilted Celeste's red lips. "I'm not interested in some girl ranger. I'm interested in you. I thought I'd made that evident."

Stepping back, Jake slipped his hands into his pants pockets. "We've been through this before. We're friends. Nothing more."

"We could be, Jake, if you'd just try," she crooned in a wheedling voice.

"I've got to go. See you around, Celeste." Jake wearily turned to leave.

Without warning, she grabbed his face between her hands and planted a long, hard kiss on his lips. "Just something to help change your mind." She turned her gaze toward the Jeep where Molly sat then back to Jake. "See you around, handsome," she cooed, strutting back into the building.

Even though Molly was looking anywhere but at them, Jake knew she hadn't missed Celeste's little scene and his blood boiled. Celeste had been after him for months. He almost dreaded coming to HQ for fear of running into her. He'd almost made it this time. No such luck.

Climbing into the Jeep, he started the engine. What could he say to Molly in explanation? Why explain at all? He didn't owe her any explanations. But deep down he knew he didn't want Molly to think he went for Celeste's type. Instead he settled on a safer topic.

"So, what'd you think of Tom?" Jake cringed. Was his tone a little too bright?

"I liked him a lot," Molly said. "He seems like a good man to work for. Caring but authoritative too."

"He is," Jake was relieved the conversation was headed toward safer ground. "I've worked for some chiefs who don't care about their subordinates except for what they can get out of them. Tom's not like that. He takes an interest in his staff. Not in a nosy way, but with caring concern. He expects the most from them professionally, but he gives in return."

"It's great to have a boss like that," Molly nodded. After a few minutes of silence, she asked, "Where does Celeste work?"

"She's a secretary in the personnel office." So much for safer ground.

~

"She's friendly. In a way," Molly said. Oh, brother! Yeah, she's friendly alright. If you're male and Jake. So what? She attempted to quell her curiosity. It really wasn't any of her business who Jake saw. The young woman was pretty… in an artificial way. She would've thought Jake was above a public display, but in all fairness to him, Celeste had initiated it.

They crossed back over the mountains in mutual silence until they reached Cherokee. Jake mentioned they hadn't eaten and it was nearly three o'clock.

"I apologize." He glanced at Molly. "Want to stop for lunch now? I'll buy."

Molly smiled at his beseeching expression. "Growing boys must eat. Sure, why not. My stomach's complaining rather loudly. Is that what reminded you?"

"No. Mine did." He tossed her a pained look.

He parked in front of a fast food restaurant built above the bank of the Oconoluftee River. The lunchtime crowd had long departed, leaving only a few customers seeking ice cream in the warm afternoon. Molly ordered a chili dog and fries while Jake ordered a deluxe burger with onion rings. After picking up their orders, they sat by a window overlooking the river.

Molly bowed her head and closed her eyes in a quick silent prayer of thanksgiving. She heard Jake open the wrapping of his food then the sound halted.

"Sorry," he said awkwardly as she opened her eyes. "I didn't realize."

Molly smiled. "It's okay. I understand not everyone says a blessing over their food, but it's how I was raised."

Jake nodded as he removed the burger wrapper. "We used to go to church too. My parents still do. I stopped going when I went off to college, and I suppose that's when I stopped praying at meals. Or anytime."

Molly swallowed a bite of her hotdog. "I can't remember a time my parents didn't take us to church. My mom was a Sunday School teacher, and we loved being in youth group."

"You didn't find it, well… stifling to be forced to attend church all the time?" Jake's curiosity seemed genuine.

Molly shrugged her shoulders and shook her head. "Not at all. They made learning about our Christian faith interesting and fun, and the church we attended was great. There are so many loving and giving folks there, always supporting one another in prayer and helping however was needed. My parents still attend there." She glanced out the window at the clear water tripping over river rocks as it churned its way downstream. Her eyes saw something much further away.

"You miss it, don't you?"

She returned her gaze to his. "You're very perceptive." A faint smile lifted her lips. "I do miss it. I thought I'd search for a church to go to Sunday. I noticed a few around town and one as you head out the North Shore Road."

Jake finished his burger then started on the onion rings. "So, where do you come from?"

"Charlottesville, Virginia. And you?"

"From over in the Nantahala National Forest near Franklin. It's one of the most popular white-water rafting areas in the country."

"Sounds familiar," Molly shook her head, "but I can't place it."

"It's almost due south of Bryson City."

"So you're a local boy! Are you a white-water rafter as well?" Molly grinned and wadded up her wrapper.

Jake shook his head, leaning back in his seat. "I've been several times, but there are other things I'd rather do. My brother runs a raft rental and guide shop, and guides tourists down the river all the time. He bugs me endlessly about getting back out there again but I manage to avoid it. I prefer the woods myself. There's no peace on the white-water river, but the woods are full of it."

"I definitely agree. I white water rafted once when I was in college. Thought I'd never get off that boat unless it was straight into the water. A lot of people I know enjoy it and they can have at it!" Molly paused before asking, "What about your family? You mentioned a brother. Do you have other siblings? Are your parents still there?"

"Yeah, they are." Jake smiled. "They love the little town where they live, and I don't think there's anything that could get them to move away. Dad has always owned an apple orchard since before I was born, and he still runs it like he did when I was a kid. I suppose I inherited my love of the outdoors from him. Mom works right alongside of him. When my brother and I grew up and left home, Dad hired a couple of hands to help on the farm. I thought he'd be disappointed when I told him I was going to pursue a career in the park service."

"And was he?"

"Not at all." He shook his head. Was he remembering that long ago conversation with his dad? "He told me I should follow my heart." When he spoke again it was more to himself than to Molly. "As long as I followed God's will."

For a few minutes he seemed to have forgotten her presence then he looked up, grinning sheepishly. "Sorry. Guess I was woolgathering. We should get back. Cal will be wondering where we've gotten to."

~

As they returned to the Jeep, Jake glanced at Molly strolling quietly at his side. What was it about her that reminded him of his spiritual roots? He hadn't thought about them for years and had pretty much forgotten his conversation with his dad. Why had that memory come flooding back? Because of Molly's mealtime blessing? He'd have to think about it later. But not right now. He needed to get her back to Deep Creek.

~

"Hi, Kate." Molly said as Jake held the door of the ranger station for her. Kate stood behind the counter, tallying up the day's fees. She glanced up and smiled.

"Hey, Molly. Hi, Jake." Molly noticed Kate's greeting for Jake seemed a little warmer than the one for her. "How was your drive to HQ? Anything good happening on that side of the mountain? Molly, I bet you met a lot of people you won't remember the next time you see them."

"You've got that right." Molly's brow furrowed. "I don't have a memory for names, and faces are even worse. Is Cal around?"

"Back here." Cal's voice came from behind the partition. "Come on back and sit down. You too, Jake."

Molly eased into the only other chair while Jake took the corner of the desk. "What's up?"

"I've been considering our conversation this morning." Cal leaned back in his chair. "It's time for another stake-out, only this time we need to bring in some rangers from the other districts. Deep Creek and Twentymile have fewer personnel than any other district in the park. I'm going to propose to Tom that we bring in most of the backcountry rangers and have a four-night long stake-out. The aides can hold down the campground and, Molly, I'll send you to Twentymile while Jake's on the stake-out. You can return if something comes up that the aides can't handle."

Disappointment that she wouldn't be involved in the stake-out filled Molly. She struggled to mask the disappointment in her voice. "Alright. When will this take place?"

"I don't know yet. I have to run it past Tom and the other district rangers and a lot of planning has to take place. We'll just sit tight for a bit."

"After our conversation with Tom this morning, I don't think you'll have any trouble getting his support," said Jake. "He's had about enough."

"So have I," replied Cal. He reached for a paper lying on the side of the desktop. "I received this notice from Ed Clark today." He glanced at Molly. "Did you stop by Oconoluftee and meet Ed Clark?"

Molly was a little puzzled. "I don't think so. The name doesn't ring a bell."

Jake shook his head. "No, we didn't stop." He looked at Molly and explained, "Ed is the District Chief Ranger for the south side. His office is behind the Oconoluftee Visitors Center. You'll meet him soon."

"Well," Cal said, "we're going to step up the wild boar trapping program. I've already contacted the NC Wildlife Resources Commission to prepare them. Tomorrow I'm heading over to Oconoluftee to pick up more boar traps." They discussed where to set the traps and a schedule for checking to see if they caught anything.

"Since I've got a lot to do with the stake-out plans, I'm depending on you two to head this up. It means more patrols, but if those poachers find out where the traps are set, it'll be a race to see who checks them first. We've got to keep it quiet. I don't even want the maintenance fellows to know. Understand?" Molly and Jake each nodded. "Jake, have you got enough corn bait down at Twentymile?"

"About a half of a sack."

"I'll pick you up some tomorrow."

After the briefing, Molly picked up her cap and daypack and headed out the door, tossing Kate a wave and a quick goodbye. It was almost five-thirty and she was ready to call it a day. The squeaky screen door opened and slammed shut behind her. The maintenance men would have to do something about that annoying door.

"Molly." Jake had followed her outside. "Wait up."

"Yes?" She spun around.

He stopped in front of her, and after a few seconds, she noticed his sudden reluctance to continue.

"Yes?" she prompted again.

"Um…. You know, about that scene outside HQ this afternoon. Celeste is just a colleague, no matter what she may want to the contrary." He took a deep breath, letting it out slowly. "She's been trying to pursue a relationship with me for a while now."

"Jake, it's none of my business concerning your associations." Molly held up a hand, halting his words. "And you don't owe me an explanation." She smiled to soften the words.

He looked like he wanted to say more, but ended with "I appreciate that."

"Thanks for taking me around today. I met some really nice people and some people that I won't remember again," she chuckled.

"Fair maiden, the pleasure's all mine." Sweeping his arm outward, he bowed gallantly from the waist then straightened again. "Well, I'd better get home. The horses will be waiting for their supper by the time I get back. I'll be here bright and early Monday morning and we'll start setting out those traps. See you then." He tipped his cap and strolled toward his Jeep. Molly waved as he drove past and headed out of the campground.

She turned and hiked up the hill, relieved that the tension concerning Celeste had been cleared away. At least she told herself it was. She just wasn't sure she believed it.

Chapter Five

As Molly patrolled the campground late Friday afternoon, she stopped occasionally to chat with campers relaxing in their campsites or walking around enjoying the late spring afternoon. She'd just circled the parking lot near the horse stables and the trailhead when Tim Young hailed her. Tim and his father, Eli, owned and operated the riding stables located just outside the park entrance. When customers rented their horses, they would trailer them to the parking lot then guide them up the trails. It was a good business and worked out well for the Young's and for the park. Molly had met Tim a few days earlier but hadn't yet met Eli.

Tim was trailering in some horses and waved a hand at Molly, motioning her to stop. After parking her SUV she climbed out and approached his truck.

"Hi Tim! What's up?" she smiled, removing her sunglasses and propping an arm on his open window.

"Hi, Molly."

Molly guessed the young man was in his late twenties. With light brown hair peeking beneath a straw cowboy hat, he seemed to have a perpetual smile on his face. Today his smile was missing.

Molly noticed his smile was missing.

"Don't know what to make of this, but there's a fella back up the road a bit. He's hunkered down and looks like something's wrong with him. Like he's sick or something." Tim pushed his hat back on his head.

"Where is he exactly?"

"Just before you get to the picnic pavilion on the left side of the road."

"Thanks, Tim. I'll check it out. See you later."

"Hope everything's ok," Tim called as Molly headed back to her vehicle.

"Me too!" She climbed into the SUV and drove to the location where Tim had seen the man. Sure enough, she spotted him crouching near a boulder, his head resting on his arms. Parking the SUV, she approached the man.

"Sir, are you ok? Can I help you somehow?"

Without answering, he began a gentle rocking motion, back and forth, never raising his head from his arms.

"Sir, if you're ill or need help, please tell me. I'll be happy to help however I can." She spoke quietly as she knelt beside him, still receiving no response. She reached out a hand to touch his shoulder. "Sir, I…."

Before she could continue, he jumped up and dashed across the picnic area back toward the campground. Molly loped back to the SUV, slamming it into gear. She'd seen the sheer terror on the young man's face, even if she didn't understand it. As she drove quickly toward the campground she flipped on the blue roof light. Grabbing the radio mic she called for assistance. Both Craig and Joe responded, indicating they were on the way.

Molly directed Craig to take B Loop and Joe to take C Loop while she drove through A Loop. Driving slowly she searched for the young man's thin figure. Without warning he appeared from nowhere, running across the road in front of her. Hitting the brakes, she watched as he took to the wooded area located between A Loop and the other camping areas. Quickly turning the truck, she headed that way.

Molly huffed out a heavy sigh and slammed the palm of her hand against the steering wheel. With him on foot and her and the others in vehicles, it would be very difficult to stop him. He dodged into places where the vehicles couldn't go. As she reached the entrance to the other camping loops, Craig drove up.

"Craig, it's going to be impossible to locate this guy in the vehicles. Head to the maintenance shed and get the dirt bike. You can follow him through the woods with that and can keep up with him better." As he drove away, Molly picked up the mic again. "Joe, what's your position?"

"I'm near the bridge by the trailhead parking lot. I just spotted him running through the woods toward A Loop. Again. What's with this guy?"

"I don't know. Hopefully we'll find out if we can stop him. Head back over and I'll meet you there."

"Will do."

After Joe signed off, her radio crackled. "Molly, this is Cal, what's happening?"

Good. Cal was back. "I don't know why, Cal, but we have a camper acting very strangely. He's running randomly through the campground. There appears to be something wrong with him. We're in pursuit, but haven't been able to pin him down."

"I'll meet you and Joe in five minutes. I'm just outside the park."

"Roger that." Cal was returning from Oconoluftee with the hog traps, and she was glad he was back. It was a perplexing situation. Like trying to grab dandelion fluff in a breeze. The young man was elusive at best.

Arriving in A Loop she found Joe waiting for her and within minutes, Cal and Craig arrived.

"Tell me what's happening." Cal jumped out of his SUV.

Molly explained from the beginning. "Cal, I wish you'd seen the look of terror on his face. There's definitely something amiss. And he's fast. Whatever may be wrong with him, nothing is wrong with his speed."

"You've got that right," Joe agreed. "I can't keep up with him."

Cal released a heavy sigh. "Craig, get back out there with the dirt bike, but stay central. If one of us spots him, you can respond quickly. Keep your eyes peeled. We'll be looking too. Where's Kate?"

"She's holding down the station and waiting for news." Molly tugged her cap off and fanned herself with it.

"Good. Call and have her search through the camper registration cards for anything that might indicate where this guy is camping or if he's even staying in the campground. Come on, folks. Let's find this guy and get him some help."

For the next half-hour they searched for the young man. Occasionally someone would spot him and then he was gone again. Several campers offered their help, looking for him on foot.

Molly was driving back toward the trailhead parking lot when Kate called over the radio. "Molly, I think I have something. It's not much, but hopefully it'll help. There's a couple staying in A-7, and when they registered, they wrote a third name on the card. Walter. The couple's names are Walter and Ruth Jones. Maybe it's them and maybe it's not, but that's the only possibility I've found."

"Thanks, Kate. I'll check it out and let you know."

~

Molly parked at the campsite where a pop-up camper stood amongst other camping gear. An older woman sat before a bright campfire, her gaze locked on the flames and her hands squeezed tightly together, knuckles white.

"Mrs. Jones?"

The woman lifted her gaze to Molly's face as she approached. "Yes, I'm Mrs. Jones." Her voice sounded strained and sad.

Instinct told Molly this woman had something to do with the young man. Kneeling near her chair, Molly spoke quietly. "Mrs. Jones, we're searching for a young man who's been seen running around the campground. I think he may need help, but I don't know why. He won't let anyone near him. Do you know anything? Can you help us help him?"

The woman's gaze returned to the fire. Tears began to form then ran down her cheeks. She nodded slowly. "Yes, I know who he is. He's my son, Walter, and he does need help. He's been in a mental facility for the past two years. He had improved so much and the doctors were impressed with his progress. They even agreed that my husband and I could bring him camping, thinking it would be good for him. But this evening something happened. I have no idea what, but he took off. My husband went after him. I've seen my son run through here a few times, but he's gone before I can call him."

Molly's heart squeezed at the woman's woeful tale. "Why didn't you or your husband call a ranger when he first ran off? We would've been happy to help, like we're doing now."

"My husband didn't want to involve anyone else. He wanted to bring Walter back himself. We didn't want it known that Walter's mentally ill." She turned terror-filled eyes on Molly. "Miss, my son needs help. Badly. This was a mistake. The doctors. Us. We made a mistake. We never should have brought him here. You've got to find him."

Molly placed a gentle hand on the woman's thin shoulder. "We'll find him, Mrs. Jones. Let me contact the others, and we'll keep searching until we find him."

"Thank you," Mrs. Jones whispered. Dropping her head into her hands, she sobbed quietly as Molly returned to her vehicle and picked up the CB mic.

"Come in, Cal," she called.

"Cal here."

"Meet me at the station. I have news."

~

"Well, this sheds a whole new light on the situation," Cal sighed heavily after Molly shared her conversation with Mrs. Jones. "We need outside help. Kate, call the Sheriff's office in town and explain our dilemma. See if they know who to contact in a situation like this."

Just then the base radio crackled to life. "Cal is this Joe. Come in." He sounded winded and excited.

"Cal here. Talk to me, Joe."

"We've got him. Between Craig, his father and me, we have him."

"Where are you?"

"In D Loop. But hurry! I don't know how much longer we can hold him." Joe's strained voice trailed off with a grunt.

"We're on our way."

Leaving Kate to make her phone call, Cal and Molly drove to D Loop. The sun had already dropped behind the mountains and little light remained. Cal clicked on the headlights, and when they reached the men, the beams lit a scene that instantly tore at Molly's heart. Craig and Joe had managed to catch the young Walter, but because of his frantic struggles were forced to hold him down. The older Walter knelt beside him, cradling his son's head in his lap, tears streaming down his wrinkled cheeks. The young man continued his struggles, making it difficult for the men to maintain their hold. His loud moan reminded Molly of a scared, caged animal. He wouldn't be released back into his parent's custody. At least not now. He needed professional help. Again.

With much care and difficulty, they managed to settle Walter into Cal's park SUV. Tears stung Molly's eyes as they handcuffed him, restraining him from hurting himself or anyone else. Walter, Sr. climbed in beside him and wrapped his arms around his terrified son, holding him close as the young man burst into heart-rending sobs.

Returning to the station, they left Walter in the SUV with his father, Craig and Joe to watch him while Molly and Cal hurried inside to find out what information Kate had learned.

"The Sheriff wants you to take Walter and his parents up to the hospital and he'll meet you there. He's already contacted the hospital and they're working to get Walter some help."

"Probably a state mental institution." Molly's voice rose with indignation.

"Molly, as much as we don't like the sound of that, we're in no position to decide." Cal placed an understanding hand on her shoulder. "We aren't trained to make those decisions. We just get him the help he needs and leave it to the experts. We can't help him, and right now, neither can his parents. We just have to let the sheriff's department and the folks at the hospital take it from here."

"I know. I just hate seeing him trussed up like that." Sadness drained the anger from Molly. She held up her hand when Cal started to speak again. "I know. I know. They're necessary measures to ensure he doesn't harm himself or anyone else, but it tears at my heart to see him so afraid and not understanding what's happening."

Cal nodded in agreement. "I know what you mean. Look, I'll go get Mrs. Jones and the fellows and I'll take them up to the hospital. Why don't you call it an evening?" He glanced at his wristwatch. "It's nearly nine-thirty. Go home and get some rest. I'll take care of the report myself, so you don't need to worry about it. Just have a good weekend, and I'll see you Monday morning."

Cal turned to Kate. "Mind sticking around until you hear from me? I'd like someone to man the station and the phones till I get back."

"Cal, let me stay," Molly appealed. "I want to see this through. Besides, I'm the one who found him. I just want to know how things work out and be here if I'm needed for anything."

"She's right, Cal," Kate agreed. "Molly should stay."

Cal peered at Molly. "Alright. I'll give you a call when I know something then you can head home."

"I'll be here."

~

Wearily, Molly sat on the high stool and propped her elbows on the counter, resting her chin in her palms. Darkness had descended and the campground was settling down for the night. During the search she'd absently noticed the evening program interpreter arrive and set up for the evening presentation. She hadn't met him yet but Cal had mentioned he presented a different program every Friday, Saturday and Sunday evening. Her family had always enjoyed the campfire programs they had attended while camping. Sometimes there was a sing-a-long by the fireside or an evening nature hike. Local ghost stories and legends by the campfire were always fun and slide presentations of animals and foliage were interesting.

Glancing out the window by Cal's desk, she spotted the glow of a campfire at the amphitheater across the creek. Quite a few campers had participated in the search for Walter, and she hoped they hadn't missed the whole program.

She glanced at her watch. Nine-thirty. It seemed so much longer than ten minutes since Cal and the others had left. She paced around the tiny office. There was paperwork she could do until Cal called but she was just too restless.

Molly dusted the office, cleaned the bathroom toilet and sink and paced some more. She made a pot of coffee and was about to pour a second cup when the station door opened. Turning, she half expected to see Cal. Instead it was a young man whom she'd never seen before. He wore the NPS uniform and the "Smokey Bear" hat worn by rangers who dealt more with the public than with wildlife and natural resources.

Removing his hat, the man laid it on the counter and flashed a self-assured smile at Molly. "Hi, I guess you're Molly Walker. You're the only one around here I haven't met yet, so I can only assume that's you."

His sparkling white smile flashed again, giving Molly the full effect of his dazzling good looks. Dark blond hair waved thickly around his head, a bit longish on his neck, but not too long. Tall and well-built, he was broad across the chest and shoulders and lean at the waist. Turquoise eyes twinkled as a dimple in his check accompanied his smile. He'd missed his true calling. He should have headed to Hollywood instead of the park service.

"Yes, I'm Molly Walker. And you are…?"

"David. David Andrews." He extended a hand. "It's a pleasure to meet you, Molly. I present the weekend evening programs at the amphitheater. We just finished up a few minutes ago, and when I saw the station lights on this late, I thought I'd stop in." He paused, his expression turning serious. "I hear you had some drama this evening. Some of the campers at the program were talking about it."

"Yes, we did." She nodded, sipping her coffee. "Can I offer you a cup? I just made a pot a few minutes ago."

"Sure, that'd be great." David came around the counter and pulled out the chair from behind the desk, taking a seat. "That's one thing about working in the park. You never know from day to day what's going to happen. You could have a run of boredom or you might get a flurry of activity. At least in your job. Mine, I suppose, is a little more sedate."

"What do you mean?" Molly cast a quizzical look his way.

"Well, as an interpreter, I deal more with the public relations side of the park. I present programs on the weekends, give tours at Oconoluftee or work at the visitor's center during the day. A lot of my time is spent in research and preparing for my programs. I don't really deal with the needs of the public except in an educational aspect. I'm not law enforcement like you are."

Molly nodded slowly. "I see your point. Do you like your job?"

"Immensely! But it's only seasonal. I teach college biology during the school months and work for the park service in the summer season."

"Wow! That must be interesting. Have you worked in any other parks?"

"I've been teaching for ten years, and each summer I've worked in a different park. The Grand Canyon, the Everglades, Yosemite and Bryce Canyon to name a few. I've been fortunate to work most of the bigger parks which has given me ample opportunity for research and experience. I take a lot of that back into the classroom and incorporate it into my teaching."

David talked on and on about his experiences and some of the research he had done. He was a pleasant enough guy, but Molly soon grew bored. He sure liked talking about himself. Not really in the mood to socialize, she grew frustrated at his relentless monologue. She was anxious to hear from Cal and find out what was happening.

Evidently in no hurry to leave, David refilled his coffee cup and returned to his seat, never missing a beat in re-telling his experiences in the Everglades. Molly tried to glean something interesting from his endless words, but had a hard time concentrating. Not once since mentioning the earlier excitement of the evening had David asked more about it.

Cal never called but finally returned about eleven-fifteen. Molly had listened to David talk the whole time. Although uninvited, he'd settled down to wait with her, never asking what kept her there so late. He had a captive audience and was taking full advantage of it.

She jumped up when Cal entered, interrupting David's latest anecdote. A hint of guilt edged her thoughts for welcoming the interruption, but it passed quickly. After all, he'd had her undivided attention all evening.

"Well?" she asked Cal as he pulled his cap off and tossed it on the counter next to David's hat. "What happened? Where are Joe and Craig?"

Cal looked exhausted and Molly felt for him. As hard as it had been to sit and wait, being present while ensuring Walter was taken care of must have been even harder.

"They just left to return home." He paused, looking at David. "Hello, David. How was the program this evening? I hope our little escapade through the campground didn't interrupt you too much."

A casual grin lifted the corners of David's mouth. "We started a bit late, but no harm done. The program went well."

Molly noticed David's even temperament. Even though he was his own favorite subject, his feathers weren't ruffled when attention was taken from him.

"That's good." Cal turned back to Molly. "Sorry I'm so late getting back. Once Walter was evaluated, it was determined he should return to his previous facility. The doctors were called and arrangements were made to transport him. The Jones' live in Pennsylvania near the facility. They're coming back to the campground in the morning to pack up and head home. Walter will already be back at the facility when they arrive."

Molly set down her coffee cup and swiped a stray tendril of hair from her forehead. "I know it's for the best. It's just so sad. His parents were hopeful because of his progress. They must be devastated."

"Craig and Joe are going to help them pack up their gear in the morning. Then we've done all we can do."

Reaching for her cap and daypack, Molly headed for the door. "We can pray for them." She looked at David who had remained quiet during the conversation. "It was nice meeting you, David. I'll see you around. Good night, Cal. Thanks for letting me know how things turned out."

~

Molly spent most of Saturday searching for an apartment where it would afford her more privacy than the duplex at the campground. Already three separate campers had shown up at her door with questions. She didn't care to be "on call" 24/7, so she drove into town, bought a newspaper and got comfortable at the drugstore lunch booth. While enjoying fresh brewed coffee and a piece of homemade pecan pie, she perused the ads, finding a few possibilities. She'd thought about calling Pam Bishop to see what she'd found, but Pam was busy with her family. Molly didn't want to interrupt her Saturday with the kids home from school.

After checking out the first two places, she immediately scratched them off her list. One, a room in a run-down motel outside of town, was just that. Run down. She suspected cockroaches and mice were already permanent residents. Would drug sales be a means of income by the human residents? The second, a very old and small mobile home in a trailer park was fairly clean, but Molly refused to live there. A couple of the occupants of the other trailers had come out to meet her. One, a large, burly man, with a cigarette hanging between his lips and a leer in his eye, made her particularly uncomfortable. She'd live in the duplex at the park before she set herself up for problems with him.

The last ad was for an apartment in the home of a widow located outside of town. When Molly arrived at the house, she found an older woman working in the flower garden bordering the wide front porch that ran the full length of the house and around one side. The old two story house sported a fresh coat of white paint. At one end of the porch, a swing swayed gently in the cool morning breeze. White wooden rockers beckoned visitors to come up and sit a while. Bright spring flowers hung in baskets above the railing. Gabled second floor windows indicated spacious rooms. So far, Molly liked what she saw.

"Mrs. Jenkins?" She approaching with a smile. A bright red cardigan topped the woman's tan dress, her gray and white hair pulled back in a bun. Smile lines bracketed her mouth and radiated from her faded blue eyes even as her lips formed a smile. "My name's Molly Walker. I'm interested in seeing the apartment you advertised in the paper."

Mrs. Jenkins set down the watering can she held as her smile broadened. "Well, how do you do? Yes, I've had that apartment for rent for some time now with not much interest. I was even thinking of removing the ad from the newspaper. I don't really need to rent, but thought a little extra income from it would be nice. I have so much room here, I rattle around most days. It's just me, you know. My husband passed away a few years ago."

"I'm sorry to hear that," Molly said.

"Oh, it's ok. I miss him, but I'm fine, really I am. I shouldn't keep you standing here listening to me prattle on. Come on in and I'll show you the apartment." She led Molly up the front steps and across the wide front porch.

Inside Molly was pleased to see that even though the house was old, it was immaculate. Mrs. Jenkins took great pride in her home. The little woman led her up a wide staircase to the second floor and unlocked a door at the top of the landing.

"The whole second floor has been remodeled into an apartment," she explained, swinging the door wide. "Here's the living room, and through that door is the kitchen. There's a full bathroom and a large bedroom, as well as another little room that can be used as an office or whatever you please. Take your time and look around. I'll be right outside by the flowerbed when you're finished."

"Thank you."

As Molly walked through the apartment her hopefulness grew. It was beautiful! The antique living room furniture was mellowed oak. The overstuffed blue and white plaid couch and armchair enticed with their softness. The eat-in kitchen sported oak cabinets, table and chairs with thick floral seat cushions. Opening the cabinets, Molly discovered plenty of space for her own dishes, pots, pans and food.

In the bedroom, a mellowed oak antique sleigh bed was draped with a white lace bedspread. Matching curtains dressed the windows. Sage throw pillows matched the thick sage-colored carpet covering the floor. The large lighted walk-in closet took Molly's breath away. Her meager belongings would surely be lost in the cavernous space! The bathroom had an old claw foot tub retrofitted with a shower. A sage shower curtain matched the window curtains. Sage towels hung from a towel bar.

The other "little room" was located next to the bedroom. A desk and office chair sat in front of a double-window that brightened the room while bookshelves lined the opposite wall. A low piled gray carpet covered the floor beneath an overstuffed armchair and ottoman that sat in one corner, an end table and lamp beside it. What an awesome place to read or nap.

Molly walked through again. Could she afford this? She attempted to tamp down the elation that was building in her stomach. It was hard not to get her hopes up. Compared to the first two rental properties, both cheap in price and quality, this was a first-rate apartment. Was that why no rental price was listed in the paper?

Lord, as much as I like this place, I want Your will to be done. If You want me here, please work out the details. If not, give me the grace to go back to the park and live in the duplex. At least until something else opens up.

If it was more than she could afford, she'd be disappointed but if she wasn't meant to be here, no matter how nice it was, she wouldn't be happy.

As promised, she found Mrs. Jenkins on her knees, pulling weeds in the flower bed. The lady looked up at her approach.

"Well, my dear, what do you think?"

"I think it's beautiful," exclaimed Molly. "Did you decorate it yourself or did professionals do the work?

Soft pink flooded the wrinkled cheeks, obvious pleasure at Molly's words. "Thank you, dear. My nephew who's a carpenter and his son did all the remodeling. Then I did the decorating myself. I love to sew and decorate. My husband used to say my talents were wasted when I married him. But I never thought so. We loved each other very much and had a happy life together. And I was still able to do the things I loved to do."

"Well, it looks like a professional did it," Molly responded with a smile. "May I ask what the rent is?"

"Well, of course you can, dear." She chuckled. "You'll need to know that for sure, won't you?" She offered an amount that to Molly seemed incredibly low.

Her heart soared! "I'll take it!"

Pleased, Mrs. Jenkins invited her to sit on the porch and enjoy a glass of lemonade while they discussed the necessary arrangements. Molly liked the older woman immensely! She soon discovered that Mrs. Jenkins was a Christian and attended a small church just outside of town. She invited Molly to attend with her the next morning and was happy when she accepted. Molly looked forward to getting to know this dear woman better. With a promise to meet her at church in the morning, Molly headed back to Deep Creek.

~

Dressed in a sleeveless pastel print cotton dress, Molly pulled her long hair back at the sides and fastened it with a clip in the back. Arriving a little early, she waited in the car for Mrs. Jenkins. At home, her church was fairly large with lots of opportunity for ministry. This church was a simple white, wood-sided building with a small steeple, Molly's ideal of the little country church.

An elderly man entered the front door and within minutes she heard the steeple bell begin to ring. Two other cars were in the parking lot when she arrived, but soon others pulled in and parked, one driven by Mrs. Jenkins. Exiting her car, Molly waited on the sidewalk for the older woman.

"Oh, my dear, I'm so happy you're here. And for Sunday School too! We have the best teacher around, next to our pastor, of course." She tittered with true happiness. "Well, do come in and I'll introduce you around. We've a number of young people your age in our church, some married, some not. For a small church, we have a nice mix of folks here." Molly smiled as the lady chattered on.

She met several more people that she knew she wouldn't remember the next time she met them, but smiled politely and followed Mrs. Jenkins to a seat. The Sunday School teacher and the lesson were very good. When he finished, she was surprised to find that time had flown. Hadn't he just started?

During the break between Sunday School and the morning service, Mrs. Jenkins continued her introductions. One was to an attractive young woman about Molly's age named Jennifer Mitchell. Long curly blond hair framed her delicate face and hazel eyes. She seemed genuinely unaware of the interest she drew from some of the young men that passed by as they talked.

"Please call me Jenny. I teach first grade at the elementary school," she explained. "I work all day, but most of my evenings are free. We should get together and do something fun sometime. I love Italian food and there's a terrific restaurant in Sylva. Want to make it a girl's night out and take in a movie?"

"Sounds good!" exclaimed Molly. "I love Italian! And Mexican! And German! And Chinese!" She laughed. "There's not too much food I'll turn down."

"She's moving into my apartment Monday evening," said Mrs. Jenkins, a happy smile on her face.

"Really? That's great!" Jenny replied. "Can I give you a hand? I get off work at five and could meet you at the campground."

"I'd appreciate that. I was planning to move by myself, but an extra hand would be nice."

The church service was similar to what Molly was accustomed to in her church at home. The pastor opened his Bible and began his sermon. A middle-aged man, he was a little heavy around the middle with salt and pepper hair and laugh lines radiating from the corners of his eyes. His voice commanded attention and Molly soon found herself riveted by his words.

All too soon the sermon ended and Molly found a longing to hear more. The sermon was the first in a five-part series, and she was glad she'd caught the first one. She'd definitely return next week.

~

After lunch, Molly changed into a pair of twill capris and a T-shirt. Pulling her hair back into a ponytail, she slipped on a faded denim ball cap and hiked to the trailhead parking lot. Cal had taken her up the dirt road on her first day, but this was the first opportunity she'd had to explore the trails on her own. It was her day off, and today she'd just be a tourist.

When on duty, she didn't really stop to think about the number of visitors to the campground, but today, when she was off duty, she noticed the place was full. Not just with campers, but local people came out to enjoy picnics and hiking. Many nodded and smiled as she passed.

The beauty of the woods, the creek and the waterfalls filled her with a serenity that comes from appreciating God's creation. The further she hiked the fewer people she passed and the more peaceful it became. She stopped to touch the delicate pink flowers on a Rhododendron bush and marveled at God's creative detail.

Her first week in the park had been good for the most part. She'd met scores of people, both staff and visitors, gone through a tough campground situation and acquired a new home. God was good! His grace was sufficient, just as He promised in His word.

Chapter Six

When Molly entered the ranger station Monday morning, she found Jake Stuart leaning against the counter talking with Joe and Cal. His disarming grin flashed, sending her heart into her throat before dropping back to a steady beat.

"Well, good morning." She dropped her daypack on the floor beside the counter. "What are you doing in this neck of the woods, Jake?"

"You've forgotten that today's agenda includes setting boar traps, huh?" he chuckled.

Molly grinned. "Yeah, I did. Sorry."

"Have a hot date this weekend that pushed it right out of your mind?" Cal teased as he sipped his coffee.

Warmth flooded Molly's face giving the impression that's exactly what happened. Three pairs of eyes watched as they awaited her answer. Perversely she responded, "I'll never tell," then walked over to pour a cup of coffee, more to change the subject than anything. "I see Joe made coffee this morning," she said after a long draw of the hot brew. "Tastes great, Joe."

He smiled. "Thanks, but I didn't make it."

"Well, I know Cal didn't make it." When Cal shook his head in agreement, her eyes met Jake's gaze over the rim of her cup.

"It's very good, Jake." Molly swallowed hard. A matter as simple as who made the coffee and an undercurrent of something inexplicable threatened to engulf her.

"Thanks," was his simple reply. A spark of something stirred in his gaze before she pulled hers away. Did he feel it too?

"Molly," Cal said, "Here's today's itinerary." Placing a piece of paper on the counter, he sketched a rudimentary map and marked "X" in several places. "You and Jake collect the boar traps from the maintenance yard then set them in these locations. It'll take most of the day, so I suggest you get started. I have to run up to Oconoluftee then I'll return here. Bill Hopper and Frank Raven will help you load the traps on the trailer, but remember, don't mention where you're taking them. I don't want anyone but the rangers at this station and Jake to know where they're located." He looked around at them and then added, "Alright, let's go."

~

Molly and Jake drove to the maintenance yard, backed the pickup to the trailer and hitched it up. Entering the shed, they found Bill Hopper and Frank Raven sitting, drinking coffee. Neither looked in a hurry to begin work.

"Morning, fellows," Jake greeted with forced cheerfulness. "We could use a hand loading those traps onto the trailer. Would you mind?"

Bill Hopper, a thin wiry man in his fifties with beady dark eyes and a long thin nose, set down his cup of coffee and stood slowly, putting one hand casually into his pants pocket. With the other one he pulled a wooden toothpick from his shirt pocket and placed it between his thin lips. "I guess we could do that, don't you, Frank?" He turned toward the younger man sitting by the workbench.

Without a word, Frank, a full-blooded Cherokee with longish black hair and muscular stature, stood and ambled out the door of the shed. He waited by the row of traps until Bill and Jake each took a corner of one then lifted the other end by himself. Molly started to offer her assistance but the task was effortless for the young Indian. He lifted his end of the trap without a grunt or a strain.

After three traps were loaded, Bill casually asked, "Where you puttin' the traps this time?"

Molly saw Jake's eyes darken and his smile became fixed as he avoided a direct answer. "Well, you know how it is. You have to find tracks first."

He didn't mention they already had.

Bill nodded slowly but said no more as a flat smile crossed his thin lips. Without another word, he returned to the maintenance shed, followed by the silent Frank.

"Thanks for the help, fellas." Jake climbed into the pickup. Molly climbed into the passenger side and waited until they were out of sight of the little building.

"Do you think they might have something to do with the poaching?" she asked.

Jake sighed heavily and glanced at her as they drove out of the park. "I don't know. Sometimes I think they might, but knowing Bill, he could just want us to think he does. It's hard to know. Most of the maintenance workers are local, and who knows but some may have an ax to grind."

They discussed the plans for the day until they were about half way out to Twentymile. After a lull in the conversation, Jake asked out of the blue, as casually as if he were asking about the weather, "So, did you have a date this weekend?"

Molly, caught off guard by the unexpected question, could only shake her head. Then she recovered from her surprise and said, "That's for me to know and no one else. Why?"

"No reason really, but I wouldn't be surprised to hear that you did. A girl like you won't remain undiscovered for long. Bryson City's a small town and word travels fast. Fellows will be coming out of the woodwork when they hear a single girl has moved to town."

An incredulous laugh escaped Molly. "I doubt that, but thanks for the kind words anyway. I've met a lot of nice people though." Then she snapped her fingers. "Which reminds me. I'm moving this evening."

"Moving? Where?" His voice was sharper than he intended.

"Don't bite," she chided with a laugh. "I found an upstairs apartment in the home of a widow named Mrs. Jenkins. She's really sweet."

~

Relief filled Jake. His blood had chilled at the thought she might be leaving the area. She hadn't been here long, but other rangers had left for better positions in other parks before. He was thrilled she was putting down roots for a while. Hopefully it would be a long while.

"Need any help moving?"

"Well, I met someone at church yesterday who offered a hand."

Jake held his breath until she told him the "someone" was named Jenny. "Jenny, huh? Can the two of you manage, or do you need a little masculine assistance? I'm old-fashioned and believe a woman still needs a man around occasionally."

"Well," Molly mused, "I tend to agree. In spite of the modern woman's philosophy, I certainly don't mind manly assistance. I'm no weakling, mind you, but if he's available, why not?"

Jake's hearty laugh filled the truck cab. "I like your philosophy, Molly."

She grinned in return. "Thanks awfully, kind sir!"

After a few miles of companionable silence, Jake said, "Cal told me what happened Friday evening. Situations like that are tough. And your first week too."

Molly shook her head at the reminder of that sad evening. "Yeah, even Cal was shaken by it. He was strong, but I could tell."

Jake reached across and squeezed her hand, quickly releasing it. "I understand David Andrews stopped in and kept you company until Cal returned."

Molly nodded. "I could tell you his life history with the park service. It's a long and detailed one."

"So I've heard," he chuckled. "I've never met him but I've heard enough. Kate says he's a handsome guy." He watched Molly's face for a reaction.

Molly smiled before returning her gaze out the window. "He's handsome, alright."

Jake frowned as he negotiated a series of curves before turning the truck onto the road leading to Fontana Dam. "We'll set a trap on the other side of the dam up in the woods. The general public can't drive across, but we have a key to the gate. Tennessee Valley Authority, or TVA, employees and security guards also cross sometimes."

The road twisted through the woods past trailheads and picnic areas. As they exited the woods, a parking lot stretched out in front of the Fontana Dam Visitor's Center. Molly made a mental addition to her growing list of places to check out on a day off.

Just past the parking lot a locked gate blocked the road across the dam. Jake handed Molly a key.

"Would you unlock the gate and swing it open? Then relock it after I drive through."

"Sure." Molly accepted the key. After following his instructions, she climbed back into the truck.

As they crossed the top of the dam, Molly spotted the lake stretching out to her right. It was a huge lake that covered many miles along the Great Smoky Mountain National Park boundary. From their high vantage point, pleasure and fishing boats could be seen scattered across the lake's surface. She glanced out Jake's window trying to see the other side of the dam.

"You won't see anything from the truck," he chuckled. "Here, I'll stop so you can take a look."

Molly jumped out and crossed to the railing that stretched along the side of the road above the dam. The nearly 500 foot sheer drop of the cement wall made her gasp. An upsweeping breeze tugged at her cap causing her to clap her hand on top to prevent it flying away. On her left near the bottom of the dam stood the power station. A river flowed from the bottom of the dam and connected to Cheoah Lake far below where she'd driven on her first visit to Twentymile.

"Quite a drop, huh?" Jake said beside her. She jumped slightly, not realizing he'd gotten out as well.

"I'll say," Molly breathed in awe, then turned her gaze to the ridge of mountains on the park side. "This is amazing, Jake! If my parents ever brought me here, I don't remember it. And I think I would."

Jake leaned his forearms along the railing. "It's not Hoover Dam, but it's the largest dam this side of the Rockies. The Tennessee Valley Authority operates 32 dams from Kentucky to Alabama and this jewel is their crowning glory."

"And what a setting for that jewel! Surrounded by these gorgeous mountains." Molly walked across the road to the other railing and looked down on the lake that was much higher on this side. "What's the story behind all this?" She waved a hand encompassing the view.

"Right after Pearl Harbor was attacked the military needed more hydroelectric energy to manufacture their military equipment. TVA built this dam as a resource for that energy. That's where the Fontana Village comes into play. Complete with a school, a small hospital and churches, it was built to house the workers and their families. They worked around the clock, three shifts, seven days a week. Two years later, the dam was opened, sending electricity to Oak Ridge, Tennessee, where research for the atomic bomb took place. Anyway, after the war, the village was turned into a resort, a marina was built on the lake and it became a vacation playground. The dam still produces electricity as well as controls flooding, which was a problem before it was built."

"Do you ever go into the village?" She wondered what was available there now.

"I use the post office and pick up a few groceries there until I can shop in town. But the park isn't connected with the village except in cooperation with managing the park boundaries on the north side of the lake." Jake paused to take a breath before continuing. "Come on. We better get those traps set. We have a lot to do."

Once across the dam, they drove into the woods as far as they could before the road faded into the trees and thick undergrowth. Jake backed the trailer into the vegetation, and then working together they dragged the heavy trap from the trailer and behind some bushes where it would be less obvious. Jake pointed out the overturned earth where wild boar had rooted around then retrieved a sack of dried corn from the back of the pickup.

"I take it that's the bait?"

"You got it," he said, setting the trap. "Just toss a handful toward the back inside of the trap and some near the entrance. Then scatter a little around on the ground. That's right. That should do it." Reaching for the sack, he returned to the rear of the pickup. "Come on. We've got five more to do."

They set two more traps, one near the Twentymile horse barn and one off a maintenance road past the ranger station. They stopped at Fontana Village for lunch before driving back to Deep Creek to get the last three traps. By the time they were done lifting, shoving and dragging, Molly's shoulders and back were screaming at her.

Returning to Deep Creek Ranger Station, they went inside to see if Cal had returned.

"I'm here," he called from the back as they asked Joe where he was. "Well, how did it go?"

Both Jake and Molly pulled up chairs and dropped into them, exhausted.

"No problems." Jake stretched his neck from side to side. "First traps set for the season. I always forget how heavy those things are."

Cal laughed and turned to Molly. "And how about you?"

"Oh, I agree. They're definitely heavy. But all in all, it went well. I'd love nothing more than to go home and soak in a hot tub." She abruptly exclaimed, hand to her forehead, "I almost forgot! There won't be a soak tonight! At least not right away." Glancing at her watch, she noted it was 4:45. "Nope. No time now." She got up as quickly as her tired body would allow and headed for the door.

"What are you going on about, girl?" asked Cal with a hint of exasperation. "Where're you headed?"

She leaned back around the partition. "Didn't I tell you? I'm moving tonight. And my help is showing up in forty-five minutes. Got to go. That is, unless you have something else you need me to do before I go."

"No, you've done your share today," Cal smiled. "And it doesn't sound like you're through yet. Where's the pickup?"

"Just outside," said Jake. "I'll take the trailer up to the maintenance yard before I park it."

"I guess you're done, Molly," said Cal.

"Bye, guys," she called as the screen door slammed behind her.

~

Molly grabbed a quick shower and washed her hair to remove all traces of the hard work of setting the traps. She had just dressed in blue-jean overalls and a gray T-shirt when a knock sounded at the door.

"Be right there." Barefoot and towel drying her hair, she answered the door, expecting to find Jennifer Mitchell.

"Jake!" Self-consciousness filled Molly as she swiped her damp hair over her shoulder. "What are you doing here?"

"You did say you could use some masculine assistance, didn't you?" His crooked grin sent her heart into a tailspin.

Molly closed her eyes for a moment and sighed. How could she have forgotten that? "Yes, I did. Sorry I forgot."

"It's okay." Jake paused before asking, "May I come in?"

Her cheeks burned. "Of course you can. Sorry." She was growing more flustered by the moment. Now why was that? No time to analyze it now.

"It's alright, Molly." Jake patted her shoulder. "You've got this move on your mind, not to mention you're exhausted from today's work. Don't worry about it." A gentle smile graced his lips as he looked into her upturned face. "Where do I start?"

He'd exchanged his uniform for blue jeans and an old T-shirt. A ball cap sat on his head reminding Molly of an overgrown schoolboy ready to play ball. The clothes must be what were in the bag he'd brought from Twentymile when they'd stopped there earlier today.

"Most everything's ready to go, but a few things in the kitchen still need to be packed. There's already an empty box in there."

"Say no more. You finish what you were doing, and I'll box them up."

~

Molly had braided her hair and was tying her sneakers when Jenny arrived. She introduced Jake then they went to work. Jake had driven his personal pickup to Deep Creek that morning and made it available to Molly. With teamwork, they had everything packed in the truck in no time. Jake swept the floors while Molly and Jenny cleaned the bathroom and the kitchen. Just like her mom had always done, Molly wanted to leave the place cleaner than when she'd found it.

She led the way to her new home followed by Jake in the pickup and Jenny in her car. Mrs. Jenkins came out to greet them as they parked in the driveway. Molly had told her approximately when they'd arrive and was surprised to find supper waiting for them.

"Come on in, young'uns," Mrs. Jenkins called from the front porch as they exited their vehicles. "I figured y'all got off work and went right to movin'. Bet you haven't had a bite to eat yet, either."

"Guilty." Molly nodded and climbed the front steps. "I was in such a hurry to get going, I forgot all about eating."

"Not to worry," replied the landlady cheerfully. "I've taken care of everything." Turning, she looked at the guy standing just behind Molly. "And who's this tall, handsome young feller? Can't say I've ever seen him before?"

Extending a hand to shake hers, Jake introduced himself. "I'm Jake Stuart, Mrs. Jenkins. It's a pleasure to meet you."

"It's a pleasure to meet you too, Jake." She raised an eyebrow in Molly's direction. "Been knowing our Molly long, have ya?"

Molly's cheeks heated at the implication in her voice. Had he noticed?

"No," Jake replied smoothly. "Only about a week. I work at Twentymile Ranger Station."

"Oh, I see. The ranger station out past Fontana Lake. Haven't been out that way in years. Got relatives out in Franklin and Andrews, but I don't make it out that way too often." She paused then added, "Well, come on in. Don't let me keep y'all standing around. The food's awaitin'. How are you tonight, Jenny?"

Mrs. Jenkins led the group into the spacious country kitchen where the table was set with a small feast. Mrs. Jenkins caught the question in Molly's eyes. "Don't you worry, dear. I just figured none of you would've eaten yet."

"But there's so much!" exclaimed Molly.

"I didn't know how many folks would be helpin' and wanted to make sure there'd be plenty. Besides," she winked at Jake, "I won't have to cook again for a week, at least."

"That's for sure." Molly laughed.

"Well, have a seat, all of you, before the food gets cold."

The foursome ate heartily, talking and laughing and getting better acquainted. Molly was going to enjoy living here.

When everyone had finished eating, Molly started clearing the table. Mrs. Jenkins laid a gentle hand on her arm.

"Leave that, Sweetie." She patted her arm. "You young'uns have enough to do without clearing all this away. Get on with your totin' and carryin'. I'll clean up the kitchen. Now go on with you. All of you."

The three set to work unloading the truck. Things went smoothly until about half-way through the load Molly decided to carry a little more than common sense would allow. Tired and wanting to be finished, she'd managed to get her precarious load up the staircase and was starting to round the corner into her apartment when she ran headlong into someone. The top of the load shifted dangerously and threatened to fall just as a pair of large hands scooped the whole lot from Molly's aching arms. A pair of dark blue eyes held gentle reproach as they met hers.

"What do you think you're doing, lady?" Jake's reprimand was softened by a half grin. "You've got help, you know. You don't have to move it all by yourself." He eyed her more closely, causing her to shift uncomfortably. "You look beat. It's been a long day, and you should take a breather and sit for a bit."

"Thanks, Jake." She *was* feeling tired and she'd probably taken too much on that last trip upstairs. "That's the last load. I'll run down and see if Mrs. Jenkins has anything cold to drink, then we can all 'sit for a bit.'"

Once again her new landlady was way ahead of her. Molly suspected she had a sixth sense about the needs of others. She was already on her way out the front door with a tray of glasses and a pitcher of lemonade. Setting it on a small table on the front porch, she filled the glasses.

"You're a mind-reader, Mrs. Jenkins." Molly reached for a glass.

"Nothing of the sort," disputed the lady. "I've moved a couple times in my early life, and I'm not too old to remember what a tiring job it is. You've got to stop and take a breather every now and again."

"My thoughts exactly," agreed a masculine voice from behind Molly. She turned as Jake reached for a glass. He winked at Molly as he raised it to his lips.

"Where's Jenny?" Mrs. Jenkins asked.

"Right here." Jenny closed the screen door behind her. Reaching for a glass, she took a seat in one of the rockers. Molly sat on the porch swing with Mrs. Jenkins while Jake sat on the top step and leaned against the railing post.

"Jake that stone step can't be comfortable," Mrs. Jenkins observed. "Why not take that rocker?"

"I'm fine." Jake took a long draught from his glass. "This lemonade hits the spot. I bet you made it with real lemons, didn't you?"

Mrs. Jenkins flashed a Cheshire-cat smile as she smoothed her hair from her forehead. "Well, yes, as a matter of fact, I did. Can't abide the fake stuff. No powder mix for me, thank ya very much."

A few minutes passed as everyone enjoyed the lemonade and the fact they were sitting.

"So where ya from, Jake?" Mrs. Jenkins asked, eyebrows raised in question.

"Near Nantahala."

"Oh, so you're a local fellow! I have a nephew that lives down that way, and Jenny has a couple cousins near there too."

"Did she tell you she's my great-aunt?" Jenny asked, nodding her head toward Mrs. Jenkins.

"No!" Molly exclaimed in surprise. "She didn't! That's great!"

"Well, I think so." Jenny chuckled. "Aunt Selma's the best aunt in the world."

"Now don't go on so, Jenny dear. My head'll start to swell." She reached for the lemonade pitcher. "Seconds, anyone?"

Jake accepted a refill. "Do you have brothers or sisters, Jenny?"

"Yes," she nodded. "Two sisters and a brother. My sisters have married and moved away, but my brother, Jamie, still lives in the area." She sipped her lemonade but said no more.

"Jenny teaches at the elementary school up on School House Hill," Mrs. Jenkins explained. "First grade isn't it, dear?"

Jenny simply nodded.

"Are you okay, Jenny?" Molly peered at her new friend with concern. She'd been quiet most of the evening, but Molly didn't know Jenny well. Perhaps she was just the quiet type.

"I'm fine," Jenny stood and headed back inside.

Molly looked at Mrs. Jenkins, perplexed. "Don't worry, dear," she lowered her voice. "It's nothing you said. Jamie's been in a spot of trouble lately and she's worried. Nothing to concern yourself with."

Jake and Molly followed Jenny upstairs. They all worked quickly and quietly until the majority of things were put away. After boxes were broken down and placed in a pile to be taken to the attic, Molly stood in the living room with Jenny, surveying their handiwork.

"It's a nice apartment, Molly," A tired smile lifted Jenny's lips. "I hope you enjoy living here. Aunt Selma's a real sweetheart and tends to look after everyone and everything. However, she respects a person's privacy and will give you as much space as you need. Don't hesitate to ask if you need something. She lives to give it."

Reaching over, Molly gave Jenny a quick hug. "Thanks. You hardly know me, but you took your evening to help me out. I really appreciate it. I suspect you're a lot like your aunt in that respect."

Jenny smiled. "I certainly hope so. I'll see you soon. Can I drop by sometime?"

"Anytime," Molly replied. "Good night, Jenny."

"Good night. Get some rest."

Molly closed the door, wondering where Jake had disappeared to. Turning from the door she found him leaning against the kitchen doorway, arms folded across his chest. "Oh, there you are! I was just wondering where you had gotten to."

"You didn't think I'd leave without saying goodbye, did you?" A twinkle flashed in his eyes.

"Not really," she admitted, smiling. "I thought maybe you were off talking with Mrs. Jenkins."

"She's a sweetheart, isn't she?" He left the doorway to cross the room. "You know, I can't imagine why you'd want to trade your government quarters for this place." He glanced around the room before returning his gaze to her.

"I don't know," Molly shook her head in mock seriousness. "I must be crazy or something."

Jake laughed. "Or something." He glanced at his watch. "As much as I'd love to stay and visit, I need to get going. It's getting late."

"Thanks, Jake. You don't know how much I appreciate your help."

He gave her a sly smile. "I could think of a couple ways you could show me."

Molly's eyes narrowed in suspicion. "Like what?"

Jake waggled his eyebrows. "Yeah, you know. Like dinner out one evening. Soon."

"Oh." Did that single-syllable word convey disappointment? Well, what had she expected? That he meant a kiss? Her cheeks warmed.

"Why, Molly! What were you thinking?" Mock shock filled his voice, his eyes alight with laughter. He strolled to the door and opened it before turning around to add, "That comes later." Then with a wink he was gone.

Molly stood staring at the door he'd closed behind him. Heart galloping at his implication, she swallowed hard and forced herself to move. *One of these days I'm going to get myself into real trouble.* Before she could move far, a knock sounded at the door. Had Jake forgotten something? She attempted to still her racing heart and opened the door.

"I know you're tired, Sweetie," Mrs. Jenkins stepped inside, "and I won't keep you but a minute. Just wanted to tell you how glad I am you've come to live here. If there's anything I can do for you any time, just let me know."

"Thank you. That means a lot. And thanks again for supper tonight. It was very thoughtful and absolutely delicious."

"Your young man stopped by a minute ago as he was leaving and told me he enjoyed it. He's a right handsome feller. Good manners too."

Molly started to reply that he wasn't her young man, but decided to let it go. "He was a big help this evening, and so was Jenny." She paused then asked, "Mrs. Jenkins, Jenny had something on her mind this evening. You mentioned she's worried about her brother. I don't want to pry, but is there anything I can help with?"

The older woman patted Molly's arm. "Keep her in your prayers, dear, but mostly keep Jamie in your prayers. He's a couple years younger than Jenny, and lately he's taken up with the wrong crowd. Don't know for sure, but I suspect he's disappeared again. He's done it once before, but then I shouldn't speculate on things I don't know about for certain."

Molly nodded. "We'll pray for them both."

"That we will. Good night, dear."

Within ten minutes Molly had her teeth brushed, pajamas on and had climbed into the bed Jenny had made earlier. Sinking into the fresh sheets, she fell into an exhausted sleep.

~

As Jake drove toward Twentymile, he recalled his day spent with Molly. She was a hard worker, eager to learn her job and about the area. Her expression of awe as she'd gazed across the wide expanse of Fontana Dam returned to him. Her eyes had been filled with wonder at the view. She fascinated him! One minute teasing and coy; the next she was aloof and standoffish. Either way, he'd enjoyed spending time with her. Even as they'd worked hard setting the traps, they'd found things to talk and laugh about.

That afternoon as she'd opened her door to find him standing on her front step, her hair had hung in damp waves around her shoulders. Had the pink glow on her face been from her recent bath or perhaps from finding him on her doorstep unexpectedly? Whichever it was, the appealing image had imprinted itself in his mind. An inexplicable desire to pull her close and kiss her slightly parted lips had surprised him. Instead he'd forced himself to turn away and ignore the fresh fragrance that had wafted around her.

Jake flipped on the radio to a news station and tried repeatedly to corral his thoughts. They insisted on returning to Molly. He'd dated a few girls through the years but none had really peaked his interest. A few, like Celeste, had pushed their attention on him whether he wanted it or not. But Molly was different. He supposed a lot of it had to do with her faith in God. *Mom would love her,* he chuckled to himself. *She'd wholeheartedly approve of Molly.*

As a child he'd given his life to Christ; a time he hadn't thought about in years. He'd grown up in a Christian home, but after leaving for college he'd allowed other things to crowd into his life, making less and less room for Christ. He'd set his Bible aside and occupied himself with his studies instead. Church attendance was a thing of the past except when he was home with his family. Praying had stopped altogether. He'd been taught to pray anytime, anywhere about anything, but it had been so long, what would he say to the Lord? And would He listen if he did pray?

Arriving at the ranger station, Jake climbed the stairs to his room and tugged a box from the back of the closet, rummaging through until he found what he was looking for. His old Bible that he'd always kept but never bothered to open. *Why not? Why did I ever allow myself to get so far from God?* Sitting on the edge of the bed, he thumbed through the pages, reading passages here and there. The markings and notes he'd made years before stood out beside the printed words. His gaze fell on a long-ago marked verse. Psalm 46:10: "Be still and know that I am God." How long since he'd done that? Stilled his heart and really reflected on who God is. Flipping through the pages he read verse after verse until, glancing at his watch, he realized it was late. But as he closed the pages, he closed his eyes and attempted a short petition. *Lord, it's been a long time since I've talked to You. I guess meeting Molly and seeing her faith lived out has made me realize just how far I've moved from You. Forgive me. Help me find my way back to You.*

Chapter Seven

The next several days passed without incident. Campers came and went, the boar traps remained empty and Molly settled nicely into her job. Cal spent a couple of hours each day on Molly's job training. In the afternoons she patrolled the campground or the North Shore Road or took one of the patrol horses up the trails, familiarizing herself with the back country.

Late Thursday afternoon, Molly was patrolling through the trailhead parking lot when she spotted a battered pickup speeding past the horse barn and across the creek. The rangers often used this road as a shortcut to Oconoluftee, bypassing town. Molly had driven it a few times over the last week but only to the park boundary.

The pickup that had long since lost any semblance of color through rust and fading, gained speed as it took the curve by the bridge too quickly, spinning its wheels and spraying gravel in its wake. A cloud of dust followed it up the back road leading from the campground to Cherokee.

Groaning, Molly flipped on her blue lights and siren and hit the gas. As she rounded the bend, the back of the SUV began to drift. Panic gripped her causing her stomach to plummet. Got to get control. She wasn't going to let these guys get away. Steering into the slide, she righted the vehicle and picked up speed. There were two men in the truck cab, but at this speed it was hard to identify any details. The dust in their wake didn't help either.

As she concentrated on the curvy gravel road and keeping up with them, Molly spotted the men glance back occasionally, but they never slowed. If they didn't stop before the park boundary, she'd have to contact the sheriff's department as they'd soon be out of her jurisdiction. Molly grabbed the radio mic, ready to click the button when they suddenly pulled to the side of the road. Stopping several feet behind them, she flipped off the siren, alerted HQ and called the ranger station for backup. After giving Joe her location, she climbed out, unsnapped the strap of her holster and drew her Glock 19 9mm sidearm. She slowly approached, stopping at the rear of the old pickup.

"Let me see your hands! Now!" Molly yelled in a loud voice. Adrenaline pumped through her veins. Her heart hammered like it would pound right out of her chest. Her first major traffic stop, and she wanted to get it right. Ticking off the procedures in her mind, she yelled. "HANDS! NOW! Driver, with your left hand, turn off the engine and throw the keys out the window. Now get out of the truck. Keep your hands where I can see them!"

The driver's door opened and a wiry young man with longish brown hair sticking out from beneath a nondescript ball cap, climbed out, hands held high. He wore a pair of worn bib overalls over an old T-shirt. His work boots looked like they'd slogged through mud and then dried, clumps flaking off as he moved.

"Well, well, well. Lookie here, Ray. We got us a new ranger." The driver glanced at his buddy still in the truck.

"What'd ya know 'bout that, Willy," replied his buddy. "A real purdy one too."

"Um-hmmm," nodded Willy. "You can say that again." His leer made Molly seethe.

"That's enough!" Mustering as much authority as she could, she steadied her voice. The smell of alcohol wafted over her from the driver and from inside the open truck. "You, Driver. Please put your hands on your head and face away from me." As soon as the word "please" left her mouth, she knew it was a mistake. She cringed inwardly.

"Listen to that, Ray. She's got manners too." The one called Willy smirked and winked with impertinence. "I like a woman with manners."

"Willy, …was that your name? Willy?" Molly asked sternly. "I guess you didn't hear me. I said put your hands on your head and face away from me." Her voice grew stronger and louder as she spoke.

"Oooooh!" Willy wiggled his fingers in the air in mock fear. "I'm so-o-o-o scared! What you gonna do? Arrest us? I'd like to see ya try."

Help, Lord! These guys are drunk and may be easy to handle, but I don't think so. I need backup! Now!

Looking down the sights of her handgun, Molly aimed at Willy. "Fellas, let's make this easy, okay? You were speeding through the campground thirty-five miles above the speed limit. You've obviously been drinking, and I suspect you have open containers in the truck. Both of those offenses are big no-no's in the park. Now we'll just stand here at gunpoint until backup arrives then we'll escort you to jail by force, or you can co-operate and then I'll escort you to jail. Either way, you're still going to jail. The second choice will make it easier for us all."

Molly heard a vehicle pull up behind her truck, but she didn't turn around hoping upon hope it was the cavalry to the rescue and not buddies of these guys.

Willy grew quiet as his eyes shifted from Molly to the vehicle behind her, to the woods and back again, calculating his options.

"What's it going to be, fellas?" Molly asked.

Suddenly Willy yelled, "None of 'em," and turned to run. In his drunken state, he misjudged the open truck door behind him, and smacked right into it. Staggering back, he tried to run around it, but Molly's reflexes were quicker than his inebriated ones. She grabbed the back of his overalls and unbalanced him, toppling him to the ground. The momentum of his fall dragged her over. Her arm banged hard on the gravel and she flinched. Hanging on, she righted herself quickly, and rolled the stunned man over onto his stomach. Pulling handcuffs from the back of her utility belt, she quickly clapped them onto his wrists.

The other man called Ray had jumped out of the pickup when Willy turned to run and had sprinted off into the woods. Fortunately, he didn't get far. Out of the corner of her eye Molly spotted Craig chasing him. Joe appeared at her side but found she had Willy cuffed and lying face down on the ground. *Thank you, Lord, for sending the cavalry.*

"You don't need my help," Joe grinned. "Handled him pretty well all by yourself."

The figure on the ground let out a string of expletives. Molly cast a glare in his direction. "Now, now. We'll have none of that, Willy," she scolded sarcastically. "I gave you your choice, and you picked the wrong one."

She looked over as Craig wrestled Ray to the ground. "Joe, you'd better give Craig a hand."

Keeping a close eye on Willy, she returned to the SUV and called HQ. Once Craig and Joe had Ray handcuffed, they seated him into the cage-enclosed back seat of their vehicle. Then they stood by to assist as Molly helped Willy into the back seat of her SUV. It was time for a trip to the county jail.

"You should've seen her, Cal," exclaimed Craig later as they sat in the station relaying the incident. "She had that guy down before he knew what hit him."

"Yeah," Joe agreed. "I was impressed. It was better than one of those police reality shows you see on TV. Definitely live action!" he added with a chuckle.

"I'm sorry I missed it." Cal laughed.

A frown tilted Molly's eyebrows. "I'm glad I could furnish you fellows with a bit of drama for the week. It was getting a bit dull around here, wasn't it?"

"Don't say that," Cal cautioned. "That's when all heck breaks loose. Everything starts happening. Enjoy the dull days. You can bet they won't last." Reaching across the desk, he handed her a sheaf of papers. "Here's the paperwork for your report. If you need any help with the technical parts, just ask."

Molly accepted the papers and winced. "Thanks, I'll do that."

"What's the matter?" Cal asked.

"Oh, I banged my arm when I took Willy down." She had felt pain but with everything that happened following the incident, she hadn't taken much notice. Upon examining her arm, there was a gash just below her elbow with blood smeared down her arm. The wound still trickled blood.

"Look at the side of your shirt and pants!" Craig exclaimed.

Glancing down Molly found blood smeared on both. Oh, boy! That was going to be fun to get out!

"Molly! Girl, what did you do to yourself? Let me see that." Cal stood and carefully examined her arm. "You need to have that checked out. Looks like stitches to me."

"Oh no, Cal, I'll be fine." But suddenly she didn't feel so fine as nausea stirred her stomach and her head swam slightly. "Just let me sit back down for a minute." Although the severity of the wound surprised her, she tried to make light of it. She really didn't want to appear weak in front of these guys. "I must've cut it on the gravel when I banged it. I'll just clean it, go home and put some ice on it."

Cal reached for his cap hanging on a peg behind his desk. "Uh-uh. I'm taking you down to see Doc Bennett right now. Come on. Fellows, the station's in your hands till I get back. I think we can make the doctor's office before he closes. Joe, call down and let 'em know we're coming."

~

Fifteen minutes later Molly found herself sitting on an examination table having her arm swabbed by a gray-haired nurse named Rose. A pair of wire-framed glasses sat low on her nose, and as she talked, she looked over them at Molly.

"Don't look so glum, honey," Rose crooned in sweet Southern tones. "Things like this happen all the time. You'd be surprised what we have to stitch up in here. And the rangers are some of our biggest customers. Besides, from what Cal said, you did this in the line of duty. Caught a couple of roughnecks trying to pull a fast one on you."

Rose tossed bloody cotton balls into the garbage can. "I know Willy and Ray. They're a pair of slick ones, alright. Glad you got 'em. Mike, the Sheriff, was really glad to see those two behind bars. Or so I heard through the grapevine."

"I'm sure he was," Molly agreed absently. "Do you mind if I lay down?" Her elbow throbbed more since Rose's thorough scrubbing.

"Not at all, honey. Here, let me adjust that pillow for you. There you go. Now you just wait right here. One of those fellows out at your station called and said you were on your way. We were getting ready to close up for the day. There are no other patients, so Doc will be right in."

"Thanks again, Rose. I appreciate your waiting for us."

"No problem." She waved a dismissive hand. "Happens all the time."

Just then the door opened, admitting a short man in his early seventies. Faded blue eyes still held a twinkle as they met hers behind wire-framed glasses. White hair swirled aimlessly around his head while his white lab coat was left unbuttoned, giving a glimpse of a green golf shirt and tan slacks.

"Ah, now this is why I just can't bring myself to retire, Rose. I'd miss all the pretty girls that come in to see me." He winked at Molly. "So what did you do to yourself, young lady?"

Molly held up her arm for him to see. "Had a little accident."

"Hmmmm. I wouldn't say it was too little. You did a pretty good job of it there. How did it happen?"

Molly quickly relayed the story, sparing the unnecessary details. Rose embellished for her. "That's right, Doc. We have a hero here. Those two lowlifes would've taken off if it hadn't been for Molly."

"Sounds interesting," he mused as he pulled out a syringe and a small vial. "Did you clean it, Rose?"

"Of course, I did." Rose defended herself with a huff. Apparently the nurse didn't take anything from anybody, even her employer.

"Alright, we'll just numb it and stitch it right up."

A few minutes and ten stitches later, Molly was given a prescription for an antibiotic. "I recommend Bennett's Pharmacy," suggested Doc Bennett.

Molly smiled. "And why would you recommend Bennett's Pharmacy, Doc *Bennett*?" she asked, emphasizing his name. "Relative of yours?"

"Well, now that you mention it, he's my younger brother. I told him I'd put a plug in for him every chance I get." He shrugged carelessly. "What's the harm? Anyway, you go home and take those pills. The antibiotic is just a precaution. Take some Tylenol for the pain. Put lots of ice on it too. If you have any problems, call me. Anytime. Rose here will get you an appointment for a week and half from now, and I'll remove those stitches. Before long, you'll be right as rain."

"Thanks, Doc." Molly climbed down from the exam table. "And thanks for staying late for me."

"Well, from what Cal said, you were just going to go home without doing anything about it. He did the right thing bringing you in. And you did the right thing by letting him. See you soon."

~

After a stop at the pharmacy, Cal drove Molly back to the campground to pick up her car. Her arm was numb from the Lidocaine injection they'd given her, and she wanted to get home before it wore off.

Mrs. Jenkins was in the kitchen preparing her supper when Molly came in. When she spotted the bandage on Molly's arm, she hurried over.

"What on earth? What happened to you, sweetie?"

Molly realized she'd be retelling this story over and over for a while until everyone knew what had happened. She was certain that half of the town had already heard of the afternoon incident. Sitting at the kitchen table, she shared the afternoon events.

When she'd finished, Mrs. Jenkins shook her head thoughtfully. "Sweetie, I know you do your own cooking and all, but why don't you go on up and get yourself settled. I'm sure you don't feel much like fixing anything, so I'll bring something up for you. I'll also fix you up an ice pack for that arm. You can take your medicine and call it an early night."

"I think I'll take you up on that, Mrs. Jenkins. Thank you."

"No problem at all. You just go up and change out of that uniform and into something more comfortable. I'll be up shortly."

Molly trekked upstairs and changed into an oversized T-shirt and sweats. She tossed her bloody uniform onto the bathroom floor. She'd take care of that later. She was lying on the couch with her eyes closed when Mrs. Jenkins knocked on the door. Without waiting for Molly's response, she entered, a supper tray across one arm.

"Now you just take your time eating, and I'll be back up in a while with an ice pack. I'll take the tray down then." Mrs. Jenkins slipped into the bathroom and returned with Molly's bloody uniform. "I'll just toss these into some cold water to soak."

Then out the door she went, closing it behind her.

Molly's arm was fully awake now and the pain robbed her of an appetite, but she ate some anyway. She didn't want Mrs. Jenkins thinking she didn't appreciate her thoughtfulness. Before long, her landlady returned with the promised ice pack, whisking away the food tray and leaving her alone. Molly tumbled into bed and as she started to doze off, she vaguely recognized the ringing of Mrs.

Jenkins phone downstairs.

~

The next morning when Molly's alarm rang she discovered that more than just her elbow hurt. The struggle to subdue Willy the day before must have been greater than she'd realized. She was sore and achy all over. The temptation to roll over and forget about work was strong, but instead she painfully climbed out of bed and dragged herself to the bathroom. A shower would have helped but she couldn't get her dressings or her stitches wet for a few days. She'd have to settle for a sponge bath.

After managing to wash, dress and eat breakfast without too much difficulty, she determined the rest of the day wouldn't be so bad. As she headed out the front door, Mrs. Jenkins called from the kitchen.

"Just a minute, dear." Her voice preceded her appearance. "I have a message from that young man of yours."

Puzzled, Molly walked to the kitchen just as Mrs. Jenkins rounded the corner. "Oh, there you are. Good morning. How're you feeling, Sweetie?"

A heavy sigh escaped Molly before she could stop it. "Like staying in bed, but I can't. I have to get to work." She paused then asked curiously, "You said something about a message?"

"Oh, yes!" The older woman pulled a note from her apron pocket. "Your friend Jake called last night. I suppose he talked to your supervisor or something. He'd heard about your accident and wanted to know how you were doing. I told him you'd gone to bed already. Said he'd call you today."

"Thanks. I need to give him my cellphone number so you won't have to take messages all the time."

"No problem, dear. I don't mind at all. Especially if those messages come from that young man, Jake. I like him. How about you? What do you think of him?" She peered closely at Molly across the top of her glasses.

"What's not to like?" Molly grinned cheekily as she sauntered out the door. Mrs. Jenkins chuckle follow her down the sidewalk to her car.

~

When Molly arrived at the station, she asked Craig to hold down the campground while she rode out to the North Shore Road.

No one had patrolled it in a few days. With Tylenol in her system, she removed the sling she'd worn except when driving.

Near the Noland Creek turnoff she noticed large dark spots on the road. Backing up, she pulled off to the roadside. After inspecting the large smears, she recognized them as bloodstains. Her own blood chilled at the sight.

Returning to the pickup, she called on the local frequency, "Come in, Cal, this is Molly."

"I read you, Molly. What's up?"

"If you can cut yourself loose from whatever you're doing, I need you to head out here." She gave him her location then added, "And Cal, it looks serious."

While she waited for Cal's arrival, Molly walked down the Noland Creek dirt road a ways, searching the ground as she went. Blood spatters and drag marks could be seen in the dirt leading back up to the highway. When Cal arrived, he examined the scene and came to the same conclusion.

"Somebody was poaching out here last night, and they got sloppy. Usually they don't leave this kind of trail." Leaving the vehicles at the top of the road, they hiked down past the gate to where the abandoned cabin stood. This was where Cal's wife, Pam, had heard gunshots just over a week ago. Searching the area, they found more blood stains along with a tuft of bloody black fur here and there. Molly discovered empty beer bottles scattered across the cabin porch and on the ground around it. A campfire still smoldered in the clearing in front of the cabin.

"Yep," Cal scowled as he tugged off his cap and wiped his forehead with his wrist. "Our friendly poachers are becoming rather careless."

"Or overconfident." Molly tapped her boot thoughtfully on the stone fire ring. She waved an all-encompassing wave around the messy area in front of the cabin. "So, what do we do with all of this?"

"We leave it for now. I'll kick some dirt over that campfire and make sure it's out, but these fellows may be back. I don't want them to know we're onto them. They may even be back to clean it up if they stop to realize the evidence they've left behind. I'll grab a couple bottles with my handkerchief and we'll put some of the fur in an evidence bag, but the rest stays. Come on. Let's go. I've got some calls to make."

~

Molly ate lunch at her desk in the station while Craig patrolled the campground. Cal had called Ed Clark, District Chief Ranger at Oconoluftee to arrange a meeting. He wanted to step up the plans for the stakeout and see if Ed could get things moving. It was quiet for the moment and after finishing her lunch, Molly read over some reports from HQ. The phone rang, making her jump.

"Deep Creek Ranger Station, how can I help you?" she answered with a cheerfulness she didn't feel. More Tylenol with her lunch had done nothing to ease the throbbing in her arm.

"You sound chipper. How do you feel?" The timbre of Jake's voice turned Molly's insides to jelly. Having jumped up to answer the phone, she quickly dropped back into her seat.

"Not as well as I sound, I'm afraid." She forced a chuckle. "But I feel better than I did last night. It was pretty tough getting up this morning."

"I'll bet. Pretty sore, huh?"

"Yeah, that too."

"Did Mrs. Jenkins tell you I called?"

"She did. Thanks. I appreciate you checking on me. I ate supper took something for the pain and went to bed." She paused then asked, "Did Cal tell you about it?"

"As a matter of fact, he did. I called the station right after he returned from taking you to Doc Bennett's office. To hear him tell it, you did quite a number on the other guy."

"That's funny. Cal wasn't even there. He's simply repeating what Joe and Craig told him. Anyway, I think the guy was too drunk to remember anything. He probably woke up in jail this morning, wondering how he got there."

"Did they have open containers in the vehicle?

"Oh yeah. Big time. Two open beers and a bunch of empties. I could smell it on them from the rear of their truck." She shuddered at the memory.

"Well, I was glad to hear you're alright. Mrs. Jenkins was very concerned about you."

"She's the sweetest thing, Jake. She brought supper up to me, and when she returned for the tray, she brought an ice pack for my arm. She's like a substitute mother."

"Well, do you feel up to dinner and a movie tomorrow night?"

Molly smiled to herself. "I think so. Yes, that'd be fun."

"Good. I'll pick you up at five. We're driving to Asheville. There's a great little Italian place there. Do you like Italian?"

"Love it."

"Good. Then I'll see you at five. And take it easy, okay!" Huskiness slipped into his voice.

Molly's heart leaped. It sounded like more than a friendly admonition, but how could that be? Surely she read too much into his words. She cleared her throat before responding. "I will, Jake. See you tomorrow."

~

Hanging up the phone, Jake leaned back in the desk chair in the office at Twentymile. He scrubbed a hand down his face then ran it through his hair. What was that all about? When Cal had told him about Molly's incident with the drunken men, his heart had chilled. But why? They'd only worked together for just over a week. Hardly enough time to elicit such an emotional response. He couldn't explain it, even to himself. From all he'd seen so far, Molly was an amazing young woman. She was new at her job but had jumped in with both feet. It wasn't his place to be concerned for her any more than for any other co-worker. Yes, he'd have called if Cal, Kate, Joe or Craig had the same thing happen to them, wouldn't he? Of course, he would. But, he admitted to himself, there was one major difference. With Molly, his heart was becoming more and more involved.

Chapter Eight

Saturday morning, Molly gazed out to see gray skies and rain spattering the window. The mountaintops had vanished beneath a shroud of low-lying clouds while the sun appeared to have taken the day off. A good day to straighten the apartment, do some laundry, iron her uniforms and catch up on her reading.

Just before five o'clock, she dressed in tan pants and a short-sleeved periwinkle blue sweater. Fashioning her hair into a French braid, she then applied a touch of makeup and slipped on a pair of loafers. With the rain, sandals wouldn't do.

At five till five, Molly heard a firm knock on her door. She opened it wide.

"Hi, Jake. Come on in." She flashed a warm smile.

Jake caught his breath then smiled eagerly. "Wow! You look…great!"

"Thanks. You didn't say how to dress, so I assumed casual would do." Molly glanced at Jake's navy slacks and a white button-down shirt with sleeves rolled to just below his elbows. "Looks like I assumed correctly."

"You did. It's not a fancy place, but the food's great and I think you'll like the atmosphere. Ready to go?"

"I see it's still raining." Damp spots littered his shoulders and shone in his dark hair. "I'll grab my umbrella."

After a quick goodbye to Mrs. Jenkins, Jake led Molly out to his Ranger pickup, holding the umbrella over their heads and opening the door for her.

Nice manners, Molly observed, pleased at the treatment. There seemed to be a steady decline in gentlemanly assistance these days, but she rather appreciated the respect that was shown when a man opened a door, stepped back to let a woman go first, or gave a helping hand.

Molly settled into the comfortable bucket seat knowing the drive would take a while. "So you go to Asheville often?"

"Not really. But I had a hankering to get out of the woods for a while. And I mean way out of the woods." He chuckled before adding, "Asheville's the nearest real city. Did you drive through there when you came from Virginia?"

Molly nodded, gazing out the rain-streaked windshield. "Yeah. It looks like a nice place….for a city."

Jake glanced at her before returning his gaze to the road. "Sounds like you like cities about as much as I do."

"I don't like the crowds and rushing around. I prefer the laid-back atmosphere of small towns and rural areas."

"Well, you've come to the right place for that. How do you like living in Bryson City?"

"I love it, although Mrs. Jenkins' house isn't 'in' town. It's a really quiet little place. I love seeing the old men sit and play checkers in the town square. You don't see that kind of thing in Charlottesville. Not anymore. But then I suppose you can't get any more rural than where you are, in North Carolina anyway."

"That's a fact. Did Cal tell you the park maintains a cabin on the other side of Fontana Lake? A backcountry ranger was once stationed there but no more. The only access is by boat or by horseback. We keep a patrol boat docked at the Fontana Marina. I use it to patrol the park side of the lake. Occasionally I've found indications of poaching activity. Sadly, there are more poachers than rangers available to patrol. I'm sure when you're at Twentymile during the stakeout, you'll have a chance to go over and see the cabin."

"Wow!" Molly exclaimed. "That is really rural. Cal didn't mention it. I'd like to go over and see that side of the lake sometime."

They talked about the park, work and their families until they reached Asheville, then Jake concentrated on traffic and finding the restaurant. Pulling up to the entrance, he dropped Molly off then drove around to park. Before climbing out of the truck, Molly handed him her umbrella. "It's coming down harder now. You'll need this."

~

As Jake shook out the umbrella under the front awning, he was grateful for Molly's thoughtfulness. But then there wasn't much he didn't appreciate about her.

The host greeted them warmly, confirmed their reservation then showed them to a table in a corner. Jake observed Molly's approving glance around the large attractively decorated room. Italian tiles covered the floor while mural scenes of Italy decorated the walls. The tables were lit by dripping candles in old twine-wrapped wine bottles. A clay pizza oven stood in a corner near the kitchen, emitting heat and light from its fiery interior. Statues and Roman vases sat on columns scattered around the room. Two violinists in traditional gypsy attire played quietly as they strolled around the room.

Jake watched with delight as Molly's eyes lit up at the room's atmosphere. "Well? What do you think?"

She returned her sparkling gaze to Jake. "You really know how to pick 'em, don't you! This is amazing. I've been to Italian restaurants before, but never one with such ambiance. Do you come often?"

Pleasure skimmed Jake's nerve endings. He'd chosen something she liked. "I've come a few times. The first time my family had a reunion here and hired one of the back rooms for a huge dinner. But it just isn't the same as bringing a beautiful girl and enjoying the romantic atmosphere with her alone."

~

Something in Jake's gaze caused Molly's breath to catch. Her heart rate accelerated even as she lowered her gaze to her menu, pretending she didn't know what he was talking about.

"What was this girl's name?" she asked innocently. Then with a sudden thought, asked, "Was it Celeste?"

She lifted her gaze back to Jake's. His sapphire eyes darkened and he glowered at her in mock disgust. "Celeste? Really? Not a chance. You can't seriously think I'd go for that kind of girl."

"Oh, what kind of girl is she?" Molly was proud of the straight face she managed to maintain. "She seemed like a very… well…a friendly kind of girl." She stressed the word "friendly."

Jake glowered, "Yeah, she's friendly alright. Nothing would make her happier than to sink her bright red talons into me. She's like a predator waiting to pounce."

Molly couldn't hold the straight face any longer. Her laugh was light and Jake's lips quirked in a grin before he started laughing too.

"Sorry. I just had a mental picture of Celeste waiting in ambush," Molly laughed, placing a hand over her mouth.

"Oh, it's nothing so sly," Jake replied emphatically. "She's too blatant for an ambush."

Molly laughed again then noticed Jake was no longer laughing although a spark remained in his eyes.

"You know the beautiful girl I was talking about was you, don't you?" he asked, his voice growing husky.

Molly dropped her gaze and was saved from having to answer by the waiter who arrived at their table.

"We've been too busy talking to look at the menus," Jake opened his and began to peruse it. "Can you give us another minute or two?"

~

When the waiter returned they placed their orders. As he headed toward the kitchen, one of the roving violinists stopped at their table, playing for Molly. Jake found himself watching her as she admired the musician's talent, entranced by his performance. In the candlelight the glow of pleasure on her cheeks warmed his heart as a delighted smile parted her lips. A surge of longing he'd never felt for any other woman filled him.

He dragged his gaze away. *This is ridiculous! I've only known Molly for a few weeks. How can I feel this way? What is it about her that fascinates me? Maybe we haven't known each other long, but I intend to remedy that.*

Molly clapped softly as the musician bowed grandly and strolled away.

"That was wonderful." Contentment eased across Molly's lovely features. "Thanks for bringing me here, Jake. This is really nice."

Jake smiled. "Good. We'll come back again sometime."

Would she want to come back with him? Not because it was a great place to eat but because she enjoyed his company?

Their food arrived quickly, surprising them both. They ate heartily as they talked. Jake learned more about Molly's home and family, pleased when she told him all about them.

All too soon it was time to go. The movie would begin shortly and they still needed to purchase their tickets.

Exiting the restaurant, they found the rain had stopped and the air had grown cooler. Molly silently wished she'd brought a light sweater. As they climbed into the pickup, Jake noted her slight shiver.

Reaching behind the seat, he pulled out a light jacket. "Here, Molly, put this on." He held it as she slipped her arms in. "It's a little cool since the rain stopped."

Molly pulled it up over her shoulders and giggled as it swallowed her up.

"So it's about six sizes too big for you. It should keep you warm," he chuckled, starting the engine.

"That's okay. Thanks for letting me use it."

The movie was a drama and one particularly sad scene brought tears to Molly's eyes. She sniffed and wiped her eyes with her fingers. Jake was sure she was trying to hide it. She leaned forward to shift slightly away. While she was forward, Jake pulled his handkerchief from his pocket and quickly dropped his arm along her seatback. As she leaned back, he handed her the folded cloth. Accepting it with a whispered thank you, she glanced over her shoulder at his arm then turned her gaze back to the big screen. Was that a smile on her lips? A good sign. At least she hadn't turned a glare in his direction.

~

Molly's heart tripped at the pressure of Jake's arm along her shoulders. The warmth that eased through her shirt was reassuring but was that what she wanted? She didn't have time for a relationship. Right? This evening was meant to get Jake out of the woods and share some fun time with a friend. No. Her career was her goal and she needed to keep that in mind. A heavy sigh slipped out. As hard as she tried to ignore it, the warmth of his arm invaded her senses. How would it feel for those arms to wrap solidly around her? No. Don't go there. She tried to force her concentration back to the movie. But that warmth sure felt good.

~

The drive home was pleasant though quiet. Each enjoying the company of the other, neither compelled to talk. Molly leaned her head against the headrest and promptly dozed off. Jake watched as her head slipped down the headrest. Reaching over he guided her head onto his shoulder, her cheek against his sleeve. He couldn't allow her head to bob around like that, could he? It had nothing to do with her gentle fragrance or the pleasant feel of her weight against him. Yeah, he could drive like this forever.

When he parked in Mrs. Jenkins' driveway and stopped the engine, Molly slowly stirred, opening her eyes. It took a moment for her to remember where she was, but as Jake gazed down into her face and she realized where her head lay, she came wide awake. Sitting up stiffly, she pushed back the tendrils of hair that had dislodged from her braid as she slept.

"Hello, sleepy-head." Jake grinned. "Have a good nap?"

Molly looked at him with wide eyes, embarrassment coloring her cheeks. "Oh, I'm so sorry I fell asleep on you. Your shoulder must be stiff."

It was stiff, but Jake wouldn't have had it any other way. "No, I'm fine. See?" He demonstrated by moving his arm around. Climbing out of the truck, he opened her door and then walked her up to her apartment. Mrs. Jenkins had gone to bed, leaving Molly to use her house key to get in.

At the top of the stairs, Molly unlocked her apartment door and opened it. Turning to Jake, she smiled sleepily. "Want to come in for a cup of tea or coffee?"

As much as Jake would have loved to, he shook his head slowly. "Thanks, but I'd better be getting home." He placed a gentle finger on her cheek. "It's late and you look tired. I'm sure your arm is sore and you need to get some rest. Can I take a rain check?"

"Any time," Molly nodded. "Thanks again for a great evening. I really enjoyed myself."

Jake smiled. "Me too."

A thought formed in his mind and he snapped his fingers,. "I have an idea! Next weekend is the Fourth of July. My family has a big picnic every year, and we go to the fireworks celebration afterward. Would you like to come with me? It's a lot of fun!"

A dubious expression crossed Molly's face. "How big did you

say your family was?"

"Don't worry. I won't expect you to know all their names the first day," he teased.

"Well, that's a relief," Molly laughed. "Okay. It sounds like fun."

"You'll have a great time." *And I'll do everything in my power to make sure you do!*

He placed a finger beneath her chin, tipping her face up. "Good night, Molly," he whispered before laying a soft kiss on her cheek.

~

Molly watched as he descended the staircase and walked out the door, locking it softly behind him. She placed her fingers on her cheek where his lips had touched ever so softly. Had she imagined it after all? No. It wasn't her imagination.

It wasn't until after she'd closed the apartment door, leaning back against it, that she realized she was still wearing his jacket. Tugging the collar up to her nose, she again inhaled the faint but pleasant aroma of woodsy aftershave that she'd reveled in all through the movie. Remembering the feel of his arm along the back of her seat, she smiled. Yep. One of the oldest moves in the book. She probably shouldn't have thought twice about it, but too late. She'd thought about it more than twice.

~

The mountains remained shrouded in low lying clouds as rain continued through Monday afternoon. By Tuesday the sky was a bright blue, not a cloud in sight. The morning air was fresh and clear. All signs of dreary weather had vanished.

Molly and Kate were on duty Tuesday morning, Kate opening up the station while Molly drove to the horse barn to see how supplies and tack were holding up. She'd just finished inventory when Cal pulled up in his patrol SUV.

"Morning, Molly," he called, strolling toward her.

Snapping the padlock shut on the tack room door, she walked over to meet him. "Good morning!" she smiled. Then noticing his serious expression, asked, "What's happened?"

"Well, we've got a problem. There's a teenage boy lost up in the mountains somewhere. He's been out since late yesterday afternoon and was last spotted in the Clingmans Dome parking lot."

"What?" Molly sucked in a horrified breath.

"Yeah, and the worst part is, he's diabetic."

"Oh, no! So what's being done?"

Cal crossed his arms on the corral fence. "Well, the local rangers searched until dark last night. A park-wide search has been underway since daylight. With Clingmans Dome being the most central part of the park, he could have gone off in any direction."

"And how can I help?" Molly propped her hiking boot on the bottom of the fence.

"I want you to hike up the Noland Creek watershed. Jake's riding a horse up from Fontana Dam. I'll hike up Deep Creek. Rangers are hiking up from all over the park. A search and rescue camp has been set up in the Clingmans Dome parking lot. Noland Creek trail will take you there. Check in when you get to the top. Throw a candy bar into your daypack. There's a good chance he may have gone into insulin shock. Keep your eyes open and keep in touch."

Returning to the station Molly grabbed her daypack. She tossed in a couple candy bars from the vending machine in the maintenance shed and filled her water bottle with ice and water. Cal called Joe to come in and give Kate a hand so she wouldn't have the campground on her own. He then drove Molly to Noland Creek and dropped her off, heading back to Deep Creek to begin his own search.

~

For the first forty-five minutes or so the trail was only a gradual climb. The rushing waters of Noland Creek tripped along to Molly's left. Here and there wild boar had rooted up the ground, leaving the area devastated and bereft of vegetation. Whoever had introduced these destructive creatures into the park hadn't done it any favors. She'd read somewhere that wild boar multiplied like rabbits. Hopefully they could put a dent in the local boar population, but it seemed to be an uphill battle.

The rippling of the creek grew fainter as the trail grew steeper. Horse hoof prints marked the trail in the mud left by the recent rain. Occasionally she spotted deer prints. One set of prints she was certain were made by a bear. They were the largest animal prints she'd ever seen. As a shiver ran up her back she glanced around to see if the owner of those prints was nearby.

As she hiked up the mountain, Molly searched from beyond one side of the trail to beyond the other for the missing teenage boy. She prayed he'd be found. Soon. With his special medical needs, his life was in danger if he didn't get help soon. But as hard as she searched, she found nothing.

After climbing steadily up the mountain trail for two hours, she noticed a change in the terrain. Between two stands of trees, the mountainous scenery stretched out in the distance. This was definitely a much higher elevation. Hardwoods began to mingle with spruce and fir evergreens as the trail meandered alternately through wooded patches then across open spaces with spectacular views. It reminded her of the day Jake had driven her to HQ. She'd enjoyed that day. Except for meeting Celeste. She could've done without that encounter. But Jake? Yeah, she'd enjoyed his company. As a matter of fact, she always enjoyed his company.

In one of the small open spaces, Molly sat on a fallen tree trunk and took out her water bottle and a granola bar. As she munched quietly and drank the cool water, a tiny brown-striped chipmunk jumped onto the log, watching her warily from a short distance. His nose and whiskers twitched with interest, making Molly smile. Breaking off bits of the granola bar, she laid it on the trunk a couple feet away. His tiny ears twitched as he sniffed, considering her offering. After a moment the chipmunk slowly made his way toward the crumbs, stopping to watch her as he progressed. Finally reaching them, he grabbed them quickly and retreated to a safe distance where he devoured them. Molly repeated this until, between them, they finished the bar.

"Thanks for sharing my snack," she said aloud as she started back up the trail. In all the quiet that had surrounded her for the last two hours, it seemed strange to hear her voice in this peaceful place. It was like standing in a huge cathedral where no one dared speak above a whisper.

After hiking for another half hour, Molly reached a paved road that wound up the mountain. This must be the Clingmans Dome road. She consulted the trail map she'd brought along. Yep. It was. And none too soon. Tiredness washed over her. She panted for breath and longed to sit down for a rest. The climb would've been easier had it been a leisurely hike, but she'd made excellent time, knowing someone's life was in the balance. Her uniform shirt clung to her back from the midday heat and the exertion of the hike. Yanking off her cap, she swiped back the sweaty tendrils of hair that were plastered to her forehead, cheeks and neck.

Replacing the headgear and adjusting her daypack, she hiked up the paved road. She hadn't gone far when a park patrol car stopped, the ranger inside offering a lift to the top. They discussed the search and rescue efforts, and she was told the boy still had not been found. When they reached the Clingmans Dome parking lot, Molly thanked the ranger for the lift, climbed out and headed over to the Search and Rescue base station set up in a tent at one side of the parking lot.

Rangers and park personnel milled about, some coming off the trail while others headed out to search. A food truck sat near the base station, providing sustenance for the searchers. Across the pavement, an olive drab military chopper perched on the tarmac. The crew relaxed in the open cargo door, helmets removed as they chowed down on boxed lunches.

As Molly approached the base station, a young man in a NPS uniform sat behind a table, a base radio beside him. He smiled when she stopped in front of the table. "Hi there. Did you hike up with the search? What's your name?"

"Yes, I did. Molly Walker, and I'm from Deep Creek Ranger Station. I hiked up the Noland Creek watershed."

"Nice to meet you. I'm Rob Edwards. So, you didn't have any luck either, huh?" A wry quirk tilted his lips.

Molly shook her head. "Nothing."

"Well, thanks for participating in the search. Head over to the meal truck and grab something to eat then hang around for a while. They've been sending some of the rangers back down the trails and even off the trails looking for this kid. They may need you later."

"Sure, no problem." Molly caught sight of the helicopter again. "Are they using the helicopter to search for the boy?"

"Yeah. That's a UH-60 Black Hawk. Impressive, huh? They've been up several times this morning searching in different quadrants. They're National Guard. The crew's taking a lunch break and refueling the chopper. They'll head back up shortly." The base radio at his elbow came to life, requiring Rob's attention. "Excuse me," he reached for the mic.

Molly wandered over to the meal truck, gratefully accepting a boxed lunch and a cold bottle of water. Heading to a grassy area beside the parking lot, she sat beneath a tree and opened the box. A ham and cheese sandwich, an apple and a bag of peanuts. Hmmm. Right about now, she would've eaten anything, as hungry as she was. It hadn't been that long since her shared meal with the chipmunk, but the operative word was shared. What she'd eaten hadn't lasted long.

As she ate the simple fare, she watched the chopper pilot and his two man crew strap on their helmets and prepare for flight. The 4-bladed rotors began to spin slowly, picking up speed and releasing a whomp-whomp sound as the blades sliced through the air, reverberating across the parking lot. The insect-like aircraft lifted off the ground, slowly circling over the valley beyond the parking lot, its noise bouncing off the mountain peaks surrounding the valley.

Molly gazed at the view beyond the chopper. In spite of the seriousness of the situation, she couldn't help but appreciate the view. The deep greenish-blue of the closest peaks faded into lighter and paler tones the further in the distance the peaks sat.

Packing up her trash, she dropped it into a trash can then wandered around the parking area, waiting… for what she didn't know. Good news. Bad news. No news. The boy's family must be frantic with worry. She prayed, both that the boy would be found and that his family would be given the strength to deal with whatever lay ahead.

The distant whirring of the chopper blades echoed around the valley as it moved about slowly, searching through the canopy of trees and open areas for the boy. She'd heard someone talking about the FLIR technology the chopper was equipped with. Equipment that could detect body heat through the tree canopy.

As Molly neared the base station again, someone commented that inclement weather was headed this way. She remembered what Jake had told her the day they drove to HQ. Bad weather rolled in quickly up here.

Thin fingers of fog began to snake around the mountaintop near the Dome, slithering down into the surrounding valleys and toward the parking lot. Within minutes, the afternoon sun was veiled and the parking lot shrouded in a thick blanket of fog. Dampness clung to Molly's face and arms. Vague figures moved about in the distance like specters, while people nearby were more visible. The whole scene faded into the mist, while the fog muffled the whirring of the chopper blades.

A chill ran down Molly's spine. Surely the pilot and crew couldn't see any better out there than she could here. Could they even see to land? Did they have equipment capable of guiding them through the fog? Would they miss the parking lot altogether and crash into the valley below? Or would they hit one of the mountains surrounding it?

So caught up in her thoughts, she hadn't heard anyone approach until a gentle hand touched her shoulder. Startled, she jumped and spun around.

"Molly, it's me. Jake." He gave a reassuring squeezed to her shoulder. "Didn't mean to startle you."

She shook her head, her hand over her heart. "No, it's okay. I was just deep in thought. I didn't hear you come up." She glanced around noting only his daypack slung over one shoulder. "How did you get here so soon? Cal said you'd be coming up from Fontana Dam. I thought it would take you longer."

"If I'd hiked, it would've, but I rode Billy Boy." Turning he pointed toward the edge of the parking lot where she barely made out a horse tied to a tree, munching on grass. "Plus, I got a very early start this morning."

"Well, at least you had company on the trail." Molly smiled. "My sole companion was a chipmunk that only wanted my granola bar."

"And did he get it?" Jake asked with a chuckle.

"At least half."

"How long have you been here?"

"Maybe a half hour or so. Long enough to get something to eat and watch the fog roll in. Does it get this thick often? It's like the proverbial pea soup."

"It's not unusual, especially at these elevations." They started toward the meal truck to get Jake some food when he stopped suddenly. "Is that a helicopter I hear?"

"It sure is. They've been up for ten minutes or so. How on earth are they going to land in all this fog?"

Jake accepted the boxed lunch from the meal caterer and scouted for a place for them to sit. "Well, I know they sometimes use colored smoke bombs to guide them in. There are several people running around over there like they're setting something up."

Molly could barely see the faint figures of park personnel where Jake had indicated, but she couldn't determine what they were doing. A plume of purple smoke rose into the air. The whirring of the chopper blades came closer but remained invisible. The smoky plume dissipated into the fog, rapidly losing its effectiveness.

"What's happening?" Molly asked.

"The slight breeze is spreading out the smoke so the pilot can't see it, but it's not strong enough to blow away the heavier fog. It sounds like they're trying to find the parking lot, and they don't sound too far out."

The purple plume had completely vanished. Within minutes another smoke plume rose from the parking lot, this time bright red. Molly prayed the chopper crew would find their way back and land safely. It was bad enough the teenage boy was still missing but a crash in the attempt to find him would be terrible.

Molly's chest tightened as she watched with bated breath as everyone in the parking lot waited, hoping the chopper crew would see the red plume. Silence descended across the pavement except for the muted whirring of the chopper blades. Molly hoped and prayed the next sound they heard would be the landing skids against pavement and not the sound of crunching metal down the hillside. The whirring continued to draw closer but still the helicopter remained invisible.

Oh, Lord! Please help them see the smoke and land safely! Please don't let them miss the parking lot!

Time seemed suspended until the shadowy shape of the helicopter appeared a hundred feet up, hovering over the landing area. A cheer rose from the waiting spectators as the skids settled onto the tarmac. As the rotors slowed their rotation, the pilot and his crew climbed out, giving the onlookers a thumbs-up. Park personnel hurried to congratulate them on the tricky landing.

"Thank you, Lord," breathed Molly, relieved. Her prayer had been answered.

Jake looked at her with a thoughtful expression she couldn't read. "You were praying for those guys, weren't you?"

"Yes, I was," she flashed a weary smile. "God knew where they were, even if they, and we, didn't."

Reaching over, he picked up her hand giving it a light squeeze. "Come on. Let's find out what's happening with the search. The chopper will be grounded for now, but I'm sure they'll continue the search on foot."

As they walked toward the base station, they watched the chopper blades slow to a stop. From the looks of the fog, the chopper wouldn't be going anywhere for a while.

Just then Molly spotted Cal approaching. "Hey, Molly. Jake. I see you two made it up alright."

"Yeah, we made it," replied Jake. "Have you heard what they're going to do now? With this fog settled in for a while, I'd say they're finished with the chopper. What about us? Do they want us to go back on the trail again?"

"Don't know yet. I've only been here a few minutes myself. Just long enough to watch the chopper land. You two hang loose while I find out."

When he returned a few minutes later, Cal filled them in. "They need us to scout around, combing down the sides of the mountain from the top. We'll head up to the lookout tower and search down the sides of the trails, more into the underbrush. Yesterday when the boy was first missing, the rangers looked along the trail edges but they didn't go too far off trail. We'll join that group."

Cal pointed a thumb over his shoulder, indicating a group forming behind him. "They're heading up shortly."

"I tied Billy Boy over there." Jake pointed at the horse waiting patiently. "It's too steep to take him to the Dome. Shall I leave him where he is?"

"Yeah. I'll tell the rangers at the base station so they know he's with you."

Within minutes Cal, Jake, and Molly were hiking to the highest point in the park. The cement lookout tower at the top had a spiral walkway winding upward to its pinnacle where a circular observation deck provided an unobstructed view overlooking the surrounding mountains. On a clear day the view was spectacular, extending for nearly a hundred miles in every direction. But not today.

When they reached the bottom of the structure, Molly looked up to see the eerily shaped observation deck with swirling fog masking its true shape. The search team spread out, working their way off trail and into the underbrush. Pushing aside low hanging limbs and checking beneath bushes, they searched carefully for several more hours until dusk and fog joined forces to shut down the search. Temperatures at the Dome had never been recorded above 80 degrees. On a good day it rarely reached that. With darkness setting in, temps were dropping rapidly.

Exhausted, hungry and thirsty, the searchers assembled back at the base station hoping for news that the boy had been recovered by other searchers. Sadly, he had not been. Food was distributed as another meal truck arrived with a fresh supply.

Molly, Cal and Jake had just finished eating when the specter-like figure of a man approached through the hazy darkness. Portable lights had been set up in various places across the parking lot, their glow dimmed by the fog. Molly recognized the man as Tom Crane, the park's superintendent.

"How's it going, Tom?" Cal climbed to his feet and extended his hand. "You remember Molly, don't you?"

Cal indicated Molly as she struggled to rise to her feet.

"Sure, I do. Oh, please don't get up, Molly. You either, Jake. Stay where you are. I know y'all are tuckered out. I appreciate your help in this search and rescue effort. Everyone's gone all out to help find the missing young man."

"We haven't had a park-wide search and rescue in quite a while, Tom." Cal scrubbed a hand down his face. "I'm sure he'll be found soon."

"We have a doctor on stand-by, Cal. Between the boy's diabetes and exposure to the elements, he isn't very optimistic he'll survive." Tom shook his head.

"We're here as long as you need us," Jake offered. "We're tired, but he's got to be found. The alternative is unacceptable."

"I appreciate that, Jake. Just hang around until we know for sure what the next step is. Cal, if you'll come with me, we need your brain power added to the rest

"Well, I don't know how much brain power I've got left, but I'll do what I can."

As Cal and Tom strode away, Molly leaned back until she rested on the ground. She was just too exhausted to care as dampness seeped through her shirt. She felt more than saw Jake lean over her.

"Are you, okay?"

She opened her eyes and nodded. "Just wake me when they've used up all that brain power and are ready to do something."

~

Jake smiled as Molly's eyes closed. "Here. Put my daypack under your head. There's a jacket inside that will make a nice pillow.

"Thanks, Jake," she mumbled as she let him slip the pack beneath her head. He watched her eyelashes swept against her cheeks, her breathing growing slow and steady. He hadn't the heart to tell her she'd have to get up soon. Her clothes would be soaked.

It wasn't long before Cal returned to tell them to go home. He chuckled when he saw Molly asleep. "I hate to do this, Molly, but you've got to get up."

Cal nudged her shoulder. "Molly, we can go home now." She didn't budge.

Jake grinned. "Let me try."

Leaning down, he touched her cheek tenderly. "Molly. Wake up, Sweetheart. It's time to go home."

Molly shook her head slowly before opening her eyes. At first it didn't register where she was, especially with the darkness that had closed in. "What time is it?" She glanced at her wrist watch. "How long was I asleep?"

"Maybe ten minutes!" Jake chuckled and held out a hand to help her up. "You were zonked out."

~

"I still am," she mumbled. Accepting his outstretched hand, she climbed to her feet, "What's happening? Did I miss anything?"

She should've listened to Jake and skipped the cat nap. It hadn't helped and the back of her shirt was soaked.

"Not really," replied Cal. "They told us to go home. It's too dark to continue the search tonight. We don't want anyone risking injury in the dark. Jake, if you're planning to ride Billy Boy home tonight, you should've left two hours ago."

"Not a problem. I've got a strong light in my saddlebag and extra batteries. What about you and Molly? How will you get back?"

"I've lined us up a ride back to Deep Creek. They'll be leaving without us if we don't hurry. Come on, Molly, time to go home."

Molly flashed a weary smile in Jake's general direction. "See you later, Jake. Call me when you get back to let me know you got home okay."

"Unless I miss my guess, you'll be sound asleep before I get back."

"I don't care. Call anyway." Molly covered her mouth as she yawned. "I want to know you got in, so I don't worry."

~

Surely she was too tired to know what she was saying, but Jake would take it. In spite of his exhaustion, a thrill coursed through him at her concern. He reminded himself it was nothing more than any co-worker would say in the same situation. Wasn't it? He shouldn't read too much into it.

Still he leaned closer and smiled into her sleepy gaze, a wink snapping one eyelid shut. "Yes, Ma'am. Your wish is my command."

Molly followed Cal to their waiting ride, but before she climbed into the SUV, she looked back as Jake mounted Billy Boy and waved. He tipped his cap in her direction then turned the horse back down the trail. He had a long ride ahead of him with thoughts of Molly to keep him company. It would be a pleasant ride after all.

~

When Molly was seated beside Cal in the back seat of the SUV, she asked, "Cal, will Jake be okay riding back in the dark and the fog?"

"He'll be fine, Molly," Cal reassured with a look she was too tired to comprehend. "Sometimes the fog stretches all the way down into the lake area. Sometimes it hangs around up here near the top of the mountains. There's a good chance he'll ride out of it shortly. And he does have a light and a compass with him. He's done this kind of thing before. Don't worry about him. He'll be fine."

Not overly reassured by his words, Molly put Jake into the Father's hands. Only He could truly look after him. She was too exhausted to examine *why* she was so concerned for Jake's safety. After all, he was just a friend and co-worker. And with that she dropped her head against the seat and promptly fell asleep.

~

Jake called at one-thirty in the morning. Molly had tried watching television while she waited for his call but soon fell asleep on the couch, an old movie playing in the background. When her cell phone rang, she was startled from sleep and grabbed it, dropping it in her first attempt to answer.

"Hello?" she croaked sleepily.

"Molly? It's Jake. I knew I'd wake you." Exhaustion filled his voice.

"That's okay. I told you to call. Besides, I was watching TV and just dozed off." That might've been stretching the truth just a tad.

"Well, I'm back safely, no problems." A yawn reached her ear before he added, "I basically let Billy Boy find his way home."

"You've got to be beyond exhausted."

"I am, but I have good news. I found the missing boy."

"What?" Molly wasn't sure she'd heard right. "Would you say that again?"

His chuckle filled her ear. "You heard me right the first time. I found the missing boy. When I was headed toward Clingmans Dome, I took the Lake Shore Trail to Eagle Creek Trail and up to the Dome, but on the way back I followed the Appalachian Trail. I'm pretty sure it was checked by other rangers, but they may not have gone far enough. He'd gone quite a ways before he became incapacitated and couldn't continue or return."

He chuckled. "Well, I have to give the credit to Billy Boy. His rhythmic gait had me nodding off. He stopped suddenly and when I tried to urge him on, he refused to move. I shone my flashlight beam around and saw something out of the ordinary just off the trail. When I investigated, I found the boy."

Molly was fully awake now. "Oh my goodness. So Billy Boy's our hero. What did you do?"

"I called the base station and they sent out the helicopter to retrieve him." Molly heard a stifled yawn. "I set up flares for them to locate us then one of the crew came down a cable with a rescue basket. They took him to a hospital in Knoxville. I haven't heard any news since I just got in. Thought I'd grab some shuteye then call for a report in the morning."

"That's wonderful, Jake. Thanks for letting me know and also that you got home safely."

"My pleasure. Just another chance to hear your voice." A pregnant silence zinged across the airwaves, then, "Thanks for caring enough to want me to call. That was…nice."

Molly's heart skipped a beat. What do you say to that? "Well….I, um…. I'll let you go, Jake. You need to get some sleep and so do I."

Jake chuckled. "Okay. Don't forget the Fourth of July picnic at my folks! I'll pick you up at nine Saturday morning. Take care of yourself and sleep well."

"You too. Good night, Jake."

~

It really was another opportunity to hear her voice. He'd thought of nothing else but Molly on his lonely ride to Twentymile. That silence had been filled with so many unspoken words. He wanted to say them, but with both of them exhausted it wasn't the time.

Instead he settled for, "Thanks for caring enough to want me to call. That was…nice." *Nice?* He winced for the second time. His tired brain wasn't pumping on all cylinders, but it didn't prevent the sweet mental picture of color-flooded cheeks. He thought he knew her well enough by now to know what her stammer indicated. And it made a pretty picture to fall asleep to.

Chapter Nine

S aturday morning, Molly had dressed and eaten breakfast and was waiting on the front porch when Jake arrived. The sun was shining and a light breeze stirred the summer leaves. She skipped down the front steps as he strolled up the sidewalk. An appreciative appraisal from his sapphire gaze took in her navy capris, red, white and blue patriotically patterned knit top and white tennis shoes.

His sharp wolf whistle that split the air set her heart to racing as did the gleam in his eyes. "Wow! You look amazing! Very….patriotic!"

Molly laughed and spread her arms wide. "Well, it is the Fourth of July weekend and it's a glorious morning! And I'm looking forward to the day!"

"Wow," he repeated. "What's got you floating like a balloon? Do we need to tie a string to your foot?"

"No, I'd just rather float." She dropped her arms to her sides. "I don't know. I'm just excited about the day. An adventure, if you will!"

"An adventure?" Jake shook his head, a grin lifting one corner of his mouth. "Not sure how my folks will take being compared to an adventure."

Molly lightly punched his arm. "Not them, Silly. The whole day! You know, going somewhere new, meeting new people, eating lots of good food!"

"Ahh! Now I understand. It's the food that draws you, not my charming company?" he smirked.

Molly flashed a coy smile. "Well, there's that too."

~

Jake was utterly captivated and delighted with her silly mood. It was going to be a good day! "You should probably bring a light jacket. It might get cool while we're watching the fireworks this evening."

"Got one." Molly hurried back onto the porch and grabbed her jacket and shoulder bag. She also picked up the jacket Jake had loaned her on their visit to Asheville.

She held it out as they strolled to his pickup. "I want to return this before I forget. I hope you didn't need it this week."

"Thanks." Jake accepted the proffered jacket. "No, I didn't. I'd actually forgotten about it."

"So, fireworks, huh? Your family does those too?"

Jake chuckled as they strolled toward his truck. "No, not exactly. Everyone drives into town to watch them. There's a softball field, and all the locals gather to watch the fireworks." He held the truck door for her. "It's usually an impressive display, for a small town."

As Molly reached to fasten her seat belt, Jake captured her arm with gentle fingers and examined it. "I see you've gotten the stitches out. Looks pretty good. Of course Doc Bennett's had a lot of practice."

"You wouldn't happen to have been stitched up by him yourself, would you?" Molly's impudent grin flashed as he released her arm.

"Oh, maybe a time or two," he evaded as he started the truck and drove away.

"Changing the subject," Jake continued, "I called for an update on the missing teenager. He had hypothermia and was in severe insulin shock when Billy Boy and I stumbled on him. He's in ICU in a hospital in Knoxville. "

"Thank the Lord you found him alive."

"Absolutely," Jake breathed a relieved sigh.

~

As Jake parked the truck at his parents' farm, Molly noticed fifteen or twenty cars parked in the driveway, along the roadside and in the front yard. Nervousness gripped her insides and her palms grew damp. She made a mental calculation. Oh boy! There were going to be lots of people to meet. Jake opened Molly's door and grasped her hand, helping her down. Thanking him, she started to move forward, but he didn't release her hand. Her eyes met his tender gaze, snagging her breath.

"Don't worry, Molly, I won't let them eat you alive. They're really a great bunch, and there's nothing to worry about."

His words were somewhat reassuring but she still fought the churning in her stomach.

"Is it that obvious?" Her voice squeaked. "I was fine until I spotted fifty vehicles parked in the yard."

Jake chuckled at her exaggeration and closed the truck door. "Just wait until the rest of them arrive."

Molly's eyes widened as she gasped.

"Come on, let's go." Releasing her hand, he led her around to the back of the house where the sounds of laughing children mixed with adult chatter.

Rounding the corner of the house, Molly spied more than a dozen children of various ages running and playing. Huge shade trees sheltered makeshift picnic tables while lawn chairs and lounges welcomed everyone to sit and relax. Several adults were doing just that. Out buildings were scattered around a large red barn and a silo at the back of the yard, while hilly apple orchards surrounded the property. An old clothesline stood just behind the house, looking as if it had seen a lot of use over the years. A roofed well stood near the back door, a galvanized bucket and a tin dipper propped on the stone ledge.

Molly loved the atmosphere here. It reminded her of her grandparent's farm in western Virginia replete with barn and silo.

Someone called out Jake's name. Molly turned and spotted a young man a few years older than Jake approaching, a smile splitting his face.

"Well, well! Looky who it is! How's it going, little brother?" He clapped Jake on the shoulder, then grabbed him in a bear hug. "It's about time you came home."

"Hey, Ben. What's up?" Jake smiled broadly, returning his brother's hug. "Ben, this is Molly Walker. She's a ranger at Deep Creek. Molly, my oldest brother, Ben."

"Welcome. It's nice to meet you, Molly. Glad you could get this bum to come home. He gets so caught up in those woods he forgets he's got a family that'd like to see him once in a while."

Molly smiled as she received a very robust handshake. "I'm happy to meet you, Ben."

Turning to Jake she feigned a serious expression. "Shame on you, Jake, for not coming home more often!"

Jake's smile broadened. "It really isn't as bad as he makes it sound."

"No?" Ben challenged with a raised eyebrow. "Wait till Mom finds out you're here. I bet you get an earful then."

"Not me, her favorite son." Jake crooned confidently.

Ben glanced skeptically at Molly. "Did this 'favorite son' ever tell you about the time he let a raccoon loose in Mom's house?"

Jake cleared his throat and took Molly's arm, leading her away. "No, and we'll leave it right there."

"Oh, I don't know," Molly replied. "Sounds like an interesting story to me."

Ben's hoot of laughter followed them as Jake replied simply. "Another time. We have people to meet. Come on!"

He was in the middle of introducing Molly around when she turned to find a woman in her sixties standing behind Jake, hands on her hips, face sporting a scowl. Her graying brown hair was pulled into a loose bun, strands of which had come out, framing her hearty features. Her cheeks were flushed red and Molly wasn't sure if it was from anger or exertion. She was slim and about Molly's height.

"Jake Stuart!" The woman bellowed reproachfully.

This had to be Jake's mother.

"Where have you been? And why haven't you been by to see us?"

Jake turned with a grin at the sound of her voice. "Hey, Mom, it's good to see you." Picking her up in his arms, he swung her around easily. "How's the best mom in the world?"

"Don't you give me that 'best mom' stuff." She huffed as he set her back on her feet. Molly had to look twice to see that she was struggling to keep the scowl on her face. Her eyes twinkled below her lowered eyebrows.

Jake bent, kissed his mother's cheek and gave her another quick hug. Her scowl gave way to a huge smile. "I never could stay mad at you. It's good to see you, Son."

"Things have been really busy at the station, Mom. You know I would've been by if I could."

She patted his cheek affectionately. "I know that, Son, but Ben put me up to it. Told me to pretend to be mad at you. He should've known I couldn't pull it off."

Molly saw Mrs. Stuart's gaze move to her. "Well, hello there. Who's this, Jake?"

"Mom, this is Molly Walker, one of the rangers I work with. Molly, this is my sweet mom." Putting his arm across his mother's thin shoulders, he gave them a squeeze.

"It's nice to meet you, Mrs. Stuart." Molly smiled, taking the older woman's extended work-worn hand.

"Molly. I like that name. It's a pleasure to meet you too, dear. And please call me Edith. We don't stand on ceremony around here. There're just too many people for that. Now you make yourself at home. And if you need something, holler. Or make Jake get it." She laughed as she poked him in the ribs. Then she patted Molly's shoulder and turned to give Jake a big wink. If it was supposed to be a surreptitious wink, she failed. Hugely! Jake chuckled as he drew Molly away to make more introductions.

"Hey, Jake!" A pretty young blond woman gave him a big hug. "Where have you been? I haven't seen you in a while."

Molly was instantly reminded of Celeste's greeting on the steps at HQ.

"Well, Shelly Bean! It's good to see you! You're looking good." Molly noticed Jake's genuine delight at seeing this woman.

"Thanks! Since the baby was born, it's been a real struggle. Believe me!"

Glancing at her trim figure, Molly couldn't believe it had been much of a struggle. When had she had this baby? A year ago?

"Shelly Bean, I want you to meet a friend and co-worker, Molly Walker. Molly, this is my kid sister, Shelly."

Shelly, who Molly now noticed favored her mom, smiled warmly. "I'm really happy to meet you, Molly. Thanks for bringing this prodigal brother of mine back to see us. And don't mind the way he calls me Shelly Bean. He's done that ever since I can remember."

Relief eased Molly's mind that Shelly was Jake's sister and not a potential love interest. "It's great meeting you, Shelly."

Jake grinned, draping an arm across her shoulders and pulling her close. "Yep, she'll always be my Shelly Bean."

Just then a young man walked up, an infant in his arms. Shelly introduced him as her husband, Tom, and the baby as their new infant of four months. Molly was fascinated by the infant, enchanted when he smiled at her. A longing tugged at her heart unexpectedly. Would she ever have a family? Kids? She clamped down on that thought. Career first, remember?

The baby suddenly frowned, turned red in the face and smiled again.

"Sometimes I really think he enjoys that." Shelly turned her nose up in disgust. "If you'll excuse me, I need to make him more enjoyable to be around."

Molly followed Jake from group to group, meeting another brother named Matt and a variety of sisters-in-law, cousins, aunts and uncles. Then came the barrage of nieces and nephews. Molly was certain she wouldn't remember a single name by the end of the day. He explained there were ten children in his father's family, and six children in his mother's family, all of whom were still living. And Jake hadn't exaggerated about more relatives arriving. They just seemed to keep coming. All with a variety of casseroles, salads and desserts to add to the already huge feast that awaited them.

At lunchtime, the food that was spread down the length of the tables was more than Molly had ever seen in one place. After filling their plates, she and Jake found vacant chairs in a group with this father, Caleb, and his brothers. She enjoyed the playful banter between the members of this family. Their love for one another was obvious and they truly enjoyed being together.

"Glad you could spend the day with us, Molly." A smile crossed Caleb's tanned, sun-wrinkled face as he stood, empty plate in hand. A faded ball cap shielded his eyes and his silvery hair from the sun. The color of his eyes remained hidden behind sunglasses, but laugh lines radiated from their corners. A little shorter than Jake, his build was stocky. A short sleeve blue chambray shirt was tucked into blue jeans. Well-worn work boots encased his feet.

"Think we're going to get an old-fashioned game of horseshoes going. Want to play?" he asked.

Molly shook her head, a smile lifting the corners of her lips.

"I'm afraid that would be disastrous for the team I'd be on, so I think I'll save myself the embarrassment and say no thanks."

After the food was taken inside for protection from insects and prying little fingers, three horseshoe pits were set up near the barn and several men gathered around picking their teams. Chairs were placed alongside the pits for viewing the makeshift tournament or shooting the breeze or both.

Molly watched Jake take aim with his horseshoe. Clapping and whistling filled the air when he made a ringer. Bowing grandly to his audience, he struck several "champion" poses. Several wolf calls and "boos" followed his actions as he returned to the pit to await his next turn.

"Molly?" Shelly stopped beside Molly's chair. "Would you mind holding Joey for a bit? The kids want me to play a game with them. He's been fed and changed, and although there are no guarantees, he looks like he's ready to fall asleep."

Molly nodded happily. "Oh, I'd love to, Shelly."

She tenderly accepted the baby, propping him against her shoulder where he proceeded to snuggle and fall asleep. With a soft touch she rubbed his little back and found herself rocking back and forth.

Glancing back to the tournament, she found Jake deep in conversation with one of his brothers. His gaze was locked on her with a look in their depths that sent a thrill surging through her. She flashed a contented smile. Jake nodded almost imperceptibly, a grin lifting a corner of his mouth.

Later that afternoon, a mixed game of softball was haphazardly organized. Playing on Jake's team, Molly soon discovered most of the players had no skill, but it really didn't matter. Everyone was joking and playing around. No one kept score and the audience applauded every play, both good and bad.

In the sixth inning however, one of Jake's cousins attempted to catch a fly ball into left field and miscalculated. The ball jammed his fingers, breaking two and stoving a third. He jogged into home and had the fingers taped together. Amidst cheers from the onlookers, he went back into the outfield to continue playing.

When the game was over, food was brought back out and everybody ate heartily, starved from their activity. Jake carried his and Molly's plates as he led her over to a wooden bench perched against the barn.

"Thanks." Molly accepted her plate. Sitting down, she bowed her head for a silent blessing, but before she could, Jake spoke softly.

"Mind if I join you in that prayer?"

Molly studied his features. He really meant it. Smiling, she nodded. "I'd like that. Do you want to pray or would you like for me to?"

"May I?" There was a reverent hush to his words.

At her nod, he bowed his head and prayed. "Heavenly Father, thank You for this food. Strengthen us with it and help us to be obedient to you. Thanks for this day and for the fun we've had and that Molly could join us. It's been a beautiful day, Lord, and we thank You for it. In Christ's name we pray, Amen."

This was a switch. Jake had told her several weeks ago he hadn't thought about prayer in years.

When she opened her eyes, Molly sat for a moment before she spoke. "Thanks, Jake."

"For what?"

Molly's smile was almost shy. "For inviting me to come today. For sharing your family with me. For the prayer. It's been a really good day."

The light in Jake's eyes yanked Molly's breath into her throat. "Believe me, lady, the pleasure's been all mine. I haven't seen my family in almost four months. Not since right after Shelly's baby was born. It's good to be back. I've needed this. And to be able to share it with you, what more could a man ask for?"

As she ate, Molly gazed out over the pleasant scene in front of them. Everyone settled down to eat as a peaceful quiet stole over the back yard. The evening sky was painted brilliant orange, yellow and gold, the distant mountains and the nearer trees in silhouette against the vibrant colors. Even as they watched, the colors deepened, adding red and purple to the mix, reminding them that night would soon arrive. Molly heard the first crickets of the evening, chirping quietly, as if not wanting to disrupt the peace that had descended over the valley.

~

Neither Molly nor Jake broke the companionable silence they shared, both realizing without words just how the other felt about the beauty around them. The brightness of the sky slowly faded to dusk as the first evening star appeared above the distant mountains. Jake reached over and twined his fingers with Molly's and was pleased when she didn't pull away. He let out the breath he'd been holding. He'd wondered if she would. She even gave his fingers a squeeze. Well, that was a step in the right direction.

"Uncle Jake! Uncle Jake!" called a young voice approaching them. A young boy about six years old ran in their direction, jolting them from their reverie.

"Well, it was nice while it lasted." Jake spoke quietly then raised his voice to respond to the approaching boy. "What's up, Mikey?"

"Dad wanted me to come get you. He wants you to come with him to the softball field to help set up the fireworks." Panting, the little boy stopped in front of them.

Jake looked at Molly with a crooked grin. "My brother, Ben, is a volunteer fireman, and it's his responsibility to lay out the fireworks and set them off every year. He should've already left to prepare for the fireworks display. I bet he got busy talking and forgot. Want to come along? I'll help him set up and then we can sit back and enjoy the show."

"Sure." She nodded.

As Jake stood he tugged Molly to her feet. "Then let's go!"

~

Jake's mom spread out three old blankets on the ground at the softball field and invited Molly to sit down. "I hope you don't mind sitting on a blanket. They're a lot easier to carry than all the folding chairs we'd need for everyone."

Dropping onto a blanket, Edith patted the space beside her. "Here, sit with me a bit until Jake comes back from helping Ben."

"I don't mind sitting on a blanket." Molly leaned back on her hands and stretched her legs out in front of her, crossing them at the ankles. "Is there any other way to watch fireworks?"

"Nope." With a soft chuckle, Edith shook her head. "This is the best way. I remember sitting with Caleb on a blanket about forty-five years ago. And as I recall it was the Fourth of July then too. He proposed to me that night. It wasn't long after that we got married. Then the children started coming along and life got busy. But sometimes it seems just like yesterday." Pausing, she chuckled again. "Listen to me prattle on. I'm sure you're not interested in my past history."

"And why not?" Molly asked. "I'm sure it would be very interesting. You've probably got a lot of stories to tell."

Edith eyed Molly, a twinkle in their midst. "Wouldn't you be more interested in Jake's history?"

Molly's cheeks warmed as she jerked her gaze across the field to where the men were gathered around the fireworks apparatus. "Mrs. Stuart," she began.

"Please. I told you to call me Edith. Everyone does." She patted Molly's hand.

"Alright, *Edith*." Molly smiled, emphasizing her name. "Jake and I are merely co-workers and friends. He invited me along today because it's a holiday and friends sometimes get together for holidays. Nothing more."

Edith nodded, pursing her lips in a way that made Molly think she didn't believe her. "Uh huh. Well, we'll see." She turned her attention toward the men as they approached. "Here come the fellas."

Caleb dropped down beside his wife while Jake sat next to Molly.

"Well, what have you two been talking about?" Jake circled his arms around his bent knees. "Anything interesting or just girl stuff?"

In the fading evening light, Molly sensed Edith's eyes on her. She couldn't stop the warmth that again touched her cheeks. Turning slightly away from Jake, she pretended to watch people gathering in the field.

Edith chuckled. "You know, just girl talk."

~

Other family members joined them on nearby blankets, all talking excitedly until it was dark enough for the fireworks to begin. Bright sparkles of various colors filled the night sky as popping sounds bombarded their ears. Jake glanced at Molly's upturned face and in the dim light from the fireworks witnessed her delight. Without warning she turned and flashed a smile, her gaze tangling with his and seizing his breath. She leaned toward him so he could hear her above the noisy din.

"Thanks for bring me, Jake. This is amazing! I had no idea that a small town could put on such a fantastic fireworks display."

As she leaned close, Jake breathed in her scent, trying unsuccessfully to steady the erratic thrum of his heartbeat. "I wouldn't have missed it for the world," he spoke into her ear, far huskier than he'd intended.

~

After the fireworks display was over, blankets were gathered and farewells and hugs were spread liberally amongst the family members. Edith gave Molly a standing invitation to return whenever she wanted, with or without Jake.

"You're always welcome, dear. And if you can get this one back sooner than later, I'd appreciate it." She gave Jake a hug. "Hurry back, Son. I love you."

"Love you too, Mom. I'll do my best."

Caleb, a man of few words, nodded in agreement with his wife and shook Molly's hand, adding his own words of invitation. Jake's siblings made their farewells, hoping to see her again soon. They teased Jake and gave Molly hugs.

The trip home was companionable. As they talked over the day, Jake told her more about his family members and Molly drank in the information. She'd truly enjoyed how his family had taken her in without a question.

Jake walked her upstairs to her door.

"Would you like to come in for a few minutes? I can make some coffee or iced tea." Molly offered, leaning against the door.

Jake shook his head. "Thanks, but I need to get back. I enjoyed you coming with me today, and I know my family enjoyed having you there."

"It was a lot of fun. And I like your family, Jake. They're a great bunch." Molly peered up at him, a soft smile on her lips.

Jake propped his hand on the doorframe just above her head and leaned in. His gaze swept her face before halting at her lips. "I'm glad you did. Before I go I'd really like to kiss you, Molly. May I?"

If she'd been able to think of something to say, the words would've been stuck somewhere in her throat. The flame in his eyes robbed her of coherent thought and all she could manage was a nod.

As Jake's lips softly grazed Molly's, her eyes drifted shut. It only lasted a few seconds but, boy, was it sweet.

When he took a step back, Molly opened her eyes. Inhaling deeply, she shoved tendrils of hair away from her face. Could he see her fingers tremble?

"Good night, Molly." A corner of Jake's mouth tilted upward, his voice husky with emotion. At least he could speak. "Talk to you soon."

~

As Molly prepared for bed, she reviewed the day's events and realized the extent to which Jake's family had welcomed her into their midst. She'd loved spending time with them. Almost as much as she loved spending time with Jake. Edith's words as they sat on the blanket had been few but carried an underlying meaning. Her own answer had rung hollow, even to herself. The memory of his kiss stayed with her as she slipped on her pajamas and brushed her teeth. Yeah, that would stay with her for a while. Her heart hammered just thinking about it.

The sudden ringing of her cell phone yanked her back from her thoughts. Grabbing the intrusive object, she spoke warily, "Hello?"

"Hi, Molly, it's Jenny. How are you?" Her friend's chipper voice reverberated through the phone.

"Jenny? Oh, hi! I'm fine! How are you?" Molly focused on Jenny's words.

"Doing fine! Had a great day today! My family gets together on the Fourth every year and we have a big picnic and fireworks. It was a lot of fun!"

"Mrs. Jenkins told me she was going and invited me, but I already had plans. I'm glad you had a great time."

"Yeah, except for one thing." Jenny's voice took on a sad note. "Jamie wasn't there. He's never missed a Fourth of July picnic before."

"I'm really sorry, Jenny." Molly didn't know what to say to encourage her friend. She'd never met him, but she knew Jamie was still avoiding his family and had been for a while. "Still haven't heard from him, huh?"

"No." Jenny sighed heavily. "Mom was pretty upset today, but she held it together really well for the family's sake. Everyone wanted to know where he was, but we couldn't tell them what we don't know."

She paused then added in a lighter tone, "Aunt Selma said you were spending the Fourth with Jake and his family. How'd that go? Have a good time?"

"Yeah, a really good time," Molly responded simply. She didn't want Jenny asking a lot of questions she couldn't answer and didn't want to. "He has a great family. More relatives than I'll ever be able to remember names for. His brother's part of the local volunteer fire department and was in charge of the fireworks. They put on an awesome display! His sister has a new infant that I held for a while. That was fun. He's such a cutie!"

"Sounds like fun. And….what about Jake? Did you enjoy spending the day with him?"

Molly's eyes closed with a wince. Good thing Jenny couldn't see her face. She'd attempted to talk about the day in general terms without going into "touchy-feely" terrain. Jake's parting kiss jumped back to the front of her mind warming her at the memory. She'd tuck that tidbit away! Definitely not for sharing. "Yeah, we had a lot of fun!" Was that light tone convincing enough?

"Molly, you're evading my question, and I think you're evading it on purpose." Jenny chided with a chuckle. "Now, how was your day with Jake? Anything good come from it? Try to evade that question."

Molly groaned. "Jenny, there's nothing to tell. We had a great day. Two friends celebrating a fun, special holiday. That's all. Really." Even to her the words sounded concocted.

"Ummhumm." Doubt edged Jenny's murmur. "'The lady doth protest too much, methinks', but I'll let it go. For now. Gotta go, Molly. I just wanted to see how your day went. Will I see you in church tomorrow?"

"Absolutely." Molly sounded far more definitive on this less dangerous topic.

"How about lunch afterwards? We can take Aunt Selma out to eat."

"Sounds like a plan. Sleep well, Jenny. I'll see you in the morning."

"Night!"

Chapter Ten

After the Fourth of July weekend, Molly noticed business slowing down in the campground. The holiday crowd had departed, leaving only the regular summer vacationers. Toward the end of the week, she'd just returned from lunch and was heading out to check the boar traps when the phone in the ranger station rang. Kate was minding the office and reached for the phone.

"Deep Creek Ranger Station. May I help you?" Kate asked in her usual cheerful voice. "Sure. Hold on a sec." She extended the cordless receiver toward Molly. "It's your lucky day! It's Jake." A dreamy roll of her eyes was followed by a dramatic sigh.

Molly grinned, shaking her head. "Thanks, Kate. Hello?"

"Hey! It's Jake. I just checked our traps, and guess what?! We got lucky! Twins, no less!"

"Twins?"

"Yeah, twins! Two piglets! Thought you'd want to come out and join in the proceedings. I've called the NC Wildlife Resources Commission. They're sending out Sam Hunter to tag and transport them out of the park. I've worked with him many times. Want to come?"

"I'm on my way." After finding out which trap the piglets were in, she hung up, grabbed her cap and told Kate where she was going.

"Lucky you," Kate sighed again.

"What do you mean?" Her comment halted Molly's exit. "I'm lucky because I get to see some wild boar piglets?"

"No, silly girl!" Kate waved a dismissive hand. "Because you get to see Jake, the hunk!" She sighed again. "He's about as good-looking as they come!"

Molly put on her cap. "I'll tell him you think so."

"No! Don't do that! I'll just settle for looking from afar." Another heavy sigh. "I don't think he even knows I exist."

Molly leaned on the counter. "I doubt that, but I know of someone who most certainly knows you exist."

"Who?" Kate's face puckered in a puzzled frown.

Just then Craig walked in, slipping his cap from his head as he entered. Molly smiled at Kate and nodded almost imperceptibly in his direction. "Hi Craig! Bye Craig! Bye Kate!"

As she walked out the door, she turned to see Kate's bewildered expression. Molly glanced toward Craig and winked. As realization dawned on Kate, she turned toward Craig, a big smile replacing her frown. Molly chuckled as she climbed into her vehicle.

~

As Molly parked behind Jake's park Jeep, she noticed the state wildlife officer hadn't yet arrived. Jake leaned against the Jeep watching the young boars in the trap.

"How long have you been waiting?" Molly climbed out of the truck.

"About ten minutes," he replied, glancing at his watch. "Sam will be here soon."

Just then the sound of tires on the dirt road indicated another vehicle approached. A large truck came into view, equipped with cages and marked with the NC Wildlife Resources Commission logo on the doors.

"Hi, Jake." An older man, tall and broad, climbed out and strolled over. From his sandy-gray hair and sun-wrinkled face, Molly guessed him to be in his early sixties.

"Who's this young lady?"

"Molly Walker. She works at Deep Creek. Molly, this is Sam Hunter. We call him when we have wildlife to remove from the park."

Molly extended her hand. "It's nice to meet you, Sam"

His huge, calloused hand engulfed hers. "Likewise. Well, what have we got here?"

Sam strolled toward the chain-link trap. "A couple of real cuties, huh? I bet Mama's not far away. This could get tricky, ya know," he added the warning.

"Yeah, I know," agreed Jake. "I have the tranquilizer gun loaded and ready in case she decides to show up."

"Good idea." Sam nodded his approval. Looking at Molly, he explained. "When these young'uns were trapped, the mother had to have been nearby. They're too young to be apart from her yet. She probably hid when she heard Jake's truck." He scanned the underbrush and wooded area surrounding them. "I'd bet anything she's out there somewhere. And when we start weighing and moving the piglets, they aren't going to go without a fight. They can get pretty loud."

Jake pulled a long, hard-sided case from the back of his Jeep. "After I called you and Molly, I returned to the station and picked this up." Opening the case he revealed a long tranquilizer rifle and several darts. "I had a feeling it would come in handy."

"Do you catch young ones often?" Molly asked.

"Often enough, but it's usually the adults we catch," explained Sam. "I'd rather catch a full-grown boar any day than young ones. They don't get half as mad when you catch them as they do when you catch their young. Those mamas can get pretty nasty."

Sam and Jake set up a mobile scale, extending it above the rear of the truck, then they worked quickly to remove two small cages. They wanted to finish before Mama Boar appeared and made her protests known. Molly knew wild boar had sharp tusks that were dangerous, even the females, and if agitated enough, they'd gore a person without hesitation.

After the second piglet was weighed, Molly tried to open the second cage so Sam could put it inside, but the latch stuck tight. She worked to pry it loose, but it wouldn't budge. It was rusted shut.

The piglet squealed helplessly as Sam held it tight. Jake had been manning the dart gun while Molly assisted Sam but handed it to her while he worked to pry the latch open. When it broke loose, he swung the door back and stepped out of Sam's way, allowing him to deposit the squealing, wiggling piglet inside. Molly handed the rifle back to Jake, but before he had a grip on it, a terrible snorting sound came from the underbrush a few feet away. A huge gray boar charged straight toward them. Within seconds it covered the short distance to where Jake stood. He'd turned at the sound, but was unable to move out of the way before the boar struck him full force, sending him flying several feet.

Without hesitation, Molly swung the dart gun around and took aim at the boar as it wheeled around for a second run at Jake. She fired, praying she'd hit the rampaging beast. The boar charged a few more feet then dropped to the ground, releasing a loud groan as it skidded to a stop.

Sam shoved the piglet into the cage and followed Molly as she ran to Jake's side.

"Jake!" Molly exclaimed, kneeling beside him. "Jake, are you alright?" She searched for possible injuries and sucked in a sharp breath as she discovered the tear in the side of his pant leg just below the knee. Ripping the fabric back, she revealed a six-inch gash on the outside of his calf bleeding profusely.

"Sam, there's a first aid kit behind the driver's seat in my truck. Would you get it, please?" The calmness of Molly's voice belied the fear that quaked her to the core.

"Sure thing, but we have to hurry. That tranquilizer won't last long. The drug Jake used acts quickly and doesn't sedate for long so there's less stress on the animal. We need to get her weighed and tagged before she comes to. She'll be madder than ever." He jogged to the truck, returning with the first aid kit and opening it for Molly.

As she applied a tourniquet above Jake's knee, he moaned, slowly turning his head. A pained expression crossed his face as his hand gingerly touched the back of his head. "Lay still, Jake," Molly directed. "I'll take a look at your head in a minute. First things first."

Edging himself up onto one elbow, he stared at this leg then glanced over at the dozing boar a few feet away. "Man, she did a number on me, didn't she? I see you got her."

Molly simply nodded as she bandaged his wound. "I think you'd better lay back down, Jake. You hit your head pretty hard on the ground."

Without argument, he did as she suggested. After the bandage was on and his leg propped up, Molly helped Sam drag the boar to the scales where they weighed her. Sam used a staple gun-like tool to attach a yellow tag to her ear.

"Come on." Urgency tinged Sam's voice. "Let's get that big cage from the back of the truck. Once we get her in, we'll winch it back up."

Working as quickly as they could, they managed to haul the boar into the cage. Once she was safely latched in, they winched the cage back onto the truck bed and loaded the two smaller cages beside it. No sooner had they strapped them down than the mother boar began to stir. Within minutes she was up and charging the sides of the cage.

"Well, Sam, she's all yours," Molly grinned, panting. She stripped her cap from her head and wiped her face with a bandanna she'd grabbed from her daypack. "Would you give me a hand getting Jake into the truck? I'll get him to the ER. Besides that gash, I have a feeling he has a concussion."

"Don't doubt that a bit." Sam's expression was pained. "She tossed him far and he hit hard."

A weak and groggy Jake was unable to help much as they assisted him into the passenger side of the truck. They moved him as carefully as possible until he was settled.

"Jake," Molly patted his cheek. "Don't go to sleep, Jake. You have to stay awake."

"I know." His clouded gaze attempted to focus on her as he winced in pain. "I'll try."

Molly looked helplessly at Sam who put a comforting hand on her arm. "Hang in there, girl. I'll follow you into town and make sure you get to the hospital. If you need anything, just pull off and I'll be right there."

"Thanks, Sam." Molly smiled faintly before climbing into the driver's seat. She drove as slowly as possible down the bumpy dirt road. Her first instinct was to drive fast, but she didn't want to jostle Jake, so she forced herself to drive with care. It seemed an eternity before they emerged onto the tarmac highway. When they did, Molly flipped on her blue lights and siren and stepped on the gas.

~

At the entrance to the ER, Molly hurried inside and asked for assistance. Sam was standing beside Jake when she returned with two orderlies. "I can't stay any longer, Molly. I wish I could, but it's going to be dark in a few hours. I need to get these animals out to the game land and ready for release." He turned to Jake. "I'll be by to see you soon, Jake. Take care of yourself!"

"You bet," replied a groggy Jake.

"Thanks for your help, Sam. I couldn't have done it without you."

"Well, I wouldn't be too sure of that." A broad smile split his face as he waved a dismissive hand. He started for his truck. "As for helping with Jake, you had the situation well in hand."

While the ER staff worked over Jake, Molly called Cal. A short time later he walked into the waiting room where Molly sat. As she relayed the events of the afternoon, the doctor came out of the ER and approached them.

"Well, Doc, how's Jake?" Cal asked.

"I'd like to keep him overnight for observation. He's conscious, but he has a severe concussion. There's quite a goose egg on his head. We cleaned and stitched up his leg but there's always a possibility of infection with this kind of wound. The gash was very deep, but I think we've got him stitched up pretty well."

"Can we see him?" Molly tried to hide the tremors she was feeling.

"I don't see why not," replied the doctor. "Just don't stay long. They'll be coming shortly to take him to a room for the night. If all goes well, he should be able to leave in the morning. Give us a call before you come to see if he's ready to be discharged."

"Thanks, Doc," said Cal. "Come on Molly. Let's go see our embattled hero."

~

Jake's eyes were closed when they entered the room. Molly cringed at the pallor beneath his tanned skin.

"Hey, Jake," Cal spoke in hushed tones. "You awake?"

Jake's eyes fluttered open. "Yeah, I'm awake. Just trying not to think how much I hurt." His eyes rested on Molly. "How's the sure shot? Wish you could've seen it, Cal. But guess what? I didn't either. One minute I'm standing there, the next a freight train hit me, then I look up to see Molly and Sam, and the freight train derailed. That boar was out cold. Don't remember much after that. Did you get the mother caged too?"

His weak voice tugged at Molly's heartstrings. She hated to see such a strong man brought so low. "As soon as you were taken care of, Sam and I weighed and tagged the boar and loaded her into the cage, and without a minute to spare. No sooner was the cage strapped down than she was up, madder than ever."

"Hate I missed it." Jake flinched as he rubbed his sore head.

"I guess they like you here, Jake." Cal chuckled. "They want to keep you."

"Yeah, I know. I'd rather sleep in my own bed, but I don't think they're going to give me a choice."

"Nope, I don't think so."

Just then, two orderlies entered the room with a bed. "I think your chariot has arrived," Cal joked.

"So I see." Jake's eyes began to droop as the pain meds in his IV began to take effect.

When the two men had transferred Jake to the hospital bed, Molly placed her hand over his. "I'll come take you home tomorrow as soon as I find out when you're ready to be discharged. If that's okay, Cal?"

She glanced at her supervisor and Cal nodded.

"That's a good plan. I have a meeting in Gatlinburg so that would help a lot."

Jake tucked her hand into his and gave it a squeeze. A light shone through the pain in his eyes and a lopsided grin tilted a corner of his lips. "I'll be waiting."

~

The next morning Molly called the hospital to see when Jake would be released. After they told her he'd be ready by the time she arrived, she hung up and turned to Craig.

"You know where I'll be, Craig. Call if you need anything. Joe will be in shortly and Kate will be in at three."

"Molly, did you mention anything to Kate about my interest in her?" Craig's serious tone stopped Molly in her tracks.

"Not exactly." She smiled. "I just kind of pointed her in your direction. Why?"

"I just wanted to say thanks." Shyness forced his eyes and chin down. "Maybe nothing will come of it, but at least I have a small chance."

"I think you have a good chance, Craig." She patted his arm. "You're a great guy, and I'm sure she's realized that too."

~

When Molly entered Jake's room, she found him resting on the bed dressed in his dirty uniform from the previous day. His torn pant leg was cut up the seam to allow his bandaged leg to fit through.

"Good morning," Molly called softly, unsure if he was awake or not.

Jake turned his head slowly toward her and started to sit up. "Good morning, lady. You're a sight for sore eyes. And I mean sore."

Why did most of his words drive warmth into her cheeks? Or was it the tone in his voice? "Why? What's the matter? Was it a bad night?"

"Not really." He clasped his fingers behind his neck. "They gave me something to help me sleep, so I rested pretty well, considering. I have a lingering headache, but that's not what I meant. I'm just glad to see you."

Could her cheeks grow any warmer? That light in his eyes did things to her nerve endings.

"Can you leave now?" She strove for a casual tone and nearly pulled it off. Jake grinned as if he knew her thoughts.

"Yeah, they said as soon as you arrive to ring for assistance." Reaching over, he pressed the call button and within minutes they were on their way.

~

Molly parked the truck behind Twentymile Ranger Station then climbed out and retrieved Jake's crutches from the truck bed. "Here you go. Now if you'll hand me the keys to the station, I'll open the door for you."

She followed him through the kitchen and into the living room. "Do you want to lie on the couch? I'm not sure stairs are an option right now. You need to prop that leg up. You had it down for the long ride out."

"The couch is fine." With care, Jake lowered himself down as Molly reached for some throw pillows to prop up his leg. She scrutinized him as he settled in.

"You're still wearing the uniform you had on yesterday. If you tell me where things are, I'll get them so you can get cleaned up and changed."

His eyebrow rose as a grin tilted his mouth. "Gonna give me a hand?"

Molly turned around quickly to hide her flaming cheeks. Her penchant for blushing was a curse. "I'll go up and rummage for a t-shirt and sweats, if that's ok."

Not waiting for his answer, she spun on her heel, Jake's chuckle following her up the stairs.

~

Jake grinned to himself. Watching the color infuse Molly's cheeks was always a delight, but he'd gone too far this time. There was a fence to mend when she came back downstairs.

As she returned to the living room, his clothes, a towel, deodorant and soap in hand, she laid them on the coffee table. As she turned away, he caught her hand and sought her gaze which was avoiding his.

"I'm sorry, Molly. What I said was uncalled for. I enjoy watching you blush, and…. well…. you did. But I shouldn't have said what I did. Forgive me?" Pouring sincere contrition into his gaze, he hoped she wouldn't stay mad at him. Her lips tugged into a reluctant smile.

"Well… I don't know." Was she exaggerating her hesitation? After a long moment she added, "I suppose so."

"Thanks." He grinned and blew out a breath, relieved she'd forgiven him. Releasing her hand, he reached for his crutches. "You know, I really do need a clean-up. Come on. Help me to the bathroom before the painkiller wears off. Please?"

~

While Jake cleaned up, Molly checked the fridge for something to prepare him for lunch. She hated to just run off and leave him to fend for himself. He'd have a hard time getting around for the next week or so.

When he was settled back on the couch, a lunch tray on the coffee table beside him, Molly grabbed her cap and turned to leave. "Hey, where are you going? Aren't you eating?" he asked.

"Not right now. Thought I'd run up and feed the horses. I'm sure they're starved after missing supper last night."

Before he could respond, she hurried out the kitchen door and up the gravel drive toward the barn. His earlier comment, although made in jest, had caught her off guard. She normally would've shaken off that kind of comment, never giving it a second thought. Why not this time? She was attracted to Jake, true, but that was all it was. Right? An attraction? The memory of his kiss returned full force. The exterior shell of her resolve to avoid relationships had cracked and Jake had slipped behind that shell. But rather than feel threatened, she felt a lightness in her spirit at the realization.

"Hello, fellows." She whistled to the horses in the pasture. They trotted over to the fence, heads bobbing and neighs resounding. "I know you're hungry, but don't be angry at Jake. He had an accident and couldn't get home to feed you. So, here I am. It's a little late, but I'll take care of you."

After pouring feed into the troughs, she forked hay into the bins. The horses ate eagerly. Grabbing a broom, she swept up the barn floor until they were finished then she curried them and picked their hooves. Releasing them back into the pasture, she watched in dismay as they rolled in the dirt.

"Thanks for nothing, fellows." Shaking her head with a grimace, she headed back down to the station.

Jake rested on the couch, his finished tray on the coffee table, cell phone to his ear. "Yeah, I know what you mean, Cal. Hey, Molly just walked in. Want to talk to her? Sure." He extended his phone to her. "It's Cal."

"Hi, Cal. What's up?"

"Jake and I were just discussing the situation and how things are going to have to be handled until he's back on his feet. We need a ranger on duty, and I'm afraid he can't be for a while."

"You're right. He has to keep that leg propped up for a few days. What do you have in mind?" She had a pretty good idea where he was going with this conversation.

"I was hoping you wouldn't mind moving out there for the duration and fill in for Jake. Although we'll be shorthanded here, I'll cut you loose from the campground. Right now Jake needs you more." He cleared his throat. "You can stay up at the bunkhouse if you'd be more comfortable. I mean…well, you know, Jake being a fellow and all. I mean… well, you know what I mean."

Molly smiled at his discomfort. "Yes, I do, Cal. And thanks for considering that. Yeah, I'll fill in for him. Okay. Bye."

Molly turned to hand the phone back to Jake and found his head back on the pillow, eyes closed. His face was pale beneath his tan, and his brows were knit together.

"Jake?" Kneeling beside the couch, she placed a gentle hand on his arm. "Is the pain bad?"

His eyes fluttered open, a faint smile tugging at the corners of his mouth. "You know, I thought I was doing okay after we got home, but right now it hurts an awful lot." He cringed as he ran a hand through his hair.

"I'll get you another pain pill then you can rest awhile." Molly went to the kitchen and returned with a glass of water and his pill bottle. "Here you go."

"Thanks." Popping the pill into his mouth, he chased it down with a swallow of water. Handing the glass to her, he asked, "What'd Cal say? Has he got a plan?"

"He does. Looks like I'll be filling in for you for a while. I'll be your eyes, hands and feet, but you'll have to tell me what has to be done and how you run the station."

"I can do that. We'll make a good team, Molly." The expression in his pained eyes and the strained smile hinted that his words might carry a double meaning.

~

While Molly drove home to pick up things she'd need for the next week or so, Jake agreed to nap. Placing his cell phone on the coffee table where he could call if he needed something, she promised to be as quick as she could be.

At her apartment, she packed her items and then went in search of Mrs. Jenkins. Molly knew she'd find her either in the garden or in the kitchen. This time it was the later.

"Hi, Mrs. Jenkins!"

The older woman turned from the stove, a wooden spoon in her hand. "Oh! Molly, dear! I didn't hear you come in." Her gaze flew to the wall clock. "Aren't you home early? There isn't anything wrong, is there?"

Molly nodded. "Yes, there is. Oh, not with me, though!" she added to ease the alarm on her landlady's face. "It's Jake. He was charged by a boar yesterday, and it gored his leg. He spent the night in the hospital, but I drove him back to Twentymile this morning. Anyway, I'm going to fill in for him for a few days while he's out of commission. I've packed some clothes to take with me," indicating the duffle bags by the door. "I just wanted to let you know where I'll be. Call my cell phone if you need anything."

"Oh, my goodness gracious!" Mrs. Jenkins exclaimed. "So sorry to hear that. I hope he'll be alright. Those boars are dangerous, and there's always the chance of infection with that kind of injury. What did the doctor say?"

"That with the proper rest and care, he'll be fine. And I intend to see he gets it."

"Good for you." A smile split her wrinkled face. "He's a fine young man, and we don't want anything more to happen to him." She turned back to the stove. "Here, take some of this beef vegetable soup to him. I made a big batch to freeze, but I'd rather you took some for the two of you to eat." Reaching into the cupboard she pulled out a large plastic bowl and lid.

"Thanks! That's very thoughtful! But are you sure? You already had plans for it."

"See this great big stock pot full? There's still plenty to freeze. It'll save you having to fix something tonight. Just reheat and serve."

Molly accepted the bowl. "I really appreciate it, and I'm sure Jake will too."

Mrs. Jenkins laid a gentle hand on Molly's arm. "I like that young man, Molly. And unless I miss my guess, you do too. I'll be praying for you both."

Molly neither confirmed nor denied, but remained silent as Mrs. Jenkins helped carry her things to the car. As she drove toward Twentymile, she reflected on her landlady's words. Yes, she was attracted to Jake. A lot. But she was just getting her career in the park service started and right now a serious relationship didn't fit into her plans.

Lord, I trained for four years and You worked things out so I could get this job. Here I am thinking about a guy that just doesn't fit into my plans. She stopped short in her prayer, realizing what she'd just said. Her plans. Not the Lord's plans.

Forgive me, Father. I do want Your will in my life. I know You have my best interests at heart. Help me seek Your will and not my own.

Chapter Eleven

After leaving Mrs. Jenkins, Molly stopped to grab a few groceries they'd need in the coming days. By the time she arrived back at Twentymile, she'd been gone nearly three hours. Gingerly opening the kitchen door, she hoped Jake was still resting. A glance into the living room told her his eyes were shut, so she quietly put the groceries away.

As she placed the last item in the cabinet, a moan sounded from the living room. Tiptoeing to the couch, she looked closer. Jake was paler than when she'd left him. He moaned again in his sleep, prompting her to lay a gentle hand on his forehead. She yanked it back in alarm. He was burning up! He'd kicked off the afghan he'd tugged over his legs earlier. She pulled back the edge of his bandage. A small gasp escaped her lips. Heat emanated from his skin and the wound was swollen and red. How much swelling and redness was from the injury itself, she couldn't tell, but the fever in the wound and on his skin told her infection had set in.

With gentle fingers, she cleaned the wound and changed the bandage as the nurse at the hospital had instructed her. Then, finding a hand towel in the kitchen, she soaked it in cool water, wrung it out and placed it on Jake's forehead. Grabbing her cell phone, she walked into the office and dialed the hospital's number. They arranged for a stronger antibiotic to be called into the pharmacy in town. She'd have to find someone to pick it up and bring it out to the station. But who? It was so far out here, but Jake needed it. ASAP. With a quick call to Cal, he said he'd find someone to pick it up at the pharmacy and deliver it.

Molly continued to wet the towel and place it on Jake's forehead. Concerned that he hadn't woken since her return, she placed her hand on his brow and asked the Lord to break Jake's fever and ease his pain. Her heart ached knowing he was in such bad shape. Lifting the towel, she gently brushed back the damp hair on his forehead. It was so soft. But the heat from his skin worried her.

Please, Father! Take away this fever!

Relief filled her when a light knock finally sounded on the back door.

"How is he, Molly?" Pam Bishop whispered as she tiptoed into the living room.

"Not good, I'm afraid." Helplessness clogged Molly's throat. She swallowed twice before she could speak. "He hasn't woken since I returned from town two hours ago. I've kept a cool, wet towel on his forehead but he doesn't wake up. I'm afraid of what the concussion and fever together may do."

"I don't know either, sweetie, but here's the antibiotic." Pam handed her the prescription bag. "Try and wake him again. You have to get this into his system."

Molly read the bottle label and dumped a pill into her palm. Pam retrieved a glass of water from the kitchen, handing it to her. Kneeling beside the couch, Molly shook Jake's shoulder, speaking firmly. "Jake. Jake, wake up. I have some medicine for you." He moaned, turning his head but not opening his eyes. Molly glanced up into Pam's concerned face.

Pam reached over and shook Jake's arm a little harder. "Jake, honey, wake up. Molly has some medicine for you. Come on and wake up, Jake."

Jake moaned again and turned his head, this time slowly opening his eyes. Pain-filled and feverish, they rested first on Molly's face then on Pam's. "My two favorite women," his words were groggy. "What did I do to deserve this?

"Absolutely nothing, you crazy man! You had us worried! Especially Molly," Pam scolded softly.

His gaze returned to Molly's face. "What happened?"

"You're running a high fever. I've been cooling your forehead since I returned nearly two hours ago. No telling how long you were like that before I got back. I cleaned your wound and changed the bandage, but you still wouldn't wake up." She heaved a heavy sigh. "You really had me concerned."

~

She was trying hard not to show the depth of her concern, but it was written all over her face. Jake's heart lurched in his chest. Did she care...? Well, of course she did! She'd be concerned for anyone in this situation.

"Sorry, Molly. I felt pretty rough when you left and I fell asleep, but didn't realize this was happening."

"I'm just glad you're awake. Here, take these." She handed him the pills and the glass of water. "I called the hospital, and they called a stronger antibiotic into the pharmacy. Pam brought them out for you."

Swallowing the pills, Jake turned glazed eyes on Pam. "Thanks, Pam. Sorry to inconvenience you, but I appreciate it."

"I know you do, sweetie. But I want your promise you'll listen to this girl and take it easy. That's what she's here for. To help you out and do the work for you. I know your kind! I'm married to one just like you. You'll get bored in a few days and want to get up, but don't do it. You take it easy. And Molly, you have my permission to sit on him if you have to."

Jake flashed a weak smile. "That could be fun!"

Molly's cheeks flamed as she rolled her eyes. From his earlier admission, she knew his words were meant to get that reaction. She cast a helpless look at Pam. "I'd say he's already on the road to recovery."

~

After Pam left, Molly warmed up Mrs. Jenkins' beef vegetable soup and found crackers in the cabinet. She made up a tray for Jake and a bowl for herself. The delicious aroma of the homemade soup caused her stomach to growl. She'd missed lunch and was starving. Hopefully Jake would have an appetite. If the fever lingered, he may not.

His eyes were closed as Molly positioned the tray on the coffee table. She laid a gentle hand on his forehead. Cooler. That was good news.

As she drew her hand away, his eyelids opened, this time revealing a brighter and more focused gaze. He grinned faintly.

"I have some food for you. Do you feel like sitting up a bit?"

Molly asked. "It might be easier to eat that way. If not, I...I can feed you," she suggested haltingly.

Another grin lifted the corners of Jake's lips higher. "As much as I'd enjoy your tender attention, I think I can sit up. For a bit anyway."

Molly's face relaxed in relief, eliciting a chuckle from Jake. Had her relief been written on her face? The light in his eyes said it had. She would've fed him if he needed her to, but the thought of such close proximity to this man was enough to send a shiver down her back. As he pulled himself into a sitting position, a grimace tightened his lips and furrowed his brow. She moved the pillows beneath his leg and resettled them then re-covered him with the afghan. *Aah! A safe topic. The afghan.*

"This is beautiful," she commented aloud, eager to shift the conversation. "I love the pine green, burgundy and cream stripes."

"Mom made it for me several years ago. It comes in handy. I can't count the times I've fallen asleep under it while watching TV."

Molly settled into the nearby armchair with her bowl of soup. "I've always admired anyone who can knit or crochet. My grandmother and mother can do both, but I never caught on."

"What do you like to do in your spare time?" Jake asked after swallowing a bite. "By the way, when did you have time to make this soup? It's delicious. Didn't think I'd be very hungry, but this is really good."

"As much as I love to cook, I can't take credit for this. Mrs. Jenkins sent it when I went home to get my things. She was sorry to hear you'd been injured."

"She's a sweet lady," Jake nodded. "And a good cook. But getting back to you, what do you like to do in your spare time?"

Molly had hoped the topic of the soup would distract him from his first question. She generally didn't like talking about herself, but this man really made her self-conscious. The kiss he'd given her on the Fourth of July proved he was attracted to her. And truth be known, the attraction was mutual. So why did a little getting-better-acquainted conversation make her uncomfortable? Was it because her career plans might be threatened?

~

Jake regarded Molly closely, eager to learn more about this

woman. She squirmed under his scrutiny.

"Oh, nothing special, I guess. Besides cooking, I love to read. I enjoy hiking, camping and traveling. I also enjoy sewing when I have a chance."

"Sewing? What do you sew?"

"Clothes mostly." A slight shrug lifted her shoulders. "My mother taught me to sew when I was very young. I used to make clothes for my dolls." Jake watched as a memory crossed her mind, a slight smile tugging at the corners of her lips.

"What do you like to read?" He placed his empty bowl on the tray.

Molly glanced at him. "Mysteries and historical novels mostly. What about you?" Her attempt to deflect the attention his way wasn't lost on him. "What are your interests?"

Besides you? Aloud he replied, "I enjoy reading too, and baseball of course. I love outdoor activities. You know. Hunting, fishing and camping."

Molly climbed to her feet and reached for his tray. "Well, in order for you to do those things again anytime soon, you need to get some rest."

Sliding back down on the couch cushions and resettling, Jake let his eyelids drift closed. Molly's movements in the kitchen while washing the dishes gave him a sense of peace and well-being. Was this what married life was like? How would it be for Molly to be there all the time? Pretty amazing, he was sure. She'd be a wonderful companion. If she'd just relax and not be so self-conscious around him. No doubt about it that she intentionally kept him at arm's length, but why? She was always friendly and kind, and goodness knows, she was doing everything she could to make him comfortable. But why was she always on edge in his presence? He fell asleep wondering what he'd done to make her react that way.

~

Hanging the dishtowel on the towel bar, Molly returned to the living room to find Jake had fallen asleep again. His even breathing indicated he was resting more peacefully, but she decided she'd better stick around a while. She'd planned to stay up at the bunkhouse, but for tonight perhaps she'd better stay here in case Jake's fever spiked again. He'd only had one dose of the antibiotic, and she'd need to wake him in a while for his next dose. For now he needed his sleep to fight off this infection.

Walking into the office at the front of the house, she clicked the button on the side of the desk lamp and glanced around the desktop. She reviewed reports and daily logs, trying to familiarize herself with things. Then a thought struck her. The horses. Glancing at her watch, she realized it was past feeding time. Not her usual job at Deep Creek, she'd have to remember that the Twentymile horses were depending on her. Looking out the window she realized the sun was merely a faint glow behind silhouetted mountains. It would be gone soon. Searching until she found a flashlight, she extinguished the lamp and left through the front door. She'd hurry in case Jake woke and wondered where she'd disappeared to.

As she entered the woods beyond the bunkhouse, darkness engulfed her. The tree canopy blocked what light remained in the sky. Cicadas buzzed in the trees and a querying call of a hoot owl sounded somewhere in the distance. The creek paralleling the road always sang a cheerful tune even in the darkness. Flipping on the flashlight, Molly made her way up the dirt-gravel road to the barn. In the flashlight's beam, she let the horses into their stalls and fed them.

"No grooming tonight, fellas. You didn't really appreciate it anyway." She referred to their earlier grooming. "Rolling in the dirt after I brushed you out so nicely. Really? Besides, I don't want to leave Jake alone too long. Look what happened last time."

When the horses were settled for the night, she strolled back down toward the station, flipping off the flashlight as she exited the woods. Glancing upward she was struck by the number of stars speckling the night sky. Out here so far from town they were amazingly bright. The Big Dipper twinkled and she was searching for Pegasus when an unexpected sound reached her ears. Stopping in her tracks, she tried to locate its position but only the creek could be heard tripping across rocks on its way beyond the station. Walking slowly again, she listened for the sound.

Approaching the station, she spotted an old model dark-colored pickup truck sitting in the station driveway just off the main road. Its headlights were off, but she could just make out the sound of the engine rumbling quietly. She stopped behind the corner of the station by the kitchen door. With no visible moon and only the stars lighting the sky, she realized they hadn't spotted her in the darkness. Low-pitched voices came from inside the truck; the unexpected sound from minutes before. Without warning the truck backed out of the driveway and slowly drove off, not turning on its headlights until well past the bridge crossing the creek.

What was that all about? Why would anyone sit at the end of the drive like that? It was doubtful they were just turning around. At this time of night so far from civilization? Uh uh. Entering the kitchen door, she locked up the station and settled into the big armchair near the couch with a book she'd brought from home. Foot propped on the heavy oak coffee table, she read until her eyes grew heavy and finally closed in sleep.

~

Pam had already climbed into bed and was propped up against the headboard watching Cal prepare to join her. "Cal," she said thoughtfully.

"Hmm?" came the low reply.

"Want to know what I think?"

"About what?"

"Molly and Jake."

"No, what?" His voice was distracted.

Pam threw her pillow at him. "Cal! Would you listen to me?"

"What?" He turned a surprised look on his wife.

"You're about a thousand miles from here. What's the matter?"

"I was just thinking about Molly and Jake," he replied thoughtfully.

"No kidding!" laughed Pam. "So was I."

Leaning across the bed, he kissed his wife's cheek. "What were you trying to tell me, honey?"

"Only that I think Molly and Jake like each other." A Cheshire-cat smile lit her face.

"Of course they do. They work together. They'd better like each other." Cal straightened up and walked into the bathroom.

"I don't mean that kind of like. If you'd seen the way Molly looked at Jake today when he was out with the fever and how worried she was, you'd understand that I mean a more serious kind of like."

After a thoughtful moment Cal leaned his head back out the

bathroom door, his toothbrush sticking out of his mouth. Yanking it out, he disappeared into the bathroom again. Pam heard him spit out the toothpaste before reappearing at the door. "You mean like they might be starting to care for each other?"

"Uh huh." Pam nodded, her smile growing bigger. "Isn't it great? I love a good romance. And they're in just the right situation for one. Besides, you work with them both. Haven't you noticed anything? Like the way they talk to each other or look at each other?"

Cal considered her questions. "No, not really. I was just thinking about how Molly's going to fill in for him."

"Figures." Pam shook her head. "Well, I'm going to do everything I can to see they get together. They'd make a great couple!"

"Now hold on, Honey," Cal sounded doubtful. "Do you really think you should be playing cupid? Maybe you should just let things work out on their own."

"Now what fun would that be?" asked Pam, rolling over and turning out the light.

~

Jake's eyes opened slowly. Where was he? Wow, his head hurt. Lifting a hand to his forehead, he found a damp towel. The fever. He remembered. Molly had been putting cool towels on his head. She'd woken him some time ago with another pain pill and the antibiotic. The lights were out except for the lamp beside the armchair. Molly leaned back in the corner sound asleep, an open book on her lap. She must've been reading while keeping watch over him. A glance at his watch said it was 3:15 am. She must've been sleeping there for hours, still wearing the uniform she'd worn all day. Tenderness swelled his heart as he watched her sleep. She was the most beautiful girl he'd ever seen. Gorgeous on the outside and a long list of amazing characteristics to boot. How could he have been so fortunate as to have her come into his life?

What do I do, Lord? I love her, and I don't want to scare her away. Please, open the door to this relationship and help me pursue it in Your way. And if it's not Your will, and You want to close that door, help me know and accept that.

Jake soon dropped back to sleep, a prayer in his heart.

~

Over the next several days as Jake recovered, Molly tried to pick up where he'd left off with his work. After feeding the horses in the mornings she checked the weather station up on the hill, recording any rainfall and reporting it to HQ. The boar traps had to be checked daily and rebaited if necessary. Three times a day she drove to Fontana Dam to write Appalachian Trail backpacker permits then did the same in Fontana Village. While there she picked up the station mail. Molly found she was on the road a lot more out here than back at Deep Creek.

At lunchtime she headed back to the ranger station and entered the front door into the office, dropping the mail onto the desk. Going through to the living room, she handed Jake a couple of envelopes.

"Here's your mail. Mrs. Willis at the post office said to tell you hello. She was sorry to hear you were down for a while. I think she has a soft spot for you. You should've heard her gushing on and on," Molly teased.

"Thanks." Jake accepted the mail and chuckled. "Mrs. Willis is the light of my life, you know. She's my fan club, although she's old enough to be my grandmother."

"Be that as it may, she's sweet on you." Molly laughed as she headed into the kitchen and returned with a glass of iced tea for him. "How are you feeling? Tired of being cramped up on that couch yet? Won't you allow me to help you up the stairs and into bed where you can stretch out more?"

Jake shook his head and accepted the cold beverage. "No thanks. I'm fine here for now."

Setting the glass on the coffee table, he slid his finger under the flap of the first envelope. The only reason he stayed on the couch was to see Molly. Upstairs, he'd only see her at mealtime and medication time. A little discomfort on the couch was well worth the reward of her presence. She'd moved to the bunkhouse the day after his fever broke, but she came in the mornings to fix and share breakfast for both of them before getting to work. Then she returned to do the same for lunch and supper.

"So, you didn't answer my question. How are you feeling?"

Jake grinned up at her. "Better every day. My head has finally stopped throbbing and the pain in my leg has lessened. It's got to be your talented nursing skills."

"Or the medications, more likely," Molly chuckled then returned to the kitchen.

"You underestimate yourself," continued Jake. "I wouldn't have gotten this far without your help, you know."

Molly returned with a reheated portion of chicken pot pie she'd made two nights prior. A side salad, a roll with butter and a homemade brownie completed the lunch tray she held. "I'm glad I could help, Jake. I just never realized how much driving you do. You must be on the road constantly, and I'm sure I'm not doing half what you normally do."

Setting the tray on the table, she turned back toward the kitchen, but Jake caught her hand before she could go.

"Molly, that isn't what I meant. At least, not completely. Yes, the job wouldn't get done if you weren't here, but it's more than that." The sapphire gaze that captured hers was sincere. "I absolutely couldn't have managed without your personal care. Thank you for everything you're doing. I really appreciate it."

Molly's heart soared. It was always nice to be appreciated for something you've done, but to have the sincerity in those gorgeous blues backing up the words? Umm. Yeah. Molly laid a gentle hand on top of his. "You're welcome, Jake. That's what friends are for. And I'll stay for as long as you need me."

Friends? Well, he'd have to work on her take on their relationship. For now he wanted to shout out loud that he'd need her forever. He settled for a smile instead.

~

One evening as Molly and Jake watched a baseball game on TV, Jennifer Mitchell called Molly. They hadn't had a chance to talk except for a few minutes on the Sunday before Jake's accident.

"Hi, Jenny!" Molly headed to the office so she wouldn't disturb Jake's game. "It's good to hear from you. How've you been?"

"Busy, I'm afraid," the other girl sighed heavily. "Even though regular school is out for the summer, I'm teaching summer school, and it's kept me just as busy. I called Aunt Selma, and she told me what happened to Jake and how you're helping out at Twentymile. How's he doing?"

"Better, I'm glad to say, but he's still taking it easy. He's started getting up more and doing some work in the office, but he's not going far from the station yet. Monday he gets his stitches out so hopefully he'll have a little more mobility. When they released him from the hospital, they said he'd need physical therapy afterward. It's too far to go in two or three times a week, so I'm sure he'll have to do it here. The wound's looking much better." She explained about the infection and the resulting fever.

"Is there anything I can do to help? I'd be happy to if you just tell me how."

"Well, I'm sure he'd enjoy a visit. He's bound to be getting tired of my constant company." Glancing out the office door, Molly found Jake's dark gaze on her. The heated look there made her heart race, her breath hitch in her throat. Had he heard what she said?

"That's a great idea!" Jenny agreed, oblivious to the tension on Molly's end of the line. "What about tomorrow evening?"

"Sure," Molly cleared her throat and walked to the other side of the office away from the door. "That'd be great. Why don't you come for supper?"

After agreeing on a time, they hung up. Molly pocketed her cell phone and returned to the living room. Jake's eyes met hers as she curled back into the armchair.

"That was Jennifer Mitchell. She's coming out tomorrow night for supper and a visit. I thought you'd like some company."

"It'll be great having her visit, Molly," began Jake, "but don't ever think that I could tire of your company, because I don't. I truly enjoy you being here."

"Thanks." She needed to change the subject. Quickly. "How about some ice cream while we finish the ballgame?"

~

Jake recognized the subject change for what it was, but he'd let it slide for now. She truly had no idea how much he loved her presence here. Heck, she had no idea how much he loved *her*. There'd come a day when he'd lay it all out, but instinctively he knew she wasn't ready. What he couldn't figure out was why. He'd just keep praying and trusting. Waiting for the Lord to open that door. "Ice cream sounds good. What flavor do we have?"

~

After work Molly quickly hurried up to the bunkhouse to exchange her uniform for capris and a t-shirt. Slipping her feet into flip flops, she returned to the station to prepare a pot of chicken and broccoli alfredo and make fresh iced tea. Slicing a French bread loaf, she spread on butter, garlic and parmesan cheese. She'd pop it in the oven as soon as Jenny arrived.

She glanced out the kitchen window at the crunch of tires on the gravel drive. Jenny parked her car next to Molly's and Jake's vehicles behind the station. Popping the bread pan into the oven, Molly pulled open the kitchen door and hurried out to give Jenny a hug as soon as she climbed out of her car.

"It's so good to see you!" she greeted her friend. "How's Mrs. Jenkins doing? I haven't talked to her since I left in such a rush the other day."

"Oh, she's fine," Jenny returned Molly's hug. Opening the backdoor of the car, she pulled out a plastic cake box. "When I mentioned I was coming out, she made this cake and sent it for you and Jake. I'm not sure, but I think it's German Chocolate. That's her absolute best!"

"Oh, my goodness!" exclaimed Molly. "That was sweet of her! You have a wonderful aunt, you know that?"

"Don't I know it!" Jenny said in hearty agreement.

"Well, come on in. Supper's almost ready."

As they entered the kitchen, Molly placed the cake box on the kitchen counter while Jenny continued into the living room to speak to Jake.

"Hi, Jake! How are you feeling?"

"Not bad. Pretty much on the mend, I think. I have exceptional nursing staff to care for me." Jake's gaze cut to Molly as she entered behind Jenny.

"I'm sure you do," Jenny laughed, turning to Molly. Warmth infused Molly's cheeks. She tucked a strand of hair behind her ear and changed the subject.

"Have a seat, Jenny. We just have to wait for the garlic bread to toast then we can eat." She headed back to the kitchen. To hide? Well, yeah, she supposed she was. It was getting harder and harder to stay neutral with Jake's gaze and comments raising her blood pressure constantly. She listened to the congenial conversation in the living room while she pulled the bread from the oven and prepared Jake's tray. Jenny set up two TV trays for them while Molly brought in Jake's food, then they filled their plates and joined him.

After Jake said the blessing, they enjoyed a companionable time of eating, talking and laughing. As Molly took the dishes to the kitchen sink, she thanked Jenny for her offer to help, but refused. "Thanks, Jenny, but they can wait. I'd rather enjoy our visit for now. In a while after our food settles, I'll cut the cake and we'll enjoy that too."

She'd just put the plates in the sink to soak when a loud roaring sounded from the driveway. Glancing out the kitchen window, she spotted a pickup truck drive up toward the bunkhouse, slinging dust and gravel in its wake. The driver gunned the engine as he drove around the bend. Molly's feet were rooted to the floor. Without seeing her, she knew Jenny had joined her at the window. Unsure of what was happening, they watched in disbelief as the pickup barreled back around the bend, engine roaring and tires spitting gravel. As it neared the station, Molly spotted something long and dark protrude from the driver's window. In horror she realized what it was. Grabbing Jenny, she yanked her to the floor.

An ear-splitting bang preceded the shattering of window glass as the truck sped away in a trail of dust. Molly and Jennifer lay face down on the floor in a sea of glass shards.

~

Through the archway into the kitchen, Jake watched in horror as the events unfolded before his eyes. What seemed like minutes to occur must have only been seconds. Forgetting about his leg, he pushed himself off the couch and hobbled into the kitchen, avoiding the glass scattered everywhere.

"Molly!" he called in a raspy voice. "Molly! Are you okay? Talk to me or I'm going to hobble right across this glass and find out for myself."

She lifted her head at the same time Jenny began to move.

"Well?" he urged as she slowly got to her feet. Glass rained from her…everywhere. Her hair, her clothes, her skin. Tiny cuts peppered her face and bare arms below her short sleeves.

"Molly!" Jake heaved a heavy sigh of relief. "Are you alright?"

He watched as she took inventory. "I wasn't shot, but I'm covered in glass. I can feel it in my hair and on my skin. I'm afraid to move."

Jenny stood, arms held out to her sides. "Yeah, me too." Her voice shook.

Molly cast a reassuring glance at her friend. "Jenny, as long as you're not hurt, it'll be alright."

Jennifer Mitchell shook her head, dislodging shards of glass. Tears marked a path down her cheeks. She stared first at Molly then at Jake, propped against the doorjamb for support. "No, it won't," she replied, barely above a whisper. "That was my brother's pickup truck!"

Chapter Twelve

Retrieving his crutches, Jake painstakingly made his way upstairs to find clothing for the young women to change into. He left them standing in the kitchen, afraid to move for fear of tracking glass around. When he returned, he noticed blood on Molly's face but couldn't determine where it was coming from.

"Molly," he said in a quiet voice so as not to frighten her. "You and Jenny remove those clothes and leave them in a pile. Here are some clothes for you to change into. I'll go to the office until you're ready. Here's a brush to try and get the glass out of your hair. Don't clean up anything yet. I'll call Cal and tell him what's happened. We'll investigate this. And, Molly, be careful. There are cuts on your face. We'll take a look after you've changed."

~

"Oh!" Molly's hand automatically lifted to her face but halted it half way up. Better leave it alone until Jake could inspect the damage. First things first. Getting out of the glass-covered clothes.

While he was gone, the girls changed, carefully helping each other remove their clothing and then brushing out each other's hair, meticulously searching for bits of glass as they worked. Molly pulled dish towels from a drawer and they washed their necks, arms, legs and feet.

"Let me check you for injuries, too, Jenny," Molly said, sweeping her friend's hair back to scrutinize her face and then her arms.

"Anything?" Jenny asked.

"I don't see any cuts. You must have moved away quicker than I did."

"No," Jenny shook her head. "You pushed me down and took the brunt of the glass. Thanks, Molly. I'll owe you a hug when we aren't covered in shards."

"Jenny," Molly began, "are you sure that was your brother's pickup truck?"

"Yeah. I wish I was wrong, but I know it was his. I can't be sure he was driving because sometimes he loans it to his buddies. Molly, why would he even be involved in a thing like this?"

Molly considered her tormented question. "Would he have known you were here?"

"I doubt it. We haven't talked in a while. He couldn't have known. I didn't tell anyone except Aunt Selma, and I know they haven't talked in a long time."

"Do you think he's capable of this? Or do you think he really did loan his truck and someone else committed this crime?"

Sadness filled Jenny's red-rimmed eyes. "I don't know, but I do know he's hanging around with people he has no business associating with."

Molly laid the brush on the kitchen counter and, taking wide steps, worked her way out of the glass and over to the other side of the kitchen. She left her flip-flops to be cleaned later. "What kind of 'buddies' does he have? Do you know who they are?"

"I don't know them well. Don't even know their names. But I know I don't care for them. Kind of slimy, you know? I've seen them out at Jamie's place before. I think he went to school with some of them."

Molly reached a hand toward Jenny, helping her across the glass. Jenny was still in shock at what had happened. And the thought that her brother may be involved had really rattled her.

"Are you girls decent?" Jake called from the office.

Molly checked to ensure they were. "Yes, you can come in now."

~

Jenny claimed an old T-shirt and a pair of sweats that Jake rarely wore. Molly grabbed the button down long-sleeved shirt and a pair of sweat shorts. Even with the sleeves rolled up, the shirt nearly swallowed her whole. Personally, Jake thought it looked better on her than it did on him, but he bit back the compliment that almost slipped out. *Now is not the time.*

"Have a seat, Molly." Jake pulled out a chair at the dining table and propped his leg on another chair. Opening a small first aid kit he'd brought from the office, he studied her closely. "Let's survey the damage."

Several cuts marred the right side of her forehead and temple, a few shards of glass embedded in them. "Does it hurt much?" Asking softly, he searched the eyes trying desperately to avoid his gaze.

He was all too aware of what the closeness of her proximity was doing to his own breathing and heartrate. Did she feel it too? Was that why she wouldn't meet his eyes?

"It stings a little," was her evasive reply.

"Well, there's some glass in there, but I should be able to get it out, if you want me to try. Or we can take you to the ER, which might be a better idea."

"No," came her emphatic reply. "I don't need the ER. I'll be fine if you take them out. Besides, you're in no condition to be going anywhere, and I'm not leaving you here alone. I'm sorry you had to get up like that."

"Like really fast, you mean? I'm not. I'd do it again in a heartbeat. And twice on Sunday," Jake chuckled to lighten the mood. Both women were shaken up, and with good reason. They'd been shot at, for goodness sake! They were holding it together rather well, considering.

Tamping down the anger that someone had purposely intended to cause harm, he reached for a cotton ball and the peroxide then laid tweezers on the table. "I'll clean up the cuts a bit so I can see the glass better. Jenny, would you give me a hand?"

From the office he'd heard the girl's conversation and hoped to distract Jenny, even for a few minutes. Unfortunately, her brother would be investigated, and Jake hoped for Jenny's sake that he wasn't involved.

"Sure," she replied at his elbow.

"There's a small flashlight in the top drawer of the office desk," he directed. "If you'll get it and hold the light for me, I could see better. The overhead light isn't the best."

"No problem."

With the small but strong beam trained on Molly's right temple, Jake removed several small shards of glass with the tweezers. Molly grimaced and gritted her teeth, never making a sound.

"I'm sorry I'm hurting you even more, but it's the only way to get them out."

"I know, Jake," she replied, eyes closed.

After removing all the shards, a couple larger than he'd expected, Jake cleaned the wounds and applied a dressing, attaching it with surgical tape.

"There you go." He gathered the implements and returned them to the kit. "We make quite a pair, Molly Walker," he chuckled. "They'll call us the 'Bandage Brigade'."

Touching a tentative hand to her temple, Molly fingered the gauze bandage and tape. "Well, I think we qualify. Thanks, Jake. And you, too, Jenny." She stood up. "Jake, where do you keep your Tylenol?"

"Tell me, and I'll get it," volunteered Jenny, getting to her feet.

~

A knock sounded on the back door but before Molly could move to open it Cal walked in.

"Well, I see there's been some action here." He scrutinized the kitchen chaos, stepped around the glass, and entered the dining area.

David Andrews followed him into the room. Now that was a surprise. Molly hadn't seen the park interpreter in quite a while, except from afar. She'd occasionally passed by as he presented his evening programs or guided nature walks up Deep Creek.

"Hello, Cal. Hello, David." She offered with a weary smile. "How are you?"

"I'm fine, but I see things aren't going well here." David nodded toward the floor and the empty window frame. "Is everyone okay?"

"Except for a little flying glass, we're good," Jake replied.

"Sorry to hear about your accident, Jake. How's the leg?" David put his hands in his pockets and leaned against the kitchen door frame.

"It's on the mend." Jake's gaze swung to Cal who'd stood quietly accessing the chaos. "Molly was hit by flying glass, Cal, but she'll be okay. However, I think it'd be wise for her to see Doc

Bennett tomorrow. She may need a couple stitches."

"Good idea," Cal agreed. "Want to tell me what happened?"

Jenny returned to the kitchen with the Tylenol bottle and slipped into the chair beside Molly as Jake related the situation. Molly noticed Jenny watching David, a puzzled expression in her eyes. When Jake had finished his account, Molly related what she'd seen, but neither mentioned anything about Jenny's brother.

Molly glanced at Jake, a question in her eyes, but with the nearly imperceptible shake of his head, Molly knew that with David there, Jake didn't feel free to tell all. Cal went outside to survey the exterior of the window. Molly followed him, leaving David inside with Jake and Jenny.

"Cal, why is David here?" she asked quietly. "As an interpreter, he wouldn't' have anything to do with an investigation, would he?"

Cal shook his head. "No, but he asked to come along for the ride. He'd just finished his evening program and wanted to tag along. I didn't see any reason why he shouldn't."

Molly nodded, not completely satisfied with the response, but remained quiet as Cal looked around. He added to the notes that he'd taken when she and Jake had related the evening's events. When they returned inside, Jake asked Cal to step into the office while Molly allowed David to engage her and Jenny in conversation. He hadn't asked but suspected Jake wanted to talk with Cal alone, without David present. As David's conversation turned out to be one-sided as usual, Jenny remained quiet and Molly wasn't given much of a chance to say anything. Not that she cared to.

~

"Cal, I didn't want to say anything in front of David, but there's something you need to know," Jake closed the office door, sat in the desk chair and propped his injured leg on the desk.

Cal sat on the desk corner. "Oh? Like what?"

"Like the fact that Jenny recognized the pickup truck used in this crime. Neither of the girls saw the driver, but the pickup belongs to her brother."

A low whistle escaped Cal's lips. "What else did she say?"

"Sometimes he loans the truck out to his buddies. Apparently he hangs out with a bunch of rough guys. She was understandably upset to see that truck involved in the shooting." He paused, releasing a heavy sigh.

"Cal, she and Molly could've been killed. Molly came away with a few deep cuts, but it might not have ended so well." Huskiness slipped into his voice. "When I think…," he stopped, shifting his gaze out the window. He didn't want to think about what might have happened. *Thank you, Lord, that they're safe. I don't know what I would do if anything had happened to Molly.*

God would always provide the strength to endure whatever came his way, but gratitude filled him that Molly had been spared.

She's Your child, Father. She's in Your hands. I want to be there for her, but I can't protect her like You can. Please look after her.

"So, it's like that is it?" A grin lifted the corners of Cal's mouth. "I suspected as much. And so did Pam."

"What? Pam? How?"

"We were talking the other evening about it. Shoot, she noticed the way you were looking at Molly the other night when she brought your medicine out."

"It's that obvious, huh?" Jake asked sheepishly.

"To pretty much everyone except Molly," replied Cal. "But you can do something about that."

Jake nodded. "In time. When she's ready. But getting back to why you're here, what are you going to do about this shooting? Neither of the girls can identify anyone."

"First, I'll question Jenny, but I don't want to talk with her in front of David. I'll make contact tomorrow and see if she can add anything. Then I'm going to pay her brother, Jamie, a visit, and see what he'll tell me, if anything." Cal stood and sauntered toward the door.

"Not much more I can do here. I'll go out and help clean up the mess, then I'll nab David and head back to Deep Creek. Oh, by the way," Cal paused, hand on the doorknob. "I have the worker's compensation papers for you to fill out for your injury. I'll email the same forms for Molly to fill out. Those bandages covered a good portion of her forehead and temple. How bad were the cuts?"

Reaching for his crutches, Jake climbed to his one good leg. Boy was it aching! With all the frenzy he hadn't paid a lot of attention. But it was fussing at him now. "Most were superficial but a couple were pretty deep. I'll see she gets to Doc Bennett's in the morning to have them checked out."

Cal helped Molly and Jenny vacuum up the shattered glass from the floor, sink and cabinets. Searching the maintenance building behind the station, he found a large sheet of plywood and nailed it over the open window frame. David watched while they worked, not offering to help. After ensuring everything was secure, Cal and David took their leave.

Since the following day was Saturday, Molly suggested Jenny spend the night up at the bunkhouse with her instead of driving the winding roads in the dark at that late hour.

"Okay," agreed Jenny, "But only because I want to make certain you get to the doctor's office in the morning."

Just before the girls headed up to the bunkhouse, Molly helped Jake settle in for the night. "You sure you two don't want to stay down here?" he asked. "You're welcome to bunk upstairs. There's plenty of room for both of you."

Molly shook her head. "No, thanks, Jake. We'll be fine. I doubt those guys will be back tonight." She turned off all the lights except for the lamp beside the couch. "I'll lock up. See you in the morning!"

"Goodnight!"

~

The bunkhouse was a small three-room building with a living area, a kitchenette off to the side, a bunkroom with six wooden bunks built onto the walls and a small bathroom with an old tin shower. An ancient wood stove stood against the back wall of the living room, it's warmth no doubt welcome on cool mountain mornings and nights. Park personnel used the bunkhouse when they were in the area and the maintenance crew used it as a place to eat their lunch when working at Twentymile. Molly was glad to be the sole occupant; however, that was subject to change at any time.

"Here are some pj's you can borrow." Molly tugged the garments from her duffle bag. "We're about the same size."

"Thanks." Weariness edged Jenny's words. "Thanks for putting me up for the night. I would've driven home, but it's nice not to have to, especially after tonight's commotion."

"I would've been worried for your safety, my friend." Molly

handed her an extra towel and washcloth. "Why don't you grab a shower first and wash the rest of the glass from your hair and skin. I'll do the same when you're done.

"Gladly." Jenny accepted the proffered items. "I've been itching ever since it happened."

When Molly had finished her shower and dressed, she grabbed her toothbrush.

"Jenny, is there anything else you'd be willing to share about your brother's situation? I mean, I don't want to be nosey, but I want to help if I can."

Leaning against the doorframe, Jenny watched as Molly brushed her teeth. "I don't know what to think sometimes. When he was younger, he always attended church with us, but lately he's become rebellious and aloof. He rarely shows up at home anymore. That's one reason I don't think he knew I would be here tonight."

"Any idea what kind of activities his friends are involved in?"

Jenny tucked a strand of damp hair behind her ear. "No, I just suspect they're not on the up and up. They always appear to be furtive and calculating. They'll be talking together until one of us approaches them then they clam up. Like they don't want to be overheard."

Jenny tilted her head. "Molly, who's the guy that came with Cal tonight?"

"David?" Molly smiled ruefully. "He's quite a talker, huh? That's David Andrews, and he's a park interpreter. He conducts nature walks and evening programs in a couple of the developed campgrounds." At Jenny's puzzled expression, it was her turn to pause. "Why do you ask?"

Brows furrowed, Jenny shook her head. "I don't know. He looks familiar."

"To me he looks like he should be on TV or in the movies," laughed Molly, putting her toothbrush away. "He's too handsome to be real, and he's his own favorite subject."

"Maybe that's it," Jenny agreed. "Maybe he reminds me of someone I've seen on TV. Anyway, he sure has a lot to say."

Molly turned out the bathroom light and followed Jenny into the bunkroom.

"Take your pick." Molly waved a hand toward the six rough-built bunks then pointed at the only one with a sleeping bag and a pillow. "Except that one."

Jenny picked up a rolled-up sleeping bag that sat on the floor. "I'm glad there was an extra pillow and sleeping bag at the station. Those bunks don't look comfortable enough to just sleep on bare."

"Would've been a rough night for sure," Molly laughed.

When they were both settled into their bunks, Molly, who was nearest the light switch, reached over and flipped it off.

"Good night, Jenny. Try not to worry about your brother. Let's pray for him and about what happened tonight. I think we both have a lot to be grateful for. We could've been seriously injured." She hesitated to mention that they both could be dead.

"You're right. I need to place Jamie in God's hands. And leave him there."

"Absolutely. I'm happy you're God's child, Jenny. It's nice to find a friend that trusts in Him too. It's a great foundation to build a friendship on."

"Thanks, buddy!" chuckled Jenny for the first time since the shooting. "That means a lot."

As they snuggled into their sleeping bags, sleep evaded Molly as she petitioned her heavenly Father for wisdom and grace to find answers to the questions marching through her head. After much tossing and turning, fatigue finally dulled her mind allowing sleep to claim her.

~

"Do you think that was really a good idea?" the man asked into the phone receiver.

"Yeah, well, I wouldn't let it worry ya none," came the careless reply. "Me and the boys have it all planned out. I, for one, owe her. I don't like what she did to me, and I intend to see she pays for it."

"It was your own fault, Willy. You know better than to do what you did. Your carelessness will jeopardize everything we've worked for, just to carry out your own little grudge."

"Look here." Willy's voice dripped with anger. "We've been in this a long time. We've got reasons for what we do, and we'll make sure they pay. I'll do everything I can to make 'em miserable. All of 'em. If I have to deal with 'em one at a time, I will. You just stick to your end of the deal, my friend. I don't think you want to cross us, if you know what I mean." The receiver clicked in his ear as the line went dead.

~

Molly waited in Doc Bennett's examination room. Déjà vu for sure.

"Well, you're back." Doc Bennett opened the door and closed it quietly behind him. "In the line of duty again, I hope."

A faint smile lifted the corners of Molly's lips. "Well, not exactly. A case of being in the wrong place at the wrong time. I was too close when a window was shattered."

"Hmmm," Doc murmured as he removed the bandage from her temple. "What have we got here? From the looks of this I'd say you were pretty close to the window."

"You could say that." Molly didn't want to reveal details that may in some way get out to the public. At least for as long as possible. It was a small town, after all, and word would spread eventually. It wouldn't take long. Since her move to the area, she'd found that news spread fast and far.

Doc Bennett examined the cuts under a light and a magnifying glass. As he probed her cheek for any elusive glass shards, Molly noticed he didn't push for further information and was glad. He dealt with enough rangers that she was sure he understood what they had to deal with, and too often it involved someone stirring up trouble. If he had questions, she was glad he kept them to himself.

"You say Jake Stuart removed the glass last night?"

"That's right." Molly had told Rose that much when she brought her into the examination room.

"Well I commend him on the job he did. I don't see any more glass, but I'd like to put a couple stitches in. The cuts are gaping instead of closing up like they should. Still bleeding a bit too. Should've stopped already." Laying the magnifying glass on the counter, he turned toward the door. "Just lay back on the table and try to get comfortable. I'll be with you shortly."

Twenty minutes later Molly walked back out to the car with Jenny who'd sat in the waiting room. Doc Bennett had deadened half of her face before stitching up the cuts. Wow, was it numb.

"Just when I got one set of stitches out, I get more." She grumbled and opened the car door.

"You won't have them long. Just over a week."

Molly looked at her with miserable eyes. "Thanks."

"What are friends for, 'buddy'." Then Jenny's teasing tone grew serious. "I'm sorry this happened, Molly. I really am."

"You know what someone failed to tell me about this job, Jenny?" A half-droopy smile tweaked Molly's face. "Just how dangerous it would be."

Jenny laughed as they climbed into the car and she started the engine.

"Anywhere else you want to go before I drive you back to Twentymile?"

"I don't want to leave Jake alone longer than necessary, but I'd like to stop by the apartment and pick up some things. With all that's happened I haven't had a chance to do laundry this week."

"No problem." Jenny swung the car out of the parking lot.

After stopping by the apartment, the girls headed back to Twentymile. Mrs. Jenkins was gone and Molly was relieved not to have to explain the bandages on her face or the story behind how they got there. Mrs. Jenkins would be appalled that Jamie's truck fit into the story.

They picked up the mail in Fontana Village then drove toward the ranger station.

As they left the village, Jenny, out of the blue, asked, "Molly, do you care for Jake? I mean really care?"

Surprised, Molly glanced at her friend. "Why do you ask?"

"I don't know," Jenny shrugged as she carefully navigated the winding road. "I just thought you might, the way you've been taking care of him and all. And then there's the way he watched you all evening. He could hardly keep his eyes off you."

Molly's cheeks burned, or at least one of them did. She couldn't tell with the injured one. Gazing out the window to hide them, she forced a light laugh. "You're mistaken, Jenny. Jake and I are just co-workers and friends. Since his injury he's needed help and someone to fill in for him. I was the logical choice. He's a *great* guy, but he's just a friend."

Jenny's raised eyebrow and half-grin were doubtful. "Are you sure that's the way he sees your relationship?"

Molly glanced at her then returned her gaze out the window, seeing none of the scenery passing by. "I don't know," she whispered.

Jenny said no more, but Molly couldn't prevent the gears of hope from whirling in her mind.

~

Jenny dropped Molly at the back door then headed home. An unfamiliar car sat beside the others parked behind the station. Had something happened to Jake while she was gone? Concern washed over Molly as she cautiously entered the kitchen door. Unsure who she'd find, she certainly wasn't prepared for the person sitting in the armchair beside the couch.

Celeste Payne spotted Molly standing in the doorway. With a feline stretch toward Jake and a seductive smile on her perfectly made-up face, she released a wicked little laugh.

"Oh, Jake, you naughty boy!" she crooned, leaning closer. "You really are a prize!"

For a moment Molly was afraid the buttons on Celeste's too-tight, too-low blouse would give way. Her too-short dark skirt had ridden up as she leaned forward. There wasn't much left to the imagination.

Jake's gaze followed Celeste's, taking in the forced smile frozen on Molly's face. He began pulling himself up from the couch. "Molly!"

Molly waived him back down. "It's alright, Jake. I see you have company. I'll be at the bunkhouse if you need me." She nodded toward Celeste, her gaze barely skimming the other woman's. "Celeste."

Pivoting on her heels Molly hurried out, yanking the back door closed behind her. Swallowing several times to prevent the tears that threatened, she practically ran up the road to the bunkhouse. Had Jake invited that woman to come? And what about all of his words of protest? Did he really care for Celeste after all?

~

Jake's eyes closed in frustration. Then they snapped open, glaring at a visually unrepentant Celeste. In fact she looked rather pleased with herself.

"What was that all about, Celeste?" Anger laced his words.

"What do you mean?" Her perfectly shaped eyebrows lifted innocently.

"When Molly walked in you acted like we were up to something. Why did you do that? You know I'd just asked you to leave."

Jake groaned inside. Well, he'd have to explain it to Molly and hope she'd understand. Did Celeste realize she'd just stepped over the line?

"I only wanted her to understand that you and I are special friends, Jake," Celeste crooned in a placating voice that turned Jake's stomach.

"You and I are *not* special friends," his voice commanded. "Certainly *not* in the way you keep trying to make it appear. We're working acquaintances who run into each other occasionally. Nothing more." He swung his legs to the side of the couch, sitting up and leaning toward her. His thunderous expression sent her retreating back into her chair. "You need to leave. *Now.*"

"But Jake. I just got here. I heard you were injured and wanted to see how you're doing. I've been beside myself with *worry.*" She sniffed and blinked back invisible tears. "I haven't been able to come until today. You know how far Gatlinburg is."

Jake stood, grabbing his crutches. Leaning over her, he grasped her arm, tugging her from the chair and urging her toward the door. "Then I'm sorry you had a wasted trip. We've talked about this before. I'm not interested in a relationship with you. End of subject."

Celeste tried tears but Jake was unmoved. "Well, I don't know what you see in that little mouse." She nodded in the direction of the bunkhouse, practically spitting the words. "She's pathetic!"

"You're the one that's pathetic, Celeste." Jake sighed wearily. "You can't force someone to care for you."

"No?" She let out an angry hiss. "We'll see."

Slamming the back door behind her, she climbed into her car. Without a backward glance she sped out of the station parking lot.

~

Molly had missed lunch while in town at the doctor's office so she grabbed salad makings and tossed them together. She attempted to ignore the rioting emotions racing through her ever since she'd witnessed the scene in Jake's living room. Returning the bottle of dressing to the refrigerator, she slammed the door. The bang reminded her of what she was doing: acting like a jealous, lovesick schoolgirl! It was none of her business who visited Jake or whom he saw socially. Besides, hadn't she already made up her mind to pursue her career, minus a serious relationship? Why should she care? Of course she didn't care she attempted in vain to convince herself.

She shook her head, physically trying to remove the scene from her mind. She'd think of something else while she tried to eat her salad. As she lifted her fork for the first bite, a knock resounded at the bunkhouse door. Answering it she found Jake balancing on the wooden steps, his crutches propping him up.

"Jake, what are you doing up here?" She scolded him gently, instant concern eclipsing her foul mood. "You shouldn't leave the station. What would've happened had you fallen on the way up here?"

"I guess I'd wait until you happened by to help me up." A crooked grin lifted one side of his mouth. "May I come in? These steps are not the sturdiest and crutches make them even less so."

"I'm sorry," Molly apologized, stepping back to allow him in. "Here I am fussing at you for coming up here then I make you stand on the steps. Here, have a seat." She indicated the couch where he could prop up his leg. "Where's Celeste?" Was her casual tone convincing? "She didn't leave already, did she?"

Jake continued to stand. "Molly, the reason I came up here is that I wanted you to understand something. I didn't invite Celeste here today. Or any other day, for that matter. She means absolutely nothing to me. She staged that little scene when you walked into the living room."

Molly moved back into the kitchenette. "You don't owe me an explanation, Jake. As I've told you before, it's none of my concern who you see."

Jake followed her into the close space of the tiny kitchenette. Uh, oh. Tactical error. Nowhere to go. With a tender grasp on her arm, he turned her around to face him. She refused to look up, afraid of what he'd see in her eyes. Hurt, confusion, love. Love? Oh, yes. She'd fought against it, but now the realization hit her, leaving her reeling with the knowledge. Witnessing the scene in the station had been like a knife slicing through her heart. For so long she'd tried to keep their relationship impersonal and professional. But would she be able to keep it up? In spite of all her protestations concerning her career, she'd fallen in love with Jake.

"Molly." Jake's voice was soft and husky. "Look at me, Molly."

Slowly lifting her gaze, Molly schooled herself to hide her

feelings. But the intensity of his smoldering gaze grabbed the breath from her. His lips opened to speak, but was interrupted by the loud and continuous blaring of a car horn.

Jake glowered out the window, never releasing his hold on her upper arms. An exasperated sigh huffed out.

"Wouldn't you know it," he murmured under his breath then turned back to Molly. "My mom is here. Come on, we'll finish this later. And we will, guaranteed."

"Your mom came to see you, Jake, not me." Molly stepped back.

"You wouldn't want me to fall on my way back down the drive, would you?" He lifted a devilish eyebrow. "You should come along to make sure I get back to the station okay. This is my first venture out, you know."

At Molly's soft chuckle, a flame ignited in Jake's eyes. *Oh, my.* "I think I'm being manipulated here, but I wouldn't want you on my conscience if something really happened."

Chapter Thirteen

That evening during supper, Edith turned to Jake. "Just how safe are you two out here right now?"

Jake sent a reassuring smile his mother's way. "Don't worry, Mom. We'll be fine. I think they're just trying to scare us."

"But who are 'they'?"

"We don't know for sure yet, but we think they're a group of local poachers trying to stir up trouble. There's been increased poaching activity lately, but it really isn't anything new." Jake attempted to change the subject. "You said Shelly was sick with a virus. Is she better now?"

Edith's expression told him he hadn't fooled her but thankfully she didn't pursue the subject. "Yes, she's better. I kept the baby for several days then Tom took over for the weekend. I'll be here as long as you need me. I'll cook for you and see that you're taken care of. That'll leave Molly to do your job."

"What about Dad? Other than having plenty to eat for a while, how's he going to make it without you there? He's so used to you being around all the time."

"Don't worry about your father," Edith waved away his concern. "He's quite capable of taking care of himself. It never hurts to be apart once in a while. Makes the heart grow fonder, as they say."

Edith passed the platter of golden-flaked meat. "Have some more chicken, Molly?"

Molly held up a hand in refusal. "No, thank you. I'm quite full. You're an amazing cook, Mrs. Stuart."

"Edith, dear," she corrected. "Remember?"

"Yes, I remember," Molly laughed.

"You'd better." Jake advised with a nod. "She's quite stubborn and won't let up on you."

"Why, Jake Stuart!" Edith stood to clear the table, but stopped with her hands on her hips, fixing a reproachful glare on him that never quite made it to her eyes. "I haven't the foggiest what you're talking about."

"Uh-huh. Right, Mom," Jake teased back.

~

Molly enjoyed the banter between mother and son, reminded of the good times her own family had when they were all together. She regretted she wasn't closer in proximity to them but knew she was exactly where God wanted her. He'd made this job possible, and she was thrilled to be here. He never promised everything would be ideal. If it were, she probably wouldn't depend on Him as much as she should, but some things were ideal. And this job was one of them.

"Molly?" Concern flitted across Jake's face. "You okay?"

She nodded. "I'm fine. Why?"

"I just asked you a question, and you looked like you were a thousand miles away. Sure you're alright?"

Realizing that Edith was watching her closely as well, she replied, "I'm sorry. I wasn't a thousand miles away but maybe four hundred. I was just thinking. My family loves to tease too. But I'm sorry I missed your question. What was it?"

"Would you take Mom up to the barn when you go to feed the horses? She'd like to see them."

"I'd be happy to. Just let me wash these dishes then we'll walk up."

~

Monday morning after showering and dressing, Molly grabbed a bagel and a banana, then taking her coffee in a travel mug she strolled down to open up the station office. Pretty sure Edith would be up she hoped Jake was sleeping in. As she rounded the corner of the building, her head was down while she rummaged through her keys. She didn't look up until she stood beside the covered stoop. Out of the corner of her right eye a movement caught her attention. Glancing up, she gasped, her eyes glued to the horrible object.

She stumbled back, one hand covering her mouth as she dropped her coffee mug to the ground. A rope noose hung from a branch of the tree that stood in front of the office. Hanging from the noose was a doe, her throat cut below the noose. A small patch of bloody grass beneath the deer reflected the morning light. It was obvious the deer had been killed elsewhere then brought to Twentymile to be hung in the tree. Had it been killed here more blood would have drained from the wound and pooled below the carcass.

Bitter bile rose in Molly's throat but she swallowed hard forcing it back down. Turning slowly, she scanned the area to see if anything else was amiss. Nothing stood out. No sign that anyone had been there. With a sprint she hurried back around the station, pounding on the kitchen door, now hoping Jake was awake.

Edith, fully dressed, answered the door. "Good morning, Molly." Her cheerful smile froze as she noticed Molly's horrified expression. Reaching out a hand, she drew her into the kitchen. "Molly, dear, what's wrong?"

"Is Jake up?" Molly gulped, her voice shaking.

"I'm right here." Jake stood in the living room doorway. Reading her expression, he hurried over as quickly as the crutches allowed. "What's the matter? What's happened?"

Molly hesitated, glancing at Edith then back to Jake. "Can I see you in the office, Jake?" her words quiet but urgent.

"Of course."

Jake followed her into the office and shut the door. He gently grasped Molly's shoulders. "What's happened? Your face is white and you're shaking."

Quickly explaining what she'd found, Molly opened the front office door for him to see. His expression hardened even as his face reddened beneath his tan. His eyes closed as he released a heavy sigh. "Call Cal and tell him about this. I'm pretty sure he'll want to see it for himself."

Molly shook her head in bewilderment. "Why? It's awful! Wouldn't he just take your word for it?"

Jake spoke deliberately. "Of course, he would, but Cal's had a lot of experience in investigating these kinds of incidents, and he may see something we might miss."

A grimace crossed Molly's features. "Why would anyone do

something so terrible?"

~

Jake recalled the bear head he'd found on the front stoop a couple months earlier. The situation was escalating. There wasn't an easy way to answer Molly's question.

"Perhaps as a warning? Most likely the poachers are trying to tell us to back off. This wasn't done by just anyone out for a mean prank. They're trying to intimidate us into looking the other way and forgetting that they poach on government property." He paused a moment before reluctantly adding, "And I'm betting it's connected to the shooting the other night."

~

Cal made short work of his investigation. After examining the deer, he snapped pictures and searched the front yard and parking lot for further evidence. Molly couldn't imagine what he expected to find, and in the end he found nothing. Cutting down the carcass, he dropped it onto a tarp which he dragged into the woods and buried. Molly fetched a few buckets of water for him to throw on the bloody patch of grass.

When he joined Molly and Jake in the office, he asked Jake, "Did your mother ask about what's happened?"

"I just explained that I didn't want her going out front until I told her it was alright to do so. Someone played a nasty prank on us and left a mess for us to clean up. She wanted to come and help clean, but I made her promise she wouldn't."

"Good idea." Cal sat on the corner of the desk. "I'm sorry you had to be the one to find it, Molly."

"You and me both," A shudder rippled through Molly, "But I did, and we can't change that. So what do we do now?"

"I was heading to Jamie Mitchell's when I got your call. Since Jenny recognized his pickup truck as the one involved in the shooting, there's a chance he may be mixed up in this." He nodded toward the front porch. "I tend to agree with Jake that this is a warning. These fellas don't like us generally but they really don't like us snooping into their covert activities."

Jake nodded. "Any more news on the stakeout?

"Yeah." Cal crossed his arms then crossed one ankle over the other. "I finally got Ed Clark's attention. Hopefully in the next couple weeks we can get one underway. Since we want to bring in so many of the park's rangers, it makes for a big scheduling problem but with Tom Cramer on our side, we'll get it worked out. Who knows, by the time all the arrangements are made, that bum leg of yours may be well enough for you to participate. Speaking of which, how's it doing?"

"The stitches come out tomorrow morning. I guess we'll see then, but it feels better." He glanced at Molly. "I'm sure Molly's anxious for me to be back in the saddle so she can get out of these woods and return to civilization."

~

As Molly sat near the front door, she was no longer listening to the conversation. How could anyone do something so terrible? How were they going to get to the bottom of this poaching problem? Jenny was certain it was her brother's truck they'd seen the other night, and Mrs. Jenkins and Jenny both had mentioned he was mixed up with an unsavory group of people. Was he personally involved? And if not personally, would Jamie point a finger at his friends if pressed for the truth?

"Molly, you're a hundred miles away again." Jake's gaze touched her face. "Where are you?"

Molly peered at the two men staring at her. "Sorry. I was just thinking about Jamie Mitchell. Cal, what makes you think he'll talk when you go to see him?"

"Well, I know he isn't going to volunteer information, but he may slip up or give something away without realizing it."

"What if his friends are there?"

"Then I won't stop. I want to talk to him alone, when he's more vulnerable and not backed up by his buddies. Don't worry, Molly. I've don't this before." He walked over, placing a fatherly hand on her shoulder. "And don't worry about that stunt out front. It'll all work out somehow."

A sudden knock on the inside office door was followed by Jake's mother's head appearing around the doorframe. "Sorry if I'm intruding, but I've got lunch on the table if anyone's interested."

Jake and Cal both accepted with alacrity while Molly declined. She'd lost her appetite and her rounds to the village and the dam had waited long enough. She needed to get to work and keep her mind busy.

~

As Cal pulled into Jamie Mitchell's driveway, he noticed his truck was the only vehicle parked there. A sigh of relief. *One hurdle down!* It appeared Jamie's buddies weren't around but it still remained to be seen. Turning off the engine of his park SUV, he climbed out, looking around as he did. It wouldn't surprise him to come face to face with a double barrel shotgun. Rusted farm implements sat near the edge of the yard while a neatly stacked wood pile stood beside the house. An old tractor sat in the small field beyond the implements, tall grass growing up around it. A stone bird bath stood in the middle of the yard, the bowl turned upside down on the pedestal.

Crossing the wide front porch, Cal knocked on the door. He didn't think anyone was home, but after the fifth and loudest knock, the door opened and Jamie Mitchell stared belligerently through the torn screen door.

"Yeah? What do ya want?" Jamie's voice was quiet. Too quiet?

"Morning, Jamie." Cal plastered a warm smile on his face. "I need to take a few minutes of your time, if you don't mind."

Jamie watched him for a full minute before responding. "Maybe. What for?" Suspicion made his eyes wary.

"Well, it'd be a lot easier to talk sitting down and not through this screen door. Can I come in?"

Jamie hesitated before reaching out a reluctant hand to push the screen door open. It squeaked loudly, grating on Cal's nerves, but without indicating his irritation, he walked in and sat on the edge of the armchair nearest the door. Jamie followed him in and plopped onto an old sofa that had seen better days."

"What do ya want?" Jamie repeated his initial question.

Cal leaned forward, propping his elbows on his knees, hands clasped loosely together. "Well, I haven't seen you around much lately, Jamie. I used to see you in town a lot and I'd run into you at Martin's filling station. What've you been up to these days?"

Jamie's thin shoulders rose in a careless shrug as he eyed Cal. "Not much. Hadn't had much reason to go into town lately." He shifted uneasily. "Now I know you didn't come out here to pay a social visit. Why are you here?"

Cal nodded. "You're right, Jamie. This isn't exactly a social call." Pausing, he sighed heavily. "Your pickup was spotted out at

Twentymile Ranger Station Friday night. Someone shot at the station with a shotgun, blowing out a window. Since your truck was used, I thought you might know something about it." He paused again, watching the young man closely. His eyes shifted slightly then shuttered. Was that surprise? Cal waited for a response. When he didn't get one, he continued.

"Jamie, I've known you for several years and I've never known you to be one for trouble, but something's going on here, and I need your help to find out what it is. Now I'm asking you point blank, were you in that truck at Twentymile Friday night?"

Jamie shifted in his seat again, visibly shaken. "No, it wasn't me," he denied. "I didn't do it."

"Were you in the truck Friday night?"

"No, I wasn't."

Cal watched him closely. "Then who was it, Jamie? It was your pickup that was seen."

"How do you know it was my truck?"

"It was identified by a witness."

Jamie shook his head vehemently. "It wasn't me. I loaned my truck to a buddy of mine." Realization dawned at what he'd just admitted.

Cal leaned forward. "If you loaned your pickup to a buddy, Jamie, then I'm sure you wouldn't mind telling me who this buddy is."

Jamie remained silent, but Cal saw the conflict as he considered his answer.

"Jamie," Cal continued in a low but firm voice, "maybe you didn't know, but your sister was at the ranger station visiting friends that night. She and one of her friends were standing at the very window that was shot out."

Jamie's face blanched as he broke into a sweat.

"That's right. Jenny was there. Both could have been killed. Don't you want to help me find out who almost killed them? Who almost killed your sister?"

Jamie slumped forward dropping his forehead into his palms, elbows on his knees. "This can't be happening," he whispered.

"Oh, it is! It really is happening. Where's it going to end? Who else will be hurt or killed before it's all said and done? You can help stop this foolishness. Help me stop it, Jamie," Cal pled in a low voice.

Jamie remained still for several minutes. Cal started to speak again, but then Jamie lifted his head. "I don't want any trouble, Cal. I didn't do nothing, and I don't think my buddy did either." Taking a deep breath, he surged forward. "I loaned my truck to Willy Cahill. He told me he had some errands to do that night. I didn't go with him! Really I didn't!"

"Can anyone give you an alibi?"

Jamie was thoughtful for a moment then his face lightened noticeably. "Yeah, my dad. Since I didn't have my truck, I couldn't go nowhere. Dad asked me to give him a hand working on his truck, and so I did."

Cal nodded. "Alright. I appreciate the information, but understand I'm going to confirm it. Now, what can you tell me about your buddy? Where can I find Willy Cahill? I need to have a little talk with him."

Fear etched Jamie's face. "Please don't mention you talked to me! He'll be really mad! He don't like people poking their noses into his business."

"Well, seeing as how this shooting was in the park and involved park personnel, I think his business is our business, don't you?"

While Jamie sat thoughtfully, Cal stood and strode to the door. "I won't mention to your buddies that I've talked with you, but I expect the same favor from you. If I find you've warned your buddies, I'm coming back to see you. I appreciate your co-operation, Jamie, but don't fight me. We're talking attempted murder here, and I don't think you want to be involved with that, now do you?"

Jamie shook his head in dejection.

"I'll be in touch. And remember, if you haven't done anything wrong, you don't have anything to be worried about. I'll be fair with you, but you have to be fair with me. I'll see you around, Jamie." Cal left through the squeaky screen door, leaving the young man to consider his words. Hopefully he'd think long and hard.

~

Twilight faded as Jake stood at the front window of the station office. What a week! Starting with Molly's gruesome discovery. What a way to begin. They'd kept busy over the next few days, she tackling the job away from the office while he resumed the deskwork. Tuesday morning his mom drove him into town to have his stitches removed. Doc Bennett had given him a clean bill of health and permission to return to work with a warning not to push too hard. Molly gladly accomplished the out-of-station duties, including a run to Oconoluftee on Wednesday to replenish the hay and feed supply for the horses.

Molly had said nothing about leaving until after work this afternoon. Her bags were already in her car and she was ready to go when she approached him in his mother's presence. She quietly stated that she needed get back to Deep Creek, pointing out that Jake was back on his feet and should be able to handle things without her. She'd waited until Friday afternoon to leave so as not to leave him in a bind. Like a sucker punch, he hadn't been prepared for her sudden departure.

With his leg mostly healed except for sore muscles and the healing scar, he knew he was up to the job now, but things weren't settled between them. The talk he'd started with her the weekend before had never been finished. A heavy sigh slipped out. He loved his mother dearly, but he wished she hadn't chosen that moment to show up.

The station phone jangled loudly interrupting his thoughts. He automatically reached for the receiver, gruffness edging his voice as he answered.

"Twentymile Ranger Station."

"What's eating you, Jake?" Cal's low voice questioned across the line.

"Sorry, I was just in deep thought is all." Jake rubbed the back of his neck, not realizing how tense he'd become. "What's up?"

"Remember I told you I'd talked with Jamie Mitchell Tuesday? Well, I've tried to visit his buddy Willy Cahill every day since then. Nothing. Hasn't been around."

"Have you talked to Jamie again?"

"Yeah, but he hasn't seen him either. I asked if any of his other buddies might know where Willy is, and after hedging a while, he gave me Ray Smith's name. Wouldn't you know it, he's not around either."

A thought came to Jake. "Aren't those the guys Molly arrested up on the back road above Deep Creek?"

"They sure are." Cal's voice was somber. "We need to find those boys."

~

Molly carried her bags up the steps of Mrs. Jenkins' house and into her apartment. Dropping them just inside the door, she plopped into the nearest armchair, feeling bone weary. It had been a long couple of weeks and it was good to be home. Later, after she'd eaten supper and unpacked, she'd find her landlady and spend some time catching up.

The overstuffed armchair did its magic and she found herself relaxing. Her mind had been in turmoil all week. So much had happened in just seven days that she was a bit overwhelmed. *I guess I haven't been depending on You very much lately, Father. So much has happened, and I haven't taken the time to bring these things to You. Forgive me! I need Your guidance and strength. These human eyes and this human heart can't see a way through.*

Jake's face sprang to mind with a clarity that almost took her breath away. The more time she spent with him, the more she lost her heart. So much so that her career plans in the park service were slipping into the backseat of her priorities. But would he expect that? For her to give up her career? Or would he encourage her to have both a career and a serious relationship with him?

She loved working in the park service, but lately things had taken a sinister turn, so unlike her expectations before coming here. Poaching was an ongoing issue, but what they were dealing with wasn't the usual problem. It had grown to a dangerous level. Far more than someone wanting to acquire game for sustenance or for a rebellious attitude at the park's expense. Someone was warning them and those warnings were becoming increasingly more malicious in nature.

Oh, Lord, lead us to whoever's involved in this so we can put a stop to it before someone gets seriously hurt. Or worse!

Molly wearily rose to her feet and went in search of Mrs. Jenkins. She hadn't planned to seek her out until later, but eating and unpacking could wait. As usual, she found her in her favorite place, her vegetable garden. In spite of the dusk that approached, the older woman was pulling weeds and picking vegetables.

"Hello, Mrs. Jenkins." Molly walked down a row of tomatoes.

"Oh, my goodness, sweetie. When did you get back?" Mrs.

Jenkins picked her way between the rows, her basket on her arm.

"Just a little while ago. It's sure good to be back. And the garden looks wonderful. It's grown a lot since I left."

Mrs. Jenkins reached up a wrinkled hand and patted her cheek. "It's wonderful to have you back, dear. I've missed you since you've been gone. Kinda got used to you being here!"

"That's sweet! Thank you." Molly linked her arm through the older woman's. "I've missed you too. More than you can know."

Mrs. Jenkins halted their progress across the back yard, looking into Molly's face in the gathering dusk. "Is something wrong, dear? You seem…well…sad. Perhaps that's not the right word, but something's different."

"I'm not sad exactly. Maybe confused is a better word."

"Well, whatever about, dear?"

Molly hesitated, unsure of what she wanted to say. "Maybe we should go inside. It's going to be dark soon."

Once inside the brightly-lit kitchen, Mrs. Jenkins set her basket on the counter by the sink then sat in a chair at the kitchen table. Pulling out the one beside it, she patted the seat. "Here. Have a seat and let's talk."

Molly sat down, leaning her arms on the edge of the table and clasping her hands together. "I don't really know what there is to talk about. I just feel confused about some things. About how I *feel* about things."

She fumbled for the right words to express herself but came up short.

A wise and kindly smile crossed the landlady's wrinkled face as she patted Molly's hand. "Are you in love with him, dear?"

Molly's breath caught but she didn't bother to deny it. How could she deny the truth? Nodding slowly, a faint smile touched her lips. "I think so. I didn't want or plan to fall in love, and I tried so hard not to. I've only just begun my park service career, and there are so many possible opportunities ahead for me. I just don't know what to do."

"Have you prayed about it?"

Molly again nodded. "Yes, but probably not like I should have or with the right attitude. I just pray a general prayer for guidance."

"Well, you know we're God's children, and as such, we can come to Him with anything that's on our hearts. Whether it's a problem, a joy, or an uncertainty, all we have to do is bare our heart to Him. That's what He wants us to do. When you were a little girl, did you ever climb into your father's lap and tell him about the bad things that happened to you?"

Mrs. Jenkins waited for Molly's nod before continuing. "And when something wonderful happened to you, did you run to him and tell him all about it?"

Again, Molly nodded. "That's the kind of relationship our heavenly Father wants to have with us. He wants us to come to Him with anything and everything. He's your Father after all. Maybe you should have another talk with Him, and tell Him the things that are in your heart. He already knows about them, but he wants *you* to tell Him."

Molly considered for a moment then reached her arms around the older woman's neck.

"Thank you, Mrs. Jenkins," she whispered softly as tears clogged her throat. "You truly are a dear lady."

Mrs. Jenkins rubbed her back comfortingly, a smile in her voice. "I've been there, dear. I'm not so old that I don't remember the hardship as well as the joy of falling in love."

A short time later Molly knelt beside her bed and poured out her doubts, fears and uncertainties before her heavenly Father, and when she got up to grab a bite and unpack, she did so with a lighter heart. Her burdens now lay at the Father's feet.

~

Monday morning Molly checked the tack and feed supplies at the barn and found the seasonals had certainly done a good job in her absence. When she walked into the office, she found Kate already behind the counter.

"Well, look who's back!" The younger woman exclaimed with warmth. Jumping off the high stool, she gave Molly a quick hug. "We sure missed you while you were gone. How've you been?"

Kate searched Molly's face, her gaze lighting on the stitches marking her forehead and temple. "I heard about the shooting. I'm so glad you weren't seriously hurt. I mean, I know you were hurt, but…well, you know what I mean."

Returning her petite friend's hug, Molly laughed. "I know what you mean. And yes, I'm fine. It certainly could've ended differently. I missed you all too. How are things around here?" She glanced around the office as she spoke.

Kate sighed as a grimace marred her face. "Just the usual citations for improper food storage. A speeding ticket or two. That sort of thing. Nothing to equal the commotion at Twentymile for sure." She again glanced at Molly's cheek. "How are the cuts?"

Molly put a hand up to the small lacerations. "They're fine. I get the stitches out Wednesday." She sat at the desk behind the counter. "By the way, how are things going with you and Craig?"

Kate beamed. "Molly, I'd never realized what a sweet guy he is. You know how it is when you work with someone for a while and then…boom! You notice how great they are!"

Molly nodded. She knew exactly how that worked!

Not noticing Molly's expression, Kate rambled on. "That's how it is with Craig. He's really a sweetheart. We've been out several times and had a lot of fun."

Molly grinned at the other girl's enthusiasm. "I'm happy for you, Kate. I knew when I told you he was interested in you that you'd make a cute couple."

Just then Cal ambled through the door, his ever-present coffee mug in hand. "Morning, ladies!" He leaned against the counter. "Welcome back, Molly. Jake called Friday afternoon and said you'd left. I wasn't expecting you this soon, but it's good to have you back."

Molly reached for a clipboard hanging on the wall beside the desk and answered evasively. "Well, I thought it was time to get back. Jake's doing great, and his Mom's there for a few more days to help around the station." Glancing up she found two pair of eyes watching her intently. "Besides," she added brightly. "I missed all of you here."

From Cal's expression, Molly didn't think he believed her. "Uh-huh. Well, it's good to have you back. Come to my office and I'll fill you in on what's been happening while you've been off playing backcountry ranger."

Chapter Fourteen

Molly's week proceeded quietly except for two incidents that left her bewildered. Late Thursday afternoon she worked alone in the office finishing up some reports that had to go to HQ the next day when David Andrews strode in the door. Thinking a camper had come in to register or to ask for information, she walked around to the counter, surprised to see David.

"Oh! Hi, David!" Molly greeted cordially, hoping upon hope he wouldn't stay long. She still had paperwork to finish and was eager to get done before heading home. "How've you been?"

"Fine, I guess," he responded. "I got in a little earlier than usual to set up for my program this evening and thought I'd wander over and see how you're doing after the incident at Twentymile last week. All healed up?"

"I'm fine. Got my stitches out, and I have orders from Doc Bennett not to come back for a while."

"That's good. Real good." David smiled, but it never reached his eyes.

Hmmm. What had him so preoccupied? "Are you okay, David? Something on your mind?"

"Oh, no! Not at all!" His casualness seemed forced, unlike his usual easygoing attitude. "I was just wondering if you'd found out who was behind the shooting that night. It was a terrible thing for someone to do, and I'm sorry you got hurt because of it."

Molly noticed his close scrutiny as he awaited her response. His sympathies were less than sincere. Cal had informed her of the situation involving Jamie Mitchell, Willy Cahill and Ray Smith, and she knew better than to talk to anyone about this investigation except Cal or Jake. David seemed to be fishing for information, although she couldn't imagine why.

"Unfortunately there's not much to tell, David, but rest assured, Cal is doing everything he can to find those involved. And thanks for your concern for me." That was a little difficult to say considering he really wasn't. She smiled sweetly although David's behavior puzzled her. Could his behavior be concern for his program tonight? Doubtful. He was generally easy-going and agitation seemed foreign to him. "Is there anything else I can do for you? If not I have some paperwork I have to finish."

"Oh, no! Nothing else. I'm just glad you're okay. I'll see you around." He donned his "Smokey" hat and hurried out the door, heading back toward the amphitheater. Hmmm. Very puzzling. It was two hours before his program was scheduled to start. Normally he'd sit down and talk, mainly about himself, of course, but not this time. He certainly was acting strange. For David.

The second incident occurred Friday morning just before she climbed into the pickup truck to drive to HQ in Gatlinburg. Cal had left the truck parked near the maintenance shed, and as she approached it, she heard her name called from inside the shed. The door stood wide open and she wasn't surprised to find Bill Hopper and Frank Raven sitting with their chairs tipped back, feet propped up, coffee cups in hand. This was usually how she found them.

"Morning, fellas." Molly greeted the two men with as much cordiality as she could muster. "Got a big day ahead of you?" She couldn't help but ask, all the while knowing they'd spend most of the day right where they were.

"Oh, yeah." Bill's weasel eyes squinted against the glare of the morning sun that backlit Molly's figure. "We've always got lots to do around here. Just can't seem to keep caught up."

I wonder why, as if I don't already know.

Bill suddenly dropped his chair back to the floor with a bang. Molly jumped. "Heard y'all had something bad happen out Twentymile way last week. Quite a mess I understand."

"Really?" Molly's antenna went up in alert mode.

Bill's eyes narrowed as his lips curled slightly before he dropped his gaze to his coffee cup. He took a long sip before answering. Frank hadn't moved a hair since she'd walked in the door. Had he even blinked?

"Well, now, Molly." Bill's voice dripped with syrupy sweetness. "The word is, something went on down there. Weren't you nearly shot? And then they left a little present by the front door. Pretty grisly, huh?"

"Where did you hear these things, Bill?" Molly words were surprisingly calm even as her gut twisted. She propped her hand casually on her sidearm holster. She had no reason to pull it and wouldn't, but she wanted to convey her authority. She didn't appreciate being toyed with.

Bill scratched his chin thoughtfully. "Now where did I catch wind of that?"

He turned to Frank. "You heard about it didn't you, Frank?"

Frank shrugged his shoulders but said nothing. Until then Molly had begun to think he was asleep.

Bill lifted innocent eyebrows, shrugging his shoulders much as Frank had done. He shook his head. "You know, I can't remember right off where I heard it. Oh, well. It's bound to come to me sometime."

"I wouldn't lose any sleep over it, Bill," Molly said in mock concern. "Well, fellas, I'd love to visit longer, but I need to be getting on. Places to go, things to do…. You know the story. Have a good one."

"Yeah, you too, Molly. And be careful. You never know what might happen." His unpleasant chuckle sent a chill coursing down Molly's spine as she walked away.

Climbing into the truck, she took a deep breath and clasped her fingers together in an attempt to still their trembling. His words had shaken her. In all actuality, the conversation could've been a casual one between co-workers, but the undertones in Bill's voice and the implications made her certain he meant something else altogether. Something dangerous perhaps? She wanted to talk with Cal just then, but he was in a meeting at Oconoluftee and she needed to get across the mountains to HQ. Hopefully he'd be around when she returned in the afternoon.

Once out of sight of the maintenance shed, she stopped the truck, pulled a notepad and pen from her daypack, and noted the conversation while it was fresh in her mind. Later when she spoke with Cal, she'd give it to him to read. Maybe it meant nothing, but again maybe it did.

~

Molly completed her business then headed down to the basement to visit Paul O'Brian in the dispatcher's office. She opened the door quietly and slipped in, so as not to disturb him if he was on the radio. Paul sat at the base station, cordless headset on, talking to someone on the other end. His dirty blond hair stood on end as if he'd continuously run a frantic hand through it. A pencil perched haphazardly behind his ear.

"Yeah, roger that, Jake," he spoke into the mic. Suddenly aware he wasn't alone, he glanced toward Molly. His face lit up. Releasing the microphone key, he said brightly, "Hey, Molly, how's it going? I'll be right with you."

He pressed the key again, talking into the microphone. "Hey, Jake, one of your pals just walked in. A really pretty one too. Bet you'll never guess which one? Over."

Molly cheeks flamed. "Is that Jake Stuart?" she asked casually, knowing full well it was. "Tell him I said hi."

"She says hello. Over." Paul released the mic key again.

"Paul, what are you talking about?" Jake's voice surged through the speaker as Paul flipped a switch so Molly could hear the conversation. Her heart leaped at the sound of his voice. "Who's there? Over."

"Your pal, Molly, my friend. Over." Paul answered with a whistle. The distance from Twentymile to Gatlinburg was far enough that the radio system required full range. In other words, the whole park could hear this conversation. She buried her face in her hands as she leaned her elbows on the counter. Paul chuckled with glee.

"Say hello for me," was Jake's simple reply. "Gotta go, buddy. Over and out."

Molly chided herself for the disappointment she felt when he cut the conversation short. Why should she be disappointed? He was talking over the park-wide radio, for goodness sake! What did she expect him to say?

Paul came over to the counter. "Well, Molly, how's the prettiest girl in the Smoky Mountains?"

"Oh, stop, Paul! You'll make me blush." She waved a hand and batted her eyelashes. "There's no need to ask how you've been. I can tell you've been up to no good."

"Who me?" Innocence masked his features. "I'll have you know I resemble that statement," he said with mock indignation, then smiled, wiggling his eyebrows. "Every chance I get."

They both laughed and then Paul sobered. "Now tell me how you're really doing."

"Oh, I'm fine. Staying busy and keeping a lookout over my shoulder. You know the routine."

"Yeah, I heard about your excitement." He frowned. "Not so good, huh?"

"No, not so good, but at least the job isn't dull." Molly attempted a lighter tone. "It could be worse, you know."

Paul shook his head. "Let's hope it doesn't go that way!"

"How did you hear about it, anyway? Word seems to spread far and wide."

"Jake was here yesterday. He came up to see Tom and stopped by. Didn't give any names or anything. Just mentioned something happened. But I knew you were out there helping him while he was laid up. Don't worry, I know better than to ask certain questions when it comes to investigations, but Jake seemed really distracted."

Time to change the subject. Molly seemed to be doing that a lot lately. "How about you, Paul. What's been happening around here?"

"Not much. A few car break-ins, park visitors feeding the bears, lightening striking a tree causing it to fall on a tent." At Molly's evident surprise, he added, "Don't worry. No one was in it at the time, fortunately. Things are pretty normal." He affected a huge yawn. "Almost boring in fact."

"Right!" Molly laughed.

"For example, just this morning, Celeste comes in here and jumps down my throat about something I had nothing to do with. I guess she was sore because Jake didn't stop in to see her when he was here yesterday." He dropped his voice to a conspiratorial whisper. "She's got a thing for him, you know."

Molly nodded. "I know."

"But that's nothing unusual, really," he said matter-of-factly. "She has a tendency to be short tempered when it comes to someone she doesn't particularly care for, and I'm afraid I fall into that category."

"Well, it's her loss," Molly replied. "She just doesn't know what a great guy you are."

"Aw, shucks!" Paul rolled his eyes and covered his face. "You're only saying that because it's true."

Molly laughed again. "I have to go, Paul. I still have a couple of stops to make before I leave the building, and I need to go to the fuel depot to fill up before I head back. It's a long walk to Deep Creek from here. I'll see you!"

"See ya later, Molly. And keep a lookout for the tiger lady. I hear you aren't on her list of favorite people either."

"At least I'm in good company. Thanks for the warning. I'll keep my eyes open."

Molly climbed the stairs to the first floor and rounded the corner to go down the hallway when she came face to face with "the tiger lady" as Paul had so aptly dubbed Celeste. She wore a hip-hugging black skirt and a ruffled white blouse that almost made Molly shift her gaze at its transparency. Celeste's makeup had been applied with great care and with, what Molly considered, a heavy hand. Her bleached hair was coiffed in a stylish fashion. Molly intended to nod her greeting and continue down the hall, but Celeste had other ideas.

Halting right in front of Molly, she forced her to stop or else appear rude, and Molly wouldn't lower herself to that level.

"Well, well, well. Look who's here," Celeste's saccharine voice contrasted with the glare that emanated from her stormy eyes. "If it isn't Miss Backwoods herself. What are you doing here? Come to see who else you can trap with that fake sweetness of yours?"

Celeste's eyes hardened and a sneer twisted her red lips as she shook a manicured finger in Molly's face. "You stay away from Jake, do you hear me? He doesn't want a little nobody like you. He wants a sophisticated woman. One that'll treat him right."

Molly's heart pounded with ire, but she simply smiled. "What are you talking about, Celeste?

"Oh, don't play dumb with me, honey. I know exactly what you're up to, but it isn't going to work. I'll tell Jake exactly what you are."

"And what would that be?" Molly projected calmness in spite of the turmoil raging within.

"You're just a…a…. Oh, I'm not going to waste my time telling you. I'll save it for Jake. I'm sure he'll be more than interested to know of your behavior concerning several of the men around here. Including that stupid idiot, Paul O'Brian. Couldn't wait to stop in to say hello, huh!"

"Celeste," Molly said with more patience than she felt. "I don't know what you're talking about. You must be thinking of someone else. But I have things to do, so I won't take up any more of your time. Have a good day."

She tried to pass the other girl, but Celeste grabbed her arm and yanked her back, hurting Molly's arm in the process. She bit her lip to keep from crying out.

"You stay away from Jake," Celeste threatened through clenched teeth. "He's mine."

Molly met Celeste's hateful gaze with as sweet a smile as she could manage. "If Jake wants you, he's more than welcome to you."

She yanked her arm from Celeste's grasp and walked down the hall, not daring to turn around. She sensed the other woman's eyes on her retreating back, filled with the hate that had been so clearly displayed during Celeste's tirade.

She finished up her business and left as quickly as possible, unwilling to run into her again.

~

After her encounter with Celeste, Molly needed something to ease the turmoil inside. A stop at Newfound Gap overlook and then Clingmans Dome might just do the trick. Her only visit to the Dome had been the day of the search and rescue when the fog had obliterated the view. But today was beautiful and clear.

The steep climb to the lookout tower helped ease the frustrated energy in her gut since her run-in with Celeste. She took time to stop and answer questions for some visitors and to say hello to passing hikers.

When she arrived at the top of the observation deck, the surrounding view in its majestic beauty reminded her whose child she was. God had seen it all. He knew the hateful words Celeste had spewed at her, and somehow it all fit into His infinite plan. Her job was to trust Him.

Molly was reminded of Mrs. Jenkins words the other evening about telling her Father all the bad things as well as the good. And so she did. With arms leaning on the deck railing, she spilled her thoughts and feelings to the Lord. Knowing that He'd created such a magnificent mountain range with all its amazing array of foliage, wildlife and fowl was an even greater reminder of His love for her. When she headed back down the path to the parking lot, her spirit was lighter than when she'd hiked up.

~

As she parked next to the ranger station, Molly hoped to find Cal had returned. She wanted to tell him about the conversation with Bill Hopper that morning, but the station door was locked. The sign beside the door indicated a ranger would return in thirty minutes. Joe was on duty this afternoon and was probably making rounds in the campground. Pulling out her keys, she went inside, locking the door behind her and leaving the clock sign in place. She reached for the base radio mic and uttered Cal's call number. He was on his way back from the North Shore Road and would be there in ten minutes. She tossed her cap on the counter and sat at the desk just as the phone rang.

"Deep Creek Ranger Station. May I help you?" she greeted in cheerful tones.

"You sure can," spoke a low muffled voice. "You tell them rangers to keep their noses out o' our business. Someone's likely ta get hurt if they don't. And it won't be no warnin' like before."

A click on the other end cut off the malicious voice, leaving Molly stunned. She slowly returned the receiver to its cradle. When Cal came in a few minutes later, he found her hunched in the chair, twisting a pen between her fingers.

"Molly? What's wrong?"

Looking up wearily, she recounted to him about the phone call and the conversation with Bill Hopper that morning. She couldn't really say that Frank Raven had participated in the conversation, but he'd been present. She handed Cal the notes she'd made.

He leaned back in his chair and sighed heavily, rubbing his eyes and looking as weary as Molly felt. "I tell you what, I'm tired. I wish this whole thing was over and done with. I'm tired of warnings and threats and the little games that are being played. I can't prove it yet, but I'm almost certain Bill Hopper's involved in the poaching. His buddy Frank Raven probably is too." He leaned forward and slapped his knee. "Dog gone it. If we could just get this stakeout finalized, maybe we could catch them."

"Any news on when?"

"As of right now it'll be next week sometime, but we haven't settled on any particular dates. It'll be over a three-day period. Some want to do it during the week, but I feel like we should be out there over the weekend. For the most part folks are off work on weekends and that seems to be when the poaching activity is the heaviest."

Standing, Molly plopped her cap on her head. "I suppose there's a possibility they'll be poaching this weekend. I almost dread Monday morning. There's no telling what we'll find."

Cal stood up and placed a kind hand on her shoulder. "Don't worry about it, Molly. You go home and have a good weekend. If something happens Monday morning, we'll handle it."

"Thanks, Cal. I'll try. It's been a long day, and I'm glad it's Friday. You have a good weekend too. Try not to let the campers get out of hand."

~

At home Molly changed into an old T-shirt and a pair of cut-off jeans then pulled her hair into a ponytail. She prepared a chef salad for supper then settled in front of the TV, searching until she found an old movie. Good. Dean Martin and Jerry Lewis should be a good laugh and a distraction from her day. After her conversations with Bill Hopper and Celeste and the threatening phone call, she was ready to forget everything for a while.

When the movie was over, she found another old comedy and hurried into the kitchen to prepare some popcorn before settling once again in front of the TV. She had just grabbed a handful from the bowl and was lifting it to her mouth when the phone rang. Leaning her head back, she groaned and dropped the kernels back into the bowl.

She reached for the cell phone and couldn't stop the weariness that crept into her voice. "Hello?"

"You sound tired." A familiar voice jumpstarted her heart rate into double time. "Was it one of those days?"

"And how." Molly told him about her day minus the run-in with Celeste. She'd keep that to herself. "How about you? How was your week?"

"Well, Mom went home Wednesday morning after making sure I had enough food in the freezer to keep me for a while. But overall it was a quiet week. Almost too quiet. I miss you not being here, you know. I kind of got used to having you around."

At the huskiness in Jake's voice, Molly forced her heart out of her throat and back into its rightful position.

He cleared his own throat and continued before she could think of anything to say. "By the way, Gorgeous, what have you got planned for this weekend?"

As warmth stole over her, she placed her hand to one cheek and pressed hard, willing her heart to settle down. "Well, I hadn't planned anything except for tomorrow morning. I'm riding one of the horses up Deep Creek. Not in an official capacity, but I'll have my walkie-talkie. I don't seem to get much of an opportunity to check out the trails during the week, so I thought I'd ride up and explore."

"Make me a promise," Jake's voice was serious. "Take your firearm with you. Considering how things are right now, I think it'd be a good idea."

"Ok. Sure. I'll do that," Molly agreed.

"How long do you think you'll be gone?"

"I don't know. A few hours, I suppose. Thought I'd bring my lunch along and take my time."

"Hmmmm." Jake's mumble reverberated in her ear. "Okay well, maybe I'll call you in the afternoon and see if you're back. Would that be okay?"

"Sure. I don't see why not."

"Good. Get some rest and be careful up on those trails. I'll see you, Dar-, um, Molly."

As she clicked off the call, Molly wondered what he was about to say. It sounded like he was going to say something then changed his mind. She wrinkled her brow as she reached for the popcorn and the TV remote. Oh well. It must not have been important

~

By eleven o'clock Saturday morning Jake had decided not to call Molly. He'd show up at her apartment instead. If she wasn't too tired after her ride, maybe they'd go out and do something. Restlessness had been his constant companion all week. In reality, since she'd left the week before. Even before his mom had left, he'd longed to hear Molly's voice and her laughter as they'd talked or shared a joke.

He kept watching for the Jeep to turn into the driveway, bringing her back from a run to the village and the dam. He'd think of things he wanted to share with her that happened during the day, but she wasn't there to share them. Emptiness filled him like never before. He'd known for some time that he loved her, and thinking of her brought an ache to his heart when she wasn't near.

But was she ready to hear him say those words? That he loved her? She seemed to be struggling with an inner battle recently, but he didn't know what that battle was. He hadn't felt he should ask, and she hadn't volunteered anything. The desire to be there for her and lend a shoulder when she needed it was strong, but until she was ready he'd continue to pray for her.

Lord, You know Molly's struggle, and I don't yet have the right to take on her struggles even though I want that right. She's Your child. Help her through it, and help me to be there for her when she needs me. You know I love her, and I want to spend the rest of my days sharing her struggles and her joys.

~

Molly got an early start the next morning. Wearing blue jeans, a T-shirt and a ball cap above her long dark braid, she'd slipped on hiking boots and brought along her daypack with her sidearm and her walkie-talkie. She'd left a message at the office for Cal, saying she'd taken Fargo and was heading up Deep Creek for a ride.

When Fargo was saddled and cinched, she'd climbed into the saddle and turned him toward the trail. She'd gone no more than fifty feet when she felt the saddle begin to slip down the right side of the horse. She pulled up the reins and started to climb off just as the saddle let loose and slid under the horse's belly, dropping her to the ground on its way down. Fargo turned a wicked eye on Molly as she picked herself up and dusted off her jeans. He nickered and blew out his nose as he tossed his head back.

"Stop laughing at me, you overgrown prankster." She swiped the dirt from the seat of her pants. "That was hardly fair, you know. After all the carrots and apples I've brought you since I've been here? And to think I'd sneak extra bites to you when the other horses weren't looking."

Molly glanced around to see if anyone had observed her less than graceful descent from the horse. Being such an early hour, she was happy to see there were no witnesses. After sliding the saddle back up onto Fargo's back, she reached for the reins, pulling Fargo's head around to look him square in the eye. "Don't do that again."

She spoke firmly and he dropped his head and peered at her with wide eyes. "It's bad manners to hold your breath while I'm cinching you. Didn't anyone ever tell you that? You need to go back and learn some good horse sense. No pun intended."

As she talked she suddenly reached around and elbowed him in the side, causing Fargo to expel his pent-up breath. As he did, Molly grabbed the cinch and yanked hard. "There. That should do it. Now let's quit messing around here and hit the trail. You should be grateful I chose you instead of one of the other fellas."

Without further incident the pair made their way slowly up the trail. With no early morning hikers they had it to themselves. Molly reveled in the clear, cool mountain breeze that wafted softly past. Even mid-summer, the mountain mornings could be cool until the sun reached past the ridges into the gullies and ravines that branched throughout the mountains. The cool air had formed a patchy haze that hugged the slopes. The spectral-like tendrils of moisture slid between the trees and along the ground. Before long the sun would warm up the haze and it would vanish, but until then Molly would enjoy the almost eerie atmosphere pervading the trail. With no animal activity present, the silence added to the spookiness. Not even the birds were singing their usual cheery song

Having long passed the upper waterfalls, Molly was several miles up when she came to the first backcountry campsite. Presently unoccupied, someone had definitely been here recently. The last campers had abandoned their garbage rather than carry it out as specified in the backcountry campsite regulations. Not only had they failed to take it with them, they hadn't even bothered to bag it. Dismounting, Molly secured Fargo's reins to a low tree branch. After his earlier stunt, she wouldn't put anything past him. Pulling a large black garbage bag from her saddlebags, she proceeded to clean up the campsite. She left the half-full bag by the trail to grab on her way back down, mounted up and headed up the trail.

As she went from site to site checking for garbage and any damage the maintenance men might need to be informed of, her mind kept slipping back to the subject that had been uppermost in her mind for some time now. Jake and her career.

She'd acknowledged to herself that she loved him, but did he share her feelings? He appeared to enjoy her company, and sometimes she'd seen something in his gaze or heard an inflection in his voice, but had she really? Or was it wishful thinking? Could she have a relationship and a career? Couples did it all the time, didn't they? Why couldn't she? But what if Jake only saw her as a really good friend? Was it truly what God wanted for her life? Molly went round and round with questions in her mind until she shook her head, attempting to dispel the tormenting thoughts.

Digging her heels into Fargo's sides, she clicked her tongue. "Let's go!" He'd been chomping at the bit all morning to stretch his legs and responded instantly. They'd reached fairly even ground, and the horse's hooves flew up the trail. They couldn't keep this up for long. It wasn't fair to Fargo to make him climb at a run, but he sure seemed to be enjoying it.

She reined him in as they emerged into an open grassy area overlooking a panoramic view. According to the trail map she'd been following, this was Newton's Bald. As she paused and gazed across the vista before her, Molly gasped at what she saw in the near distance. Engrossed in her thoughts and in checking the campsites, she hadn't noticed the sun disappear. The mountains maintained their bluish hue, fading to lighter hues the further away they were, but what concerned Molly was the sky above them. It was darker than the mountains below. Up here on the grassy bald there was little vegetation to stop the progress of the wind that seemed to bring the storm ever closer. Lightning flashed across the dark skies, and with nothing between her and the storm, she could now hear the growing rumble of thunder. Reaching into her daypack to retrieve her rain-suit, she rummaged around until understanding dawned on her. It wasn't there!

"Oh, no!" Molly gasped, glancing back at the approaching storm. It was hanging in the bathroom at her apartment. She'd needed it this past week and afterward had hung it from the towel bar to dry, never replacing it in the daypack. "How could I be such an idiot?" she spoke aloud. "Lesson learned. The hard way." Fargo nickered in agreement as he stamped a hoof in agitation.

Zipping up the daypack, she glanced at her watch. One o'clock! Wow! She had been preoccupied!

"Come on, Fargo, we have to get out of here! We're going to get soaked! Let's just hope lightning doesn't hit a tree while we're riding underneath." Fargo tossed his head up and down and whinnied loudly, as unhappy with the situation as she was.

Pulling the reins sharply to the left, she guided Fargo back to the trailhead. The thunder grew louder. Unwilling to risk Fargo slipping on the rocky trail as they descended, Molly forced them to a walk. They'd just have to get wet.

They'd gone no more than a mile when the heavens opened up and began to pour. Within seconds, Molly was drenched. Because of the bill on her cap, her eyes were the only dry spot. Rain slipped down her cheeks and neck. Before long her feet were squishy in her hiking boots, and they became slippery in the stirrups. "Come on, Fargo." She patted the wet hairy neck of the horse picking his way down the trail. "It's just you and me, buddy. We can do it." She was pretty sure this pep talk was more for her than for Fargo.

She'd tucked her radio into her daypack to keep the majority of the rain off but suddenly she heard it crackle to life. With very little radio activity during the morning, she'd paid little attention to it, but when she heard her call numbers and then her name, she pulled it from the pack.

"This is Molly. Go ahead. Over," she called loudly over the din of the pouring rain.

"Molly, this is Cal. What's your location? Over."

Giving him her location, she told him about the storm. "There's quite a bit of lightning, Cal. Every time I see it, the hair stands up on the back of my neck."

Cal's chuckle resounded across the radio waves. "Ten-four, Molly. I'm sure it does, but listen, HQ has a report of a lightning fire started north on Thomas Ridge. I was hoping you were still near Newton's Bald. I know it's pouring and you're likely soaked, but I need you to ride back up and take a look. Give me a call and tell me what you see. Over."

"I'm on it. I'll call you shortly. Over and out."

Returning the radio to the daypack, Molly again turned Fargo's reins, heading him back up the trail. "Why do I get the feeling I should've stayed in bed this morning?" she asked the back of Fargo's head.

When they were once again on Newton's Bald, Molly reached into her daypack and rummaged for her binoculars. "Hallelujah! At least I put something back the last time I used it!"

With her own eyes, she scanned the northern horizon for any indication of smoke or fire. Was that smoke in the distance? It was hard to tell in the rain. She focused the binoculars on the spot in question. It took a couple tries of wiping the lenses with a rag from her pack before she could make anything out. Her heart froze. In the binoculars nearer view there was indeed a fire. Not only could she see smoke near the summit of Thomas Ridge, but flames licked at the tops of the trees.

Hopefully the heavy rain would put it out quickly. It wasn't unusual for a lightning fire to start in the mountains, but the rain usually extinguished them without the rangers having to take action.

"Cal," she called over the radio. "Ten-four on the fire. So far it doesn't look like its spread far, but it isn't just smoke. Looks like it's four or five miles from here on Thomas Ridge. What do you advise? Over."

"I'm on the phone with HQ now. Yours is the confirmation call, but you're too far away. Fire crews will head up Oconoluftee River Road and get right on it. You head back to Deep Creek. I can hear the thunder in the background when you talk, and unless I miss my guess, you're in enough danger being out in the storm. Come on back. Over and out."

"Roger that. I'm on my way. Over and out."

Feeling like a lightning rod on this grassy bald, Molly wanted to get down off this mountain as soon as possible. Turning Fargo back to the trailhead, they once again picked their way back down the slippery mountain trail.

~

Jake parked in Mrs. Jenkins driveway and climbed out of his truck, almost running up the front walk and taking all three steps at one time. Mrs. Jenkins must've been near the door, because she immediately opened it

"Jake, dear! It's good to see you. Come on in." She held the screen door wide for him to enter. "How's that leg doing?"

"It's doing great," he chuckled. "But then I had a good nurse, you know."

"Don't I know," replied the good woman with a wink. "Our Molly is quite a girl."

"That she is," he agreed with a hearty nod. "She isn't by any chance back from her ride, is she? I didn't see her car."

"Oh, I'm afraid she's not back yet." Mrs. Jenkins smiled and placed a gentle hand on his arm. "I hate to disappoint you, Jake, but I don't think she'll be back for a while. She took her daypack and had her lunch packed in it. Said she'd be back sometime this afternoon."

A wry expression tilted an eyebrow downward as he nodded. "Yeah, that's what she said on the phone last night, but I was hoping she'd have left early and might be back early. It's just past noon now."

"Why don't you come in and have lunch with me while you wait." Mrs. Jenkins suggested as she tugged him toward the kitchen. "Maybe we ought to have a little talk."

Chapter Fifteen

When Molly dragged herself into Mrs. Jenkins house, she knew Jake was there. Not only was his truck parked outside, but his laughter from the kitchen mingled with that of her landlady. Following the happy sounds, she walked in to find Mrs. Jenkins sitting in a chair, arm resting on the counter. The cabinet beneath the sink was open, and a pair of long blue-jean clad legs stuck out at an odd angle. An occasional chuckle and a metallic clang filtered from the recesses of the cabinet beneath the sink.

Mrs. Jenkins spotted Molly standing in the doorway and gasped. "Oh, my goodness!" She sprang from her chair, forgetting the activity beneath the sink. "Molly, dear! What in the world happened to you?"

Jake immediately extricated himself from the cabinet and stood up. From their expressions of shock, Molly determined she must be a frightful sight

"Molly!" Jake pulled out a chair and grasped her shoulders tenderly.

"What happened, Sweetheart?" Had he realized the endearment had slipped out? Now wasn't the time to think about it.

"I better not sit down, Jake. I'm soaked. Through and through. I'd hate to mess up Mrs. Jenkins chair cushions."

"Oh, piffle! Sit down, dear." Mrs. Jenkins urged her into the waiting chair. "Now tell us why you're soaked and muddy. Here, wipe your face with this."

She held out a kitchen towel, but before Molly could reach for it, Jake nabbed it, knelt beside her chair and gently wiped water and mud from Molly's filthy face.

"What happened, Molly?" Jake's gentle tone prompted as he pushed back strands of hair that had long ago pulled from her ponytail and plastered to her cheeks.

His solicitous touch evoked warmth in her cheeks, causing her breath to catch in her throat. Hopefully there was still enough mud to cover the tell-tale blush.

As she recounted the day's events, Mrs. Jenkins poured a glass of lemonade, setting it in front of Molly.

"So that's how I got soaking wet." She reached for the cool glass. "As to why I'm so muddy, we have Fargo to thank for that. This must have been his day for pranks. After the cinch incident, I guess he thought he'd get me back. About a mile from the barn, he stopped suddenly, sending me flying over his head. The saddle and stirrups were wet and I slid right off."

"Are you hurt?" Huskiness edged Jake's question as his eyes scanned for injuries. His penetrating gaze scrutinized her face.

His intensity robbed Molly's breathe. Seized up. Yep. Just plain seized up. That's how her lungs felt.

"Would you stop looking at me like that?" she exclaimed heatedly. "I'm having enough trouble talking, much less breathing, as it is." She colored again at his delighted grin and chuckle. "Besides, I landed in a huge, messy, gooey, deep mud puddle. I think that was Fargo's intention, by the way. 'Let's not hurt her: let's just get even' says he, with a wicked nicker!"

"Well, praise the Lord you weren't hurt, dear." Mrs. Jenkins pressed her hand to her heart.

"Amen to that," Jake exhaled heavily, never removing his eyes from Molly's face. "And what about the fire?"

"By the time I got down the mountain, the crew up on the Oconoluftee River Road had it out, with some help from the rain. Cal took one look at me and sent me straight home. He wouldn't even let me into the station." Indignation colored her expression. An overwhelming desire to put her head down and cry her eyes out filled her. Taking another deep drink of lemonade, she batted her eyes quickly and forced that desire away.

"Next on the agenda is a shower. A nice hot one. Not that I need one or anything. I can almost feel the steam rising from my clothes." She glanced over at the sink. "What's happening here? You two sounded like a couple of kids on a holiday when I came in."

Jake laughed, glancing down at his own clothes. For the first time Molly realized that he, too, was rather wet.

Not nearly as wet as me, though.

"Jake's been busy helping me with some improvements around here." Mrs. Jenkins waved an all-encompassing hand. "He showed up at noon looking for you, and when you weren't here, we had lunch. Then he offered to help with some chores around the house. He fixed the back screen door that always bangs when it shuts. He restrung my clothesline and then went to town and got me a new faucet at the hardware store. Unfortunately, when he first started to put it in, we forgot to turn off the water. Needless to say, he got a bit wet."

The memory sent the lady into a fit of chuckles.

"Not to mention the kitchen." Jake raised an eyebrow. "It was like Old Faithful all over again."

"Shore was," agreed the landlady, between chuckles.

The mental picture made Molly laugh. "I didn't realize you were such a handyman," she teased, taking a step out of the doldrums that had enveloped her most of the day.

Jake cocked an eyebrow and gave her a wicked grin. "You'd be surprised what a *handy man* I could be to have around."

There goes my breathing again.

"Yes…well…I'm going to…get a shower." Molly stood abruptly and headed for the door.

Minutes later she poised beneath the gentle pressure of hot water, reveling in the flow as the grime and filth washed away. Scrubbing her hair and her body until it tingled, she rinsed, quickly dried off and dressed in a pair of knit capris and a baggy T-shirt. Towel-drying her hair, she pulled it up with a large clip, leaving tendrils falling against her cheeks and neck.

She tossed the filthy clothes in the wash and cleaned her hiking boots, placing them in front of a fan to dry. It would take days for those to dry out. She'd have to pick up another pair before returning to work Monday morning.

A knock sounded at the door, and she knew without a doubt it would be Jake, but when she opened the door she wasn't prepared to find he'd also showered and changed into dry clothes.

At her quizzical expression, he explained. "Mrs. Jenkins is a resourceful lady. She had a shirt that belongs to her great nephew and loaned it to me. While I took a quick shower, she threw my jeans in the drier. They're still a bit damp, but nothing I can't live with."

He paused. "Can I come in?"

"Oh, sorry. Come on in."

She saw Jake's gaze immediately zero in on the pair of deformed boots drying in front of the fan. The rain had morphed them into a misshapen mass of leather. "You know it'll take days for those to dry out." His lips twisted in a wry grin. "And they'll never be the same."

"I know," Molly sighed. "I'll get another pair after church tomorrow."

"Why not tonight? Let's go grab a bite to eat then I'll drive you over to Sylva where you can shop till you drop if you like. Or are you too tired after your day?"

Molly was weary but she knew part of that was due to the fact that she hadn't eaten lunch. She'd been too preoccupied before the storm and too wet afterward. Her lunch was still wrapped in a soggy mess in her daypack. "That'd be great, thanks. But we won't shop for long. I'd drop sooner than you think."

~

The following morning Molly sat beside Mrs. Jenkins as people filled the little country church. It seemed more like Easter or Christmas with all the people streaming in, but nothing out of the ordinary was happening. Just more people were attending than usual.

As they stood to sing, Jake stepped beside her, taking the last available seat in the pew. With a quick whispered "Good morning," he picked up the hymnbook and held it for her as the congregation began to sing "When the Roll is Called Up Yonder." When the hymn was finished and they sat down, Molly found herself squished between Jake and Mrs. Jenkins. To make things a little easier, Jake placed his arm along the back of the pew behind Molly's shoulders.

"A little crowded this morning, huh?" He whispered in her ear. "But not uncomfortable."

Molly caught his mischievous grin and a raised eyebrow. "Behave yourself," she whispered back, playfully elbowing him in the ribs. He chuckled softly, much to her embarrassment.

Concentrating on the sermon was a lot harder than usual, Molly found, given the proximity of the man beside her. *Thank goodness the church is air conditioned.*

After the last amen, Jake grabbed Molly's hand and guided her through the crowd, stopping occasionally to speak to one person or another. When they'd finally spoken to the pastor and were out in the hot sunshine, he walked her to her car, never releasing her hand. Asking for her keys, he unlocked and opened the door before turning back to her.

"Have any plans for today?"

"No, not really." She shrugged and shook her head.

"Good. Then I have. How about going tubing with me? It's supposed to be really hot today, and it'd be a cool way to spend it."

"Tubing? You mean down Deep Creek?" A smile lit her face.

"Exactly. I'll bring along a picnic lunch, and we'll have a great time."

"Okay." Molly's smile deepened. "Sounds like fun. I've seen campers and visitors at Deep Creek tubing a lot, but I haven't had a chance to try it myself."

"You'll love it." Jake squeezed her hand.

After driving Mrs. Jenkins home, Molly hurried upstairs and dressed in a swimsuit, a baggy T-shirt and capris then followed Jake to Deep Creek in her car. Parking his truck by the creek where they'd get out at the end of the trip downstream, they took Molly's car to the tube rental kiosk just outside the entrance to the campground. Renting two huge rubber inner tubes, they piled them on top of the car and drove to the trailhead parking lot.

They spread a blanket on the ground beneath a tree near the creek, and opened the picnic lunch Jake had brought. Excited to get on their tubes and begin their downstream cruise, they didn't linger over the meal, but ate quickly, packed the remains away and pulled the tubes from the top of the car.

"Now this is the hard part," Jake explained. "We have to carry them or roll them up the dirt road to the place where we get in. But it's worth the effort."

Molly removed her T-shirt and capris and tossed them into the backseat beside the food hamper. A wolf whistle sounded beside her. "Wow!" Jake exclaimed. "You're a knockout, lady!"

Her swimsuit was certainly considered modest by current standards, but his compliment made her self-consciousness. Choosing to hide behind silliness, Molly dropped a quick curtsey, and batting her eyelashes coquettishly, fanned her face with her hand. "Why, thank you, kind sir."

They joked and teased all the way up the trail until they reached the fork below the waterfalls. Wading into the cold mountain water, they held their tubes firmly to prevent them from floating away with the strong current then Jake held Molly's tube as she climbed in. Dropping back into the hole in the middle of the tube, her arms and legs stretched over the sides.

Molly squealed as the water splashed over her. "Wow, this is cold!"

She shivered as Jake held onto her tube and his at the same time. He laughed as he climbed onto his own tube, one foot still holding them in place.

"Are you ready for this?" He shouted over the sound of the rushing water.

"I don't think so. I think I'm having second thoughts!" Molly laughed. "Remember, I've never done this before."

"Well, it's too late now." He shoved her tube out into the rushing current then pushed himself off. They floated along with the current for a few minutes until they came to a short waterfall, about four feet high.

"Hang on!" Jake called from right behind her. "Don't let go!"

Pointing her toes downstream, Molly braced for the drop over the edge, hanging on for dear life. Happy when she landed still on top of the tube instead of under it, she let out a victorious yell. She spun around to see Jake as he went over. Slipping off the tube, he went under, but came up in time to save his tube from floating on without him. His dark hair plastered to his head as he spit water. Molly giggled excitedly, goosebumps covering her arms and legs.

"I thought you said 'don't let go'!" She reminded him pointedly, laughing at his wry expression.

"Right." He climbed back onto the tube.

They continued downstream, passing lots of tubers, from elderly to young children. Everyone was having a wonderful time. Parts of the creek were quite bumpy as they passed over rocks and fastmoving water. Then it would transform into a gentle flow allowing them to drift along peacefully, meandering through deep pools. Here Molly laid her head back and relaxed, trying to still her chattering teeth.

Once she felt her hand grasped lightly and squeezed. Opening her eyes she found Jake's smiling gaze. They floated on until she found herself beached on a rock. Jake tugged and pulled her loose.

"Thanks. I thought I was going to get stuck for good."

"I wouldn't let that happen." Sincerity filled Jake's words as his gaze probed hers. Her breath hitched again. That seemed to be happening more and more.

The entire trip down the creek took about forty-five minutes. They passed beneath the bridges in the campground and spotted campers and tents arranged along the creek bank. Small children played at the water's edge; their mothers close by. They noticed an elderly couple floating by, holding hands. Molly found herself relaxing as she adjusted to the cold water. It was wonderful to just float along, her hand in Jake's. A smile tilted up the corners of her lips.

Jake reached across and let his fingers graze her cheek. "What's that smile for, lady?"

"Oh, nothing really. I was just thinking how contented I feel right now. Makes me want to float on forever."

"Sounds good to me, but I have a feeling Cal would want to know where we were come tomorrow morning. And I hate to call a halt to all the fun, but we're almost at our exit point. It's just up ahead."

Molly spotted the top of Jake's truck parked near the creek. "Aw-w-w. That went too fast," she said as they made their way toward the creek bank. "We'll have to do it again some time." Her teeth chattered behind cold lips.

Jake climbed from his tube and reached out a hand to help Molly up. They dragged the tubes along with them and threw them into the back of the truck. Unlocking it, Jake reached inside and pulled out two huge beach towels. Draping one around his shoulders, he then tossed one around Molly's, tugging her toward him.

Probing her gaze, he said softly, "You're something else, you know that?"

His arms encircled her as he slowly lowered his head until his lips met hers. Molly was certain time stood still as his warmth reached out and enveloped her. She thrilled at the cool touch of his lips on hers. When he lifted his head, Molly's eyelids slid open. She was aware of that something in his gaze she'd seen before but had always been afraid to name. Maybe she still was. Maybe she was afraid it wouldn't be real. Or maybe she was afraid it was.

Releasing her abruptly, he rubbed himself down with his towel. "Let's get these tubes back and get you home. We need to talk."

Those four words sent a shiver down Molly's spine

In less than forty-five minutes they were climbing the stairs to her apartment. Molly unlocked the door, and Jake followed her inside. She turned to ask if he wanted something cold or hot to drink, but he shook his head and caught hold of her hand, tugging her down beside him on the couch.

Entwining his fingers with hers, his eyes devoured her face. "Molly, I think it's time we talk things out. I know something's been bothering you lately, but I can't believe it's something we can't work out between us. And whatever it is keeps me at arm's length. I've loved you since the day you startled me, causing me to lose my balance and fall on the ground. I looked up and fell again, but not on the ground. I fell in love. I haven't been the same since."

Drawing her hand to his lips, he kissed her fingers. "Molly, I have to know how you feel, and I have to know what's been bothering you."

She couldn't believe her ears. "You love me?" she whispered. Had she heard him right?

"Read my lips," he chuckled then grew serious as he enunciated each word slowly so there'd be no mistake. "I love you, Molly Walker. Could you ever love me back, Darling?"

Reaching her hand up, Molly cupped his cheek. "Oh, I do love you, Jake. I've tried hard not to, but I can't help it. I didn't want to fall in love, but you weren't the only one that fell. I fell hard. And you want to know what's been on my mind lately? Well, this is my first job with the park service. I was afraid of a relationship because I was afraid of losing my career. I had it all planned out, and love didn't fit into that plan. But you know what? I was making the plans and not allowing God to lead me in His plan for my life."

She paused and looked into his eyes, stroking his cheek with her soft fingertips. "I know great-grandpa Murphey would be happy that I'm a park ranger, but he found love in the park. I'm sure he'd be happy that I have too."

He caught her gently caressing fingers in his own and brought them back to his lips. Then with a moan he pulled her into his arms, laying his lips on hers, first cautiously then deepening into a kiss that expressed more than words ever could. Releasing her, he cupped her face between his palms, resting his forehead against hers. His love was laid out plain for her to see.

Molly flashed a teasing smile. "You know, I ran into your girlfriend last Thursday. She told me to stay away from you."

"My girlfriend?" Jake looked puzzled at her words.

"I ran into Celeste when I was at HQ. She warned me away."

Jake snorted and drew Molly close. "I can't ever have you thinking she was my girlfriend. She never meant anything to me, Molly. I avoided her like Typhoid Mary, but unfortunately she'd always find out when I was at HQ, and she'd seek me out."

Molly smiled happily, snuggling into his embrace. "I know, Jake. Although the day she came to Twentymile I wasn't so sure."

"Don't I know it," he replied with a rueful grimace. "And when I came up to the bunkhouse to talk it out with you, my mom shows up. Perfect timing, huh? Then before another opportunity presented itself, you left."

"I had a lot to think about." Molly glanced down at her hands resting against his broad chest.

"I know that now. And I know you want a career, so why can't we share that career? After all, we are in the same profession. Will you marry me, Molly? I can't envision a future without you in it in every way. I want to be there to share the problems and uncertainties. And I want to share the joys and passion for life that being with you brings." Reaching into his pants pocket, he pulled out a small burgundy velvet case and opened it for her to see. "Will you wear this ring, Molly? Will you be my wife?

~

He couldn't prevent a niggle of apprehension as Molly glanced from the case to him and back again. She removed the gold and diamond circlet displayed in the case and held it between her fingers. "It's beautiful, Jake," she breathed an awed whisper then she looked back into his dear face. "But when did you…?"

"The day you left Twentymile. You left so quickly and without warning I was devastated. Everything seemed so empty with you gone, even with Mom still there. So after work I drove to Asheville and found a jewelry store. I saw this one and it looked perfect for you. I knew how much I loved you, so I decided to just hang onto it until I could find the right time to ask you. It may not fit–I had to guess at the size–but we'll have it sized later."

Pausing momentarily, he stood up and walked across the room, raking his hand anxiously through his hair. He had to have some space between them. She said she loved him, but would she marry him or would she reject him for her career.

"Well, Molly, will you marry me?" His voice came out hoarse as he thrust his hands deep into his pockets.

A smile curving her lips, Molly's eyes shone with love and his heart leapt.

"Yes. Yes, I will, Jake. But you have to come back over here and put this on my finger," she said softly, indicating the gold ring.

Jake released the pent-up breath he hadn't realized he'd been holding as he awaited her answer, then caught it again at the love shining in her eyes. He reached down, scooped her into his arms, pulled her close and kissed her tenderly. His hand found the clip holding her still damp hair and released it. He ran his fingers through the silken strands, breathing in the fragrance of it. After a bit, he drew back, and taking the ring, slid it onto her finger. A little loose, but they'd deal with that later.

Then looking deep into her eyes, he spoke clearly so there'd be no misunderstanding. "Sweetheart, I want you to know that whatever the Lord wants you to do about working in the park service, I'll support you one hundred percent. Even if that means following your desire for your great-grandpa Murphy's memory. If we both apply to a park but only one gets a position, then we won't go. I won't go to a job where you can't work with me, and I don't want you to go without me."

Molly placed a gentle finger against his lips to silence him. "Jake, I'll go with you no matter what or no matter where. And if it means I don't stay with the park service then that's fine. I think great-grandpa would understand. He was a family man himself, remember? Besides, there are other things I could do, you know."

She smiled shyly, dropping her gaze.

His brow furrowed. "Oh, yeah? Like what, Sweetheart?"

"Mmmmm. I like the sound of that." Molly's lips curved into a gentle smile. "I wouldn't mind trying my hand at motherhood."

Jake's heartstrings strummed as the light in her eyes sent a thrill through him.

She caught her lip between her teeth. "Do you think you could handle being a father? Someday?"

Jake remembered the day at his parent's farm when Molly held Shelly's baby. He'd thought then how natural she looked holding the infant and how his heart overflowed with love for her. She'd be a great mother.

"In a heartbeat." He whispered softly as he drew her close.

~

Later that evening as the sun descended behind the mountains, Jake left for Twentymile and Molly ventured downstairs to share her wonderful news with her landlady. As usual she was out in the garden, plucking green beans and tomatoes from their vines.

"Oh my!" Molly exclaimed. "You've got some big tomatoes there. How do you grow them so big?"

Selma Jenkins chuckled then turned back to place the tomatoes in her basket. "A lot of hard work and love, sweetie. Mostly hard work, but I love it. I grew up working in my folk's garden, and I suppose you could say that's all I know to do."

"Well, I have some news I wanted to share with you. Do you have a few minutes?" Molly thought her news would burst out without waiting for her, but she tamped it down.

"Why certainly I do. Let's go around and sit a spell on the front porch. I do love this time of evening when the sun's going down and the lightening bugs come out. Did you ever catch 'em when you were young? We did. Every night we'd be out with a jar. But before we headed inside to bed, we'd let 'em go so they'd be there to catch again the next night."

As they strolled around to the front porch and settled in the rocking chairs, Mrs. Jenkins added, "Hmmm, listen to those crickets. Can't stand the pesky creatures, but I do love the song they sing in the evening." She glanced over at Molly. "So what are you smiling about? Something to do with your news? What'd you want to tell me?"

The words crowded into Molly's throat vying for escape, so instead she simply held out her hand, displaying the gorgeous diamond ring.

Mrs. Jenkins eyes grew round and huge. "Oh, my lands! That's an engagement ring, Molly, dear. Where'd you ge…." She stopped herself as realization dawned on her. "Did that young man, Jake, give that to you?"

Molly nodded. "Yes. With the loveliest proposal you could ever imagine."

Mrs. Jenkins took her hand and examined the ring in the fading light. "These old eyes don't see so well in the daylight, but they see terrible in the gathering darkness. Can I take a better look when we go inside?"

"Certainly, you can."

"Oh my, but he's a keeper, dear. Reminds me of my dear departed husband. He was a wonderful man. And Jake seems just like him. I can tell he loves you. That's why it didn't take long for me to figure out where you got that."

She nodded toward Molly's hand. "We got to talking while he was here fixing my sink. He loves the Lord too. Have you set a date?"

"No, not yet."

"Well, don't wait too long. No time like the present, I always say. You're both young but you don't want to wait to begin your life together."

"I doubt we'll wait long."

Mrs. Jenkins lifted herself out of the rocker and pointed a finger in Molly's direction. "Good. You want to enjoy those babies while you're young, you know."

Then the landlady headed for the screen door, leaving Molly to pick her chin up off the floor.

Chapter Sixteen

Molly almost floated into work Monday morning. Kate stood at the counter as Molly walked in, her eagle eyes zeroing in on the gold and diamond circlet on Molly's left hand.

Hurrying around the counter, she squealed with delight. "Oh, Molly! Did Jake propose to you?"

A huge smile split Molly's face. "Yep! He sure did!"

Kate squealed again and grabbed her in a big hug. Cal came around the partition to see what all the commotion was about.

"Well, congratulations, girl," he said in his quiet voice after Kate explained. "He's a fine man. You've got the best. And Pam'll be tickled pink. Now I can tell her she doesn't have to worry about playing matchmaker."

"What?" asked Molly, surprised.

"You betcha! She had it all planned out. Was going to fix you and Jake up herself, but I guess you two beat her to the punch. She'll be really happy to hear about this." After a moment he added, "On a more serious note, come on back. I've got news for you."

Cal explained there was to be an organizational meeting at the Oconoluftee conference room at one this afternoon. Everyone that was participating in any way with the stakeout would be there as well as Tom Cramer and Ed Clark.

"You can ride over with me, but don't mention it to anyone, and I mean anyone. If you run into Bill Hopper or Frank Raven, mum's the word."

"No problem," Molly agreed.

~

The Oconoluftee conference room was filling with rangers and pertinent park personnel when Cal and Molly arrived. Glancing around the room, Molly spotted Jake. He'd already scoped out her and Cal's entrance and was making his way across the room toward them. After greeting Cal, he snagged Molly's hand and guided her to a pair of vacant chairs near the middle of the room. Without concern that they were hardly alone, he leaned over and planted a tender kiss on her lips.

"Hi," he whispered. "How are you?"

"Wonderful." She whispered back. "Cal said I'm floating like a tube down Deep Creek.

Jake's mouth slipped into a crooked grin. "Kind of feel that way myself."

Nearly forty-five rangers from all over the park had gathered, both from all the backcountry stations as well as from the various campgrounds. It grew quiet as park superintendent Tom Cramer took the podium at the front of the room.

"First, I want to thank all of you for coming today. This is the largest stakeout this park has ever had. When your supervisors approached each of you about participating you must've wondered what the outcome will be. We certainly don't know that, but with a group this large, we can make a consolidated effort to stop these poachers who are plaguing the park. We can't stop them all with one stakeout. The park's a big place, and we're only concentrating on one major area, but hopefully word will spread and they'll get the message."

Turning to Ed Clark who sat behind him, Tom added, "Ed, let's get started. Time is of the essence."

"That's right, Tom." Ed Clark replaced Tom at the podium. Accessing a laptop on a small table beside the podium, he turned on an audiovisual large screen projector, and a map of the Fontana Lake area appeared on a screen on the wall. With a laser pointer he indicated the marks where rangers would be stationed during the stakeout. "As your supervisors have probably told you, Fontana Lake is a major problem area because poachers can easily cross the lake and enter the park. However, with forty-five rangers participating, we should be able to concentrate in that area successfully.

"Let me warn you concerning the nature of poaching in this area. Until recently it's been generally for one reason: to provide food for families at the park's expense. However, within the last few months the type of poaching has become more malicious and some of our rangers have been shot at. We surmise there may be a less obvious reason."

Ed paused to let his words sink in. A growing murmur spread across the room before quieting down again. Molly's gaze dropped to her lap then she felt the gentle squeeze of her hand. Glancing up, she caught Jake's wink. In spite of the memory of that awful night, she couldn't hold back a small grin.

Ed continued. "These poachers have left several grisly reminders that they're out there, and they want us to leave them alone. Well, that isn't going to happen."

The laser pointer was again directed at the map. "Two ranger patrol boats are always docked at the Fontana Lake marina and we've been granted the use of twenty more. Over the next three nights some of you will help dock those boats in strategic places along the lakeside opposite the park boundary. The stakeout will begin Thursday evening."

He went on to explain how and where each ranger would be stationed and how the stakeout would proceed.

"We've made up a list of code words to be used on the radio specific to this stakeout. Except when absolutely necessary there will be radio silence. Texting will be used to stay in touch."

Ed handed a stack of papers to an assistant. "These are your individual assignments with the co-ordinates for your assigned locations and a list of the radio codes. Parker, here, will call out your names. Raise your hand and he'll give you your assignment. And I can't stress enough that the success of this endeavor requires that no one, and I repeat no one, outside this room can know what we're doing."

A low murmur circulated the room as names were called and assignments given.

Molly whispered to Jake. "Have you ever participated in anything like this before?"

Jake squeezed her hand again. "Yeah, but not on this level. I'm not sure anyone here has. Hey, don't worry. It's all been well planned, and hopefully, well secured." He raised his hand as his name was called. Accepting the papers, he glanced through them.

"Well, what's your assignment?" Molly whispered.

"Looks like I'll be staking out Hazel Creek. Remember I told you about the cabin we maintain across the lake? I'll be in that area."

"Here, Molly. Here's your assignment," Cal's low voice came from right behind her. She accepted the papers, wondering why Cal was handing her the assignment instead of Ed's assistant. As she perused the page, disappointment crept over her.

"Well, what does it say?" Jake asked.

"I'll be manning the Twentymile station. Issuing backcountry permits, feeding the horses and staying near the radio." She despised the disappointment that crept into her own voice, but she couldn't help it. The prospect of participating in the stakeout had filled her with anticipation but now that fizzled away.

Jake's fingers tipped her head back so he could see her eyes. "Hey, beautiful, don't be disappointed. No matter what your job is in a stakeout, it's important. The support group, and you aren't alone in it, is just as important as the stakeout team. Without them, the stakeout team wouldn't be able to function. Cheer up, Sweetheart. I'm glad you'll be at Twentymile instead of Deep Creek. When I come in for a bit of sleep or supplies, I'll find you there waiting for me." Draping his arm along her shoulders, he gave her a squeeze. "If you were on the stakeout, I might not see you for days."

"Well, if you can see the bright side, I suppose I can too." A wry smile lifted one corner of her lips.

"Break it up you two lovebirds. Behave yourselves." Cal whispered loudly as he slapped Jake on the shoulder. "Congratulations, buddy! You've got good taste. I can hear those wedding bells ringing already."

Ed Clark returned to the podium and the room grew silent again. He fielded questions from the group, making sure everyone understood the plan. Before adjourning the meeting, a smile crossed his normally serious face and his eyes locked on Jake and Molly.

"Before you go, folks, I just want to announce that two of our rangers have decided to get hitched. Jake Stuart and Molly Walker are taking the big step. Let's give 'em a hand."

Warmth flooded Molly's cheeks as a resounding chorus of wolf whistles and applause filled the room. Jake's arm that lay across the back of her chair gave her another squeeze. When her gaze met his smiling eyes, embarrassment fled and she was reassured. He'd always be there for her, and she for him. Not a doubt in her mind!

~

As the meeting adjourned, Jake and Molly strolled outside to wait for Cal while he talked with Tom and Ed. Several times they were stopped for a quick congratulation or a commiseration for her and a slap on the shoulder for him. As they strolled toward the Deep Creek SUV, Jake spotted David Andrews climbing out of his car and heading in their direction.

"Afternoon, Molly. Jake." His curious glance took in the various rangers as they left the building or climbed into vehicles. "What's going on? A party? Gee, and I wasn't invited."

"Afternoon, Dave." Jake replied, more amiably than he felt. He'd never cared for the program interpreter, and he couldn't put a finger on a reason why. His gut told him there was just something about the guy. Bad vibes? It seemed silly when he thought of it that way. "No, no party. Just one of those meetings the rangers have occasionally. You know, to pass on pertinent information concerning the district."

David nodded. "I see. Anything I should know?"

"I'm sure your supervisor will pass on anything he thinks is necessary." Jake gave a casual shoulder shrug in spite of the hairs standing up on the back of his neck.

"Right," agreed David. "I'm sure he will."

~

Molly had a funny feeling David didn't really agree. He turned to her suddenly with a charming smile. "You know, Molly, I've been planning to give you a call and ask you out to dinner. I know you were at Twentymile for a while, but now that you're back, we should get together sometime soon."

Molly smiled back, attempting to exhibit her own charm. "Oh, I'm sorry, David, but that won't be possible. Not anymore. You see, I've just become engaged."

Holding out her left hand, she displayed the diamond ring.

The urge to laugh out loud filled her. David looked like he'd swallowed his tongue. He quickly recovered from his surprise, drawing a smile across his handsome face.

"Oh, really? Well, that's…that's wonderful news!" he oozed more of that Hollywood charm. "And who's the lucky guy that beat me to the punch? You, Jake?"

"That's right. I'm the lucky guy," Jake placed a possessive arm around Molly's shoulders. "She's graciously consented to become my wife."

"When's the big day?"

"We haven't decided yet," Molly grinned. "It only happened yesterday."

"That's my luck," David replied with a wry smile that Molly didn't believe for a second. "The proverbial day late and all that stuff. Well, I've got to be going. Again, congratulations."

David ambled back to his car and climbed in. With a careless wave, he was gone.

"That was one of the fakest conversations I've ever been a part of," Molly observed in a whisper.

"Yeah," Jake nodded. "And did you notice he didn't finish whatever business he had here? He came from his car and afterward went right back to it. Strange, wouldn't you say?"

~

"Well, what else ya got for us, my friend?" Willy Cahill asked, pushing his hunting cap back on his head. Leaning into the car's open window he placed his face closer to the man inside. In spite of the darkness surrounding the car, there was enough light from the dashboard lights for the man inside to see his expression. "I sure hope you're leveling with us. Because if you ain't, you know what could happen, right?"

"Yeah, I know," the man in the car replied quietly. "But I need the money by tomorrow night. I've got to have it."

Urgency laced his words as he thrust a nervous hand through his hair.

"Now don't you worry none. We're your friends, ain't we? We'll take care o' you." Willy leaned to the side to spit on the ground and then pinned the man with a dark look. "You do your part, and we'll do ours. Pretty simple if you ask me."

He paused before asking, "Is there anything else?"

"That's all I know," came the agitated reply.

"Well, maybe we can use it to our mutual benefit, huh? I reckon if she's going to be getting married maybe she'll let her guard down. You just keep your eyes and ears open. And I'll have that money to you by afternoon."

As he straightened up, the man in the car sped off in a cloud of dust. Staring after the car, Willy watched the taillights become mere specks in the darkness.

"Chump," he chuckled. "Yeah, we'll do our part."

~

Jake sat on the corner of Cal's desk. Cal leaned back, feet propped up and hands clasped behind his head. Molly sat in the chair beside the desk.

"Still nothing on Willy Cahill?" asked Jake.

"Absolutely nothing." Cal shook his head, heaving a sigh. "His wife claims he's away visiting relatives, but she wasn't convincing. More likely she's covering for him."

"How about his buddy, Ray Smith?" Molly asked. "Anyone seen him around?"

"I'm afraid not." Cal sighed heavily, dropping his feet to the floor and leaning his elbows on the desk. "It's like they've vanished."

"When they heard you wanted to question them concerning the shooting, they probably went into hiding, which tells me they must've had something to do with it." Jake rose and walked over to the window, gazing out past the mini blinds.

"You and I both know that isn't enough to get them into a courtroom, Jake. They'll find an alibi if they have to fabricate one." Cal picked up a pen, twirling it between his fingers. "I warned Jamie Mitchell not to say anything to them, and I doubt he has. He was pretty scared after I talked with him, but I'm worried he'll skip town too. Then there goes our valuable link." He looked at Molly. "And I'm a little concerned about you too, Molly."

"Me?" she asked, puzzled. "Why me?"

"Those fellows weren't too happy when they found themselves in jail and you were the one who put them there. Strike one, a park ranger and strike two, a female park ranger. Sort of went against the grain, if you know what I mean."

"Yes, I know what you mean, but I don't know why that should worry you."

"These fellows are known for holding grudges and getting even," he explained. "I don't like not knowing where they are and what they're up to."

"My sentiments exactly." Jake turned from the window and thrust his hands into his pockets. "Who's to say it wasn't you they were aiming at the night of the shooting? Maybe they were attempting to exact vengeance for your arrest. After all, it cost them a lot of money for the amount of bail that was set."

"Jake," Molly chuckled. "Let's not get carried away here. How would they have known I'd be there? Although Jenny was there, Jamie certainly didn't know she would be. If he had, I doubt very seriously he'd have loaned them his truck. No. More likely it was a drive-by-warning to stop harassing them about poaching. That certainly seems to be the purpose of the hanging deer. I don't doubt for a minute they're probably involved in the poaching. I mean, it stands to reason. But me? I think they have bigger fish to fry than to worry about me."

"I wouldn't be too certain," advised Cal. "Just promise you'll watch your back. With this stakeout coming up, Jake and I won't be around to do it for you."

Molly smiled first at Cal then at Jake. "Don't worry, guys. I promise to watch my back."

"Now, why don't I feel reassured?" Jake glowered.

"Well, here's another interesting bit of information." Cal switched subjects. "I have an FBI buddy in Washington, DC and I had him run a check on Bill Hopper and Frank Raven. Frank's background is pretty clean. He grew up on the Cherokee res and has stayed out of trouble for the most part. No major infractions. He lives with his wife and his mother-in-law.

"He hunts up in the mountains, but there's no proof he hunts in the park. With the reservation backed up against the park boundary and the Blue Ridge Parkway, it'd be easy enough to do."

"And what about Bill Hopper?" asked Jake.

A sly smile tilted the corners of Cal's mouth. "Well now, that's the really interesting part. You see, Bill had a younger sister that left here years ago when she was teenager. She'd gotten in the family way and was sent to live with a distant relative in western Kentucky. She never returned. But her son did. And you'll never guess who that is."

"Who?" Molly moved to the edge of her seat.

"David Andrews." Cal waited for that information to sink in.

Jake retook his seat on the corner of Cal's desk. "You mean to say that David Andrews is Bill Hopper's nephew?"

"The very same." Cal nodded. "He went to college and began teaching. Bill helped him get into the park service several years ago. But here's the real kicker. He returned to be near his dear old uncle to get financial help. Apparently David's something of a gambler. His luck hasn't been too good lately. Huge gambling debts."

"That's interesting," Jake agreed. "I knew there was something about him I didn't like from the get-go, but I never knew why."

"And what about Bill?" Molly asked. "Anything about poaching?"

"Like most mountain folks, he's a big hunter. But *unlike* most of them, he's been known to hunt in the park. He's never been caught, but he likes to brag. There are folks who say he has too. However, without further proof, it's his word against theirs. He's lived here his whole life, and knows these mountains well. His grandfather owned property here before the park was established. When the government came with money in hand, he sold out, picked up his family and moved out. Bill's dad thought his father was cheated out of what should rightly have come to him. He transferred that bitterness onto the park, choosing to believe the park forced them out. He passed that bitterness on to Bill, who picked it up and ran with it."

"But he's a park employee," replied Molly. "Why work for an organization you hate?"

"What better way to get back at them than to become a loyal and trusted employee," reasoned Jake, his expression wry. "I wouldn't put it past him to hunt while he's up in the backcountry on maintenance jobs."

"Exactly," agreed Cal, "but at this point it's all still conjecture. Let's not get off on a rabbit trail here. Let's try and keep our focus on this stakeout."

~

Later that afternoon Molly returned to the station after patrolling the campground. When she walked inside, she found Kate sitting with elbows on the countertop, chin resting in her palms and a contemplative expression on her face.

"What deep and mysterious thoughts are passing through that head of yours?" Molly teased. "You look like you're a couple hundred miles away."

Something was on the younger woman's mind. She wasn't her usual bubbly and cheerful self.

A wry smile lifted one corner of Kate's mouth. "Well, maybe not that far away, but I'm certainly not here today. My body may be but my mind isn't."

Molly pulled up a chair from the desk. "Ok. Spill it. What's on your mind?"

Kate shook her head, gazing at her clasped fingers. "I don't know. I suppose I'm just feeling uncertain about some things."

"Like about Craig maybe?" Molly probed kindly.

Kate nodded. "Yeah, I guess so." Then she shook her head again. "Oh, I don't know, Molly. I'm so confused, I don't know anything anymore."

"Why don't you start at the beginning and tell me about it."

"Well, since you made me aware of Craig's feelings for me, I've really grown to care for him. We've enjoyed the time we've spent together, and I thought maybe our relationship would grow."

"Well, isn't it?"

"Yes, but now what? Here we are in August, and we'll both be heading back to college in a couple weeks. In opposite directions. And we won't see each other for who knows how long."

"I'm sure you've heard of that new invention called the cell phone," chuckled Molly. "You can call each other anytime. Then there are holidays when you can visit. It can work if you both really want it to.

"Is that it, Kate?" Molly lifted an eyebrow in question. Do you want it to?"

"Of course I do, but things are just so uncertain. What if it doesn't work out? What if he goes back to college and meets someone else? I'm not sure I could handle that."

Kate's pleading gaze plucked at Molly's heart.

"You know, Kate, I've recently been going through some doubts and uncertainties of my own. I've just graduated from college, and now I'm on my way to a good start in my career. Then I met Jake and fell in love with him. I didn't want to and even tried not to. It wasn't in my plans. But I found he loves me. And even now I'm not sure how the future will work out, but I know it will."

"But how? How do you know that? What's your assurance?"

A smile lit Molly's face. "Because I've put my trust in God, and He has my best interests at heart. No matter what doubts and uncertainties I face, He's my stronghold, my rock and the foundation of my faith. The Bible compares our faith to a house that's built on a solid foundation. Storms come and winds blow, but because it's built on that strong foundation, that house cannot fall. When I'm faced with hardships or difficulties, and I can't see a way through, my faith in God helps me weather the storms. He gives me peace here." She patted the area over her heart.

Kate nodded. "I can see that peace in your eyes, but I don't understand it. You say it comes from God. But how?"

"True peace only comes in knowing God and having a close relationship with Him. And the only way to know Him is through Jesus Christ His Son."

"I remember hearing that in Sunday School when I was a child, but my parents never attended church. I went with a neighbor girl I hung around with, but after a while I stopped going. I became too wrapped up in other things, and since my folks didn't go, I didn't either. But I don't know what to do, Molly. I need that reassurance you have. I've always believed there was a God and thought that was enough. I thought if I stayed out of trouble and kept my nose clean, everything would be okay. But sometimes I feel so alone, and I can't handle it anymore. How do I know God?"

Molly had always perceived Kate as a self-assured and bubbly person, never giving any indication she was troubled and lonely. Reaching over, she placed a gentle hand on her arm. "Oh, Kate. You don't have to feel that way, and you don't have to carry your burdens by yourself. God's shoulders are a lot bigger and stronger than ours are, and He's just waiting for you to ask Him to take your burdens. He wants a close relationship with you, and He cares about everything you face.

Molly stood and moved to lean on the counter next to Kate. "People often have the idea that God sits up in heaven and looks down on the happenings here on earth much like we do when we look down and see ants crawling around in the dust. But He isn't that way. That's why he created people: to have a close relationship with them. When Adam and Eve sinned in the Garden of Eden, that broke the fellowship between them and God. Every person after that was born into a sinful world with a sinful nature. The Bible tells us the penalty for sin is death. Eternal separation from God. But God still wanted that close relationship He created us for, so He sent His Son, Jesus Christ, to come down in a human body and take our place in death. When He died on the cross, He took on Himself the sins of the whole world, from Adam to everyone born after that."

"But why would He do that?"

"Because He loved us so much that He was willing to sacrifice His Son for us." Molly's smile broadened. "You can have this same peace for yourself. He holds it out for all to take. No strings attached. If I had a present for you and held it out for you to take, all you'd have to do is reach out and take it. It'd be yours. That's what God has done. He holds out the gift of salvation, and all we have to do is accept it. Jesus paid the price for that gift long ago when He died on the cross."

Kate remained thoughtful. "You said Jesus was the only one who could pay the price. Why?"

"Because He was perfect and sinless. Everyone who was ever born was born sinful. But not Jesus. And the most wonderful thing of all was His resurrection. He defeated death and rose again. If we die, we go into eternity, either to heaven or to hell, but because of His sinless sacrifice, He holds out the gift of everlasting life, just as He has. Not only do we gain His peace in our lives, one day we'll spend eternity with Him. We don't have to face eternal punishment for our sins."

"How do you know all this, Molly? What if it's all just another religion? The world is full of them."

"Faith. I have the faith to believe it's true. Look around at the religions of the world. They all require their followers do something to gain entrance into heaven. It's all based on what you have to *do* to work your way in. God took care of that for us through His Son. He just wants you to accept Christ's payment for your sins and have the relationship with Him that He's planned from the beginning."

"I don't know, Molly. It sounds so amazing but a bit overwhelming. I suppose it's something to think about."

"Please do, Kate. May I pray for you that you'll make the right decision?"

"Sure. That would be....comforting, I think, knowing that you're praying for me." She flashed an awkward smile. "Thanks, Molly. I don't know yet what I'm going to do, but thanks for listening and for answering my questions."

"Ask anything, anytime. I'll be happy to help. And if I don't know the answer, I'll help you find it. But remember, I'll be praying."

Chapter Seventeen

Molly, I don't like the idea of you staying out at Twentymile by yourself during the stakeout." Jake called Molly after work Tuesday evening.

"I know you care, Jake, and I appreciate that more than I can say," she replied, "but I'm not sure what we can do about it. That's my job during the stakeout. And besides, I'm not thrilled about you being out in the woods with poachers running around."

He chuckled. "Touché, Sweetheart. But do something for me, and realize that it won't be the best solution, but I'll feel a little better about leaving you out there."

"What's that?"

"Give Jenny a call. Ask her to come spend a few nights with you. Just tell her I'm away for a few days and you're there to cover the station for me. You can't tell her about the stakeout, of course, but you can tell her you'd like some company."

"That might work," she agreed. "Summer school is over and regular classes won't start for another couple of weeks so she won't have to contend with work. Let's just hope she doesn't have any other commitments."

A pause ensued from Jake's side of the conversation. "Jake? You still there?"

"Yeah, I'm here."

"Is something wrong?" Her concern grew.

"No, Sweetheart. Not at all. I was just thinking what a lucky man I am to have found you." The huskiness in his voice brought warmth to her heart. And to her cheeks. "I love you, Molly, and I plan to spend the rest of my life showing you just how much."

Heart soaring at his words, her eyes grew misty. "No luck involved, Darling. I'd say God had a plan for us all along."

~

"Well, Bill, What'd ya hear?" Willy Cahill asked the man sitting across from him. They were meeting in Bill's old, secluded hunting cabin out in the Nantahala National Forest. Willy and Ray had been hiding out there since Willy's wife told him Cal was looking for him.

Bill Hopper tilted his chair onto its back legs. With a long draw on his cigarette, he blew smoke into the air, watching as it spread out and dissipated. "Well, now," he began his slow reply. "I think I've some news you just might want to hear."

"Yeah? Like what?" Curiosity lit Ray's face as he straddled an old wobbly straight back chair, arms folded along the back.

"It seems our little pigeon's going to be out at Twentymile for a few days. Stuart's heading out of town, and she's moving back down there to run things while he's gone. Seems like things might play into your hands just like you wanted 'em to. She'll be out there all by her lonesome, with no one to holler to for help."

"And where'd you hear that?" Suspicion narrowed Willy's eyes. "How do you know it's true?"

"I heard Cal telling her Stuart's going away and she needs to get down there and take care o' things while he's gone." Bill chuckled. "They didn't know I was there. I'd come up behind the maintenance shed just as they were walking by."

"Well, that's good. Real good." Willy flashed a wicked grin. "I can't wait to see her trussed up like a turkey with her hands tied behind her back, just like when she handcuffed us and threw us in jail. And I want to see fear in her eyes. I want her to know what it feels like."

"Yeah," agreed Ray with a hearty nod.

"But first," Willy continued, "we're goin' hunting while Stuart's away. We'll set up camp over on Hazel Creek, but we don't want to get too close to that cabin the rangers keep up over there. We'll camp up in the woods beyond it, out of sight of the lake where we've got lots of room to hunt in."

"You coming hunting with us, Bill?" Ray asked, hand waving in the smoky air.

"Maybe so." Bill blew another stream of smoke. "When ya going?"

"How about Saturday night?"

"Ok," he nodded with a shrug. "Then we can take care of our little pigeon Sunday night. I think Stuart'll be gone for about a week from what I heard Cal say."

"Won't they get suspicious when she don't show up for work Monday morning?" A quizzical expression twisted Ray's features.

"Oh, she'll show up," said Willy with a wicked chuckle. "Don't you worry none. She'll show up."

~

"Jenny, its Molly. How are you?" With cellphone to her ear, Molly opened the door to her apartment and tossed her daypack onto a chair then threw herself onto the couch.

"Oh, I'm fine." Molly detected the smile in Jenny's voice. "I saw you in the crowd at church on Sunday but when I looked for you after the service, you'd disappeared."

"Sorry about that," Molly apologized. "I kind of got whisked away before I could speak to you.

"Oh? By whom?" Jenny laughed as her sarcasm dripped through the phone.

"Jake. He invited me for a picnic at Deep Creek and then we went tubing."

"How fun! Did you like it? Have you ever been tubing before?"

"No, never, but it was a lot of fun. The only thing I'd change would be the temperature of the water. It was freezing!"

Jenny chuckled. "Yeah, it is. But by the time you're finished tubing, you're so numb you can't feel anything anyway. So you had a good time?"

"Yes, we did. And I have something else to tell you." She paused for effect.

"Ok," Jenny said. "So, what is it?"

"Jake proposed to me."

A loud gasp that threatened to suck the air from the room was followed by a squeal. "Oh, Molly, I'm so happy for you both. When I was at Twentymile I could tell he was in love with you. It was in his eyes every time he looked at you." A dramatic sigh filled Molly's ear. "How romantic! Isn't love wonderful? But then how would I know? I've never been in love."

Molly chuckled. "The right man will come along someday, Jenny. You just wait and see."

"Maybe. Anyway, when's the wedding?"

"We haven't gotten that far yet." Molly paused before continuing. "Jenny, look, the reason I called is that I have a favor to ask of you."

"Sure. You know I'll be happy to do it if I can."

"Thanks, Jenny. Jake's going away for a few days, and I have to head back down to Twentymile while he's gone. I'd love some company or it's going to get awfully lonely out there. Could you pull yourself away from your schedule and come stay with me? I'd have to be away part of each day, but most of the time I'll be around. We can visit in the evenings and on the weekend. Maybe even get in a good hike or two. What do you say?"

"As for my schedule, I'm not overly booked for dates or anything, so…sure. That'd be no problem. I'd love to. I need to do some reading and lesson planning before school starts, and I can do that while you're working. Anything I can bring? How about I help with groceries? What do you like besides Italian?"

"Anything will do, but don't get a lot. It'll just be the two of us, you know."

"Okay. When are you heading out?"

"Thursday morning, so if you want to show up sometime in the late afternoon we can prepare supper, eat and watch a good movie."

"Sounds like a plan. It's going to be fun." Jenny chuckled. "See you Thursday."

~

Molly parked her car beside Jake's pickup truck behind Twentymile Ranger Station. Climbing out, she gazed around. Where was Jake? As she'd driven past the front of the station she noticed the "Time of Return" clock was on the wall by the door. The office was closed. She stood for a minute soaking in the peacefulness that always surrounded this place. The creek, with its constant melodious sounds as it tripped over rocks was always soothing. On her last visit she'd determined to one day grab a lounge chair and a good book and park it under the shade trees by the creek. Maybe there'd be time during this stay, but somehow she doubted it.

Closing her eyes, she leaned her head back and propped herself against the side of the car. Oh, it was so peaceful here! The birds were singing like there was no tomorrow, and the light breeze rustled through the trees. The only sounds were those made by nature, and she reveled in it.

"Do you know how beautiful you look standing like that, your face turned up to the sun like a flower seeking sunshine?" Jake's voice asked from beside her. Molly started, surprised to find him leaning against the car beside her.

"Oh, Jake! You startled me! I never heard you come up!"

"Must be that Cherokee blood running through my veins." Chuckling, he pulled her into his arms. Lowering his head, he placed a tender kiss on her lips. "I've missed you. I know it's only been four days, but that's a long time when you're away from the one you love."

"Don't I know it!" Molly nodded in hearty agreement. "How have you been?" Reaching up, she stroked the hair back from his forehead.

"Lonely." He heaved a dramatic sigh. Then his eyes grew serious as he added in husky tones. "I can't wait to marry you, Molly." He slid his hand beneath her ponytail and tugged her closer for another kiss. This one curled Molly's toes. Her heart raced, threatening to burst with the love she felt for this man.

~

Jake slowly lifted his head, drawing in a deep breath. Yep. He slammed the brakes on the yearning Molly stirred within him. What he felt was reflected in her own eyes. They'd have to set a date soon.

Grasping her hand he led her into the station office and leaned a thigh against the corner of the desk. "We need to go over some things before I head out. You know the routine here, and I want you to stick with it as much as possible. Since radio silence is to be maintained except when absolutely necessary, you won't have to monitor the radio constantly, but keep your ears open and use it as you normally would. We know the poachers monitor our radios and they'll grow suspicious if they're not hearing the normal chatter."

"When will everyone be in position?"

"Most everyone should've moved into position during the night.

I wanted to hang around until you got here and make sure you're settled okay. Did you get hold of Jenny?"

Molly nodded. "She'll arrive sometime late this afternoon."

"Great."

"What time are you heading out?"

"In a few minutes. I'm going to drive down to Dean's Marina at the other end of the lake and park my truck. I have a couple of fake magnetic business signs for the doors. No one will be the wiser. I need you to take the ranger boat from Fontana Marina and ride over to meet me. You'll take me across to Hazel Creek. My stakeout partner, Eddie Hayes, from Cades' Cove should already be there. After you drop me off, head back to Fontana and park the boat. It should look like a routine patrol to anyone monitoring your movements. And we know they do."

Molly looked thoughtful. "Won't they see you in the boat and suspect something? Since you're supposed to be out of town?"

"There's an old tarp in the back of the boat. I'll duck under it until you pull into Hazel Creek, then when I get out you take your time and meander the lake boundary on your way back to Fontana. That'll reinforce the notion that you're on patrol." Picking up a map from the desk, he held it for her to see. "Here's the route to Dean's Marina. Don't go all the way in. There's a hidden cove here." He stabbed the map with his finger. "I'll be waiting for you there. That way no one at the marina sees me get into the park boat."

"Wow! Covert to the max," exclaimed Molly with a laugh. "Ok, Skipper, I'm ready."

~

Locking up the station, Jake hurried to his pickup where he'd already loaded his backpack with supplies. Molly climbed into the park Jeep and away they went, each in the same direction until the road split toward Fontana Dam. Molly blew a kiss in Jake's direction before following the road to the marina.

After parking the Jeep, Molly grabbed her daypack and strolled over to the dock. A bait and tackle kiosk sat on the floating dock, several rows of boat slips positioned around it. The ranger's patrol boat and the park maintenance boat were docked in two of the slips.

"Hey, Mike!" Molly waved casually to the man behind the

counter of the kiosk. "How's business?"

"Hi there, Molly. Not bad, not bad." Mike laid down the newspaper he'd been perusing. She was always amused when Mike talked. His long walrus mustache covered his mouth, making it appear that his mouth wasn't moving when he talked. "Lots of fishing boats on the lake recently so business is good. How've you been? Life been treatin' you alright?"

"Oh, I certainly can't complain." Molly leaned her forearms on the counter.

"Wouldn't do any good, would it? Nobody'd listen. So where's Jake? He usually comes down every couple o' days to patrol."

"He's away for a few days so I'm filling in for him."

"Well, if you need any help with that boat, you just let me know." Then he added quickly. "Not that I don't think you can handle it, mind you, but I know you don't use it as much as Jake does."

"It's okay. I understand." Molly chuckled. "And thanks for the offer. I may have to take you up on it sometime. See you later."

"See ya." Mike tossed a casual wave and picked up his newspaper.

As Molly stepped aboard the park motorboat, she retrieved the key from her pocket and started the motor. Releasing the mooring ropes from the dock, she settled behind the wheel, reversed the throttle and slowly moved out of the slip. When the boat was well past the entrance to the slip, she eased the throttle forward and moved slowly away from the marina. At the channel entrance, she throttled forward, skimming the boat across the glassy lake. Having fastened the map to a clipboard that was attached to the dash, she glanced at it occasionally, reassuring herself of the correct course. The length of Fontana Lake extended over sixteen and half miles and fingers of tributaries spread out in every direction. Even the tributaries had tributaries. It'd be easy to get lost on this lake and many a fisherman and boater had done just that.

A few pleasure boats and several fishing boats were on the lake. Pulling her binoculars from her daypack, Molly glanced at the occupants, ensuring their activities were benign. Passing a small motorboat, she was delighted to see an elderly man help a young boy land a large-mouth bass. Further on, a water skier maneuvered through a series of acrobatic stunts, never losing his footing in the process.

Thirty minutes later, Molly entered the hidden cove near the entrance to the channel to Dean's Marina. Jake stood leaning against a tree on the bank. Throttling back, she edged the boat to the bank. Jake tossed his backpack in then hopped onboard.

With a quick kiss he then knelt on the floor of the boat. "I see you found me with no problems. Notice anything suspicious as you came east? You weren't followed, were you?" His eyes scanned the entrance to the cove.

"No. I kept watch. Once I thought I'd picked up a tail, so I turned into a tributary. The boat continued on past. I followed for a bit but they headed further east." Molly tugged at his ball cap. "I think you'd better get beneath the tarp."

He laid another quick kiss on her lips. "Yep. As much as I'd rather loiter here with you a while, we need to get going. Eddie's going to wonder where I am."

Grabbing his backpack, he crawled to the back of the boat and tugged the tarp over it and him.

Molly waited for his muffled "Let's go," then she slipped the boat out of the cove and throttled the engine, heading west. At the entrance to the channel leading to Hazel Creek, she inspected the surface of the lake. She passed a boat with two fishermen casting toward shore, and although she kept a close watch on them, they remained where they were. She continued up the channel then turned the boat into a short tributary that led to the Hazel Creek trailhead. She drove the boat up to the edge of the water and cut the engine.

Jake flung off the tarp and grabbed his backpack, tossing it onto the rocky but dry shoreline. He turned to Molly. "Thanks, sweetheart. You did great."

"Thanks. Will you be staying in the ranger cabin?"

"No, it's too risky. If we occupy the cabin, the poachers may come over and figure things out." He pointed up to a ridge part way up the mountain. "We'll be up on that ridge sitting in a camouflaged blind with netting and vegetation. We'll be virtually invisible."

"How will you sleep?" A crease appeared between Molly's brows.

Jake pointed to his backpack on the shore. "Bedroll. Eddie and I will take turns keeping watch and sleeping."

He reached up a gentle finger to smooth away the crease. "Hey, sweetheart, don't worry. We'll be fine. Remember whose hands we're in. And Lord willing, we'll catch these guys and put them where they can't hurt anyone or anything ever again."

Jake tipped her chin up and looked into her eyes. "Are you going to be okay?"

Molly plastered on a smile she wasn't feeling. "I'll be fine, Jake. You just make sure you come back safe and sound. Do you hear?" She touched a finger to his cheek.

Capturing her fingers in his own, he drew them to his lips and kissed them. Then leaning closer, he tenderly kissed her. "Don't worry. I have a lifetime of memories to make with you. I'll be back. And I expect another one of those when I see you."

"I think I can handle that." Molly winked and blew him a kiss.

With a groan he jumped out of the boat, hefted his backpack onto his back and hurried up the trail. Turning at the edge of the woods, he waved and then disappeared into the trees.

When he was gone, an unexpected wave of intense loneliness hit Molly. How silly. They hadn't seen each other for several days before, and she hadn't felt this way. Why now? Because of all the uncertainties of the stakeout, perhaps? She wouldn't be alone. Jenny would be arriving in a couple hours. Which reminded her she needed to get back. She still had things to do. The horses would need care and she still had backcountry permits to assign. Glancing at her watch, she realized she had just about enough time to get back across the lake and drive up to the top of the dam to meet any backpackers who'd be expecting a permit to camp in the backcountry.

Easing the throttle into reverse, Molly slowly turned the boat around then headed back out into the channel and across the lake. She'd just have to stay busy, plain and simple. Yes, she'd miss Jake terribly, but there was work to do, and she had a front to maintain. That was her job. Business as usual. The poachers wouldn't be able to pick up anything from her activities that was for sure. *Oh, Lord, please keep Jake and the other rangers safe during this operation. And help them put a stop to the poachers.*

Chapter Eighteen

Jake and Eddie settled behind their camouflaged blind on the southern boundary of the park overlooking Fontana Lake. All Thursday night, Friday, Friday night and Saturday morning nothing of consequence happened.

Using earbuds while listening to the park radio, they'd noticed even normal radio traffic seemed limited. Rangers were scattered all across the park side lake boundary but texting was kept to a minimum and very little was said concerning the stakeout. Between them, Jake and Eddie talked little, whispering occasionally but mostly texting when necessary. Jake suspected he'd have permanently impaired vision from the constant binocular surveillance. He'd scanned every face in every boat that came anywhere near their area of the lake, but no one approached the shore.

The food supply held up pretty well, but with two more full days to go, it'd run out before the weekend was over. Eddie urged Jake to take the boat he'd hidden near the entrance to Hazel Creek Cove and retrieve supplies. While at the station he could call HQ for information on the stakeout. Eddie had left old clothes and a hat in the boat to discourage recognition when he left the hideout. He handed Jake his truck keys.

"I'll have the rest of this food eaten by the time you get back," he whispered. "So hurry," he added with a grin.

Flicking him a two-fingered salute, Jake ensured his walkie-talkie mic was securely attached to the shoulder clip. "Call if there's a problem. I'll be back as soon as I can." Leaving the cover of the blind, he hurried to the hidden boat down below their hiding place on the ridge. He moved as silently as possible and cautiously approached it. Finding old clothes and a slouch hat, he quickly pulled them on over his uniform, adding his own sunglasses. The motor fired up on the first try and he slipped out into the channel, taking a circuitous route back to the marina. Since Eddie worked on the other side of the mountains, no one would recognize or pay attention to his truck leaving or coming back. Should be simple enough.

While sitting in the woods with nothing to do but watch the lake, Jake had a lot of time to think and pray, both of which he did concerning Molly. His heart hammered at the thought he'd see her again in a short while. Boy had he missed her.

~

Molly had urged Jenny to sleep in as long as she wanted to. There was nothing she had to do this Saturday morning and she could sleep while Molly took care of the horses and cleaned their stalls. Tossing back the covers, Molly got up and dressed in a pair of jeans and a sleeveless chambray button-down shirt. After pulling her hair back into a ponytail and donning her work boots, she sliced up two apples and dropped them into a Ziploc bag then grabbed a banana for herself. The horses would love the apples. While always pleasant, the short hike up to the barn was particularly nice this morning with the breeze rustling the trees in gentle rhythm with the water tripping over rocks in the creek.

The horses approved of their morning snack before receiving their usual hay and oats. While they were eating, Molly mucked out their stalls. Jake was conscientious and kept them cleaned out well, so it didn't take long. She finished by brushing down the horses and picking their hooves. Making their coats glisten was a point of pride with her.

Molly had just finished the second stall and had retrieved the curry comb to groom the horses when she heard a twig snap on the dirt road near the barn. Spinning around she found a stranger standing near the corner of the barn, one shoulder leaning against the rough wood.

Molly's heart surged into her throat then settled somewhere near her stomach. Wracking her brain to think what to do, she remembered her handgun was at the station! What an idiot! Now what? Could she make it to the nearest horse and jump on his back before the man could get to her? So far he'd done nothing threatening. But would that change? She took in his old army boonie hat slouched low over eyes hidden behind dark glasses. He wore an old army field jacket and several days' growth covered his lower face, giving him a rough appearance.

The man reached up and removed the dark glasses, revealing a sapphire blue gaze that no amount of disguise could hide from her.

"Jake?" Molly's heart raced as a grin lifted the corners of his mouth.

"The one and only." Jake smiled, eliciting a relieved sigh from Molly.

The feet that moments before seemed rooted to the ground suddenly became animated as Molly raced to throw her arms around his neck. "Oh, I'm so glad it's you, Jake. I thought some strange man had found his way back here and was watching me, possibly with nefarious intentions."

Jake's arms slipped around her, holding her securely against him. Oh, they felt so good! It had been a long two days.

He pulled back only far enough to look into her eyes. "I guess you missed me a little bit, huh?" His gaze drifted from her eyes to her lips and then his lips followed the same path, lingering to enjoy their sweetness. "Oh, sweetheart, have I missed you!"

Molly leaned her head on his shoulder and settled into the circle of his arms. "How long can you stay?"

"Not long enough, that's for sure." He dropped a kiss onto her brow. He released her and took her hand. "Are you finished here? Can I help with anything?"

Molly shook her head. "No. The only thing left is to groom the boys, and I can do that later. If you don't have much time, let's not waste it on grooming horses."

As they strolled back down toward the station, Jake held onto her hand, swinging it lightly between them. "Eddie sent me back for food supplies. He's about to eat us out of house and blind. He doesn't just sit very well. Seems to always need something to do, and since there isn't much to do, eating is the activity of choice."

Molly laughed. "Is that all that you came back for?"

"Well, that, a few stolen kisses and stakeout news. Heard anything?"

"Not much. There were a couple of poachers picked up on Forney Creek, but not the guys we're specifically looking for. They were caught field dressing a wild boar. In the park, of course."

"Ah. My favorite animal!" A wry smile lifted one corner of Jake's mouth.

"Why don't you call headquarters? With the radio silence mandate in place, you'll have to go to the top. Maybe they can give you more information."

As they approached the back of the station, Jake reached for the doorknob. "I'll do that. But I really need to hurry. Can you see what's in the cabinets that might make a good meal or two? Or six? Nothing in crinkly wrappers or cans, unless you can open them and put them in plastic containers."

With a soft laugh, Molly turned him toward the office and gave him a gentle push. "Go make your call. I'll see what I can do. And go quietly. Jenny's asleep upstairs, and I don't know when she'll wake up. She thinks you're out of town."

~

Molly placed unopened jars of peanut butter and jelly, a bag of bread repackaged in a plastic container, a bag of orange sections, four bananas, and a large container of trail mix into a daypack. She added several plastic containers of fruit and pudding and plastic ware to suffice. If they went through all that in two days, then they needed to just go home. She placed two large bottles of water and a jug of peach tea beside the pack.

"So, what do we have here?" Jake returned to the kitchen and peeked into the daypack. "Hmmm. Looks good."

"I hope it'll be enough." Reaching over, Molly grabbed the last three apples sitting in a basket on the counter and added them to the bag.

"It'll be fine," Jake whispered with a soft chuckle.

"So what'd you find out?"

"I spoke with Ed Clark. He said there have been several arrests for poaching made all along the lake boundary, but when he read the names to me, I didn't recognize any of them." He shook his head. "I was so hoping to nab Willy Cahill and Ray Smith. And Bill Hopper would've been an added bonus."

Molly placed a hand on his arm. "Jake, it could just be they aren't out hunting this weekend. They move to their own tune and not when we want them to. The weekend hasn't been a bust. With the arrests that've been made, I'd say it's been successful."

Jake heaved a heavy sigh. "I know you're right. I just want these guys stopped. If they aren't caught in the net this weekend when we're highly manned, it'll be so much harder when we're back to regular manning. They keep slipping through, and I want to put a stop to it."

~

Jake's return to the stakeout sight had been uneventful, and Eddie was happy to have a new supply of food. Jake waved away the twenty dollar bill Eddie offered to help pay his part.

"No problem," he whispered. "You shared your fare with me, so in reality, I'm paying you back."

"Thanks, Jake."

Eddie pulled out his pocket knife and made a couple peanut butter and jelly sandwiches, handing one to Jake. They munched quietly as Jake surveilled the surface of the lake.

"Anything happen while I was gone?" he whispered. "Or did you just nap?"

Eddie pretended to guffaw at the slur, all the while not making a sound. Then he whispered, "Funny. No, nothing happened. Just like the last two days. Absolutely nothing."

They finished their sandwiches as well as an apple each, then sat back to wait. As the sunlight disappeared and darkness crept along the ridge, Jake pulled out night vision goggles. It would make the surveillance of the lake far easier in the darkness. Flipping his ball cap around backwards, he settled the headgear over it. Turning the activation knob, the eerie green phosphor screen illuminated, bringing into view the lake and the surrounding vegetation. He never ceased to be amazed at this wonderful invention that made a huge difference in law enforcement and military operations.

Scanning the woods around them and then the surface of the lake, he started to turn away to look again when he spotted a pinpoint of light. As he watched, it moved steadily and smoothly across the surface of the lake.

"I've got some light and movement, Eddie." Jake nudged his partner. "It's coming from the southwest moving parallel to the shoreline of the channel."

Eddie pulled out a second NVG and settled it over his cap. "Got visual. Looks like it's going to pass on by the entrance to Hazel Creek." Jake strained to hear his faint whisper. "Can you make out how many subjects are in the boats?"

Jake searched the green image in his field of vision, making adjustments to gain a clearer visual. "Not for sure, but looks like three. You?"

"10-4. The third's half hidden behind one of the others."

"They're moving out of sight," said Jake. "Nobody just goes out cruising the lake at this time of night for the fun of it. They've got to be up to something. Did you notice any fishing gear? I know some folks use lights to fish at night, especially on this lake."

"Couldn't see that much detail. As far as that goes, I couldn't see if they had rifles or shotguns, either," Eddie groused in a soft voice. "What do you say we head east on foot wearing the NVGs and see if we pick up where they come ashore."

"Good idea. I'll head east through the woods and you head east past the ranger cabin. Keep your radio handy on the local channel. I'll use vague messages so if anyone's monitoring the channel, they won't understand. You do the same."

"Roger." Eddie slipped out of the blind and hurried quietly through the woods. Jake ensured his earbud was in tight and his radio was set to the local channel, then he faded into the darkness.

~

"What if somebody sees us?" Ray asked in urgent tones. "I don't want nobody to see us, Willy."

"Shut up, Ray. Ain't nobody goin' to see us. It's pitch black out and we're across the lake and up a channel deep inside a cove. Ain't no way they'll see or hear us. So quit your sniveling. Come on."

Bill Hopper stepped out of the boat behind the others. "There's just something satisfying about coming out here on park land and huntin'. We need to get us a few more bear to meet the quota, and whatever we can get tonight will add to that."

Willy tied the motorboat to a tree branch hanging along the water's edge. "How many more do we need, Bill? Thought we were getting' close on the total."

"We are. We have until the end of next week to get five more.

Mr. Ching's getting pretty impatient and says that's the longest he'll give us. If we don't make the deadline, then we better just move to South America and fade into the jungle. You just don't mess with these Chinese mafia fellows. They'll kill ya as soon as look at ya."

"What!" Ray's voice squeaked with the exclamation. "I don't like this no more, Willy. We need to get out of it. I don't want nobody killin' me!"

"Shut up, Ray." Willy smacked the back of his friend's head. "You're in deep like the rest of us. Let's just find the bears and kill 'em. Where ya goin' to set up, Bill?"

"Up on that ridge. There's a cave up there. Staked it out when I was hunting up here last year. I've seen a couple bears around. Might be other caves nearby too. It's a good thing we put on these ghillie suits. We'll fade into the vegetation and they'll never see us. Ray, did you spray yourself with that scent-away stuff? We don't want 'em smellin' us."

"Yeah, I did, Bill. But this ghillie suit itches."

"Oh, shut up, Ray," said Willy. "It'd been better to bring my six-year-old than you."

~

The NVG made travel through the woods fairly easy. Jake was able to avoid sticks and twigs just like he would've in the daylight. Moving with deliberate, stealthy movements through the woods, he surveyed the perimeter around him. No sign of anyone yet, but he remained vigilant. Crossing a fallen log with care, he paused momentarily to get his bearings. A shot rang out, the echo ricocheting through the mountains. Startled, a sick feeling settled in the pit of his stomach. He hurried in the direction of the sound, hoping that whoever had fired had missed their target. It was definitely inside the park.

The sound had come from the ridge northeast of his position. Climbing nearly straight up to the ridge, he wanted to have the advantage of higher ground. If he could get above them, it'd be easier to make his approach and possibly an arrest than if he approached from below. If they did get an animal, then he'd hopefully have the element of surprise. Not wanting to haul out a complete carcass, they'd be rushing to field dress the animal.

Reaching the top of the ridge Jake paused to scout the area. A dim light just east of his position glimmered. Two men were indeed dressing out a bear. He unsnapped his holster as he moved in. With stealthy steps he slowly crossed the ridgeline until he was twenty feet above them. Carefully he made his way closer until he was ten feet away. He removed his sidearm from the holster and slipped the NVG up onto his forehead. He waited a minute for his eyes to adjust back to the dim light.

"Toss the knives away and hands behind your heads," he said firmly. "No sudden moves. And do it NOW."

The two men stopped slicing at the carcass and paused. Neither moved.

"I said toss the knives away and hands behind your heads," he yelled. "I won't say it again."

Both men, still on their knees by the bear carcass, pitched their skinning knives away and held up their hands.

With a steady gun held on the two poachers, Jake pressed the walkie-talkie mic button at his shoulder. "Come in, Eddie. I have two visitors to the area who are in need of help," he hoped Eddie would understand his altered terms. "They have a pet with them."

"Got you loud and clear." Eddie's soft voice sounded in his ear. "I heard that report, and I'm on my way. Nearly there."

The area was faintly lit by a small lantern sitting on the ground by the men. Studying the scene, Jake spotted a 30.06 rifle leaning against a tree four feet from one of the men. They were faced away, so as of yet, he had no idea who they were.

"Ok, slowly turn and lay face down on the ground, hands behind your heads." Jake edged forward, cutting the distance in half. "Slowly, now. No sudden moves."

The two men did as they were told and with grunts of displeasure lay face down. Jake walked over and kicked the knives farther away, keeping his handgun trained on the prostrate men.

Eddie called from the darkness. "Don't shoot. I'm coming in."

"Keep them covered while I cuff them," Jake instructed. "But keep a watch. I haven't seen the third man yet."

As Eddie covered the men with his sidearm, Jake holstered his, reached for the cuffs tucked into a pouch on the back of his utility belt and proceeded to cuff the first man. Neither had said a word to this point.

"Here, use my cuffs." Eddie removed the handcuffs from his

belt and tossed them to Jake. He snagged them and cuffed the second man.

"Ok, fellas, let's get you into a sitting position." He helped the first man roll over and sit up, recognizing him as soon as the light illuminated his face.

"Well, well, well," Jake said, a pleased smile on his face. "I was hoping to run into you sometime this weekend, Willy Cahill. So glad you could drop by, and with evidence, no less. And who's your buddy here. It wouldn't be Ray Smith, would it?"

He helped the second man into a sitting position. "Yep. Thought so. When you find one cockroach, you'll usually find more. Where's your other buddy?"

"What other buddy?" Willy spoke for the first time. "Just us out here enjoying the night. Found this here bear layin' on the ground. Since somebody else killed it and left it, thought I'd grab me some steaks for my wife's birthday dinner."

"We heard the report of a rifle a little while ago, and you're saying you didn't fire this rifle? Ballistics will confirm it was fired."

"That rifle? Ain't ours. We must o' scared away whoever shot the bear and left this rifle leaning against the tree." Willy continued to weave his story on the fly.

"Well, I'm betting they'll find your fingerprints on it and if not yours, then Ray's." Jake pulled his phone from his pocket, walked over and snapped pictures of the rifle against the tree, the bear carcass, and the bloody skinning knives. Then pulling a pair of rubber gloves from his backpack, he slipped them on and picked up the rifle, preserving any fingerprints that would be found on the weapon.

Racking the bolt back, he ejected the shells then reached down and picked them up. Pulling an evidence zip bag from his backpack, he dropped them in, marked the bag and stashed them in the backpack for later examination. Slinging the rifle over his shoulder, he approached the bear carcass and examined the skinning job. Only they hadn't been skinning the bear. Both paws were removed and the abdomen lay open, partially revealing entrails. "Well, what were you fellas doing here? Doesn't look like you were skinning this bear for fur or meat. What were you looking for?"

Only the sound of cicadas and crickets competing for volume could be heard as neither man responded. Their refusal to answer only validated Jake's suspensions that something else was going on here.

"Not going to answer, huh?" Searching the ground around the carcass, he found a small zip bag with a bloody object in it. "What's this?"

Again silence.

"You know your silence won't really matter, right? Forensics will answer the questions you won't." Jake placed the zip bag inside an evidence bag and tucked it next to the shells. Then looking for the bullet hole he dug out the slug that killed the bear, dropping the bloody, mangled object into another zip bag. Then in a larger evidence bag he placed the dissected bear paws.

Standing up, Jake secured all the evidence then turned to his partner. "Eddie, let's get these guys back across the lake and locked up. Come on, fellas. Move."

~

As Bill Hopper slipped through the darkness toward the sound of the rifle shot, he hoped Willy or Ray had gotten a bear. They needed to fill their quota and fast. He liked living where he'd grown up and had no desire to hide away in South America somewhere for the rest of his life. After checking out their find, he'd head up to the caves and try to scare up another bear.

Spotting a light in the darkness he edged toward it, but instinct cautioned him to approach carefully. For one thing he didn't want those crazies to mistake him for a bear and shoot him. But in the dim light of Willy's lantern were four men, not two. And on the ground was indeed a bear. The two other men looked like rangers and unless he missed his guess, one of them was Jake Stuart. Swearing beneath his breath, he dropped silently behind a bush and watched as his cohorts were arrested and hauled toward the lake. There wasn't much he could do for them now, but one thing was for sure, he'd make Jake Stuart pay. Yep. That sweet little ranger lady of his would help him make sure of that.

~

After church Sunday morning, Molly and Jenny shook the pastor's hand at the church door then climbed into Molly's little SUV. Selma Jenkins hadn't been feeling well and missed services.

Jenny had called her Saturday evening, discovering that her aunt was suffering from a stomach bug. Molly suggested they drop by the grocery store and pick up some chicken soup from the deli and take it to her. It would never equal the quality of her cooking, but at least she wouldn't have to cook.

As they left the store, the sunshine and warmth of the late summer morning filled Molly with happiness. It was wonderful to see Jake even for the short time he was at the station the day before, but she was looking forward to this stakeout being over so they could get on with their lives. For now she hoped it was worth all the time and effort that had been expended. Apparently it was since several poachers were arrested as well as a couple of marijuana growers. She'd been surprised when she called HQ this morning for an update, and they'd told her that. Two men were growing the vile plant within the park boundary in a remote area, but the rangers had nipped that in the bud, thankfully.

"You're awfully quiet this morning," Jenny said. "I hope you're not coming down with something. Or are you missing Jake?" she asked with a sly smile. "I'm sure it's tough with him out of town."

Molly glanced at her friend. "You guessed it. I do miss him. It's like life is sort of cock-eyed, you know? We're not even married, and I feel like a part of me is missing."

"Well, I suppose it is. He's a part of you now. Your world is starting to revolve around him." Jenny paused momentarily. "Have you thought any more about a possible wedding date?"

"No, not yet. Until he's back in town and things settle down, we won't really be able to discuss it. My mother has given me some suggestions," Molly chuckled. "I'll take them into consideration, but Jake and I will have the final say."

Molly parked in her usual spot and they hurried to the front door of Mrs. Jenkins' house.

"Knock, knock," Jenny sang out as they opened the door and went in. "Aunt Selma? Where are you?"

"In here." They followed the sound of Mrs. Jenkins voice into the living room. She lay back in her recliner, a light afghan pulled over her legs. "Well, what are you girls doing here? Thought you'd be out at Twentymile."

"We came into town for church and thought we'd stop by to check on you. Heard you were a little under the weather. How are you feeling?" Molly placed a gentle hand on the older woman's brow. "Thankfully you're not feverish."

"Nope, no fever," she replied. "Just some stomach discomfort and some, well…other issues."

"We brought you this." Jenny held out the large Styrofoam container of chicken soup. "I know you can make much better, but this way you won't have to fix yourself anything."

Mrs. Jenkins held out her hand. "What is it?"

"Chicken soup."

"I'll put some in a bowl if you like," offered Molly.

"Oh, that's mighty sweet of you two, girls. I'll have some in a bit."

Molly and Jenny visited for a while and then before they left, Molly went to her apartment to grab a few things.

"I've been missing you, Molly," Mrs. Jenkins said as they prepared to leave. "I know that young man of yours is out of town and needs you to fill in for him, but the house seems so quiet without you. Not that you're loud, mind you," she added in a rush. "Just miss you, is all."

Molly leaned over and gave her landlady a hug. "And I miss you too. You get some rest and get well. I'll be home soon." She dropped a kiss on the wrinkled cheek.

"Bye, Aunt Selma." Jenny gave her aunt a hug and a kiss as well. "And behave yourself. I want you well the next time I drop in. Love you."

"Love you, girls. Thanks again for stopping by."

~

Once Jake and Eddie dropped their prisoners at the town jail for incarceration, they drove out to Deep Creek to call HQ for directions on dealing with the evidence. Something was beyond odd about what Willy and Ray were harvesting from that bear. Paws and a small internal organ? A forensic scientist would determine exactly what it is, and hopefully why it was so important to the poachers. Ed Clark, who was called from his warm bed to get back with Jake and Eddie, finally called with instructions. Lock the evidence in the station safe and head back out to the lake. Another ranger would pick it up shortly and take it to the state crime lab in Asheville for forensic analysis.

"Ok," Jake said, hanging up the phone. "We have our marching orders. Back to the blind. Chances are if Willy and Ray were in the park hunting, Bill Hopper may also show up. And if not, we may catch others." Without a doubt, this stakeout had been successful, but he wanted Bill caught, in the worst way.

~

After supper, Molly hiked up to the barn to feed and water the horses. She spent a little time with them, humming in a soft voice as she curried their coats and loved on them. She enjoyed her time with Billy Boy and Blackie. She loved riding but hadn't had a chance since she'd been back. Maybe in the morning she'd take one of them out after issuing camping permits at the dam. A good trail ride would help kill time as she waited for Jake's return.

The sun had dropped behind the mountain peaks as she walked back down to the ranger station. Hopefully Jenny would want to take an evening hike. She glanced at the sky. They might get a short one in before it got too dark.

"Jenny," she called as she entered the kitchen door. "Where are you?"

Footsteps sounded on the stairs from the upper floor just before Jenny appeared in the living room. "I'm here. What's up?"

"Want to go for a hike before it gets too dark?" Molly propped her hands on her hips. "It's a beautiful evening, and I have the urge to hike off some edginess. The crickets are chirping, the breeze is blowing softly, and I know this gorgeous weather won't last much longer. It's almost September after all."

Jenny leaned against the doorframe as Molly talked. "Bet I know what the cause of that 'edginess' is. Sure. A hike sounds like a good way to end the weekend. Let's go. But let me run out to the car and grab a light jacket. The mountain nights can be cool."

~

Molly stood on the back stoop as Jenny went to grab her jacket. Glancing up she saw that night was quickly approaching. This wouldn't be an evening stroll but a night hike. A chuckle slipped out. It'd still be fun. Jenny had become a good friend, and she enjoyed the time they spent together. Hmmm. Maybe she should grab a jacket too.

Before she could think twice about it, a dark truck roared up and stopped a few feet away. The headlights were off. Remembering the night of the shooting, hairs prickled on the nape of her neck as dread filled her. Surely not again. Glancing out at Jenny's car, she hoped she'd realize something was wrong and stay hidden. Molly turned to rush back into the station to grab her sidearm, but before she could take a step, a hand settled over her face. A sharp stab on her upper arm immediately followed. What was that? Had she been stuck? Oh, no! A needle? Why would they….? Her vision swam as her ears began to ring. What had they done? Why?

Bill Hopper's cruel laugh came just behind her head. Was he the one holding her?

"Not so tough now, huh, ranger lady. This should take Jake Stuart down a peg. Yep. See if it don't."

Molly's vision faded into blackness as every muscle in her body went limp. Her last conscious thought was to send a single-word plea heavenward. *Help!*

Chapter Nineteen

There had been no other encounters with poachers, hikers or any other humans since Jake and Eddie returned to their stakeout blind in the late hours of Saturday night. By Sunday evening, they both were ready to pack it in and head home. Jake was so exhausted he was sure he'd sleep for three days straight. That'd never happen, but a good night's sleep would suffice. After receiving a welcoming hug and kiss from Molly, of course. That thought revived his efforts to pack up and head back to the station.

Eddie dropped him at Dean's Marina just as darkness descended. With a weary wave to his stakeout partner, he climbed into his pickup and drove as quickly and safely as his fatigued brain would allow him to. Hopefully Molly would have some leftovers from her and Jenny's supper. Oh, how he longed for a real meal. Four days of jerky, fruit and sandwiches was more than he cared to repeat anytime soon.

As he pulled into the Twentymile driveway and passed the station, he noticed several ranger vehicles parked haphazardly in the back parking lot and in the driveway, some with blue lights flashing. What in the world? Had something happened? Molly's car sat in its usual place. Could it be Jenny?

Parking as close as he could, he climbed out and hurried into the kitchen where he found Jenny slumped in a kitchen chair, tears streaming down her crumpled face. Cal stooped beside her, looking up at her and speaking in a quiet voice. A couple rangers stood nearby while others could be heard in the station office.

"What's going on here?" Jake asked as he halted beside Cal and Jenny. "Are you alright, Jenny? Where's Molly?"

If possible, Jenny's face crumpled further as her hands covered her face.

"Jenny?" Fear gripped Jake's heart even as his mind refused to believe what was evident. If Molly were here, she'd be by Jenny's side.

Cal stood up, placing a hand on Jake's shoulder. "Molly's been kidnapped, Jake."

"What?" Incredulity sucked the air from Jake's lungs. How could it be? With a sudden flashback to the night of the shooting, he knew it was possible, and he had a good idea who was responsible.

"Who did it?" he ground out, anger replacing disbelief.

"We suspect Bill Hopper and possibly David Andrews. Jenny wanted to be reassured that her brother Jamie wasn't involved, so we called and he's at home. Said he didn't know anything about it. I've sent a ranger over to question him further. She didn't recognize the truck, but she got the license plate number. She couldn't see any faces because they were backlit by the kitchen light when they took Molly."

Jake was pacing back and forth as Cal talked, but stopped, leaning both hands on the kitchen bar. "So who does the truck belong to?

"Bill Hopper. Jenny says there were two men who took Molly. Apparently they doped her. Jenny saw one of them cover her face just before she went limp."

Jake strode back to Jenny's side and knelt down. Tamping down his anger and angst, he spoke in a quiet voice, "Jenny, I know you've already told Cal everything, but would you repeat it to me? I need to know. Please?"

Wiping her eyes on the sleeve of her jacket, she looked at him, sniffing several times before mustering words. "Oh, Jake, I'm so sorry. I was outside by my car getting my jacket. We were going on an evening walk."

Starting at the beginning, Jenny repeated the account right up to the call to HQ and waiting for someone to arrive. "Jake, could I have done anything differently to save her from being kidnapped? What could I have done?"

Reaching up a gentle hand, Jake brushed back wayward tendrils of hair that had escaped her blond ponytail. "Jenny, you did everything you could. Had you come out of hiding and made a move toward them, you'd most likely be with Molly right now, who knows where. But you had the presence of mind to take in the details and get the license plate. Now the authorities will do all they can to get Molly back."

Jake's fists clenched. "*I* will do all I can to get her back."

He dug deep and managed a slight smile. "You just hang in there and remember what Molly would tell you to do in this situation. Do you know?"

A soft smile eased the tension in Jenny's face as she nodded. "She'd remind me to pray. So that's what I'll do."

"You bet. You've done all you can to this point. Now pray. For her safety and for us as we look for her. Just remember that the Lord knows where she is. Ask Him to lead us to her. Okay? Will you do that?"

"Of course, I will. And let me know if there's anything else I can do. I'll be here."

~

Leaving Jenny in the station, Jake and Cal walked outside toward the vehicles. "Jake, you haven't had much sleep in the last four days. Why don't you try and get some rest while we begin the investigation and search, then after you've rested, you can join us."

"You've got to be kidding, right?" Skepticism filled Jake's voice as his arm swung in an all-encompassing arc. "How in the world do you think I can rest when Molly's out there somewhere? No way. I'm heading to Frank Raven's home in Cherokee. Maybe he can shed some light on where Bill might've taken her."

"Ok, Jake. Didn't figure I could dissuade you from coming along. Frank's was going to be my first stop. I also sent rangers to Bill Hopper's house and David Andrews' apartment to see if they're home. Everyone's innocent until proven guilty."

"Yeah, that's the law," Jake agreed, "but we both know what we're going to find. You drive." He climbed into the passenger seat of Cal's SUV. "If I start nodding off, I won't pass up a catnap."

~

Frank Raven lived up a dirt mountain road on the east side of the reservation in a small log home. Few details could be seen in the darkness, but the outside lights illuminated enough to see it was well kept. Lights were on inside, so surely someone was home. After climbing out of the SUV, Jake and Cal climbed the steps onto the covered porch and knocked at the front door.

As they waited, they glanced around the yard. A small barn surrounded by a corral perched near the house with the shadowy shape of a horse standing in the open doorway. An old dog lay by the fence. He'd raised his head when they drove up, but hadn't bothered to get up and investigate the visitors. Not much of a watch dog, that was for sure.

The front door opened, drawing their attention back to the house. An elderly Cherokee woman stood in the doorway and opened the screen door. "Yes? May I help you?"

"We'd like to talk to Frank. Is he around?"

Before the woman could answer, Frank appeared behind her, standing a foot taller than her diminutive size. "Cal. Jake." He nodded in greeting. "You're looking for me?"

"Yep. We sure are, Frank," Cal said, hands on his hips. "We have a very serious situation, and we're hoping you can shed light on some things. May we come in?"

"What kind of serious situation?" Although the woman had left the doorway and returned into the house, Frank remained still, his features never shifting.

"A life and death situation." Jake fought the urgency that coursed through him. He wanted to get to Molly now. Would they reach her in time? "Someone's life may be at stake."

Cal placed a calming hand on his shoulder. "Jake's pretty concerned, Frank, but what he says is true. Molly Walker was kidnapped this evening, and we think Bill Hopper was involved."

Jake watched Frank's expression for any minute reaction, but saw none. Frank's gaze shifted from one face to the other before he pushed the screen door open and nodded. "Come in."

Following him into the living room, they took the seats he offered on the couch and in an arm chair. The elderly woman had disappeared, but a younger woman came in and greeted their guests.

"Hello," she smiled.

A noticeable softening touched Frank's features as he looked at the young woman. "Jake, Cal, this is my wife Sue. Honey, these are two of the rangers from our district."

The woman nodded pleasantly. "It's an honor to meet you. May I get you something to drink? Tea or soda, perhaps?"

"Nothing for me, thank you." Jake was eager to get on with the investigation. Too many distractions. He just wanted to get on with finding Molly. His heart hammered in frustration. Being exhausted probably wasn't helping.

"No, thanks," Cal said. "If we could just talk with your husband for a bit, we'd appreciate it."

"Of course." Sue turned toward the door. "I'll leave you then. It was nice meeting you both."

After she left the room, Jake and Cal took their seats, Frank sitting across from them.

"So, Molly Walker's been kidnapped. How can I help?"

"Well, Bill Hopper is our prime suspect and we're hoping you can shed some light on his activities and where he may have taken her." Cal started at the beginning and explained the evenings events surrounding Molly's disappearance. As he talked Jake observed Frank for any indications that he already knew what had happened. Nothing. Either his native blood kept his features stoic or he just didn't know anything about it.

When Cal finished, Frank nodded slowly. "I've long suspected Bill of something more than just the occasional poaching. He's shifty, that one. He brags about hunting in the park and the animals he takes down, but bear seems to be his greatest achievement. And not just one or two, but many."

Frank shook his head in confusion. "What would be his purpose for kidnapping Molly Walker?"

"For one thing she dared to arrest and jail two of his cohorts, Willy Cahill and Ray Smith," Jake responded. "I don't think they liked being bested by a female ranger. Some men take that kind of thing personally."

"I think it goes further than that, though," Cal added. "Whatever Bill and his nephew David have been up to, it's far more than just Molly arresting Willy and Ray. Do you have any idea what could be behind Bill's poaching?"

Frank thought for a moment, his face remaining impassive. He looked first at Cal then at Jake. "I think he's killing bear and selling parts for money. I'm not sure what parts or who he's selling them to. When he didn't know I was within earshot, I heard him talking to his nephew about it. No details but what he said made me think that."

"So you knew David was his nephew?"

Frank nodded. "He slipped up one day and said something. I asked about it and he acknowledged that David was his sister's son. Tried to pass it off as unimportant."

Cal mulled that over. "Do you know if either Bill or David has a place where Molly may have been taken? Somewhere remote perhaps?"

Frank nodded again. "Bill has a hunting cabin in the Nantahala Forest. It was his uncle's and he inherited it on his uncle's death."

"Do you know its location or have any information that could help us find it?" Jake pushed forward to the edge of his seat.

"I've never been there but he told me it's out Joyce Kilmer Road near Lake Santeetlah. He hunts and fishes there. When he's not hunting in the park."

"Is it in his name?" Cal tugged his cell phone from his pocket.

"I would assume so." Frank shrugged. "He's divorced and has no children. His uncle passed a decade or more ago, so I can't imagine it would be in anyone else's name."

Jake surged to his feet and grabbed Frank's hand, pumping it in a vigorous handshake. "Thanks, Frank, I really appreciate your help."

As he and Cal headed for the door, Frank asked, "I've heard rumors. Is there more to your relationship with Molly Walker than mere co-workers?"

"Those aren't just rumors, my friend," Cal clapped Jake on the shoulder. "This man is about to tie the knot with Molly."

"If we can find her." Fear tinged Jake's words.

"You'll find her." The first smile either of them had ever seen on Frank's face appeared from nowhere. "Don't worry, Jake. Bill Hopper is a lot of things, but I can't imagine him harming Molly."

"I pray you're right." Jake grabbed hold of Frank's confidence and held on tight. *Please, God, let him be right.*

~

Molly's head pounded as she struggled through the blackness that tried to hold her within its grasp. She felt as though she were floating. It took a while for her to realize she lay on a hard mattress, a flattened pillow beneath her head. Something tight bound her hands together, as well as her feet. Why couldn't she move? Why did she feel so…disoriented? Fear knotted her insides. Heavy eyelids refused to open as she attempted to recall what had happened. Jenny had been at Twentymile. They were going for an evening walk. Jenny went to grab her jacket from her car, and then…. What? Someone else had been there. A truck. Just as she realized their presence, everything had gone blank. Where was she? Was she still at Twentymile?

A sound nearby drew her attention. Was someone there? Jenny? A chair scraped across a wooden floor. A second endeavor to open her eyelids proved more successful. Faint light attempted to illuminate the darkened room as she caught movement several feet away.

"Ah, you're awake." A familiar voice spoke with kindness, but her muddled mind refused recognition. "Good. I know my uncle will be glad to know that. Are you thirsty?"

The sound of water pouring into a plastic cup reached Molly's ears as she strained to see the owner of the voice. Footsteps approached the bed where she lay, and then the friendly, smiling face of David Andrews appeared beside her.

David?

"It'll be difficult for you, but I'm sure I can help lift you up if you want a drink of water."

As he spoke a door opened and then slammed as another person entered the room. From her position, it was impossible to see who it was. Before David could help her into a sitting position, a figure flew into view and violently knocked the cup from his hand. As droplets of water flew in every direction, the angry face of Celeste Payne dove close to Molly's.

"She gets nothing to drink, Dave. Do you hear me? Nothing!"

David cowered momentarily before he reached for the plastic cup that had landed on the foot of the bed and turned to walk away. Water had peppered Molly's face and clothes, running down her cheeks and soaking into the fabric. Her throat and mouth were parched and a drink would've been welcome. A sigh escaped as she licked her lips to retrieve the few precious drops that remained there. Why was Celeste here? What was her connection with David and Bill Hopper? They were up to something involving Bill's poaching, but Celeste? It didn't make sense. Hadn't she just been after Jake? Molly swallowed down the fear that Celeste's anger had kindled.

Celeste pulled back to stand above Molly but watched her with narrowed eyes. "Stay away from her, David. Do you hear me? She's poison." The last word was spat in contempt. "When Uncle Bill gets back, we'll see what he has to say about things." Turning her back on Molly, Celeste strode away, high heels clicking on the wooden floor.

Closing her eyes, Molly attempted to relax the tense muscles that had bunched at Celeste's appearance. Hard to do when her hands and feet were tie strapped. Opening her eyes again and ignoring the pounding in her head, she inspected the room, but between the low light and her prone position, it was hard to see. The wooden walls were covered with an aged patina and an old pot-bellied wood stove stood against the wall across from the foot of her bed. A cabin, perhaps? Not very large. Close to the stove sat a kitchen table and chairs. She glanced to her left. A window on the wall by the bed indicated it was dark outside. It was just growing dark when she was taken. How long had she been here and how long had she been unconscious? A few minutes? A few hours? More than a day? What had they knocked her out with?

An unintelligible male voice murmured from across the room. Was it David again or someone else?

Celeste spoke in a raised voice.

"No, dear brother. That's not what we're going to do. Uncle Bill will be here soon, and he'll decide. I'm sure he has a plan. So just sit back and shut up. Read a magazine or something. And don't go soft on me. She's more trouble than she's worth and you need to remember that she won't be around for long anyway."

Molly's heart lurched in her chest as the last phrase sank in. They weren't planning to keep her here long. Did that mean they were going to…kill her? Celeste's tone indicated she was pleased about that part, whatever it was.

The sound of the door opening came again then it was slammed shut, causing Molly to jump. What in the world?

Heavy booted feet stomped in her direction then Bill Hopper's face hovered beside the bed. If looks could kill, she'd already be dead. A sneer twisted his lips as his eyes narrowed. Reaching over, he pulled a wooden chair next to the bed and plopped onto the seat. Leaning forward, he placed his elbows on his knees, clasped his hands together and glared at her.

"You and those rangers think you're all so high and mighty, don'cha! First you arrest Willy and Ray for some trumped-up charges so you can be the big hero. Now your Jake Stuart's done arrested 'em again. And for what? A little night hike in the park? And he is your Jake, ain't he? Went and got yourself engaged to him. What do you think about that, Celeste?" He tossed the last words over his shoulder.

"I'm thinking she connilved somehow to get him to ask her," Celeste snarled as she appeared behind Bill's shoulder, "because he's in love with me. Not her. ME." She tossed her blond curls with contempt.

"Now, now, Celeste. Settle your feathers. You won't have to worry about her for much longer."

Wariness stole through Molly as she listened. Again talking about her not being here much longer. She really hoped that didn't mean what she thought it did. So why were they keeping her here?

Celeste stomped away only to return immediately, a pistol in her hand. She aimed the barrel at Molly's face. Panic seized Molly at the wild anger in the woman's eyes. Molly clasped her fingers together to hide their trembling. What in the world? Was Celeste crazy?

"Let's just shoot her now and be done with it." Celeste pulled back the hammer and took deliberate aim.

Bill jumped up from the chair, knocking it over in his haste. Putting a hand on top of the gun, he pushed down, lowering it and her hands. "Now, just hold on a minute, girl. Don't go off halfcocked. Yes, we'll deal with her. But we have to wait till the right time, and I'm not ready. I want Jake Stuart to know we have her. I want him in agony."

Celeste turned to stare at her uncle. "But I want Jake Stuart! And that's why I want to kill her. Right now *she's* got his attention. I want to remove her from the picture so I can have it." Her voice grew more shrill as she spoke.

"Do you think he'll want you if you kill her?" David's voice carried from just outside of Molly's vision. "Why would he? He's in love with her."

"He won't know it was me, you idiot!" Celeste screamed. Then her demeanor and voice changed in an instant to sweet and demure. "I'll be right there to console him. He'll turn to me when I lavish him with sympathy and an understanding shoulder."

"Sure he will." David's dry sarcasm came across clearly.

"Shut up, the both o' you," Bill snarled. "I don't need this bickering right now. I gotta change my plans now that Willy and Ray are taken. And I can't think with you two going at it. Your mama, bless her soul, wouldn't be too happy with you two if she was still living." He grabbed the pistol from Celeste, un-cocked it and slipped it inside his jacket.

"Go sit down and let me think. You got your women's magazines. Read one."

The young woman stomped away, huffing as she went. Molly switched her gaze to Bill to see what his next move would be. He picked up the chair, setting it back against the wall.

"I'll be back." He glared first at Molly then looked at his niece and nephew. "Hold down the cabin while I'm gone. And *don't* kill her. Not yet, anyway."

As he left the cabin, slamming the door behind him, Molly let out a sigh and closed her eyes. *Oh, Lord! I need help here! Please! I need help!*

~

Oh, Lord, we need help! Jake prayed silently. *Please! We need to find Molly before something terrible happens. Lead us to her! Please!*

Cal hung up his cellphone and snapped it into its holster on his utility belt. Opening the truck doors, he and Jake climbed into the cab and drove away from Frank's home. "I called HQ and they're going to put out an All-Points Bulletin on Bill Hopper and David Andrews. They're also going to search for the location of Bill's cabin. If it's in his name, they'll find it. We'll head into the Nantahala Forest. It'll get us closer so that when we have the location, we'll be right there."

"Good." Jake closed his eyes to continue praying.

As they reached the outskirts of Bryson City, Cal's cellphone rang, a shrill sound in the quiet truck cab. "This is Cal." He answered then listened as the caller spoke.

"Yep. That's great, Ed. Can you send backup to that address? Thanks a bunch. I'll get back to you when we know more." He hung up and replaced the phone at his side.

"What did he say?" Jake sat up straighter, his head pounding from exhaustion, but he'd see this through. He wouldn't stop until they found Molly, no matter how long it took. He had to. For her sake.

"They found the location of Bill's cabin. Ed called with the information. Here, plug it into the GPS." Cal rattled off the address as Jake entered it into the device on the truck's dashboard. "He's sending out the Sherriff's Department and more rangers. The deputies will call shortly with a rendezvous location so we can coordinate a rescue plan. I want to take these fellows down and fast."

~

Cal pulled into the Serene Waters Mountain Lodge driveway and followed it around to the back. Three sheriff deputy vehicles sat at the rear of the parking lot of the rustic resort. As Cal parked beside them, two other park vehicles pulled up. Exiting the truck, Jake and Cal approached the other vehicles as their occupants also climbed out.

"Hey, Jake, Cal." Cory Ryan, the lead deputy, shook their hands. "Sorry to hear about your troubles. We're here to back you up. What can we do to help?"

"Molly Walker, one of our rangers, was kidnapped earlier this evening and we have a suspect." Jake crossed his arms over his chest. "It's most likely Bill Hopper, one of the Deep Creek maintenance staff. We have the location of his cabin where we think he's taken her. His nephew is probably involved and may be there as well."

Jake briefly explained what had transpired and how time was of the essence.

"We've never been out there, so we're unfamiliar with the lay of the land," Cal added. "Can you help us out?"

"You have the address?" Cory asked.

Cal handed him a slip of paper.

"Hmmm. Hey, fellows." Cory addressed the three other deputies present. "Anyone recognize this? I've been out Black Bear Road many times but don't recognize this address."

"I was out there once," commented one of the deputies. "Drunken disorderliness. They were having a pretty big party and messing with boaters on the lake. What'd you say the owner's name was?"

"Bill Hopper," replied Jake.

"Yeah, that sounds familiar."

Cory reached into his SUV and pulled out an area map, opening it on the hood of the vehicle. "Here, can you pinpoint it and give us some information about the surrounding area? We need to conceal our approach. If they have her inside, it's imperative we do this as stealthily as possible."

After reviewing the map, they pulled together a plan and then climbing into their vehicles, implemented it.

"Here we go," Cal said, starting the truck engine.

"Yeah, here we go." Jake's heart tightened as he struggled to hold out hope.

~

Molly had no idea what time it was. Her wrists and ankles hurt from their tight confinement and her head was still pounding. It was still dark outside the window with no indication that daylight was on the way. As the cabin quieted down with only the occasional murmur from the other side of the room, she grew sleepy. Most likely the effects of whatever they'd knocked her out with. She wanted to stay awake and alert to whatever might be coming. If there was an opportunity to escape, she wanted to take advantage of it. Staying awake was more difficult than she'd expected. She hadn't realized she'd nodded off until the door opened and slammed shut causing her to jump again.

Bill Hopper stormed over to the wood stove where an old percolator coffee pot sat warming. He grabbed a cup from the hooks hanging beneath a plain shelf. After filling it, he glanced in her direction, glared then thumped over to wherever David and Celeste were. They'd grown quiet and she assumed they'd fallen asleep.

"Can we kill her now?" Celeste's strident voice reverberated against the wooden walls. "I'm tired of staying here. I want to go home. But I want to get rid of her first."

A pause indicated Bill might be considering her suggestion. No, no. That's a bad idea. Molly's heart hammered and her ears began to ring as panic surged through her. Was he going to let her do it?

Closing her eyes, Molly prayed for what seemed like the hundredth time then a verse she'd memorized as a child came to mind. "Be still and know that I am God. I will be exalted among the heathen; I will be exalted in the earth." Oh what peace those words brought! He was God and she was his child. He'd never allow anything to happen to her unless it was His will. And if His will was for her to die this night, then His will be done. The surrender that filled her in itself brought peace. Was anything as sweet as the peace that passes all understanding?

The cocking of a pistol hammer sounded nearby. Very nearby. Molly's eyes snapped open to find Celeste standing over her, pistol only inches from her forehead. Another scripture came instantly to mind. "Yea, though I walk through the valley of the shadow of death...."

~

Jake, Cal, the other rangers and the sheriff's deputies surrounded Bill Hopper's cabin and found hidden positions. Jake crept around back and unobtrusively peered into a rear cabin window. A quick scan of the cabin revealed David Andrews sitting at a kitchen table, his attention on the cell phone in his hand. Behind him on an old twin bed, Molly lay with her hands and feet bound. Her eyes were closed, but she was moving, attempting to stretch the muscles in her shoulders.

Thank you, Lord! She's still alive!

Another furtive glance didn't indicate that Bill was in the cabin, but it looked like a door led to another room. Could he be in there?

With one more quick perusal, he slipped back into position behind the woodpile stacked near the back entrance to the cabin. He spoke softly into the shoulder mic attached to his uniform shirt.

"She's in there. Looks like just David Andrews is with her. It's quiet, like they're waiting for something. I suggest we lay low for a bit. There's a door to another room, and I'm not sure if Bill's in there or not. I'll keep a watch. If he isn't then we need to see if he shows up. We *have* to capture him."

"Acknowledged." Cal's whispered reply came through Jake's earpiece. The rest of the officers acknowledged as well, and they settled down to wait.

Jake moved back to the window to watch for further activity.

He'd only been observing for a few minutes when Cory Ryan's voice sounded softly in his ear.

"Heads up. Vehicle approaching."

Jake slipped back behind the woodpile and watched as headlights lit the side yard of the cabin and a motor rumbled to a stop. The headlights extinguished.

"It's Bill," Cal said. "Be alert, fellows."

Jake pulled the bill of his service cap low over his eyes in an attempt to shadow his face as much as possible and moved back toward the window. The front door of the cabin slammed as Bill stomped over to the wood stove and poured a mug of coffee.

Hot anger surged through Jake at the hatred visible in the man's eyes as he glared at Molly. What would Bill do? The urge to rush into the room, guns blazing was nearly uncontrollable, but he tamped it down, forcing himself to wait until the right moment. He couldn't jeopardize her life or the lives of the other officers.

Bill disappeared from view and Jake heard murmuring. Was that a woman's voice? He cast a glance at Molly. Her lips weren't moving and her eyes were still closed. The voice was vaguely familiar and growing more raucous by the moment.

"There's a woman inside other than Molly," Jake reported to the others, "and she seems pretty agitated."

Without warning a blond woman flew at Molly, the pistol in her hand pointed straight at his love. Jake's blood pressure soared.

"It's Celeste Payne and she's pointing a pistol at Molly's head. Move! Move!" he directed into his mic as he surged toward the door.

Jake rushed the backdoor of the cabin as the deputies followed his lead. Cal and the other rangers rushed the front door. The word "freeze" echoed through the cabin several times as the three perpetrators stood in shocked stillness. Disbelief marked Bill's face then the shadow of hatred slipped a mask over it. He spat in Jake's direction but the spittle fell short. Celeste had turned at the unexpected intrusion but suddenly twisted back toward Molly.

"I don't think I'd do that if I were you, Celeste." Jake's easy tone belied the turmoil in his gut. Rushing forward, he grabbed the gun from her fingers, un-cocked it and slipped it into his waistband. He had to get to Molly.

As Cal and the other officers handcuffed Bill Hopper, David

Andrews and Celeste Payne and read them their Miranda rights, Jake hurried to Molly and cut the ties that bound her hands and feet. Then very unceremoniously, he lifted her into his arms.

"Molly, sweetheart! Are you alright?" His gruff voice vibrated with relieved emotion.

"I am now." Molly's voice croaked with emotion as she tucked her head beneath his chin. A perfect fit. She wrapped her arms around his waist and hugged him. "I didn't think I'd see you again until you got to heaven because that's where I thought I'd be in about a minute."

He released an exultant chuckle. "Oh, sweetheart! I knew the Lord still held you in the palm of His hand, no matter where you were. And He brought us here in the nick of time." Then he whispered, "Thank you, Lord!"

Molly pulled away enough to look at the activity in the room. "Looks like you brought the proverbial cavalry."

"Whatever it took."

"Were you the least bit worried you wouldn't find me?" Molly tilted her head to one side and cast a curious gaze on him.

His breath hitched as he remembered the despair that had threatened to consume him. "Yeah, I was worried. A lot. My faith faltered because I didn't know if we'd find you in time. Thank goodness God doesn't do things in relation to our faith alone. He's so much bigger and mightier than that."

"Jake Stuart, you haven't heard the end of this, do you hear?" Celeste's shrill voice rang out over the din in the room. "She can't have you! She's just a tramp who came between us and she can't have you!"

Jake tugged Molly closer as Celeste's words reached them. He tucked her head beneath his chin to convey his protection. He'd always be there to protect her.

Celeste's voice faded as she was led from the room by Cory Ryan.

"Pipe down," Cory said. "I don't think he really cares."

"Bill Hopper, you're under arrest for kidnapping and illegal poaching. I'm pretty sure you'll also be charged with selling bear parts on the black market." Cal cuffed the former maintenance man. "You have the right to remain silent…."

As the Miranda rights were read, Bill remained silent but cast a hatred-filled gaze at Molly and Jake. Cal led him out to one of the deputy patrol vehicles.

Jake helped Molly up from the bed and supported her as he led her out to Cal's SUV. "Come on, Sweetheart. I know a young woman waiting at Twentymile for news of your rescue." He kissed her temple. "Jenny thinks she could've done more to prevent your kidnapping."

Molly stopped in her tracks, looked up at the love of her life, and shook her head. "Jake, there's nothing she could've done without getting herself kidnapped too. I'll tell her that when I see her."

Dropping a quick but tender kiss on her lips, he nodded. "Let's go home."

~

A few days later Molly sat in the Deep Creek Ranger Station attacking an overdue stack of paperwork while Kate and Craig helped campers. Kate registered a family for a three night stay and no sooner had they departed to set up camp than Cal strode in followed by Jake.

"Well, do you want the good news or the bad news?" Cal hung his cap on the nail above his desk.

"No bad news, thanks." Molly turned as Jake leaned down and planted a firm kiss on her lips. "I only do good news, and that definitely was good." She batted her eyes at him as he dropped onto the corner of her desk, a satisfied smile on his face.

"Alright, you two. Give the love stuff a break," Cal groused.

"Ok, I'll ask," Kate said. "But I prefer good news to bad too. So...."

Cal sat in the chair behind the counter. "So, Bill Hopper has been officially charged with kidnapping a federal officer, poaching on government property and selling animal parts on the black market."

"But what actual evidence is there that he's been poaching on government property?" Molly asked. "He's never been arrested for it."

"We have two eyewitnesses who are willing to turn states evidence against Bill," Jake said. "Both Willy and Ray are ready to talk."

"Then there's Frank Raven," Cal added. "He's heard Bill brag on several occasions how he poaches. He's willing to testify against him."

"Why didn't he come forward before now?" Craig asked.

Cal shook his head. "He had to work with the man. There was no proof. It was his word against Bill's. Now there are actual witnesses."

"So what's the bad news?" Molly held onto her seat. "I have a feeling I'm really not going to like it."

"You'd be right," Jake said. "Remember that Eddie and I confiscated both bear paws and some type of internal organ from the bear that Willy and Ray poached? That organ was a gallbladder. There's a black market for bear paws and gallbladders in Asia. The gallbladders are used in what is termed the Traditional Medicine trade. The highest price paid for one gallbladder several years ago was $45,000.

"Without going into too much detail, the by-product is used in various medical uses from digestive disorders to blood purification. The population of several bear species has suffered due to this particular black market. Some bears are even kept in confinement to get the necessary bi-product. As for bear paws, it's a delicacy in Asia with presumed health benefits. The price of bear paw soup can bring in hundreds of dollars on the lower range and thousands of dollars on the higher range."

Molly's chin dropped in astonishment. She glanced around and noticed incredulous disbelief was written all over Kate's and Craig's faces too. "You're kidding, right? There's got to be a catch line here somewhere."

"Nope," Jake shook his head. "It's all absolutely true. You can't make this stuff up."

"Then that really is bad news." Kate slumped against the counter. "And our arrest of three poachers isn't going to make much of a change in the grand scheme of things."

"No, it won't," Cal agreed, "but it'll give the bears in our area a chance to make it. Warnings to poachers will be posted and written up in the local newspapers. If we crack down and pursue them more vehemently, we may be able to make a difference here anyway."

"And what about Celeste and David?" Molly asked. "What will happen to them?"

"David will be charged with accessory to the crime of poaching and kidnapping a federal officer," Cal said. "He says he left the black marketing to his uncle. He will, however, need to seek help with his gambling. And the men he borrowed money from to gamble? They're also being investigated. Could be a whole other crime ring to bring down. David's testimony could earn him a lighter sentence. But we'll leave that with the FBI."

"And Celeste has been charged with accessory to kidnapping a federal officer." Jake shook his head. "Unfortunately, I think some of that may be my fault."

Molly stood up and wrapped an arm around his shoulders. Her heart ached at the dismay written on his face. "What do you mean, Jake? You didn't make her kidnap me."

"No, but I never really put my foot down when she came onto me. I should've set her straight from the beginning. I was *never* attracted to her and I mostly just avoided her."

"Jake, you had no idea she was as unhinged as she's proven to be." Molly grasped his hand and squeezed. "You certainly didn't know she was capable of kidnapping or brandishing a weapon with intent to murder."

"Nope, no one could've known," agreed Cal. "And by the way, Molly, you'll be called as a witness in this case against all three."

Molly nodded and leaned her head against Jake's shoulder. "I know. It won't be fun."

"No, but it could certainly be satisfying," Craig said, a smile on his ruddy face.

~

"It's such a relief to have this case settled." Molly cuddled beneath Jake's arm as they swayed back and forth on the porch swing at Selma Jenkins. "We still have the trial, but just knowing that three poachers and their accomplices are behind bars brings tremendous satisfaction. Craig was absolutely right when he said that a couple weeks ago."

"It certainly does." Jake tugged her closer. He couldn't get enough of this woman and wanted to march her before the preacher and soon. He relished the thought of spending a lifetime getting to know her even better. Was one lifetime long enough? Well, it's all he had and he'd make the most of it.

The leaves on the trees were starting to change as fall waved hello and summer bid them goodbye. In the higher elevations of the mountains, the leaves already had a head start and cooler air had moved in. But for now, the caress of the mid-September breeze was refreshing.

"So when do you want to set the date for the wedding?" Jake asked. "I'd say tomorrow's fine, but I guess you have a few things you'd want to do to get ready first, huh?"

A laugh escaped Molly as she leaned back to peer up at him. "Tomorrow? Well, I'd say let's go for it, but I think mom wouldn't be happy with that. Since I'm the only daughter in the family, she's got visions of wedding plans dancing in her head. Hey, how about a Christmas wedding? It gives us time to plan without waiting too long. That's just over three months away."

Jake groaned then sighed. "Three months seems like an eternity when all I want is to marry you and get on with our life together, but a Christmas wedding could be fun." He added with a chuckle. "Sort of like giving myself a present."

~

Molly smiled with contentment, her heart threatening to burst with joy. Jake was eager to marry her. And she was just as eager. What a blessing that God had brought this man into her life and that he loved her. When she'd first arrived in the Great Smoky Mountains, she had no idea that her life would take this turn. With her career all mapped out and knowing what she thought she wanted in life, she was happy she'd surrendered her will to that of Christ's. He loved her and wanted what was best for her, and Jake's love was just that. Oh, what peace to be in God's will!

"Yeah, it is sort of like that." Reaching her hand up, Molly tugged his head down closer until her lips met his in a light kiss.

Jake pulled back slightly, revealing his smoldering gaze. "Merry Christmas to me," he whispered then lowered his head in a kiss that made her long for Christmas to come early this year.

Dear Reader,

If you enjoyed reading this book and want to help me to continue writing and publishing more books for your enjoyment, please take a moment to leave a review. They are very important to authors. We depend on them to let other readers know what they think about our books so they in turn will know whether or not to purchase and read them. Should you not care for it, I would appreciate an email to me rather than a negative review. And remember, the author has no control over prices, so please keep that in mind if you're not happy with the cost.

Thank you again for reading my story. I hope you enjoyed it.

For His glory,

J. Carol Nemeth

Don't miss the next book, <u>Canyon of Death</u>. Read the first chapter!

Prologue

Wow, this trail is treacherous." The tall hiker planted his foot against a large rock to steady himself and surveyed the canyon wall along his left side. "Did you see which way the mountain goat went? I lost sight of him just over there."

"Yeah. He slipped behind that huge boulder." His shorter hiking partner pointed to a large, craggy formation, nearly twice the height of an average man, just below their position. He scratched his goatee-covered chin before yanking off his ball cap and wiping his arm across his forehead. "I wanted to snap his picture but he disappeared. Want to check it out and see if we can catch him back there?"

"Why not? We've gotten some amazing pictures out here. Let's go for it."

Both men edged carefully down to the "boulder" that turned out to be part of the canyon wall. The trail led to the right and away from the wall just before this point creating a divide between the wall and the trail. Scrub vegetation covered the side of the formation.

"Hey, long legs. You jump first then you can catch me," chuckled the shorter of the two hikers.

The taller hiker rolled his eyes and easily jumped across the divide, grabbing hold of the side of the rock formation. Pushing the vegetation aside, he pulled out a flashlight and glanced around the opening before turning back to his hiking partner.

"I don't see any snakes. Go ahead and jump. You'll make it. I'll give you a hand."

When the second hiker was safely inside the opening of the formation with his partner, they turned to take stock of the situation.

"Are you sure he went this way? Looks like a dead end to me."

"I'm positive he came back here. It has to go somewhere."

The short man slid his hands further behind the vegetation, feeling for a fissure in the cliff face.

"Are you sure you want to be doing that? I mean, there still might be snakes and stuff out here, man. Don't get yourself bit. I can't carry your sorry carcass back up that trail." He nodded in the direction they had descended.

His hiking partner turned with a victorious smile as he tugged a clump of vegetation away. Behind it an opening in the rock was large enough for a man to walk through without ducking his head or having to enter sideways.

"Looks almost like it was put there. Intentionally."

"Yeah. Like it was chiseled out. Let's see where it goes." The taller man slipped through as his partner held the vegetation back.

As the hikers slipped into the opening, they realized they were in a small tunnel that ran approximately twenty feet before curving inward along the canyon wall. Light streamed from around the bend lighting the tunnel without the use of their flashlights.

The tunnel walls were dry and smooth, and the floor was scattered with fine rocks and sand. Around the bend, the tunnel opened into an enormous room that hugged the side of the Grand Canyon.

"Oh, my…are you seeing this, man?" The tall hiker gaped at the sight before him.

"I'm seeing it, but I'm not sure what I'm seeing. Do you think the park service knows about this?" His partner's chin dropped in awe. "There's no signs or postings on the rim or anything."

"Or on the trail map."

The mountain goat long forgotten, the hikers carefully explored the brightly lit cavernous room. Cliff dwellings built into the back wall extended several hundred feet in length. Various sized round holes in the floor indicated rooms were likely positioned beneath as well. A large overhang in front of the massive room allowed light in but would hide it from the outside. Lower views of the canyon could be seen but nothing above the overhang. Whoever had lived here hadn't intended to be seen by the outside world.

"I think we better tell someone about this, man. If they already know about it, that's one thing, but if not…"

"Let's snap some pictures. Stand over there by that low wall.

That's it."

With pose after pose on their digital camera, the hikers decided to get back and report their find. Who knows? One day they just might be famous.

Chapter One

"Rock of Ages, cleft for me,
Let me hide myself in Thee"

The faint melodic words floated on the morning breeze as Kate Fleming made her way toward Mather Point. She was about to catch her first glimpse of the Grand Canyon and her heart ticked an upbeat in anticipation. She'd waited a long time for this moment.

"Let the water and the blood,
From Thy wounded side which
flowed,"

The closer Kate got to the south rim of the canyon, the stronger the words grew. Definitely feminine in tone, there was a slight crackle as though she was elderly. It held a quality that indicated the a cappella soloist sang straight from her heart.

People dressed in heavy winter clothing meandered about as they snapped pictures and took selfies with the canyon behind them.

"Be of sin the double cure,
Save from wrath and make me
pure."

As the Grand Canyon came into view, Kate sucked in the cold morning air in awe, chilling her throat and lungs. Placing her gloved hands over her nose and mouth, she warmed them up again.

The Grand Canyon was the most amazing thing she'd ever seen. Gorgeous earth tones blended with blues, pinks and shadowy purples. With the morning sun still in the eastern sky, long shadows were cast on the western side of ridges and peaks. As a strong, cold breeze blew up from the canyon, Kate zipped up her olive-drab uniform parka and jammed her "Smokey-Bear" hat further down on her head.

"Could my tears forever
flow…."

"Shut up, old woman! I don't want to hear you singing."

The angry voice came from Kate's left, drawing her attention from the spectacular view. An elderly woman stood by the chain-link fence which protects visitors from going over the edge of the canyon at the overlook. Her rheumy eyes were focused on the horizon between earth and sky, her thin, arthritic hands raised toward heaven as tears streamed down her wrinkled cheeks. Two young men stood beside her, anger marring their faces.

"Shut up, old woman," one of them yelled. "Stop your screeching!"

Kate quickly approached them to see what the commotion was about. The woman certainly didn't seem to be bothering anyone.

"Excuse me." Kate put as much authority in her voice as she could muster. "What are you two doing here? This lady isn't bothering anyone."

The guys spotted her uniform, belligerence oozing from their expressions. "Well, she's bothering us. I don't want to hear her singing about…God." The last word was spat out with disgust. "She's gotta stop."

Kate laid a kind hand on the woman's arm. "Ma'am, I hate to interrupt you but can I hear your side of this situation?"

The woman's faded blue eyes turned to Kate, tears still wet on her cheeks. "Of course, my dear. I'm eighty-six years old. All my life I've seen pictures of the Grand Canyon, but I've never been here before. Well, now that I'm here, I can't help but be in awe at the wonder of God's creation. He did this." She waved a hand in the direction of the natural wonder spread before them. "It didn't just happen. All I wanted was to praise Him for how marvelous and mighty He is. One look at that view and anyone with half a brain knows God made it."

The two young men sputtered in anger at the pointed remark.

Kate held up her hand. "Fellows, this is a really big canyon. I mean, really big. There's plenty of room for you to see it and for this lady to sing as she desires. Why don't you just move along to another location and enjoy the view. Leave her in peace to enjoy it in her own way."

They cast angry glares in the woman's direction as they shifted their daypacks higher on their backs and left the canyon rim, hopefully to find a spot elsewhere.

"Thank you, miss." The old woman settled a gnarled, arthritic hand on Kate's arm. Gloveless, it felt cold even through Kate's parka sleeve. "I just don't understand how folks can look at that view and not give credit where credit is due. God made it, and He made it for us to enjoy. I just don't think some people want to believe He exists. It's sad really."

"Yes, I think you're right, ma'am." Kate patted the woman's thin shoulder. "And thank you for the reminder. You might want to go inside and warm up though. It's pretty chilly out here. Are you here alone?"

The woman smiled. "No, my son and daughter-in-law are here with me. They went to get coffee, so they'll be back shortly with a cup for me. I just didn't want to leave this view. I want to drink in as much as I can as long as I can."

"I understand," Kate nodded with a smile. "You have a wonderful day, ma'am."

Before Kate realize what she was doing, the woman reached out thin arms and wrapped them around her. Then she stepped back and smiled, contentment written across her wrinkled face.

"Thank you, my dear. These weary eyes have seen a lot of things during my lifetime, but this was the last thing I truly wanted to see before the Lord calls me home. I don't know if that'll be tomorrow or next year or the next, but I'm happy that I got to see this marvel of His handiwork."

Kate started to walked away, then stripping the gloves from her hands, pressed them into the woman's hands and hurried away before she could protest.

As Kate strolled along the canyon rim, she could hear the

woman's voice once again lift in praise. She reflected on her words. Kate hadn't given God much credit lately. She believed in Him, had even put her trust in Him, but He'd let her down. Pain sliced through her heart as memories flooded her mind. Nope. She wasn't going to think about all that right now. Whether God put this view here for her to enjoy or not, she could still appreciate the beauty before her. And she wanted to forget. Oh, how she wanted to forget.

Pushing the memories from her mind, she glanced at her watch. She needed to get to the visitor center to meet with Tasha Johnson. Kate had arrived yesterday afternoon. Just long enough to be assigned living quarters and to begin to learn her way around Grand Canyon Village and some of the government offices, but she hadn't yet met Tasha.

With a last long appreciative glance at the canyon, she left it behind and made her way to the visitor center near Mather Point. In spite of the cold wind that swept across the south rim, bundled-up visitors scurried from one overlook to the next, searching for that subtle difference in the scenery. Kate could appreciate that. She was sure she wouldn't get tired of the view any time soon.

Kate slipped inside the visitor center where it was much warmer. Straight ahead was a long information desk with a few park staff members answering questions and passing out park maps. To the right was the entrance to a theater where a video played every few minutes telling about the Grand Canyon National Park and its natural splendor. Exhibits of small wildlife and historical information were arranged to the left. Park visitors meandered about looking at these exhibits and taking in the video in the theater. So, where would she find Tasha Johnson?

"Kate Fleming?"

Kate turned at the soft feminine voice that spoke her name. A young African-American woman met her questioning gaze with a smile. Her flawless ebony skin, black eyes surrounded by long lashes and beautiful white teeth between full lips was striking. Her short, curly black hair set off her beautiful features.

"Yes, I'm Kate Fleming."

The young woman held out her hand. "It's nice to meet you at last, Kate. I'm Tasha Johnson. We've been expecting you."

Kate shook her hand. "It's a pleasure to meet you, Tasha."

"Have you been out to see the canyon yet? That's usually where everyone makes a bee-line to as soon as they arrive." Tasha chuckled. "And no wonder. I've been here three years and still can't get over the view."

"Yes. I just came from Mather Point. It's amazing. I'll be spending a lot of time soaking in the sights." Kate had wanted to work at the Grand Canyon for a long time, and she'd finally made it. But she hadn't planned to come alone. Shoving those painful memories away, she concentrated on Tasha's words.

"Well, I hate to rush you into your job, but I'm going to take you out to the sight and introduce you to the archeologists." Tugging on her parka and her uniform ball cap, Tasha eyed Kate's "Smokey-Bear" hat critically. "If you've got your ball cap, I think you'd better wear it. Much better suited to where we're heading. Good. You're wearing hiking boots. You'll need them."

With a quick trip to Kate's car to exchange hats, the women climbed into Tasha's park SUV.

"As my assistant, your help will be invaluable in keeping an eye on the archaeological team," Tasha explained.

"You're the park liaison, right?" Kate wanted to make sure she had her supervisor's title correct.

"That's right." Tasha flashed a smile. "I have a few projects I'm overseeing, so I need you to keep me informed. You'll be my liaison to the archeological team. My eyes and ears, so to speak. If they have questions you can't answer, bring them to me and we'll get them answered. There are regulations they must follow. I need you to ensure they follow them. If they don't, tell me and I'll deal with it."

"So, what is the team looking for? Anything in particular or just digging until they find something?"

"Oh, no. It's something in particular. A couple of hikers stumbled on a lost Anasazi city a month ago. The park invited the archeological team to investigate."

"What about the hikers? How did they find the site?"

"They were hiking on the Hermit's Trail and followed a mountain goat. It disappeared behind a rock formation and when they went to investigate, they found the city. They snapped a lot of pictures, too, but we confiscated them. No way could we let that out to the public."

"Won't they talk?"

"Probably, although they signed an agreement not to." Tasha stopped the SUV next to a gate with an electronic keypad. She entered a four-digit code and the gate swung upward, allowing them to proceed. "This is Hermit's Road and it's closed to the public except during the winter months. They just closed it last week, so we don't have to worry about competing with tourists anymore. Only park personnel and shuttle buses as well as the Hermit's Rest Gift Shop employees drive out here now. And of course, the archeologists. I'll give you the combination so you'll have access. You'll be driving out here all the time."

They followed the road along the south rim of the canyon to the Hermit's Rest Gift Shop and overlook. Tasha drove a half mile further down a dirt road behind the gift shop and parked beside a building comprised of two mobile construction trailers placed side by side.

"This is the archeologists' office." Tasha climbed out of the SUV. "You might find one or more of the archeologists here but usually they're on-site so it's harder to find them."

"Ok. Good to know." Kate exited the SUV and followed Tasha toward the trailhead. "So, they're not here now?"

Tasha glanced at the dark windows. "Probably not."

Kate's eyes were glued to the view before her. A completely different and amazingly colorful configuration of ridges, peaks and plateaus met her gaze. Tasha's chuckle beside her drew her attention back to her companion.

"Sorry. I'm just in awe of…well…this." Her hand moved in an all-encompassing arc. "It's… gorgeous."

"Yes, it is," Tasha sighed. "I just love it here. But," she pointed at the trailhead, "this is a very treacherous trail to descend. It's not maintained by the park as much as the other trails. So take your time and watch your step. It's going to take some getting used to."

Kate and Craig had hiked a lot of trails in the three years since they'd started dating, and she was confident she was in shape and could tackle it. This did look daunting. What would Craig have said to this bit of adventure? A pang sliced through her heart as it always did when she thought of Craig.

She swallowed hard. Don't go there. It hurt too much.

Tasha eyed Kate closely and laid a hand on her jacketed arm. "Are you ok, girlfriend? Your face is mighty pale. Want to take a minute before we head down? It's not that bad, really."

Kate met Tasha's concerned dark gaze and was touched. The young woman hardly knew her but had read Kate's expression like she'd known her a long time.

Kate flashed a smile in spite of the tears that threatened to spill from her eyes. "No, I'm fine. Really, I am. I just…remembered something…someone. It's okay. I'm ready when you are." She pulled her sunglasses from her jacket pocket and tugged her ball cap lower over her eyes. It probably wouldn't help hide the pain at the memories of Craig, but it was worth a try.

Tasha considered her a moment longer before nodding. "Okay. If you say so. But if you have a problem, just tell me."

Kate understood that she wasn't just talking about the difficulty of the trail. Did she mean she could talk to her about other things too? Would Tasha be a friend she could trust? Time would tell. But some things were just off limits. Totally.

The path down the Hermit's Trail was indeed difficult. In some areas they had to crawl over rocks and boulders while in other places the trail smoothed out for a few feet. Kate concentrated on following Tasha and pushed personal thoughts from her mind.

At a particularly steep and precarious spot on the trail, Tasha stopped and pointed at a large formation on the left of the trail.

"That's the huge boulder the notorious mountain goat disappeared behind. Funny how that goat lost his one claim to fame. We'll never really know what happened to him. But he led the hikers to one very spectacular archeological find." She laughed between gasps for breath. "Come on, girl. We're almost there."

A wide, wooden board had been placed across the divide from the trail to the entrance to the formation, and Kate followed Tasha across to it, waiting for her to disappear behind it. Taking another look at the colorful scenery as she waited, Kate reached up to grab hold of the rock. Her foot slipped and before she knew what was happening, she slid toward the cliff edge several feet below were the trail turned to the right and the canyon wall remained on the left. Her fingers grasped for anything that would hold her, but she continued to slide.

Tasha's voice rang out in fear. "Kate! Grab onto something!"

Kate's heart lodged in her throat even as she slid toward the edge of the cliff. While she scrabbled for a handhold, her mind screamed the words: *Lord, help me!*

Read the rest here

You might also enjoy Mountain of Fear by Cynthia Hickey. Read the first chapter!

Prologue

The sound of the hammer echoed over the small Ozark mountain. He struck the nail once, twice, three times, securing the paper to the door frame of the new camp store. He stood back and read the printed words.

WARNING

By order of the Righteous Survivalist Group,

under Command of General Duane Watkins,

any trespassers on this mountain will be shot.

This land is being reclaimed by its rightful owner.

The breeze whistled through the trees, ruffling the paper's edges. The wind teased it some more—pulled it free and let it drift to the ground. The young man bent to grab it when the wind snatched it from beneath his fingers.

He watched it skitter away. The wind gently lifted the warning, let it dance upon the dirt-packed surface in front of the store, then carried the paper wafting and twirling, into the forest.

Taking a few steps to retrieve the paper, he changed his mind. He looked out over the campground. The lake shone black and smooth in the falling dusk. Fire pits were clean, swings hung silent. The windows of the store were freshly cleaned and almost invisible.

He whirled in the opposite direction. He'd done what he'd been sent to do. It wasn't his fault the freak breeze had sprung up. The boy looked again for the paper. The scrap of white shone from the top of an evergreen tree. He shrugged. It'd blow down tomorrow.

After walking several miles, he entered a campsite. Ten men huddled in silence around the dying embers of a fire. Several of them, clothed in camouflage, sat assembling automatic weapons. The rest cleaned an assortment of rifles and handguns. One man drew a knife across a whetstone, the sound rasping in the still air.

One man sat alone, head bowed with no weapon at his feet. The weight of the world appeared to be on his massive shoulders. "Is it done?"

"It's done." The young man swallowed past the lump in his throat.

Without looking up, the man said, "Go on home, boy. Your work here is done."

"But, I want to stay."

The man's head jerked up. His eyes hardened. "Do what you're told. Your granny is waiting."

The young man released his breath with a huff and turned, walking away. "Still don't know why I can't stay."

"Cause I'm the boss here, and I said for you to go." The big man stood. "It ain't safe for you here. I don't want you messed up in this."

"Too late for that." The boy muttered other words under his breath and stomped to a waiting truck.

The words "Find me a hostage," drifted to him on the early afternoon breeze and his eyes shifted to where the big man barked orders to a smaller man wearing fatigues.

1

"Well, that's it then."

Rachel Kent stood back and shut the door on the rented U-Haul, closing the door on the last fifteen years of her life.

All that was left of her material possessions she'd packed into the U-haul with the panoramic picture of the Grand Canyon painted on its side. Her two whining offspring sat in the cab of the truck, their Cairn Terrier between them.

She rested her forehead against the closed door of the trailer. The coolness of the metal soothed her aching head. A lone tear trailed down her cheek. Sniffing, she rubbed her hand roughly across her face before the other tears welling in her eyes could follow their leader.

Squaring her shoulders, not looking back, she strode to the driver's side of the truck. Yanking the door open, she climbed into the front seat. Her daughter, Melanie, fifteen going on twenty-one, sat staring straight ahead, her long, blue-striped hair hanging down her back. Rachel cringed, noticing the faded jeans Mel wore were ripped at the knees. The cropped tee shirt wasn't much better. Once a bright fluorescent pink, it had faded to a dull orange-pink. It was a direct contrast to the stripes in her hair.

Rachel's twelve-year-old son, Dustin, bobbed his head to the music on his headset. He jerked his chin up, acknowledging his mother's presence, and continued to pet the small wheat-colored dog lying beside him. The dog raised its head to greet Rachel, then rested his chin on his young master's knee.

"Tell me again *why* we're doing this," her daughter demanded before Rachel had clicked her seatbelt across her middle.

"Mel, we've gone over this until I'm sick to death of talking about it." Rachel slammed the heavy door, turned the key in the ignition, and started the truck. "I can't find any work here. Not something that will pay the bills anyway. Your father's life insurance is almost gone. We need to move. We're going to stay with my parents for a while. They're very excited about getting to spend time with you and Dusty.

"Right." Mel folded her arms across her chest.

Rachel turned her head to look at her daughter. "Melanie, please try to understand. I'm doing what I think is best. I'm not excited about leaving behind my home, either. It hasn't been easy since your father died."

"Oh, and you think it's been easy for Dusty and me" Mel stared out the passenger window.

"Don't be so dramatic. You'll make new friends. You're a very likeable person." *Except to your brother and me*. Rachel backed the truck carefully down the driveway, watching the car she towed through the rearview mirror. She frowned as she backed through one of the flower beds. It didn't matter. She wouldn't be there to enjoy them. "Besides, this is at least a three-day drive. It'll give us a chance to spend quality time together. I miss the time we use to spend together as a family."

"Dad died. We're not a family anymore." Mel's words hung heavy in the air of the truck cab.

Rachel opened her mouth to speak. No words issued forth, and she clamped her lips closed. Ignoring the pain her daughter's words caused, she put the truck in drive. A horn blared as she merged onto the highway. Smiling an apology, Rachel met the gaze of the outraged driver and waved. She steered the truck back into her own lane.

It wasn't long before Dusty and Mel fell asleep. Rachel listened to the music of the droning tires and passing cars. Occasionally, she'd find herself drifting into the next lane, her heart stopping each time a car horn blared.

I shouldn't be doing this. You should be driving this truck, Dennis. She sniffed against the tears stinging her eyelids. *What were you thinking?*

Dusty interrupted her melancholy reminiscing. "Mom?"

She glanced over and smiled, pleased to have someone to talk to. "Yes, Sweetie? Did you have a nice nap?"

"I have to pee."

Rachel sighed. "Don't use that language, Dusty. You know I don't like it."

"Well, I do. Have to go, I mean."

"Now?"

"Of course now," Mel cut in. "He wouldn't have told you otherwise." She ran her fingers through the striped strands of hair, smoothing them against her head.

"Mel…" Rachel narrowed her eyes.

"Yeah, I know. Watch my mouth. Be respectful." The girl turned to stare out the window.

Rachel patted Dusty's knee. "I'll pull over at the first rest stop we come to. Will that be okay?"

Dusty replaced the headphones on his head, and nodded.

Rachel glared at her daughter, hazel eyes clashing with blue. Mel rolled her eyes and turned away.

It's going to be a long trip. Rachel turned her attention back to the road. *Am I doing the right thing?*

A short time later they pulled into the parking lot of a rest stop. The towed car bounced over the curb as Rachel took the corner too sharply. "Sorry," she muttered.

Mel opened the door and climbed out before the truck came to a complete stop. She slammed the door behind her, not leaving it open for her brother to follow, and headed alone to the restroom.

Rachel pulled on the door handle and shoved the door open. "Melanie Elizabeth Kent! You almost shut your brother's fingers in the door." Rachel struggled with the clasp to her seat belt. Releasing it, she slid from the truck, wincing as her short-clad legs stuck to the vinyl seat. Mutt bounded past and Rachel grabbed his leash.

She reached over and plucked the headphones from Dusty's head. "You go first. You can hold Mutt's leash when I go."

"Sure, Mom." He flashed a quick grin and sprinted toward the restroom.

Rachel followed at a more sedate pace, allowing the dog freedom to nose around and lift his leg on every bush they passed. She glanced several times toward the restrooms. As time passed, she worried, shifting from foot to foot, and gnawed her lower lip. She breathed a sigh of relief when Dusty appeared and took the dog from her.

"Stay close." She put her hands on Dusty's shoulders and turned him to look at her. "There are a lot of strange people hanging around here. Transients stay in these places all the time. I'm always hearing things on the news. You yell loud if someone bothers you, and I'll come running."

"Okay, Mom." He flashed another of the face-splitting grins she loved so much, the ones where his eyes disappeared and his face lit up. He sprinted back to the truck, tugging on Mutt's leash.

Rachel watched him until her full bladder screamed for release. She pushed open the restroom door.

Mel stood next to a cracked and dirty mirror running her fingers through her hair. She didn't acknowledge her mother. She withdrew a stick of eyeliner from her pocket and lined the already heavily lined lids.

Rachel peered under the three stall doors and, not seeing anyone, chose the closest to the exit door. She glanced around for toilet seat liners, grimaced when she saw the dispenser was empty, and lined the seat with toilet paper.

"You did line the seat, right, Mel?"

Her daughter's heavy sigh hung in the air between them. *Were all teenage girls this trying, or did I just get lucky? Yes, it was definitely going to be a long trip.*

"Mother?" Mel whined, her voice reverberating through the tiled room. "I'm ready to go now. What's taking you so long?"

"May I please use the restroom in peace? Since when are you so worried about me being with you?"

Mel sighed again, louder, and Rachel heard her stomp out of the restroom.

Rachel shook her head. "It all has to be on her terms." She read the names and phone numbers on the walls, frowning at some of the crude language.

Someone posted a warning about the coming Armageddon. Another scratched in a No Trespassing, Violators will be Prosecuted. Rachel squinted, trying to make out the rest of the words, but someone had scratched through them, writing Ha Ha in black marker.

She flushed the toilet with her foot and backed into the swinging stall door to push it open. Turning on the faucet, Rachel glanced into the mirror and frowned. Where had that tired-looking woman come from? Reaching up, she pushed her bangs to the side, out of her eyes. Hazel eyes shone back at her.

"Mother!" Mel's voice rang with impatience through the door.

"I'm coming, Mel." She used a paper towel to open the door,

careful of the germs that might be lurking there. Wadding up the towel, she tossed it in the trash can and let the door slam behind her. "I thought you weren't in a hurry, Mel."

"I don't want to just stand here. People are staring."

Rachel laughed and strolled past her. "It's probably the bright blue stripes in your hair, or the several pairs of earrings you're wearing. Maybe, it's the holes in your jeans."

"Okay, Mom. I get the picture."

"You could've waited in the truck if you didn't want people staring at you." She glanced toward the U-Haul. She couldn't see Dusty. Rachel whipped her head around. "Where's Dusty? He's supposed to be in the truck."

"How should I know? Am I my brother's keeper?"

"Yes. As a matter of fact, you are." Rachel scanned the playground, her heartbeat accelerating.

Several people walked dogs in the pet area. More supervised young children on the play equipment. A few men smoked cigarettes while standing around trash cans. Smoked butts littered the ground around their feet. One met Rachel's gaze and winked. She frowned and continued to scan the area.

A woman stood, bent slightly, scolding her child. The woman's shrill voice rose above the surrounding noise. An elderly couple walked a small dog, saying hello to everyone they passed.

There he was. Over by the slide. Rachel released the breath she held. She called his name and waited to make sure he'd heard her before walking back to the truck. She turned the key and switched on the air conditioner while she waited for Dusty and Mel to join her.

Leaning forward, Rachel rested her forehead on the steering wheel and waited for her racing heart to slow to normal. *Why do I worry so much*? A tap on the window startled her, and she bolted up.

The man who'd winked at her, stood staring, his nicotine-stained teeth showing as he smiled through a scruffy beard.

Rachel took quick note of her children approaching the truck and waved to them to stay where they were. She cracked her window, just enough to speak through. Turning to the man, she asked, "Can I help you?"

"Howdy, little lady. My name's Rupert. Your boy told me y'all were going camping. Which campground? Maybe I can show you the way." He placed another cigarette between his lips and flicked open a lighter.

Cigarette smoke invaded Rachel's space, tickling her nostrils. Her heart thudded. "That's our business."

The passenger door opened and Dusty and Mel climbed in. *Don't they ever listen?* Rachel hit the automatic lock button, causing the man to laugh.

"Looks like you're headed across country."

"Maybe." Rachel locked eyes with the man's blood shot ones.

He winked again. "I bet I'll be seeing you again real soon."

Rachel watched him stroll away as she raised her window. She threw the gear shift into reverse and backed out. A horn blared. Rachel yelped, slamming her foot on the brake. She glanced into the rearview mirror as another driver leaned on his horn and sped passed them.

"Mom, be careful."

"I'll see what I can do, Mel." Her hands tightened on the wheel, knuckles turning white, as her heartbeat returned to normal.

Seven o'clock that evening, she steered the truck into the parking lot of a cheap hotel close to the freeway. The garish neon sign flashed a red vacancy.

"They probably don't even have cable here. Or a pool." Mel's eyes widened like saucers.

"We don't have time for you to swim anyway." Rachel turned off the truck. "We're just staying the night."

"There's a Denny's restaurant across the street." Dusty unhooked his seatbelt. "You can eat whatever you want."

"I'm not a bottomless pit, you know. Like you."

"Stop fighting, please." Rachel opened her door. "Stay here while I get the key to a room."

A bell tinkled as she pushed open the glass door. The woman behind the counter barely acknowledged Rachel, not turning from the game show on her small television. She waved a hand toward a peg board, telling Rachel to go ahead and pick a room. "One bed or two?"

"One, please." She needed to save money wherever possible.

"Bottom floor or second?"

"Bottom."

"Room four, eight or ten."

Rachel glanced outside, noted the room closest to their U-Haul and took the key to number four. "Thank you." She handed the woman her credit card.

The woman nodded, temporarily diverted from her show, and slid the card through the credit machine, making a carbon copy of Rachel's card. She passed the paper and a pen across the counter.

Signing her name, Rachel carefully tore off her copy and stuffed it into the pocket of her jeans. "Thank you, again."

"Welcome." The woman switched her attention back to the television.

Mel and Dusty were still arguing when Rachel popped the trunk on the small car they towed. "Both of you stop fighting and give me a hand with these suitcases."

"Tomorrow night we're camping. Right, Mom?" Dusty took the larger suitcase from her hand.

"Day after tomorrow. I'm excited about the KOA I've chosen." Her mind drifted to the man in the baseball cap, and she shuddered. Hotels were safer. You could lock your door against the outside world. "It's new and built right by a lake. The brochure is really lovely. We'll arrive there by early afternoon. That'll give us time for a short hike." She handed the other suitcase to Mel. "I want to stick to our schedule as much as possible. Grandma and Grandpa are expecting us on a certain day, and I don't want to worry them."

"Mom, isn't that the man from the rest stop?" Mel stopped, looking over Rachel's shoulder.

Rachel turned, her heart in her throat. Standing at the end of the row of rooms, was the man from the rest-stop. He tipped the brim of the faded baseball cap he wore, and grinned.

She ushered her children to their room. "I'm sure it's a coincidence. There aren't many motels around here."

The glow of the man's cigarette burned brighter as he took a drag. He lifted a hand to wave, and Rachel slammed the door closed. Her heart thudded painfully. *Is he following us?* She struggled to remain calm and fisted her trembling hands at her sides.

Mel stopped just inside the room. "Green and orange bedspread. Who decorates these places." She gasped, turning to Rachel. "One bed,

Mother? You have got to be kidding me. I have to share a bed with you and Dusty? That's sick. If my friends ever found out I shared a bed with my brother they'd…"

"I'll sleep in the middle, Mel. I couldn't afford a room with two beds. Our money has to last until I find a job."

"This trip just gets better and better." Mel dropped the suitcase by the door and flopped across the bed. "Where's the remote?"

Dusty looked around the room. "I don't think there is one. Oh, yeah. Here it is. It's chained to the TV." He went to hand it to her, the chain stopping just short of Mel's outstretched hand.

"I give up. Let's go eat."

Rachel stopped her. "I was hoping to have sandwiches."

"Again? Please, Mom. Denny's isn't that expensive."

Rachel looked from Mel to Dusty, who smiled, hope shining in his blue eyes. She nodded. "Fine. But let's make it quick. It's getting late, and I have another day of driving tomorrow."

"Do we have to walk?"

"It's across the street, Mel." Rachel grabbed her purse from the dresser.

She ushered the kids out of the room, taking care not to leave the key behind. They were almost across the parking lot when Rachel saw the man again.

He stood in the shadows, turned in their direction.

Her heart stopped. She faltered, catching her foot in a pothole.

Mel shot her a look and shook her head. "Geez, Mom. What's wrong with you?"

"Nothing." Rachel quickened her pace to catch up with Mel and Dusty. She grabbed each of them by the elbow and dragged them across the street, glancing back over her shoulder. The man was gone.

They slid into a corner booth at the restaurant, and she diverted her attention to the menu. She scanned the salads, made her choice, and then waved to the waitress to let her know they were ready to order.

She rolled her eyes as Dusty and Mel ordered hamburgers and fries. What did they think a hamburger was if not a sandwich? She shrugged. Pick your battles, her mother always told her. The problem was…Rachel allowed Mel to spur her into a lot of them.

Rachel returned their menus to the waiting server and leaned against the back of the booth, watching the waitress walk back to the kitchen. *Didn't she know those black slacks were too tight on her? And that hair. How did anyone get it teased up that high?* Was Rachel's self-esteem so low she felt compelled to criticize someone else?

Leaning forward, she propped her chin in her palm. At a nearby booth, another mother sat with three small children, one of them a squalling infant.

Mel stuck her fingers in her ears to drown out the baby's cries.

Rachel rubbed her temple, willing the dull pounding to go away. The waitress plopped their food on the table, shot them a quick smile, and spun around to wait on another customer. Rachel picked at her salad, halfway listening to the sibling squabble going on around her. At least it wasn't her two this time. They were both totally involved in their burgers.

A gust of cool air blew across their table, and Rachel glanced up to see the capped man enter the restaurant. Her fork suspended in midair as he took a seat at a nearby table. Yellowed teeth flashed a smile in her direction.

"We're finished." She grabbed her purse and jumped up from the table.

"Mom," Mel clutched Rachel's arm. "It's him again."

"Him who?" Dusty spun around.

Rachel grabbed her children by an arm and pushed them through the door ahead of her.

The man's laughter followed them out the door and into the street.

"I get the shower first." Mel slammed the hotel room door behind her, the force shaking the picture on the wall.

"Fine," Dusty retorted. "I pick what's on TV."

"Whatever!"

"Don't use all the hot water!" Dusty yelled back

Head pounding, Rachel rummaged in her purse for an aspirin. She glanced around the room for a glass. There wasn't one. She tossed the pills in her mouth and swallowed, grimacing against the bitter taste.

How easy it seemed to be for her children to push aside the fact that the stranger in the ball cap may be following them. Rachel sat on the side of the bed. They might be in the middle of nowhere, but his showing up everywhere they went was too much of a coincidence for her to feel comfortable.

Later that night, after wedging a chair under the door handle, Rachel lay squeezed between Dusty and Mel. She listened to her son's quiet snores and the low murmurs of her daughter. With tears rolling down her cheeks and dampening the pillow beneath her head, she cursed her dead husband.

*

Wesley Ward placed a plastic mug of water into the tiny microwave and pushed the start button. Leaning against the counter, he ran both hands through his hair as he waited for the timer to buzz. He removed the mug from the microwave and stirred in two teaspoons of instant coffee. Taking the cup of hot coffee to the wooden table in the center of the room, he sat.

A manila folder lay before him. He picked it up and scanned the contents for the second time. *Ex-military, huh? Yep, this is one bad dude.* Wesley raised his head and peered out the small window into the deepening dusk. *And this is one solitary cabin. No wonder the other forest service ranger quit.* He lifted the mug by its handle, grabbed his rifle from over the fireplace, and carried them with him outside.

The clearing around the ranger cabin sprouted green with scattered wildflowers. A cottontail rabbit bounded across the ground.

The crisp mountain air felt wonderful as he breathed in a lung full. *How long until they discover I'm here? Will they try to ambush me or meet me head on? Will they even care?* Wesley shook his head.

A hawk soared above him, capturing his attention. He watched as the bird floated on the breeze, dipping and gliding.

Wesley propped the rifle against the door jamb and sat on the top step, continuing to watch until the hawk disappeared from sight. He ran the contents of the file through his mind. He knew Moe was on this mountain; the question was where.

He sipped the now-warm coffee. *What is the man up to?* Wesley shrugged and emptied the mug into a nearby bush. "I'll see what I can find out tomorrow." He laughed at himself talking out loud with no one to hear. "Just the way I want it."

He heard a squawk from the radio inside the cabin and pushed himself reluctantly to his feet. Wesley opened the door, stepped inside, turned, shook his head, and grabbed the rifle. "Can't leave you out here."

Placing the rifle and mug on the table, he answered the radio.

"Ward here."

A man's voice came through the line. "We got nothing."

Wesley set his jaw firmly. "Nothing? At all? You don't have others working on this?"

"Nope. Just you. Doesn't warrant the manpower, but I'll see if I can get someone up there to help you."

Wesley shook his head. With his free hand, he swung the small wooden chair around and straddled it. "How can one man disappear? Much less one man with a group of followers?"

"You tell me." The man's voice held a hint of humor. "That's what I'm paying you for."

Rolling his head, Wesley worked the kinks from his neck. "I'll go scouting tomorrow. The last ranger said he kept receiving threats. Somebody wanted him to leave this mountain. Pronto. I haven't been contacted."

Wesley rose from the chair and paced the small room. "I'm fine alone. Don't send anyone else. It's easier for one man to remain inconspicuous. I want the element of surprise."

"Is that your final answer?"

He laughed. "Yes, Sam, that's my final answer."

"You shouldn't be alone now, Ward. You need to focus on something other than what happened."

"I am focusing on something. Moe."

Sam snorted.

"You're like an old mother hen. I've got plenty of supplies. This assignment is mild compared to what I'm used to. You know that. Man, you were there!"

"You got to work through it."

Wesley squared his shoulders. "I'm fine. I'm dealing with it."

"You're alone too much," Sam insisted.

"Yep. I like being alone. Nobody nags you. Besides, I have a partner…"

"God."

"Yes, I'm talking about God."

"Okay. Anyway, I don't nag."

Wesley laughed again and leaned his back against the counter. "You do too nag me. You're the only one I let get away with it." He grabbed his mug from the table and refilled it. "Gotta go, man. Don't worry. I'll find Moe." *Or he'll find me*. He put the mic down and smiling, refilled his mug and lifted it to his lips.

Read the rest here

Author's Notes

It's an unfortunate and sad fact that poaching exists and is done for many reasons. Various animals are hunted illegally but as I've addressed in my story, the black bear is one of them. I've also addressed a particular reason that the black bear is hunted. However, the black bear isn't the only bear hunted for its gall bladder and bear paws. Various species of bears are hunted worldwide and their parts are sold on the black markets to Asian countries for medicinal purposes and for food delicacies. This has been occurring for many, many years. Various law enforcement agencies have been working together to put a stop to the poaching and the black market sales. Through their efforts there has been a decline but unfortunately it does still continue. Let's hope that one day this practice will eventually be eradicated completely and that the bears will be able to remain in the wild where God intended them to be.

A native North Carolinian, J. Carol Nemeth has always loved reading and enjoyed making up stories ever since junior high school, most based in the places she has lived or traveled to. She worked in the National Park Service as a Park Aid and served in the US Army where she was stationed in Italy, traveling to over thirteen countries while there. She met the love of her life, Mark Nemeth, also an Army veteran, while stationed in Italy. After they married, they lived in various locations, including North Yorkshire, England. They now live in West Virginia, where, in her spare time, Carol and her husband enjoy RVing and sightseeing. Carol and Mark are active in their church and enjoy their two grown children, son-in-law, and three grandchildren.

Yorkshire Lass - Buy Link https://amzn.to/2Ivddxd

Dedication to Love - Buy Link https://amzn.to/2IJMnBF

The Peaceful Valley Wounded Soldiers Anthology Buy Link https://amzn.to/2Kb6QRa

www.facebook.com/J.CarolNemeth

https://twitter.com/nemeth_jcarol

https://amzn.to/2AbdKRa

https://www.goodreads.com/author/dashboard